W9-BAC-341

GLORY

GLORY

BOOK ONE OF THE GOLDENWING CYCLE

ALFRED COPPEL

A TOM DOHERTY ASSOCIATES BOOK
NEW YORK

TOR

GLORY

Copyright © 1993 by Alfred Coppel

Edited by David G. Hartwell

Design by Diane Stevenson—SNAP·HAUS GRAPHICS

This book is printed on acid-free paper

A Tor Book
Published by Tom Doherty Associates, Inc.
175 Fifth Avenue
New York, N.Y. 10010

Tor® is a registered trademark of Tom Doherty Associates, Inc.

Library of Congress Catalguing-in-Publication Data

Coppel, Alfred.
    Glory / Alfred Coppel.
        p.   cm.—(Goldenwing cycle ; bk. 1)
    "A Tom Doherty Associates book."
    ISBN 0-312-85469-2
    1. Life on other planets—Fiction.   2. Space ships—Fiction.
I. Title.   II. Series: Coppel, Alfred.   Goldenwing cycle ; bk. 1.
PS3553.064G57   1993
813'.54—dc20   93-12452
                                                                       CIP

First Tor edition: May 1993

Printed in the United States of America

0 9 8 7 6 5 4 3 2 1

Once again—for Elisabeth.

———

a broad and ample road, whose dust is gold,
and pavement stars, as stars to thee appear
seen in the galaxy, that milky way
which nightly as a circling zone thou seest
powder'd with stars.

him that yon soars on golden wing . . .

John Milton
PARADISE LOST

———

1

IN THE OORT CLOUD

She is a Goldenwing and her name is Glory. *Her bones are titanium plated with gold, and fragile as those of a bird. She wears a skin of monomolecular fabric; each strand of the thread from which it is woven is a single long molecule. Delicate as it is, it has withstood micrometeoroid strikes, asteroid collisions, and the dust between the stars.* Glory *is far older than her syndicate. She has outlived many syndicates before it.*

She was built in orbit around the Moon, one thousand seven hundred of Earth's years ago. She is still one of the most beautiful artifacts ever made by Man.

Glory *was completed in the last year of the Twenty-first Century— near the end of the Exodus and in the midst of a religious revival. The story is told that she was christened with holy water and blessed by a bishop. It may be so. In the last years of the Exodus there was a jihad. Christians were hunted down and slaughtered in the streets of a mostly Muslim world.*

Glory *was commissioned to carry preachers, priests, monks, and nuns to the safety of the stars. Her first destination was Ross 128/2, a world called Aldrin.*

They named her Gloria Coelis—Glory *of Heaven. On her maiden voyage she carried four thousand New Catholics and seven thousand Protestants stacked in honeycomb holds, in frozen sleep, to sanctuary, eleven light-years from Earth.*

Yet even as Glory *spread her sails to the tachyon wind, the Exodus was ending. The homeworld, sick with religious slaughter and drained of her most adventurous souls, had grown weary. It would take a thousand years for the planet to restock itself with freedom and enough courage to continue the colonization of the stars.*

At the completion of Glory's *maiden voyage, she became the property of the men and women who sailed her, the first syndicate. Many changes of command later, she has become the ship of Duncan's syndicate—a fifth generation of Wired Starmen.*

Glory *and her people have been in space, with only short stays downworld, for twelve ship years. A working span for Starmen, many lifetimes for landsmen, who live by a different measure.*

The tachyons which flow from the galactic center are the only particles in the known universe that exceed the speed of light. The hectares of skylar sails a Goldenwing flies impede tachyons and transfer a fraction of their enormous energy to the ship. And as a Goldenwing approaches lightspeed, time dilates. Objects in motion experience time more slowly than objects at rest. The laws of relativity are strange but inflexible.

At this moment, Glory *is transiting the Oort Cloud of the system Luyten 726. She is slowing, but still moving at a fraction of the speed of light. In two shiptime days of twenty hours each, she will assume high orbit over Planet Luyten 726/4, known as Voerster. And on a hilltop on Voerster, where* Glory *is being watched nightly by an old astronomer whose dream it has been to live long enough to see a second Goldenwing, a month will pass before* Glory's *shuttles descend to the capital town of the Voertrekkers.*

Time dilation plays strange games with short-lived humans.

It is their spread of sail that gives Glory *and her sisterships the name of Goldenwing. Skylar is gossamer-thin and the color of sunlight. From* Glory's *ten-kilometer-long hull rise a half dozen slender masts. Angled at ninety degrees are her two mains. They rise fifty kilometers from carapace deck to masthead. There are three mizzens of thirty kilometers each and a foremast of ten. The monofilament rigging gleams like a spider's web in the starlight of the Oort Cloud. The trim of* Glory's *tops and skysails can presently be monitored only by the hundreds of imaging devices scattered throughout the rig.*

The radio environment surrounding the ship carries the chittering voices of the monkeys, small cyborgs who scurry through the rig performing the myriad tasks needed to keep a sailing ship moving at her best speed. Their voices are high-pitched, simian. They speak a language created for them by Glory's computer, part machine clicks and tones, part animal chirps and growls. It is exactly suited to the monkey-brained cyborgs; Glory is semisentient, and she provides for all her creatures.

Seen from the bridge and from the dorsal apertures in the hull, the eternal sky seems dominated by the eighty million square meters of bright skylar Glory flies. But that is only illusion. The Wired Ones know that humans are insignificant intruders among the stars.

In orbit around an inhabited world a Goldenwing is seen sailing across the night, a golden creature, wraithlike, silent, a vision of light and breathtaking, commanding beauty. It is a sight landsmen think themselves lucky to see once in a generation.

"There," mothers tell their children. "Your great, great great grandparents came here"—from Earth, or Gagarin, or Christa McAuliffe—"in one of those beautiful things. Perhaps in that very one."

There is fear in the women's voices. Wired Ones make demands. On Search they may ask for a child. Children chosen tend to submit willingly to the surgery and training. To those left behind they become an object of awe. On some worlds, like ice-covered Lalande 2, the chosen have been remembered as gods.

A Goldenwing in the sky is a promise of adventure, and of escape from the subsistence worlds where colonists struggle to survive. But now Goldenwings are very few, and the paucity echoes with ancestral sadness. A rare Goldenwing awakens memories of the blue Earth, and touches watchers with the melancholy of humanity's restless roaming.

The age of the sailing starships is nearly ended. They have performed great services. They have carried humanity to the near stars: to triple Centaurus, to Barnard's Star, Wolf, Lalande, to Sirius A and B, to the Ross pair, to Indi, to 61 Cygni, to the Luyten Stars. But it is nearly done now. It will take Earth thousands of her swift years to repopulate sufficiently to launch a second wave at the stars.

The colony worlds are primitive; few have progressed beyond hand labor and agriculture. It is not an easy thing to people an empty galaxy.

But it is an article of faith among Goldenwing crews that when Earth is reclaimed by her far-traveling children, they will not come in cold-sleep, aboard sublight sailing ships. They will come in new vessels, swifter than light, and armed with new sciences developed under foreign suns.

But this tomorrmow will not dawn in Glory's time. Nor in the time of Duncan's syndicate. On some colony worlds interplanetary ships are built and manned. But Glory and her sisterships are the work of Earth, the homeworld. The golden starships and their Wired Ones, though fewer this century than last, are still the reaching hand of humankind.

There is a dead man in Glory's hold 1009. For him, relativity has ceased at last to have meaning. He was a member of Glory's fifth syndicate before he became the astroprogrammer for the syndicate captained by Duncan Kr. Han Soo was eighty, shiptime, when he died of a stroke. He was born on Earth, in a land called China, eighteen hundred years ago.

Glory has sailed from Sol to Barnard's Star, to Proxima, then to Wolf, and now to the Luyten Stars. A round-robin voyage takes Glory five years uptime.

The tachyon winds are constant. As once her clipper ship precursors were driven by the trades across the oceans of Earth, Glory is driven by the great Coriolis force of the epochal spin of the Milky Way galaxy.

With starlight reflecting from her great wings, Glory traverses the Luyten Oort Cloud—the Luyten solar system's vast englobature of frozen rock and ice far beyond the orbit of Luyten 726/9, the gas giant Drache.

Glory tacks and points to intercept Planet Voerster, fourth from the Luyten sun.

Starmen, it is said, are made, not born. Physically, this is certainly true. Each has undergone neuropsychosurgery and a socket implant. And each began life as a downworlder. Almost without exception Starmen are recruited as children by other Starmen on Search downside. There are women Starmen, but they are few. Fertile females are not surrendered willingly by colonial societies with empty worlds to populate.

Aboard Glory in this syndicate period there is a single woman. Anya Amaya—her name, in the language of New Earth, where she was *born—is pronounced with a kind of musical elision. She is native to the tenth planet of Proxima Centauri where women must breed at thirteen. When* Glory *appeared over New Earth Anya had reached the age of fifteen and had not yet borne a child. Considered useless by her femina-group, she was—in the manner of New Earth—offered for sale.*

It was her blind good fortune that Glory's *computer detected a talent; Duncan's syndicate bought her the moment she was put on the market. She has now been in space, Wired, for four uptime years. On New Earth nineteen years have passed and Anya is forgotten. The cold women of New Earth do not bestow godhood on Goldenwing crews. They are far too sophisticated for that.*

Starship syndicates are pure meritocracies. On Glory, *once her neurosurgery and implant healed, Duncan and* Glory's *computer have made Anya Sailing Master.*

At this moment Anya lies nude in her pod on the bridge. Her body twitches and quivers like a sleeping cat's. Through the thick cable connecting the computer to the socket in the back of Anya's skull, she and Glory *are exchanging billions of bits each second. As Sailing Master she is overseeing the work of the monkeys, the set of the sails, the process of sloughing off speed, the availability of the crew, the distance of proto-comets, the gravitational effects of distant bodies.*

At this vast distance from the Luyten star, and so lightly tasked, Anya has time for personal concerns.

She has been humoring the old astronomer on Voerster. His name is Osbertus Kloster, and he is related to the ruling family of Voerster. Anya has been in communication with him for weeks. By burst code alone. Relative time-scales must be matched before voice communication is possible.

But Osbertus has used his primitive radio dishes to send excited greetings and information about the astronomy of the Luyten 726 system. His greatest accomplishment as a scientist has been a plot of the six gas giants of the outer Luyten solar system. He has carefully and in great detail informed Anya of the known facts about Erde, Smuts, deKlerk, Wallenberg, Thor and Drache. It is his contribution to a great event: the arrival at Voerster of a Goldenwing.

Using Glory's computer, Anya Amaya has had the astronomy of the Luyten solar system plotted for weeks. But ever tactful, the girl has pretended that Osbertus Kloster has provided Glory with vital information.

Now she is giving gentle orders to the monkeys who are swiftly reefing and backing the sails so that Glory may begin to bleed off excessive delta-V. Once done, Glory will slingshot around the outermost giant—Drache—and overtake Voerster, arriving exactly two twenty-nine hour days before Voerster's apastron, when the season of storms ends on Voerster's stratospheric highlands.

Anya Amaya joyously uses the astronomical assets available to her to achieve an elegant solution to a problem in celestial mechanics. This ability is the talent Glory's computer discovered. It is the reason that Anya Amaya is Sailing Master. All Starmen are talented. It is a requirement of their craft. Anya Amaya and her captain, Duncan Kr, are more talented than most.

Glory's cold-sleep combs were empty. They had been empty since the last colonists awoke on Aldrin, long ago. The only human thing in the combs was the dead astroprogrammer in hold 1009.

A strange man, Han Soo, with a horror of drifting in interstellar space for eternity. Duncan had promised him a burial in soil. If not the soil of China on Earth, then what soil the colonists of Voerster would allow a man of Old Earth.

The Goldenwings suffered from an ancient malady. They were no longer "economically viable enterprises." Without colonists to transport, what could a ship carry that might be ordered by one generation and delivered to another? This vulnerability to market forces was slowly forcing Goldenwings into dismantlement and oblivion. Circling Columbia, the colony world of the 61 Cygni system, the Goldenwing *Starbolt* slumbered away eternity as a space museum, visited by the precocious children of a technologically advanced society. On Wheat, the prairie world of Beta Indi, the bones of Goldenwing *Potemkin* lay like fossils surrounded by fifty million hectares of grain. But *Glory* sailed on.

She carried timeless things. In her holds were ingots of rare elements, old books and works of art, bolts of silk and tapestries, gemstones from Barnard's Star, and polished slates from Lalande. There were a few technological supplies now far out of date at home, but still useful to colonists on less favored worlds.

Glory was certain of a welcome on Voerster. She carried frozen animal embryos for the kraals and farms of Voerster's savannahs. There were horses, beef cattle, goats, sheep, and dogs. On Voerster's single continent there were only the few animals descended from the stock brought by the First Landers. Offworld stock had not prospered on Planet Voerster. And there was a sea of wild grass. But there were no trees, no insects, no flowers, and no native mammals. The indigenous life-forms were necrogenes struggling, against their nature, to survive.

A Voertrekker of Voerster could do without native flowers and insects. He could live without trees. But he could not survive without a replenishment of his stock of Terrestrial farm and domestic animals.

A great many of Voerster's five-hundred-day years before, an ancestor of the present Voertrekker-Praesident had ordered a vast shipment of genetically engineered animals from the captain of a Goldenwing named *Nostromo*.

The old Voertrekker's descendant now awaited the arrival of the shipment. The *volk* of Voerster could always be counted on to be stolidly patient and to take the long view of things.

On Voerster, the long view was the only view. Thirteen hundred planetary years before this time, colonists from South Africa had been landed on the single great continent by the Goldenwing *Milagro*. The voertrekking whites had fled from the plague-ridden horror of Africa. Miraculously, they had persuaded several thousand blacks to join them in cold-sleep and colonization. "Look about you," they said to the kaffirs. "See what Africa has become. There is talk of democracy, but what is real is the repression, plague, tyranny, and death you see all about you. On Luyten we promise you opportunity."

For the first three hundred years the promises were kept and

Voerster prospered. There were some who saw a threat in the assumption of that name, called it code for oppression to come. But the whites wished only to honor their tribal leader, they said, who had led them skyward.

The Great Kaffir Rebellion exploded 301 years after Landers' Day. It began as a riot and ended in a ten-year war between the races. Civilization was staggered, knowledge was lost. A population laboriously built up to number ten million whites, sixty million blacks and fifteen million persons of mixed blood was savagely reduced to one-twentieth of that number. Science, except for the technology of war, languished. The medical arts stagnated. What had been a burgeoning technological society reverted to rustication. And there it remained, slowly dying, a sad replica of the world of apartheid the first white colonists of Voerster had secretly longed for.

The crew of *Gloria Coelis* knew little of Voerster's history. The planet had not been visited since the brief call by Goldenwing *Nepenthe* more than fifty years before. But what *Nepenthe* might have discovered about Voerster, only *Nepenthe*'s syndicate knew. Goldenwing syndicates dealt with one another through agents. Space is simply too vast for chance encounters.

Anya Amaya, her eyes open but unseeing, caused the mizzen foretops to be furled preparatory to tacking the ship out of the Oort Cloud. Her move, so neatly done that it took only a score of monkeys racing up the rigging and out onto the spars, was watched and admired by the Captain.

Duncan Kr was a man with a natural appreciation of elegance, and the Sailing Master's skill was worthy of her talent. Within a solar system Anya sailed *Glory* like a zero-gravity dancer.

Duncan's pod lay next to the Sailing Master's. There were others, one for each member of the crew, but at the moment they were empty. Like Anya, Duncan lay nude in the pod's glyceroid medium, hard-wired to the computer.

His globe of awareness was far larger than Anya Amaya's. Her responsibility was to sail *Glory*, who was *yare*. Sweet to sail, quick to the helm, swift and manageable. Duncan's talent and responsibility was larger. His computer-enhanced awareness englobed the entire vessel and the millions of cubic kilometers of space around her. Duncan sensed the Luyten 726 solar system almost in its entirety. He felt the turbulence of the Oort Cloud, cluttered with hurtling rocks and clumps of ice. Duncan was aware of collisions, close passes, the surge of gravity tides and centripetal forces.

There were twelve planets circling Luyten out to a distance of 5.6×10^{12} kilometers. The outer six were gas giants. Of the inner six, only one was habitable. Voerster, fourth from the sun, was not an easy world. Space had not provided Man with any worlds as good as his own. Soon Duncan would begin to sense the life on Voerster, still a billion kilometers sunward.

Closer at hand, Duncan was aware of the subtle bioelectric spillages from the living things aboard *Glory*. He felt the faint, spectral plasmas formed by the frozen animal embryos in the hold—the feral, joyous, psychic auras of the ship's family of cats—the strongest from Mira, the young queen who has been given her own small remote interface with *Glory*'s computer. A sardonic joke by Dietr Krieg, the German neurocybersurgeon.

Wired, Duncan shared the protothoughts of the simian-brained cyborgs who inhabited the rig. Duncan even detected the melancholy grace notes released by Han Soo's slowly dissolving synapses in the comb.

Sentience, Duncan thought, was fragile. But final death in the cold of space can be a slow business.

As Master and Commander—the syndicates were always drawn to ancient ranks and titles—Duncan was aware of all *Glory* contained, including her crew.

He shared Mathematician Jean Marq's troubled sleep as he sweated through his nocturnal bout with remorse. Each night of every voyage the Frenchman returned to a sunny field long ago in Provence where, over and over, he committed rape and murder.

Dietr Krieg, a saber-blade of a man recruited at the advanced age of thirty-four downtime years, was not sleeping. Duncan felt him nearby.

Dietr, too, was presently hard-wired to the ship's computer. But he was not concerned with *Glory* or the Oort Cloud or anything whatever pertaining to Luyten or the voyage. Krieg's passion was medical knowledge for its own sake. Unlike the others of the syndicate, he never felt a twinge of regret or loneliness. He could as easily have worn a black SS uniform in the Dark Century of Earth, performing grotesque experiments on living men and women. He would have done this without heat or rancor, but with a vast curiosity—much the same sardonic curiosity he expressed when he fitted Mira, a four-year-old Abyssinian cat, with a computer interface. Krieg's only truly human trait was his sense of the prodigious.

As *Glory* transited the dangerous Oort Cloud, Krieg reclined in his quarters, wired to the computer and absorbing a new medical program he had acquired at the last planetfall, on Gagarin. His brain was receiving information at billions of baud. Duncan, aware of the neurocybersurgeon, knew he would not be able to retain data absorbed at such speed. Duncan knew that Krieg knew it, too. But the surgeon was addicted. Hunger for knowledge of his art was what had enticed him into space. "Downside," he had once said to Duncan, "how long could I live? Eighty years? Ninety? How much could medicine progress in that time? But if my years are *uptime*, I can suck medicine dry."

Perhaps, Duncan thought. *There are many wonders. But Dietr lacks a heart. There are things he will never know.*

An impression of fear brushed Duncan's consciousness. It came from young Damon, the last recruit of the *Glory* syndicate. Damon Ng, fifteen and newly Wired. It was his task to back up the monkeys, to handle whatever problems they could not. It was the most menial task aboard *Glory* and the most physically challenging. The Rigger must go EVA many times each voyage and must often climb to the tops, fifty kilometers from the hull of the ship.

Damon Ng was chosen on Grissom, the second planet of Ross 154, a forested world of thousand-meter-tall trees. The natives of Grissom spend all their lives under a green canopy. They see the stars rarely. Damon, like many of his generation on Grissom, was raised on fantastic tales of space and Starmen. When the *Glory* syndicate dispatched Krieg and Han Soo downworld on Search, the young man begged his family to give him to *Glory*.

He quickly discovered that without the comforting ceiling of green leaves above his head he was neurotically acrophobic. A climb into *Glory*'s rigging never failed to call up a choking panic. Yet he went extravehicular at every opportunity, determined to conquer his fear.

It was Dietr Krieg who had introduced Damon to the process of "desensitization." No psychiatrist, Krieg was curious about the efficacy of such therapy. When Duncan questioned the wisdom of sending a terrified Rigger EVA, Dietr said, "It is an old Earth method, Duncan. If a horse throws you, you must get back into the saddle."

Duncan asked drily, "Does it work?"

"It may," Dietr Krieg replied. "But how would I know? I am a neurosurgeon, not a feelgood."

At the moment there was a minor tangle at the blocks of the starboard mizzen top. A monkey could clear it easily, but Damon Ng was determined to master his phobia. Duncan allowed it because to shield young Damon would be to destroy him. A frightened man between the stars was a menace to himself and to his syndicate.

At this moment Damon was at the mizzen top, untethered, clearing the block and weeping with silent terror.

Duncan feels still another faint, faint sending from the brain of Han Soo. In the cold it takes a life many days to complete its dying. The sending carries the faint scent of soil, the smell of earth. Duncan will ask

———

permission from the Voertrekker-Praesident to lay Han Soo in the ground of Planet Voerster.

Duncan suspects there may be trouble about this. The Afrikaaners who settled Voerster are as bigoted now as they were when they abandoned Earth. But Duncan is prepared to demand a suitable grave for his dead astroprogrammer.

Duncan Kr—it was once Kerr—*is a tall man, long-boned and pale of skin with shaggy dark hair. His face is homely, but finely modeled. He has eyes that are clear, pure blue and set in deep sockets that by now, in his fortieth year, are nested in tiny webs of wrinkles. He has the face of a man grown accustomed to seeing great distances.*

His people, Clan Kr, were very long ago Scots from the islands of Earth called Hebrides. But for seven generations Clan Kr had lived in a bleak seaside village called Chalkmeer, a settlement of stone huts and a stone pier on the north coast of the continent of Sin on Thalassa of Wolf 359, eight light-years from Earth. Thalassa is a world of saltwater and stone, a perpetually wintry world with a single, great satellite that raises tides of two hundred meters once each forty-day month. Huge tides and storms dominate the single enormous sea of Thalassa. Sin is the only continent. It is gray-green with oxygen-producing lichens. What remains of Thalassa is a gray-green ocean. The land is all rocks and mountains, and it lies under snow for two-thirds of the long, 900-day year.

As a colony Thalassa has not been a success. Life is too difficult and the colonists too few. Humanity is slowly, inexorably losing its grip on the planet. But Duncan's people have always been seafarers and fisherfolk. They are stolid and determined—despite the fact that the colony actually began to die the day the sleepers left Goldenwing Aristotle's planetary shuttle and stood to stare in silent dismay at their world.

But for generations they have endured, though each long year there are fewer of them.

Until Duncan was eleven, Earth Standard, he, like all the few children of Thalassa, trolled for the red-furred fishes of the deep ocean. These sad creatures cried out in pain when they were gaffed into the boats, and Duncan, a natural empath, felt their pain and sickened.

His parents were dour, but not unkind. They had no time for therapies and disappointments. Duncan was put to work ashore, to help the women of Chalkmeer grow barley in the interstices of the rocks on which the village perched above the sea.

Duncan was one of six children of a marriage group consisting of four men and a dozen women. The dour Scot settlers grudgingly had chosen this form of marriage as a hedge against the sea, which killed men and left widows.

Duncan was willing and strong for his age, and he might have lived out a life there by the Thalassa Sea in the rocky village of Chalkmeer.

But when Glory *appeared in Thalassa's night sky, the clan met at the Scone Stone by firelight, and as the flames leaped skyward, considered how best to deal with the Starmen.*

Glendora Kr, the clan's Yearleader, mounted the Stone and spoke to the gathered people. "The Starmen have come back, as the Computer predicted that they would do. But we have no goods to sell nor money with which to buy. We have no items they can carry into the sky, for the fishes have surrendered only enough furs to suppy the grand folk of Sin. The Wired Ones, they know many things. They surely know our state. Then we must consider: why are they here?"

Rob Kr, thought to be Duncan's father, spoke up. "They have come on Search. They will ask for one of our sons or daughters." He regarded his fellow clansmen soberly. "They will never take a child unwilling, but if we refuse them they will never return." He glanced up at the windswept night sky.

Glory, *in synchronous orbit over the land of Sin, was a bright golden star near the limb of Bothwell, the great moon of Thalassa. "They will descend in a shuttle that rides on fire. The Good Book Program describes it all. I put it to you that we must let them leave us satisfied we have treated them with respect." He looked sadly around the circle of the burning stone fire. "We all know that one day—who can say when?—our children or our children's children will need the goodwill of the Starmen. So let us select a child, and ask that they choose that one and no other, for the great sea is broad and we are few." Rob Kr sat himself down in silence.*

Katryn M'donald, the mother of twelve strong daughters, said to the Yearleader: "What Rob says is so. The Starmen must always smile on us."

Glendora, still standing on the Stone, said to Katryn, "Do you offer one of your girls?"

"I will if I must."

The clan children, all who were old enough to attend the meeting at the Stone, murmured, some fearfully, a few expectantly.

Rob Kr stood again. "I have the candidate. My Duncan loves the sea but hates the hunt. He is one we can spare." Rob was known as a loveless man, but the clansmen whispered at this and the Preacher murmured, "'Take now thy son, thine only son Isaac, whom thou lovest, and get thee into the land of Moriah; and offer him there for a burnt offering upon one of the mountains which I will tell thee of.'"

"That is a brave thing you do, Rob," said Glendora, who was Duncan's birth mother. "It is fit that I join you in it."

And when the Starmen rode their shuttle down and the then-captain of the Glory, a man old even in uptime, named Washington, with black skin and white hair, was met with fish and salt (the gifts of submission on Thalassa), Glendora Kr called Duncan and offered him to the Starman.

It had been a hundred and fifteen long years since last a Goldenwing paused at Thalassa, but the clansmen knew the ritual. Washington felt young Duncan's skull gently and then asked, "Will you travel with us, boy? To the stars?"

"Oh, yes. Yes, sir," Duncan replied.

The choosing was not complete until Duncan had been examined for suitability by another ancient Starman, a neurocybersurgeon. When this was done, Duncan's forehead was painted with a star and Chalkmeer launched into three days of bittersweet celebration.

The clans from kilometers around were represented and there was even a delegation from the Meeting House in Edinburgh. The Starmen, all of whom were aged, said that they had postponed their Search until reaching the Wolf Stars because great Starmen were born under the sign of the Wolf. It may have been flattery, but if it was it was well intended and the clansmen of Chalkmeer were pleased. In those few days Duncan was treated with more love and affection than he had ever known in his father's cold croft. After the feasting Duncan was taken to a newly built, clean croft and there given aphrodisiacs mixed in strong beer, and for three nights until Moon Bothwell waned, he was visited by each of the nubile girls in Clan Kr, so that his genes would not be lost to the breeding pool.

Then he was decorated with garlands of barley, wrapped in red furs and escorted to the shuttle with songs and bagpipes.

It is many years uptime since that day and those nights by the great ocean. On Thalassa eighty years have gone by. Rob and Glendora Kr are dead. The sons and daughters Duncan spawned in the ceremonial croft have grown old with families of their own. Like all Starmen, Duncan imagines that one day he will revisit the world of his birth. He will not. When Starmen do return to their starting points, they find only weathered headstones over the folk they once knew.

2

DEORBIT DAY IN VOERSTERSTAAD

Frowning with peevishness, Ian Voerster, Voertrekker-Praesident and leader of the majority party in the Deliberative Assembly, sat wrapped in furs as the open electric carriage turned the corner at the Gate of Advance and started down the long, narrow avenue toward the Kongresshalle.

Sedate, he thought. That was the word for the progress of his limousine. If the ornate wagon made fifteen kilometers in an hour it was doing well. Once there had been cars on Voerster that ran on petroleum. But the Rebellion had put paid to all that. The theories remained, but the war with the kaffirs had destroyed the infrastructure of a once-technological society. In the case of hydrocarbon fuels, the Rebellion had smashed the refining and cracking plants brought in pieces from Earth on the *Milagro*. And like so many other things, the tools to rebuild them were simply not available. Nearly a thousand years after the kaffir uprising, Voerster remained a rustic planet. A backwater. Ian Voerster often dreamed the dream of many Voertrekker-Praesidents before him. If only a Goldenwing could be captured and used exclusively to resupply Voerster. But it would never happen. There were too few Goldenwings, and space was too vast. If a Goldenwing called twice in a century, it was a near miracle.

At close intervals along Advance Street, police militia in dress uniforms stood at attention. It was what was due the Head of State since the Rebellion, but Ian Voerster viewed the scene with distemper. The driver, a kaffir called Joshua, and the plainclothes bodyguard, a Trekkerpolizei of the Wache—the Security Troops—named Ryndik, sat like bookends, one ebony, one white, on the driver's bench. Ian Voerster prized kaffirs able to remain silent—a gift rare among the garrulous blacks. Ryndik, too, spoke seldom—so seldom, in fact, that there were rumors around Voertrekkerhoem that the bodyguard had been captured by wild kaffirs who cut out his tongue. The rumor was as untrue as it was grotesque. Such atrocities had not been perpetrated on Voerster since the Rebellion. But silent kaffir and laconic policeman sat dispassionately together on the carriage bench, wrapped, as was Ian Voerster, in furs against the bitter sea wind that blew across the city from Amity Bay.

Actually, Ian Voerster's white servants all loved ceremonial occasions. The Voertrekker chose them from families of soldiers and policemen who had a taste for the panoplies of power. Whether or not kaffir Joshua or any other loved Voertrekker holidays and ceremonies, the Voertrekker-Praesident never wondered or cared.

The crowd of kaffirs and white *lumpen* lining the streets of Voersterstaad had shown minimal respect, but they had been sullen. Deorbit Day marked the anniversary of the departure of the Voertrekker colony ship from Earth, and for this reason the Convocation always began at the hour of breaking orbit from Earth's Moon. In that place, long ago, the hour had been 1322 hours Greenwich Universal Time. The First Landers had immortalized the event by setting the opening of the summer Convocation of the Deliberative Assembly to 1322 Western Province Time. The fact was that no one had any idea of the relation, if any, between the two times. Ian Voerster was fond of quoting the Law of Unintended Consequences. In the case of commemorating Deorbit Day with a Convocation, the First Landers could not have foreseen the Great Kaffir Rebellion or the Security Laws which followed, namely the Kaffir Curfew—a law, passed by the Deliberative Assembly, enjoining all kaffirs to be in their townships by 1800 hours. Since the Rebellion, all Voertrekker ceremonials were scheduled to begin after the kaffirs were out of sight. Except the Deorbit Day Convocation, whose hour had been established long ago and very far away.

The effect was to force the races to share this one Convocation. Voertrekkers disapproved, because it seemed an improper mixing of white and colored. Kaffirs disapproved because inclusion in this occasion made them acutely aware that they were excluded from the others on Voerster. The Preachers of Elmi seemed to delight in telling their black congregations that they should love Voerster because it was as much theirs as it was the Voertrekkers'. So Elmi, as white as a snow-peak, was said to have believed. The thought irritated the Voertrekker-Praesident. The cult, for generations only an annoying kaffir fantasy, was now fashionable among University students and even some Kraalheeren.

In his heart Ian Voerster, like many Voertrekkers, disliked sharing Deorbit Day with the kaffirs, but as the Voertrekker-Praesident, Ian was the guardian of traditions, which demanded that the Deorbit Day Convocation ceremonials be paraded before kaffir and Voertrekker alike at the hour stated by the First Landers. Even after so long, the Rebellion still loomed like a threatening shadow over the rulers of Voerster. But courage, too, was a tradition among Voertrekkers, and it would have been bad form to admit that the inhabitants of the townships still had the power to make Voertrekkers tremble.

Beauty had not been a consideration when the state's architects designed the government buildings of Voerster. Public construction was designed to be daunting to the eye. It was. The Kongresshalle and the surrounding structures—the Ministry of Defense, the Treasury, the Police Academy, and Home Barracks—had all been designed after the kaffirs were put down and confined to the townships. The architecture was as massive and suspicious as Voertrekker society—resentful and alert.

The *halle* had the look of nothing else on the planet. Not even the heavy buildings of Pretoria University, two thousand kilometers across the Sea of Grass on the eastern shore of the continent, were so uncompromising. Voertrekker taste naturally ran to stone lodges and bermed manor houses. Dwellings, while always built to larger-than-human scale, crouched low to seek shelter from the constant winds. But the Kongresshalle was arrogant. Its high facade was lined with galleries of blind stone arches, each constructed to collapse on an advancing enemy when the keystone was removed. Above the arches, gray stone walls were pierced with narrow gun-ports high above ground level. Truncated towers stood at each corner of the vast structure, and from each flew the Voertrekker flag—a white cross on a field of black—and under the planetary flag, the banner of one of the four provinces.

It was an intimidating building. With the Wache and police barracks and the armory, the Kongresshalle covered a half dozen hectares of some of the best agricultural land on a planet not known for fertility. Ian Voerster accepted this as a proper sacrifice made to preserve the values of Trekker society.

Like most Voertrekkers, the Voertekker-Praesident was a farmer. Also like most Voertrekkers, he led a life of privilege supported, on this bleak and wintry world, by the vast labor force of kaffirs descended from the breeding stock brought from Earth by the First Landers. From the first day on Voerster, the Voertrekkers had made it plain to the kaffirs that the promises made on Earth would be kept in abeyance until the society was properly established. They were still in abeyance. The Rebellion had put fulfillment even further away. The kaffirs gave their labor and withdrew their trust. And so it had been for a thousand years. So it would be forever.

Yet even for the privileged mynheeren class, life on the Sea of Grass was harsh. And however hard life might be for the kraal owners of the Grassersee, it was infinitely harder for the descendants of the First Landers who had settled on the stratospheric lands of the Planetia, where the mean altitude above sea level was fifty-five hundred meters and the atmospheric pressure less than half what a normal man needs to breathe.

The *volk* of the Planetia had all but become a race apart on Voerster, and it was this separation that Ian Voerster was resolved to reverse. The Highlanders were vital to the defense of the State should the kaffirs ever rebel again. Yet they were a deadly danger if allowed to develop further in isolation.

Voerster stared gloomily at the police guard standing along the roadway. Lowlanders, every one. Assuming a Highlander willing to accept Grassersee discipline could be found and put in the Trekkerpolizei or Wache ranks, he would have uglified the neat ranks of the Trekkerpolizei and Wache. Shorter than normal men by a head, the Planetian was built like a wine tun, with a grotesquely distended chest and limbs like the stone pillars of the Kongresshalle. His skin was white, but hidden under a pelt that resembled the coat of an ebray.

The records had been lost, but most medical men on Voerster believed that the Planetians were descended from men and women who had been genetically engineered for the brutal environment of the high plains. Ian Voerster believed it. To a Lowlander, Planetians were human—but only just. There were other physical adaptations among the *volk* of the stratospheric Highlands: an epicanthic fold protected their pale eyes against the glare of the Luyten Sun at high altitude and many were polydactyl on both hands and feet. Under their pelt, the skin had a bluish, anoxic tinge. They were as unruly and vicious as they were unprepossessing.

For a moment Ian Voerster slipped into thinking as a father. He permitted himself to consider the hellish life to which he intended to doom Broni Ehrengraf Voerster when he betrothed her to Vikter Fontein, the Planetian Kraalheer of Winter.

But only for a moment. His ironclad sense of duty and Voertrekker self-righteousness immediately suffocated his conscience. Voertrekkers were not like the other descendants of Earth. They were a *volk* with a vision, a people with a sense of themselves and their duty.

The first Voertrekkers had proved that on Earth, centuries ago on the long trek north from the Cape Colony. The Voertrekker of Voerster today could certainly do nothing to tarnish that steely resolve and awareness of race.

*

The carriages of the one hundred congressmen—each as polished and decorated with gold leaf and appliqués as Voerster's—lined the edges of the roadway. The kaffir drivers had erected banks of solar cells facing the afternoon sun, and each machine appeared to be sucking energy through a cable, replenishing feeble batteries. Electric carriages were used only on holidays and for ceremonial occasions. Little wonder, thought Ian Voerster. It was a sign of the sorry state of Voertrekker science. That was another matter Ian Voerster had always intended to see to, but even after eight years as Voertrekker-Praesident, he had no real notion of how to begin. *Once we were a race of urbanites*, he thought rebelliously, *but now we are a nation of farmers and rustics. It is a mistake to try to make Voerster into something it can never be.*

Kaffir Joshua stopped the carriage directly in front of the stone stairs leading into the first gallery of the Kongresshalle. As Ian Voerster alighted, there was the customary delegation on hand to welcome him. Guildsmen in silver chains from the crafts, academics in caps and gowns, and inevitably, his neighbors from the Kraalheer High Council, a hugely outdated committee that still was, theoretically, in command of distribution among the kraals of supplies from Earth.

The trouble was that no supplies had ever arrived from Earth. In the last two hundred years, the only Goldenwing calling at Voerster had been the *Nepenthe*. She paused briefly in orbit, nineteen years ago. The visit had not been the one awaited, despite the optimistic predictions to that effect from the then-only-middle-aged Astronomer-Select. The last Voertrekkers on Earth had become extinct a thousand years ago. The colonists in Luyten had no agents or relatives who might tend to their affairs on Earth. But the present Voertrekker-Praesident's Great-granduncle had dispatched an order to the homeworld by the captain of the *Nostromo*, a Goldenwing that had called at Voerster a hundred and twenty years before the appearance of *Nepenthe*.

It had been assumed that the appearance of *Nepenthe* was the arrival of that long-ago order. It was not. Had Osbertus Kloster not been related to the Voersters, he would certainly have been dismissed. *Nepenthe* did not carry the supplies ordered by Great-granduncle Titus Voerster. *Nepenthe* brought nothing, stopping only long enough to deposit on Voerster a single, very large, and slightly demented Wired Starman named Black Clavius. Ian Voerster, at that time new in his office and uncertain how to deal with the unprecedented situation, solved his dilemma by doing nothing. For the last nineteen years a grounded Starman, with kaffir skin and the odd notion that he could speak with God, had roamed Voerster preaching foolishness, mingling with the Preachers of Elmi, and practicing shamanism. He was still at it.

The disappointment still rankled Ian Voerster.

The Voertrekker-Praesident was enfolded by the Kraalheeren for his ceremonial walk into the Kongresshalle. In his sabertache lay the latest of the daily reports he had been receiving from Osbertus Kloster at Sternberg. There actually *was* a Goldenwing approaching. And this time, the astronomer assured his cousin the Voertrekker-Praesident, it was the *Gloria Coelis*, carrying the cargos for which Planet Voerster had waited so long. That was the good news, Ian Voerster thought grimly. The bad was that the Starman syndics intended burying a yellow man in the soil of Voerster. No person, black or white, on Voerster had ever seen an Asiatic. And who knew what other outlandish demand the Starmen might make?

But the main business of this day, Voerster thought, was not about Starmen and their strange ways. His first and most important meeting after the tedious business of the Convocation was done, was with Vikter Fontein.

The Kraalheeren convoyed him closely (like a tarted up prisoner, he thought) into the Great Room crowded with two hundred of his peers gathered for the trimestrial democratic sham of the Convocation of the Deliberative Assembly.

The interior of the room was paneled in polished brownstone, somberly reflecting the heavily dressed splendor of the assembled Voertrekkers. There were three Convocations each year, holdovers from the early days when the First Landers opted for their own peculiar brand of parliamentary government. The Deliberative Assembly had never managed self-government. The nation of Voerster—the only nation on the only continent on the planet—was an oligarchy. It had never been anything else.

Ian Voerster settled into the uncomfortable Machtstuhl—the Chair of Power—a narrow throne made of valuable wood (and a source of aching buttocks to a long succession of Voertrekker-Praesidents). The legs of the Chair were carved into representations of the incredibly ancient Roman fasces, the bundle of rods representing the power to chastise, and the ax representing the power to kill. Earth-images.

The chaplain began his long and certain-to-be-dreary New Lutheran Invocation and the Assembly stood with heads bowed. There were never any seats on the floor of the Great Room. An ancestor of Ian Voerster, infuriated by seventeen hours of speech-making, had decreed that in future, all delegates to Convocations would stand for the duration of the ceremonials. Later, in the separate meeting rooms scattered throughout the gloomy pile of the Kongresshalle, the delegates could sit for their inevitable wrangles. *But thank the Lord God*, Ian Voerster thought, *here they must stand until their legs ache.*

His somber eyes fixed on the corner of the Great Room where the delegates from the Planetia stood shoulder to shoulder around the commanding figure of Vikter Fontein. No bowed heads there.

Fontein, bulky even for a Planetian, returned his gaze with a steady, dark hostility. The Voertrekker-Praesident frowned. To retain the fidelity of the high plains he must win the loyalty of that savage man. *Broni, child, forgive me*, Ian Voerster thought, knowing that even if his daughter did, his wife, the kraalheera of Ehrengraf, never would.

———

3

AT STERNHOEM

Five hundred kilometers from Voersterstaad's lights stood the Sternberg—the Star Mount. As mountains went on Planet Voerster, Sternberg was unremarkable in all respects but one. The hill—for such it was, with slopes covered with the primitive grasses of the plain that surrounded it—was six hundred meters high. On the summit stood the single dome of the National Observatory of Sternhoem. The top of the Sternberg was the highest ground between the Great Southern Ocean and the Shieldwall of the Planetia. Here, above the Grassersee lived the current Astronomer-Select of Voerster, Osbertus Kloster, sixty local years old and a cousin of the Voertrekker-Praesident.

Inside the observatory dome stood an Earth-built, copper-tubed, twenty-six-inch refracting telescope. It was a matter of great pride to each succeeding Astronomer-Select that the instrument had come to Voerster aboard the *Milagro*. It was more than a thousand downtime years old and in beautiful condition.

For generations the holders of Sternhoem had been pensioned academics from the University of Pretoria. Some had been Osbertus' own forebears. Sinecures ran in families on Voerster. Most holders had been content to do the local astrometrics Astronomers-Select had always done. One measured the precession of Voerster's seasons, charted the annual pattern of sunspots on the surface of Luyten 726, and searched fruitlessly for the brown dwarfs believed to be a part of the Luyten 726 astronomical triple. The dwarfs could not be found with the equipment available, and they were so distant that their effect on Voerster was almost nil—and would be so for the next five hundred thousand years. The brown dwarfs became a kind of scientific Holy Grail, distant, improbable, legendary.

Osbertus spent his first years at Sternhoem searching for the brown dwarfs as all Voertrekker astronomers were bound to do. But with the passing of years he had become fascinated with radio astronomy.

Voerster had gone into shock during the Rebellion. It had still not recovered. Many sociologists believed it never would. There was hydroelectric power generated by the rivers that plunged down the sheer cliffs of the Planetian Shieldwall, and steel was still made on Voerster. There was coal and iron and a low level of science and technology. But the passage of a thousand years had strange effects on post-Rebellion society. Time had become detached from the people's lives. The Rebellion—a seminal experience for Voertrekkerdom—never really receded into history. It was as though it had happened last year. And the advances Voerster had laboriously made in the years between the arrival of the *Milagro* and the Rebellion were never recovered. The population stagnated. Intellectuals feared Voertrekker society was moribund. It had lasted a thousand years after the Rebellion through the grim miracle of the Voertrekker mind-set. According to the gloomy demographers of Pretoria University, it could not last another five hundred.

But with diligence and sacrifice and that same dogged determination that characterized the Voertrekker breed, Osbertus Kloster was single-handedly able to resurrect the science of radio astronomy. Crude parabolic dishes, fashioned by the Astronomer-Select and his kaffir work force, dotted the crest of the Sternberg.

From Sternhoem to Durban on the southern coast the distance was seven hundred kilometers. Pretoria lay two thousand two hundred kilometers due east. And between the observatory and the nearest part of the northern Shieldwall lay another thousand kilometers of the Sea of Grass, empty but for a half dozen isolated kaffir townships.

Osbertus Kloster was an improbable innovator. He was nearly

fifty years old on a planet where a year was made of 510 twenty-nine-hour days. An Earthman would have said he was in his seventies. Kloster was also overweight, unmarried, shy, and cursed with a face and manner so amiable that he was customarily taken for a fool. He was not a fool, but he had long ago discovered that a poor relative of a ruling family on Voerster was almost certain to be thought one. His mother, now ten years deceased, had been Ian Voerster's great-aunt. Using family influence, she had obtained a University eduation for her three sons. From Pretoria one went to the clergy, the second to the army. Osbertus presented a problem, but fortunately Klosters had been scientists in times past. She prevailed upon The Voerster to give Osbertus the sinecure of Sternhoem. And at Sternhoem he remained, humble and grateful.

Nineteen years ago Osbertus had nearly lost his post when he mistook some unrecognized electronic emissions from the Goldenwing *Nepenthe* as indications that Vorster's long, long awaited shipment of farm animals and other goods from Earth was about to arrive. When *Nepenthe* only paused long enough to maroon the Starman Clavius, the then-new Voertrekker-Praesident Cousin Ian had been furious, claiming that Osbertus had made him look a fool.

Osbertus learned caution from the incident. But he also learned to take great pleasure from the presence in the Sea of Grass of the marooned Starman Black Clavius, who had never, in all his years of wandering exile, failed to stop at Sternhoem to discourse and drink *greena*, the bitter grass brandy of Voerster, with Osbertus.

Once, to Osbertus' great delight the Starman said, quite without urging, "God is pleased with you, Mynheer Osbertus. You are a Voertrekker of a very different kind."

On Voerster, the word *Voertrekker* did varied service. The inhabitants of Voerster called themselves Voertrekkers. They were ruled by *the* Voertrekker-Praesident. Most of their monuments incorporated the word Voertrekker or the idea of Voertrekkerdom. Many centuries ago, the people from whom the Voertrekkers of Voerster sprang had left southern Africa to found a Free State. Those who led this great migration were called *Voertrekkers*—literally "those who travel in front."

In the Age of the Exodus, Bol-Derek Voerster, leader of the embattled and finally defeated Successor State, engaged the Goldenwing *Milagro* to carry the folk and their laborers to a recently discovered world in the Luyten system. The old Boer died of shock awakening from cold-sleep. But it was declared that the patriarch's dying wish was that the world be known as *Voerster* and the perople as Voertrekkers "*until the end of time or the Day of Judgment, whichever comes last.*"

If Bol-Derek had lived long enough to see the Planetia, to which a third of his colonists—the less affluent—were assigned, Osbertus Kloster wondered if he might have been less grand with his prediction.

In Kraalheeren circles it was said that Bol-Derek's true genius had been his ability to entice Successor State kaffirs to join the migration to Luyten. It was a Kraalheeren joke that Bol-Derek must have promised the blacks all the grass they could smoke and forty hectares and a mule. But the truth was that Bol-Derek promised them what the Successor State had never delivered: equality, freedom, land, and escape from an Africa grown plague-ridden and chaotic. But Bol-Derek did not survive the awakening from cold-sleep, and when the *Milagro* landed the seeds of the Great Kaffir Rebellion were planted in the soil of Voerster.

The Observatory of Sternhoem and all it contained was considered the property of Mynheer Astronomer-Select. His sinecure included possession for life (at the Voertrekker-Praesident's pleasure) of Sternhoem and all its chattels.

Voertrekker society maintained the colonial fiction that *all* property and worldly goods were owned in common, to be used for the common good. This did not prevent the accumulation of wealth, but it did tend to stifle dissent. Since Landers' Day no one but a male of the Voerster tribe had ever governed from the Machtstuhl or lived in Voertrekkerhoem, the presidential kraal.

A Voertrekker folktale told of Voerster's only female ruler. The story was that once, near election time, a single generation after the Landing, the only candidate, Bolger tum der Voerster, died of a surfeit of *greena* and eel. Though grieving as a wife should, his young bride, a cousin named Elmi Voerster Ehrengraf, disguised herself as her husband, won the election, and assumed the mantle of Voertrekker-Praesident. It was said that she lived out her life as a man, ruling for fifty years. She was reputed never to have left the gloomy galleries of Voertrekkerhoem until taken out in her bier at the age of one hundred and twenty-three. Her austere kindness to the *lumpen* and the kaffirs was legendary, and the source of the mythology surrounding the Cult of Elmi.

The story was probably apocryphal, but Osbertus Kloster had always rather hoped it was true. Black Clavius found it highly amusing but never ventured an opinion on whether Elmi was the stuff of fantasy or flesh and blood.

Eliana Ehrengraf Voerster, the Voertrekkerschatz and, in Osbertus Kloster's opinion, the most beautiful mynheera on Voerster, liked to smile her dazzling smile and say that it should be true, that Elmi must be real. "I would not be related to a shadow," she said. "Even the shadow of a saint."

Around the observatory buildings Osbertus Kloster's kaffirs performed a never-ending labor, building larger and ever larger parabolic radio dishes of steel and wire. The discovery of new high-grade chrome deposits on the penal lands of the Sabercut Peninsula had turned ordinary iron into good quality steel, making the larger dishes possible.

The beds had also been a source of an academic triumph for Osbertus personally. Several years before the discovery, he had presented a rather daring paper at Pretoria stating his belief that in ages past epochal changes were caused by Luyten 726 being a triple star system. The brown dwarf theory again, but with a difference. Perturbations of the system caused by the millennial approaches of one or more of the dwarfs caused, he contended, periodic bombardments of Voerster by large meteors, some of which were the source of the chrome and other rare (on Voerster) elements to be found on the Sabercut.

His fellow academics had first sneered at him and then censured him for presenting a "frivolous" paper. They had refused to reverse their motion of censure until commanded to do so by Ian Voerster, who had decided to give Cousin Osbertus the sinecure of Sternhoem.

The Voertrekker-Praesident had sourly asked him if his theory that bombardment from space was caused by the brown dwarfs was *really* anything more than a guess. It was a guess, but an inspired one.

Radio astronomy became Osbertus Kloster's true love and obsession. The work with the radio dishes continued to open before him a vast panorama of the universe in terms no Voertrekker had imagined since the destruction of the books and computers in the Rebellion.

The dishes outdid the old refracting telescope and were first to discover the approach of the new Goldenwing, though it was now visible as a streak on a photographic plate. In a week's time the *Gloria* would be clearly seen in the Sternhoem refractor, and in two weeks, seen with the naked eye in Voerster's wind-scoured sky.

Having completed his nightly observations, Osbertus Kloster now developed his latest set of glass-and-silver-nitrate plates. The Goldenwing was still beyond the orbit of Drache, but the spectrograph of the light reflected from the starship (How the hectares of golden sails must *gleam*, he thought.) was still blue-shifted. This meant that the vessel was closing Voerster at a goodly percentage of the speed of light.

The signals coming from the Goldenwing were steadily growing stronger and more distinct. It sent a thrill though him to realize that in the far reaches of the solar system there was a young person capable of understanding his clumsy attempts at

Anglic—the *lingua franca* of space. Hunched over his desk in the cavernous dark of the observatory dome, listening to the whir and click of the telescope's ancient equatorial drive, he told himself that he was the most favored of men upon Planet Voerster.

Cousin Ian would be pleased with the new ephemeris. It meant that the beasts ordered so long ago for the farms of Voerster were at last at hand, and who knew what other trade treasures the Goldenwing might have in her cavernous holds? But Ian would give no sign of pleasure or anticipation because he was a dour, dark-minded man who feared another disappointment.

Mynheer Osbertus Kloster wondered what Black Clavius would say when he learned that Wired Men and Women, people like himself from the near stars, would soon walk the soil of Voerster. Perhaps he already knew, Osbertus thought, leaning back in his chair and gnawing absently the pencil he held. He had always suspected that the *Nepenthe* syndicate had marooned Clavius because he had extrasensory powers. But that was only conjecture. The *Nepenthe* had arrived unheralded and departed without a Search. She would not be seen again over Voerster for centuries, perhaps millennia. Osbertus wondered why Clavius had remained on Voerster among the kaffirs. It would be a natural thing to seek one's own kind, even among the stars. But the truth was that Clavius was slightly mad.

But, Osbertus thought firmly, *all* Starmen were peculiar. Clavius was the only Starman the Astronomer-Select had ever actually met face-to-face. But how could Goldenwing crewmen not be strange when they carried embedded in their skulls a terrifying sign of the supernatural?

Clavius wandered the savannahs with his Book of Gospels, his knapsack of homeopathic cures, his musical instrument, and his deep sonorous voice. He was revered in the homelands, where the blacks called him *"Starkaffir."* Even in Voersterstaad there was a kind of clique among the sons and daughters of the elite, devoted to meeting with Clavius and listening to his outlandish stories. The young mynheeren gathered in the parks and commons to hear Black Clavius preach, sing, and spin tales from offworld. Many of the young people were also followers of the Cult of Elmi. Shocking, really, thought Osbertus. A kaffir cult, a kaffir Starman, and the young of the best families on Voerster. Where would it end? he wondered.

Osbertus sometimes attended these meetings incognito. He regarded the marooned star sailor as a perpetually replenished well of information about a vast life he, Osbertus Kloster, could only imagine. And he always made certain that Sternhoem was generous with its hospitality when Clavius appeared. The aging astronomer, even more than the young fashionables, yearned to know about the lands in the sky.

Osbertus pushed the green-shaded lamp away and rubbed at the bridge of his ample nose. All around him was the echoing silence of the observatory dome, catwalks lighted at intervals by red night-lamps. The astronomer's desk was of wood, real wood. When a rare near-tree was felled on Voerster, the logs went to the cabinetmakers of Voersterstaad where artisans cut and polished it until it was almost indistinguishable from the wood brought by the original colonists. Earth wood existed on Voerster only in tiny bits, now used for jewelry. But Osbertus Kloster's desk was from Earth, brought aboard the *Milagro*, along with the Machtstuhl, now in the Great Room of the Kongresshalle in Voersterstaad.

The desk belonged in a museum, and Kloster's great-great-grandfather, a previous holder of the Sternhoem sinecure, had pridefully placed it on display in the grand foyer of the observatory. But when Osbertus became Astronomer-Select, he had had the desk carefully moved upstairs to the base of his beloved telescope so that the two artifacts Osbertus cared about could share one space.

The telescope was shut down and unmoving and had been since the tenth night-hour. It troubled the astronomer that the telescope was so lightly used. But the fact was that the government of the Voertrekker State was penurious and indifferent to astronomy—to all science, except agronomy. Even medicine on the planet progressed—when it did progress—in the footsteps of the plant geneticists.

The native animals of Voerster were all necrogenes. It was interesting to speculate how things would change after the shuttle of the *Gloria Coelis* unloaded ten thousand or more frozen placental mammals for the farms and kraals of Voerster. And wasn't it odd that the word the mynheeren used to denote their estates was a word the homeworld Zulu had once used to describe the enclosures where they confined their cattle? Such matters intrigued the Astronomer-Select. Pondering was his avocation.

He looked thoughtfully into the upper darkness of the dome. The long tube of the refractor seemed to vanish into the gloom. Osbertus had caused Buele to hand-crank the dome closed because who knew what damage might be done by the night to the twenty-six-inch objective lens far above his head? Of course no harm had come to the telescope in all this time, but if—*if* some ill befell the irreplaceable glass, what would Osbertus Kloster do? Suicide as a form of apology was not unknown on Voerster. Osbertus shuddered.

The astronomer had nearly reached the age of retirement. Sixty was a goodly age on Voerster, where the years were 510 days long. He grimaced as he considered. How typically Voertrekker. *We do not live the short traditional years of Earth, but the ponderous years of Luyten 726/4.* Five hundred ten and an awkward fraction days long. Osbertus could not even begin to imagine what it would be like to live on a world where a year was a miserly 365 days long, and there were real seasons. On Voerster there were none. Spring was cold, summer was also cold, and fall was colder still. Winter was frozen. Voerster was not a kind world, but it had its own sort of spartan beauty. Clavius said it was a world to build character.

The astronomer looked again at the sheaf of calculations he had painstakingly completed using the same arithmetic the First Landers had brought with them from home. He sighed, dreaming of the computers he read about in the old texts. *We have the theories but not the means*, he thought sadly, returning to his labor.

By his revised calculations, and always assuming the ship approaching the outermost gas giant in the system would choose to slow at a constant rate, the *Gloria Coelis* would be in orbit around Voerster in two months, three days, and ten hours.

What changes would the Goldenwing bring? Mynheer Osbertus had always been the butt of criticism because of his yearning for change. Cousin Ian, *The* Voerster (his family title, which he bore in addition to his political title of The Voertrekker and his legal rank of Voertrekker-Praesident), quite disliked changes and greatly relished the power of disapproval. He believed with all his God-fearing heart that dissatisfaction led to brashness, arrogance, hauteur, vainglory, and self-love. These qualities resulted in sinfulness, ineptitude, and wickedness. So Church and chaplain taught, and so the Voertrekker-Praesident believed.

Osbertus had small brashness, little arrogance, and despite being a mynheer, almost no hauteur whatever. A certain vainglory and self-love he could not deny. But he wished that The Voerster could find it in his heart to be more tolerant of a poor relation. More than once Cousin Ian had threatened to close down Sternhoem. But for the intercession of Cousin Eliana, he quite possibly might have actually done it. He had not yet forgiven Osbertus for his personal disappointment in the *Nepenthe* affair. He probably never would.

Osbertus spoke aloud, "But a Voertrekker who has discovered *two* Goldenwings in a lifetime surely has a right to a *bit* of vainglory?" His cherubic face twisted into a comic opera laugh. "No?" he said to the darkness. "Then a kind word, surely."

He heard a noise at the door, which stood at the end of a long, helical steel ladder attached to the outside of the building. It was Buele, his helper and general handyman, come with Osbertus' late night cup of steaming, *greena*-spiked kava. Buele was not a clever person, but he had a good heart. Osbertus had rescued him from an asylum, where the mentally inept were used for farm labor, and none too gently—since, the resident minister had pointed out, "They feel very little."

"It is time again to signal Voertrekkerhoem on the telegraph, Buele," Osbertus Kloster said. "I want Cousin Eliana to know that the Goldenwing will arrive when I said it would arrive." He wanted all the news about the Goldenwing to come from him. Was *that* vainglorious? he wondered innocently. Why should he not be in love with Eliana Ehrengraf? Every other mynheer in the world was.

He knew that it would be the sleepy duty clerk who would receive any message from Sterhoem, and that he would file it to be read by the Voertrekkerschatz in the morning. Ian was in Voersterstaad, conscientiously fulfilling duties he loathed.

But Buele did so love to work the telegraph key. For all that he was feebleminded, he knew the code and the Astronomer-Select of Voerster did not.

The name *Buele* had been given the boy when Osbertus took him from the asylum, and though it was a cruelty, it suited him. It was a cruelty *because* it suited him. The word meant "lump" or "boil." And that was what Buele was, a lump on the reputation of Sternhoem, and a boil on Osbertus Kloster's patience. It was Buele who spilled precious photographic plates and smashed them, Buele who dropped a stone maul into the cogs of the telescope drive and put it out of action for seven weeks in midwinter—the time of best seeing. Buele frightened the land-girls on the nearby kraal of the deKupyers and was very nearly arrested by the Trekkerpolizei. The list of Buele's faults and omissions was long, but Osbertus was still glad of his presence.

Osbertus was a lonely man with a reputation for being featherbrained and even, on occasion, a bit subversive. Buele was company. Buele was, in fact, the best Osbertus could expect.

Which is odd, he thought. *I am, after all, a cousin of the Voertrekker-Praesident*. The Voerster acknowledged the relationship. It probably explained why Osbertus was allowed to have opinions about the inner troubles of the Voerster family.

Osbertus thought of the life that was led in the vast cold

-----

rooms of Voertrekkerhoem as "the family darkness." On Voerster, marriages were alliances rather than love matches. A dynastic marriage was rather rudely spoken of by the kaffirs as "blood-breeding." The land went with the blood and the land was all, even though there was a whole planet to be populated.

There had been blood-breeding between the Voerster family and the Ehrengrafs for five generations. The dark and beautiful Eliana Ehrengraf had lived for half of her twenty-two years—the long years of Voerster—at Voertrekkerhoem, wife and consort to the Voertrekker-Praesident. But the match had not been a fruitful one. The Voerster's sons had died in childhood, of a genetic fault that might have been his, or Eliana's—who could say? Their only living child, the golden Broni, was tubercular, given to long spells of sickness, and so fey as to be suspected by the *lumpen* of witchcraft. If she were truly a witch, Osbertus thought, then why did she not heal herself?

Osbertus loved the fragile Broni, and for as long as he could remember, he had been *in* love with the dark vision of her mother Eliana, whose melancholy beauty should tear any man's heart and did, all save her bitter husband's.

"The Kaffir is in the neighborhood," Buele said. To Buele, Black Clavius was always *The Kaffir*.

The information brought a flash of pleasure to the Astrono-mer-Select. "See to it that an outside light is left burning, Buele." For years a burning light at the door to the observatory had been an invitation to Black Clavius,

"Yes, Mynheer. And shall I send the message to Voersterstaad now?"

"Not to Voersterstaad, Buele," Osbertus Kloster said patiently. "To Voertrekkerhoem."

"I know where that is," Buele said with enthusiasm.

"Then go send the message, Buele."

Presently Osbertus, standing at one of the windows level with the inner catwalk, heard the click of the telegraph key and looked thoughtfully out at the starlit savannah. All six of Luyten

726's gas giants were in the sky, blazing like first-magnitude stars against the constellations of the Ploughman, the Virgin, and the Hanged Man. Voerster was without a major satellite and clear nights blazed with stars.

Mynheer Kloster wondered again what new things would come to Voerster when the people of the *Gloria Coelis* arrived. He found himself anxious as a schoolboy awaiting a treat. The visit of the great Goldenwing would be, he felt certain, one of the most memorable occasions in a long and sadly unremarkable life.

4

ON THE SAVANNAH

Black Clavius walked the game path with a swinging stride, staff in hand. His familiar Starman's pack—known to all the township dwellers as a source of succor and help for pain—hung from his great shoulders. From it depended an ancient, beautifully inlaid balichord. The instrument's strings thrummed musically at each step as Clavius strode toward the distant light on the dark shape of the Sternberg.

The sky giants, drops of molten light, were ranked across the heavens from zenith to horizon. Drache the Dragon shone with pure white brilliance; Thor, the War God, had a bloody hue. Wallenberg, deKlerk, and Smuts were like blue diamonds. And Erde was a magnificent green, the green of emeralds, the green of stormy seas. At this time of the year the configuration of the gas giants changed nightly as a radically elliptical orbit swung Voerster swiftly past the slower-moving outer planets.

The kaffirs, of course, had different names for the giants. Drache was Angatch, the supreme and terrifying god of Madagascar. The companion five giants were called *razanes*, for the ghostly attendants of Angatch. Individually they were named Chaka, Tutu, Nampa, Mbutu, and Mandela. An eclectic pantheon, to be sure, Clavius thought.

The Starman wondered whether it was fit that he should be tolerant of so many pagan images in the religion of the kaffirs, or if he should speak out. He had been thinking of this and, as he walked, discussing it with God, whom he knew well.

"'O, Lord, rebuke me not in thine anger, neither chasten me

in thy displeasure. Have mercy on me, O Lord; for I am weak: O Lord, heal me; for my bones are vexed.'"

The verse was a favorite of Black Clavius, one he addressed to God whenever he suspected he had not been as upright as he should be. Clavius often addressed himself to God in the words of the Psalmist, who had also been a favorite of the Almighty.

The cold was deep out on the savannah, but Clavius took no notice. He loved to walk under the thickly starred night sky of Voerster. And he loved to confound God with his skill at remembering the Book. He looked with affection at God's face, the diamond-bright sky.

There were other Books, of course. In his travels he had found many. But it was the language of the First Book that gave him the most pleasure. Sometimes it seemed to him that when he spoke to the Lord in the language of the Book, the Lord used the same language to reply in a voice undimmed by distance or time. What were parsecs and centuries, after all, to the Creator of the universe?

The dust of the savannah trail underfoot had the pungent smell of the native necrogenes. How strange it was, and how very sad, that the beasts of Voerster—warm-blooded or cold—were all born in the belly of the parent who must inevitably die as the young ate its way into the world, to be sustained in its first days of life by the corpse of the lifegiver. The ways of the Lord were prodigious indeed. Clavius understood that each world that had been given life made its own sacrifices to pass it on. Compared to the placental mammals of Earth, the beasts of Voerster had a far more difficult racial choice. They had only self-immolation to drop into the sacred balance of life. Was that really fair? Clavius understood that the necrogenes were one of God's experiments, probably discarded with hardly a second thought from the Almighty.

From time to time Clavius felt it his duty to remind God that he owed more kindness to all creatures, even to the primitive creatures of Voerster.

And what about Voerster's adopted children? Clavius wondered. Voertrekkers and their kaffirs colonizing Voerster had not been God's idea, but Man's. Still, the father should protect the child. On this subject, God had been silent all night.

Clavius had been walking southeast for three days and four nights, but he was unwearied. On Earth he had massed one hundred thirty kilograms. Here, under .96 gravity, he massed slightly more than one hundred twenty. But that still made him a very large and heavy man on Voerster.

His head was covered with nappy, tightly curled hair turning gray. He had a face that was the color of purple grapes and his irises were black, set in eyeballs white as eggshells.

He had received a summons from the mynheera Eliana Ehrengraf Voerster, a person of great spirit and physical beauty, and one of the most unhappy women Clavius had ever known. The messenger said that the mynheera Broni was ill once again and that the Voertrekkerschatz begged his help. The mynheera Eliana had sent Clavius a *carnet de passage* for the dirigible flight from Windhoek to Voertrekkerhoem. But Clavius had refused it. Voertrekkers grew uneasy and unpleasant when they found kaffirs in restricted places, even though it was technically against the law to do more than confine kaffirs to the townships after curfew. The Starman had always found this facet of Voertrekker life fascinating. In a society built entirely on separation of the races, it was actually illegal to "discriminate." Refusal to serve a kaffir, for example, in any restaurant designated as racially open, resulted in severe legal sanctions.

The *luftschiff* transport system of Voerster was, by law, open to all. But it was still too new, too scientific, to be integrated. And in any case, Clavius thought, it was not fitting that the *volk* of Voerster be troubled by a giant of a man from offworld, who was himself still learning tolerance.

"'But as an hired servant, and as a sojourner, he shall be with Thee, and shall serve Thee until the year of jubilee,'" Clavius said aloud in his bass drum of a voice. "But jubilee, Lord, when shall that be?"

Then, because he did not wish to be overcritical of God, he added: "'When I consider the heavens, the work of Thy fingers, the moon and the stars, which Thou hast ordained: what is man that Thou art mindful of him?'"

There were times he was sorely tried considering how God ran the universe. But it was a big place He had made, and it took a deal of minding.

And the Lord did mind, did look after His creations. Poor, earthbound David, singer and poet that he was, had had no idea how magnificent the works of the Lord Jehovah really were. "You do care, Lord. You do pay attention most of the time. You even look after this poor black man marooned nine light-years from Earth, where he was born. And you send me dreams, Lord. I don't always understand them, but that's not surprising, considering that You are God and I'm only a Wired Man put aground by an impatient syndicate. But You gave me a gift of healing to make up for it, and I thank You for that." It was a humbling thing that the Lord of the Universe, the builder of the nebulae and quasars, cared—even a little bit—about Black Clavius.

The plain across which Clavius walked had originally been named the Copernica. The Shieldwall had been the Midcontinent Fault and the high plain had been named for the first true astronomer, Planetia Galileo Galilei. But the Voertrekkers, with their penchant for renaming everything they possessed, called the savannah on which most of the Voertrekker kraals were located "the Sea of Grass," and the land above the Shieldwall simply "the Planetia." The Highlanders took perverse pride in the killing land they ranched.

Clavius had made his way there, as he had to every corner of the populated continent of Voerster. The high kraal owners had regarded him with cold curiosity. They were men and women who for years on end did not leave the high tableland, and had no wish to do so. Clavius had visited the high-plains kaffirs and found them as proud of place as were their mynheeren. Human beings, Clavius thought after the long and arduous journey back to the savannah, had a great capacity for misery.

Dressed in the rough homespun of the working kaffir, Black Clavius walked with a space-devouring stride. In the long years downworld he had traveled constantly and had never been lost. A map of Voerster's sky was imprinted on his brain, alongside the words of the holy Books he favored. The Hebrew Bible, the Talmud, the New Testament, the Koran, the Bhagavad Gita—all were filed away line by line in memory. Like all astroprogrammers aboard Goldenwings, Clavius was an eidetic. He could forget nothing. And the weight of his memories made him slightly mad.

He looked to the spot low on the eastern horizon where dim Sol could be seen on a clear night. It was not possible this night. The cold air was too turbulent. But still, the star that gave birth to mankind was there, even if unseen. Clavius found it amusing that the Lord of Hosts had chosen a planet of that unimportant star as the birthplace of his chosen people. "How come You picked that one, Lord? There were plenty of others. Millions upon millions of them. Or did You put them in other places, Lord? Did You hide a tribe or two in the Lesser Magellanic Cloud, or perhaps nearer to home in the Hercules Cluster?"

It gave Clavius pleasure to indulge in these speculations. It made him feel much nearer to his Maker, and somehow in the Lord's confidence.

Clavius had spent the last fortnight in a kaffir homeland east of Windhoek, on the North Sea coast. The folk had been generous, as always, and his presence appeared to give them great joy.

Kaffirs always seemed to know when he was coming. As he approached a township he would be met by swarms of black children who would close in about him and escort him to the longhouse in the center of the kraal where the adult kaffirs would have foregathered to await him.

Then there would be singing and dancing—oh, the dancing!—how he loved the dancing. Even if food was short in the kraal, there would always be roasted tubers and fresh tender

---

meat of the native beast called a "faux-goat"—meat sliced thin while the necrogene still lived, causing it nobly to imagine it was being eaten by its own needy young.

Necrogenesis was a harsh fact Clavius had had to learn about when the *Nepenthe* abandoned him on Voerster. But he understood now that each world had its truths and most of them were very hard.

On Voerster no necrogene ever bore more than one off-spring, one clutch, one litter.

It was surprising to Clavius that the Voertrekkers never learned a lesson from the self-sacrifice of the native life. But they did not. Instead of sacrificing themselves for their sons and daughters, they immolated their children for power or dynasty or simply for property. Though the kaffirs called the Voertrekker way of marriage "blood-breeding," sometimes they were a great deal more explicit and vulgar than that. "The Trekkers blood-fuck only in the missionary position," they would say with gales of laughter. It was true. In his years downworld, Black Clavius had never encountered a Trekker couple matched in love. He thought that a great pity.

Black Clavius had heard that another Goldenwing was approaching Voerster. To see one Goldenwing in a lifetime was about all any man living on one of the planets of near space could expect. Goldenwings were becoming ever more rare. But two ships to one world in ten years really was remarkable. Clavius was eager to talk with Mynheer Osbertus about it. The black Starman never forgot that he was Wired, a man of deep space. The interface socket under the woolly hair was a defining and unchangeable part of his life. If he lived a thousand uptime years he would always yearn for the ecstasy of awareness a Wired One experienced when the mind was enhanced and expanded by interfacing with the incredibly sophisticated and sensitive computer aboard a Goldenwing.

Machines like that were no longer built. Even before Clavius was Chosen on Earth by the *Nepenthe* syndicate, astrogational computers for tachyon-sailing starships had not been built for at least a generation. Very little had been built on Earth during the years of Clavius' childhood there. The homeworld had spent itself on the holy wars and the Exodus to the stars. Now Earth lay exhausted, a garden grown rank with the remnants of the great dream.

Well, in the twenty-five years of the Exodus, Clavius thought, sixty planets had been planted with human seed. Not all the colonies were successful, but enough were so that in another thousand years or ten thousand (What did time matter?) another Exodus would begin the cycle all over again.

Meanwhile Earth waited, Gaia supine—but not dead. Like the necrogenes of Voerster, she gave herself to her ungrateful offspring.

The Nachtebrise was rising. After midnight the winds of the Grassersee always blew west to east. The kaffirs of the Sea of Grass put sails on their carts to travel on the Nachtebrise.

Clavius could hear the wild grasses rippling, heads still heavy with pods. In another week, the spore pods would sprout wings and fly with the wind for three days of fantastic soaring. Dirigible passengers often reported seeing flying grass at five thousand meters. Then the wings would fail and for a day the sky would rain spores. The Sea of Grass would begin to turn emerald green with the first rains of autumn. On Voerster it was the beginning of the natural yearly cycle.

It was, all told, a rather lovely world, this Voerster, Clavius thought. Not an easy world, no. But possessed of a certain nobility, like the morose folk it sheltered.

The light at the door to Sternhoem gleamed brighter as Clavius approached. He could see no light from the observatory proper, so he assumed that Osbertus had ordered Buele to close the dome. The old fellow had a horror of exposing the telescope to the night sky unless it was actually in use. What strange Voertrekker tabu was that? the black Starman wondered. But no matter, Osbertus was good company and a good man. He, too, was deeply concerned about Broni Ehrengraf Voerster. In a world without much love, the old astronomer bestowed what he had to give on The Voertrekker's daughter and her mother.

———

5

IN THE WAKE OF THE DRAGON

With the red-shifted stars from which *Glory* fled shining down through the overhead skylight, Starman Jean Marq slept.

The hot Provençal sun burned down on the familiar, rock-terraced hillside, throwing hard, black shadows from the dry vines. The vintage would be bitter without rain, without pity from the sun. The Earth was weary, even the ocean level was low. The weather had been changing for a thousand years, and as it changed, Earth itself became more inert, as though determined to survive by husbanding what strength was left in the soil and air.

Even the wild grasses were sere, but in Amalie's russet hair he could smell thyme and marjoram, and on the damp cloth of her bodice the sweet female smell of her sweat.

He had followed her down the terraces in great, slow, dreamy leaps as though he, and she, could fly like the ravens that circled overhead, crossing and recrossing the swollen yellow disc of the sun.

Jean Marq watched her now as she flew down the mountainside. Back straight and slender as an arrow, brown bare legs flashing, full skirt lifted to show her white thighs. He could hear her laughter as he followed her with his breath coming hard and his heart pounding in his chest. Why did she run from him, he wondered, and why did her flight seem magical?

Amalie filled his days and tormented his nights. She was only a farm girl, a peasant tied to the land by tradition and family and French law, while he was a rising star of the ancient Sorbonne's faculty of mathematics. The social distance between them was stellar, but he knew that he would give his life and his privileges to possess her.

She stopped, chest heaving, to wait for him. Dampness glued the cloth of her blouse to her breasts, hard as melons. The nipples were a dark announcement of her nubility, thrusting against the wet cloth. Her best shirt, Marq knew; his gift. White chambray with red thread worked in a pattern around the collar and across the breast. Bright, like a trickle of blood.

She called mockingly to him and he felt light, as though he could launch himself into space and fly like a spear to her, pierce her, embrace her, explore her as the sunlight did.

A peasant, yes. But a land-owning peasant. Jean Marq was French enough to care a great deal about that. For centuries France had slowly been slipping back into the medieval mystery of her beginnings. Perhaps, he sometimes thought, it had been the same when the continent began to awaken after the great plagues of the Fourteenth Century killed forty million souls and left vast tracts of field and forest abandoned and silent save for the cry of birds and the rutting roars of the stag.

Now two-thirds of the population of Earth were gone to the nearer stars. There was a great stillness in the abandoned cities, a melancholy peace on the breast of the empty land. Yet the great schools persisted. The Sorbonne, Cambridge, Columbia—the universities still produced scientists.

Marq was on holiday after the demanding ordeal of winning his tenure. He had come south to Provence for the sun, the sea, and the stillness.

He had met Amalie Delacroix and had had no peace since his first view of her working in her father's terraced vineyard. She tormented him with her body, naked under skirt and blouse. She tormented him with looks and touchings and simply by being Amalie, eighteen and a woman. She even tormented him with long, speculative statements on how she would, if she could, apply for her passage to the stars (to which, in this time, every citizen of Earth was entitled), and spend a year or maybe two in cold-sleep so that she could awaken to a world alive with fiery young men who would not be afraid, as some were, to take her by force and make love to her.

Jean Marq listened and the sweat rolled down his back and his loins filled and he hardened and asked himself, "Does she mean what she says? is that what she wants?"

He would lie awake at night, sick with longing and perhaps even with love, though Jean was not a loving man.

Marq stirred in his pod and moaned. Oh, Jesu. Again he was following Amalie down the stone terraces of that ancient, vanished Provence. The great terraces that were like steps built for some dark and malevolent god.

He stood on a terrace above, her, looking down at the flash of leg and thigh with which she favored him as the wind lifted her skirt. He felt the heavy pounding beat of his pulse in his throat and behind his eyes. His penis was hard and full. He called out to her, "Amalie, Amalie, attendre!"

The sound of his call echoed down the terraces and reached the cliffs that fell away to the empty sea. Somewhere there was laughter.

She had vanished and panic surged. Why did she mock him so? He felt the sharp stone shards through his light sandals, and then she was behind him—and her pungent woman scent was in his nostrils, and her arms were around him.

Let it be different this time, he thought in his dream. Please, God, let it be different.

He turned and they kissed; she curious, he hungry, searching. Her tongue flicked his, ran across his lips. Her breasts pressed hard and damp against his naked chest. They sank to their knees and she allowed him to open her blouse and search her nipples with his mouth. She tasted of salt and sun.

"Je t'aime . . . je t'adore."

Oh, God, he heard her laughter.

She said, "Enough now, Jean." She pushed his face away from her breasts and sat back on her heels, her nipples glistening in the bright sunlight.

She frowned and said, "Now look at what you've done. You've torn my blouse. You are worse than the laborer's boy."

A thing of orange light flashed in his head. The stone terraces, the sky, the sea, the vineyard vanished, and there was only Amalie and her naked slobbered breasts. Love and hatred exploded. He threw himself upon her, lifting her skirt until it gathered around her waist.

"Stop this, you fool," he heard her say. She always said it in exactly the same way, without fear, with a touch of contempt.

The sun pierced his bare back with spikes of light. Close to, behind her russet eyelashes, he could see her eyes, green and shot with flecks the color of gold, pupils narrow against the sun and then dilating with fear. He felt himself penetrating her, driving into her without mercy or charity, tearing her tender hymen and feeling her heave beneath him in screaming protest.

Engorged to bursting, he drove himself into her again. The circling birds joined their screams to hers. He felt her clawing at his face and then, quite suddenly, she was still, limp, and he emptied himself into her.

"Amalie, Amalie, je t'adore—"

He lifted his weight from her and looked down into her flushed and sweat-streaked face. Her eyes were open, staring over his shoulder at the sun. A trickle of blood ran down her cheek from her hairline, and another leaked from her ear.

Jean Marq said, "Amalie?"

Then he lifted his right hand which was clenched around a smooth stone taken from the terrace. It was smeared with her blood . . .

He felt ten tiny needles piercing the skin of his chest. They burned like fire. He opened his eyes in terror and looked into the tiny cat face of Mira.

The animal's small head sprouted a hair-thin platinum wire. That damned Boche Krieg's demented experiment. The cat knew what a man was thinking. Predator's thoughts filled Marq's sleep-pod. Mira's slit pupils dilated in a mad parody of the dream-Amalie's. The cat's eyes became bottomless. Marq had the crazed notion that Mira was threatening him, warning him that if he displeased her she would somehow disclose his dream to Duncan.

Marq made a savage sound in his throat and struck at the cat, but she was far too swift. She released her hold on him and leaped, weightless, across the compartment to land on the fabric wall and cling there, still looking at him. Mira had been born in space, had lived all of her life in free-fall. *Glory* was her universe.

Jean Marq sat up in the open pod and hugged himself to stop the inner shivering that dominated his naked body. Would the dream never end?

Mira hissed at him and launched herself into the transit tube. Marq hated the cat and she hated him. Krieg's cybersurgery and the computer made it possible for her to tell him so. Each time he dreamed of killing Amalie, the small beast knew and came to judge him. With the others aboard the *Glory*, she was gentle and affectionate. Even with the icy Krieg. But with Marq, who had murdered a female creature, she was a tiny fury.

Still shivering in the cold air of his personal compartment, Jean Marq arose and slipped into a skinsuit. Among the clutter of his personal gear he found his stash of Dust. Duncan knew that he had brought Dust aboard, because Duncan knew everything. But Masters seldom interfered with the vices of their crewmen. Only if they reduced the efficiency of the ship did they enforce their authority. Duncan Kr was not a disciplinarian. He ruled by example, not by threat.

Marq broke the seal and inhaled deeply. Dust gave him no pleasure. What it did was dull remorse.

He pushed off and floated to the terminal in the wall and plugged in. *Glory* told him the state of voyage, ship, and crew.

Duncan and Anya Amaya were conning the ship. *Glory* was tacking away into a region of the Oort Cloud swept almost clean by the gravity of Drache, the great white gas giant that guarded Luyten 726's outer marches. Young Damon was EVA, surrounded by monkeys. What did the youngster find to talk about with those half-machine, half-animal things? Some Dust would do *that* one no harm whatever. Ng's acrophobia was like a stench in the ship, Marq thought.

The neurocybersurgeon had unplugged himself and was relaxing in his pod, dreaming up who knew what Germanic grandiosity. He was listening to Wagner. The *Liebesnacht*. The bulkhead microphones picked up the music. There was no real privacy anywhere aboard a Goldenwing. For safety's sake, no crewman could ever be out of touch.

On impulse, Marq asked that *Glory* show him the frozen corpse of Han Soo in the hold. The computer imaged the old Celestial's still face and Marq saw it clearly. He felt a pang of deep sorrow. Han Soo had been Marq's only friend aboard the *Glory*.

Marq closed his eyes and studied the calm, distant face. It was like an ivory carving: the smooth features, closed eyes behind sloping epicanthic folds. Those eyes, Marq thought, had opened first in the valley of the Yangtze River. And they had closed for the last time eight light-years from Earth, after a life that a downworlder would think was as long as forever.

We share the emptiness, Old Man, Marq thought. *You sleep dreaming of Earth as I do. But you will never awaken more.*

The computer showed him that Duncan and Anya were both naked in the bridge pods. Though it was common practice among Starmen to go nude if they chose, it still sent a shaft of sensation through Marq's loins to sense the image of the naked teenaged girl conning the ship. She would never have bared her breasts to the sun of Provence, he thought, yet she lay naked as a newborn in her working pod without a second thought. She slept with Duncan and Krieg and Damon without prejudice. And she would have done so with Jean Marq, too, but for Marq's need to do penance. Anya Amaya's New Earth open sexuality was like a splinter in Jean Marq's flesh. Eros was a demon, a destroyer of men.

Marq told the computer to inform Duncan that he was awake and ready to stand his watch. Then he detached the computer drogue from his socket and allowed the heavy cable to retract into the fabric wall.

His face was stubbled and there was a sour taste in his mouth, but he did not wash himself or clean his teeth. Marq deliberately neglected his body. He seldom shaved, washed infrequently. He almost never visited the spinning segment of *Glory*'s hull where gravity to order was simulated by centrifugal force and the Starmen could exercise with weights and springs. Han Soo had once told Marq that his physical neglect was deliberate, a self-inflicted punishment. Jean Marq accepted that judgment.

Since there was really no God, it fell to each man to pass sentence on himself for his sins.

He was vaguely hungry, but as always, the thought of suckling on the feeding tube nauseated him. From time to time young Damon, who fancied himself a great chef, would open the vast galley—designed to feed thousands—and create a sumptuous meal, a feast for monarchs. But the daily business of nourishing the crew was handled by *Glory* herself, who did not much care whether or not food was elegant, only nourishing. Jean Marq, once a gourmet, likened eating ship's fare to the consumption of offal. With the need to recycle everything on long-duration voyages, the simile was not pure hyperbole.

Marq turned from the terminal and caught a glimpse of his doll in her half-open drawer. "She" was a quasi-living, speaking paracoita (a name given such devices by an ancient writer named Wolfe, who speculated vastly about Earth's future), an almost ludicrously buxom product of the sex laboratories of Yoni Island, on Nightwing in the Ross Stars. Driven beyond endurance by abstinence early in his first voyage, Jean had purchased the grotesque artifact. She was a low-level android designed to perform coitus on demand. "Better than Lefty's sister," the vulgarians of Yoni had said of their product. But Marq, shamed by what he had done, never used her. She rested in her transparent case, a plastic sepulcher decorated with erect phalluses and gaping labia.

To use the paracoita, he felt, would be to abandon the last of his humanity. He intended to set the thing adrift in deep space, but somehow had never managed to do it. Uptime passed and the paracoita traveled with him, reclining in her case, silent but ever ready, acquiescent, and virginal.

Bareheaded and barefoot, Marq launched himself into the transit tube that had swallowed Mira. It was a fabric entrail, one of thousands that wound through *Glory*'s inner spaces. It was kept open primarily by air pressure, although there were titanium ribs at intervals. If punctured, the tube would pinch shut to isolate the damage until it could be repaired by a monkey, or if the damage were really serious, by a member of the crew in space armor. To a man as practiced as Jean Marq, a transit tube was like the barrel of a gun to a bullet. He, and all the others, could literally fly through *Glory*.

Duncan Kr lifted himself from the glyceroid and floated free. Without bothering to dress he moved to an auxiliary panel and activated the spar cameras. A holocube came alive with the computer image of *Glory*'s rig. Sails gleamed gold in the light of the Luyten sun—still distant with a barely discernible disc. The intricate web of the monofilament rig made a fantastic pattern of silvery threads against the black of space.

The star *Glory* was approaching looked slightly bluer than it was and the stars astern were red-shifted. *Glory* carried a substantial percentage of light-speed, though she was using her backed royals and main t'gallants to bleed off velocity. The sails nearest the hull coruscated with a shower of inhibited tachyons. They created a glow of St. Elmo's fire along the spars. The effect was startlingly beautiful, even to an old hand like Duncan. The golden fire transformed *Glory*'s top hamper into a living design, glittering against the night.

Still connected, Duncan said: *"Anya. Jean can take over now. Disconnect."*

"Yes, Duncan." The thought was clear and without overtones. When Anya sailed, she was a sailor, nothing more.

Duncan studied the holograph of *Glory*'s rig. To his practiced eye the location of the hundred or more monkeys was clearly visible. And so was Damon, falling free, a dozen meters from the mizzentop. Duncan could read his fear from his spread-eagled position and the pulsebeat of apprehension that leaked through from the telemetry to the computer interface.

"Damon. This is the Master. Use a tether, damn it."

"Don't be angry, Duncan." There was a mental quaver in the transmission.

"I'm not angry. But use a tether when you are EVA from now on. That is an order."

"Yes, sir."

"That should make him happy."

Duncan turned to see Jean Marq on the bridge. When the Master did not reply to Jean's comment, the Frenchman said, "He does it on purpose, you know. He enjoys being terrified."

The glow from the holocube showed the Mathematician's stubbled face and hollow eyes. The cadence of his speech made Duncan aware that he had Dusted immediately upon waking from his nightmares.

"I know why he does it, Jean," Duncan said. "Are you fit to take your watch? I can stay on if you want."

"I am all right, Duncan. Are we about free of the Oort Cloud?"

"We are in Drache's swept space."

"In the wake of the Dragon," Marq said. "How fitting." His eyes flickered as Anya rose from her pod and pulled her drogue free. It retracted into the Conn Panel and the girl floated out of the pod and stretched, Mira-like, arching her back and extending her arms and legs. Her fine, dark hair formed a cloud around her small, well-shaped head. She smiled at the Frenchman and said, "Hallo, Jean. Rest well?"

Marq wondered if she had been spying on him. But no. He knew that Anya was more sensitive to *Glory* and all her sailing parts, than to the living things inside her. Except, perhaps, Mira. She loved the cursed animal and her brood of kittens. It disgusted the mathematician that Mira's pregnancy, too, had been arranged by Krieg with a vial of frozen genetically enhanced cat sperm. Marq looked away from the naked Anya as tiny fires raced through his nervous system. Dust and sexual arousal had conflicting effects. Marq wondered if that was why he Dusted.

Duncan removed his drogue and suffered that familiar diminution of vision when he separated himself from *Glory*. He turned again to watch the holocube in which a tiny Damon approached the masthead complex of blocks and halyards aswarm with monkeys. Who were probably setting things to rights, Duncan thought sardonically; the halyards were beyond Damon's merely human efforts. Through the rig one could see the distant shape of Smuts, another of the gas giants, making a transit of the Luyten sun. *Glory's* speed was still affecting the apparent celerity with which things were happening in downtime. As the great planet moved across the face of its primary in uptime seconds, downtime hours were passing. Earlier, in deep space, the time dilation would have been greater.

"Any word from below?" Jean Marq asked, taking the Master's drogue and preparing to connect.

"I sent Colonist Kloster the latest ephemeris," Anya said, twisting in air and heading for the transit tunnel.

Marq settled the drogue into his socket with practiced movements. His awareness did not encompass all, as Duncan's had. Some men were less sensitive than others. But he was sufficiently aware of *Glory* to be left safely with the conn.

"I relieve you, Master and Commander," he said formally. Tradition, ritual, and the Master's privileges were vital aboard a Goldenwing. They were the elements of the Wired Ones' law, without which life in deep space was impossible.

Duncan waited until the Frenchman had settled into the warm glyceroid before closing the hatch on the pod.

He spoke to a wall microphone and said, "An Amber Watch should be sufficient, unless you think differently." A vessel's condition of readiness was described by the hue of the Watch. Green for sailing an interstellar sound. Amber for a state of wary alertness, required in locations such as the Oort Cloud. And Red for those rare times when the Coriolis force exploded into the violence of tachyon storms, far rarer in deep space than the hurricanes and typhoons on old Earth.

"We won't make another midcourse correction until we are well inside the orbit of Thor. There is some debris in Drache's trojan point, but nothing massive."

The words *"Marq aye"* whispered from the speakers. Duncan patted the covered pod and left the bridge.

———

Anya was waiting for him in the transit tube. "Are you tired, Duncan?"

"No."

"Good. The dorsal?"

"I want to check on Han Soo first."

"I'll come along," Anya said. She had been fond of the old Celestial. He had been teaching her calligraphy at the moment of his death.

Duncan led the way down the transit tube into the ventral sections of the ship, past the banks where the Donkeys, the EVA tractors, were kept. The tubes were lighted by a single fiber-optic thread spun through the fabric in a spiraling design. As one flew through the tube the peculiar lighting made it appear that the tube, rather than the observer was in motion. It could be unnerving to the unwary. Duncan paused at the valve to hold 1009, where Han Soo's frozen body was tethered in a vast emptiness.

The air in the hold stood near the absolute zero of space. Duncan opened a compartment and handed Anya a coldsuit and took one for himself. It was a plastic body coverall with hood and faceplate that could protect one for a few minutes. Long enough, the theory went, to allow one to contrive other measures for survival. The theory was absurd, but the coldsuits were useful.

Duncan opened the transparent valve and floated into the dark hold. The suit had a small light fixed to the helmet. In its glow Duncan and Anya Amaya could see that Han Soo was exactly as they had left him after preparing his body for a cold hold.

"I keep expecting him to open his eyes and speak to me," Anya said.

"Han Soo has said all he will ever say," Duncan said.

It was a deep trauma for all when a Goldenwing lost a crewman in space. Terrible if by accident, almost as bad if, as in the case of Han Soo, the cause was natural. There was something about the vast isolation of a ship between the stars that made the

———

loss of a single life a wrenching, melancholy thing to experience. Han Soo himself had once wondered aloud: "What must a lone soul experience, being cast out of its body in these emptinesses? How fast do you imagine a soul can travel across these spaces, if it is going home?"

Duncan made the Sign of the Fish over Han Soo. It was a completely spontaneous gesture, a remnant of his almost forgotten childhood, when he worshiped with his marriage group in the stone kirk on the cliffs overlooking the great sea of Thalassa.

Anya Amaya saw and smiled. On New Earth there had been no religion. The people had considered themselves totally rational beings, without the need for psychic crutches. Only in the matter of female fertility were they fanatical. But Anya was a tolerant girl, aware of Duncan's peculiarities, and slightly in love with him despite them all.

They left the cold hold and returned the suits to the locker. They flew swiftly "upward" past the spin section, through the empty comb holds to the highest level under *Glory*'s dorsal surface. They floated into a compartment, large, as all spaces on *Glory* were, but warm and dark.

Anya somersaulted to a stop and floated in between fabric deck and titanium frame overhead.

"How shall it be?"

She knew the answer, of course. With Duncan it was always under the stars and the rig, the two things he loved most in all the universe. Young Ng preferred it dark, the more womblike the better. Krieg favored a blaze of interior light that turned the space into a large laboratory, and his performance was usually as cold and brilliant as his surroundings.

Jean Marq? Anya could only guess. He was a man with a badly damaged libido. Once, quite by accident, she had glimpsed the entombed paracoita he kept in his compartment. She thought it the saddest thing she had ever seen.

She made a dancing spin in the darkness and passed a hand across the light sensors. A section of the overhead opened,

---

became transparent. Instantly the space was filled with the overwhelming presence of the stars. *Glory's* sails, hectares of them, reflected the light of the Luyten sun endlessly, the repeating patterns gilded by the golden skylar. The rig, seen from this angle, was like an expanding maze of a web spun by some magical cosmic spider. And through it shone the red-shifted stars behind and the blue-shifted stars ahead. The effect was breathtaking. Duncan's upturned face showed his joy. Anya floated to him and rested her small, pointed breasts against his back, her arms around his neck.

"How you love it," she said.

"Yes, I do."

"What a lovely man you are, Duncan Kr," she said.

Many kilometers above the hull's curving flank, and resembling a fly in a web, Damon Ng prepared to work his way slowly downward. The name *Damon* had been assigned to him by *Glory's* computer when he first reported aboard for his cybersurgery. His birth name was Eight; he was the eighth of a clone raised to young manhood under a thousand-kilometer-long canopy of green on the large island of Nixon on the planet Grissom, second from the sun Ross 128.

Damon's mother was a machine of sorts, not of metal and glass, but of fibers and sap and chlorophyll. An incubator tree. Women on Grissom were rare in the early days and the practice of cloning humans, considered immoral on the once-crowded Earth, was adopted. Young clones were raised in nests provided by the incubator trees. The human parents from whom the cloneable cells were taken did not involve themselves with the young. Nurture was left to specially trained individuals who guided the nesting generation through life as far as puberty, at which time the clone's specialty in life was selected.

Damon, however, was Chosen by the Starmen, and he willingly abandoned his life under the towering trees.

Now he struggled against his acrophobia every minute of

every hour of every uptime day. At this moment his ordinarily ruddy face was livid with fear despite the tether he had fastened to the rig at Duncan's order.

He could feel himself shaking, his stomach cramping, his suit tainted by the smell of urine. He had wet himself when he had drifted a dozen meters from the mizzentop. Going *outside* was an agony. Even an hour in *Glory*'s observatory with the transparent dome brought the cold sweat.

It was Krieg who had told him that it might be possible, if he persevered, to desensitize himself by going extravehicular at every possible opportunity. However, there were no guarantees, Krieg had said dispassionately.

Damon ordered the importunate monkeys away and saw that they had already cleared the halyard. Gibbering softly with fear, he disconnected his tether from the top and snapped the lead onto a running stay. Intellectually he now knew that it was impossible for him to drift away from *Glory* as he descended the several kilometers to the hull, but the assurance did not appreciably lessen his dread.

He tongued his radiophone to life inside his helmet and instructed the monkey cyborgs to resume their normal routine, which entailed patrolling the rig for six hours, then returning to the monkey comb—familiarly called the Monkey House—for two hours of recharging and self-maintenance.

Damon touched his reaction controls and backed away from the mizzentop, taking great care not to entangle himself in the maze of stays and braces. Above him the starboard mainmast towered, all sails set. The maintop was twenty kilometers farther away from *Glory*'s hull than was the mizzentop, where Damon Ng floated on his tether. Thirty kilometers below, lost in the geometric complexity of the mizzen spars, lay *Glory*'s long, fabric hull. She resembled the antique airships of Earth that Damon had seen in the teaching spools on Grissom. Dirigibles were the approved method of transport on Voerster, he had heard, though nothing he would encounter there was nearly as impressive as the great airships of ancient Earth.

————

He felt a flash of golden light across his cheek and his faceplate darkened automatically. He looked again at the rig and for a few moments he forgot his fear. Jean Marq, who was now alone on watch, was backing the entire sail plan, resetting the huge mains, the smaller fores'ls, and a flaming array of stays'ls, stuns'ls, jibs, and spankers to face Luyten 726 so that *Glory* might use the photons streaming away into deep space to help slow the ship. For close maneuvering inside a solar system Goldenwings routinely used light-pressure to assist the driving force of tachyons on their sails.

But the evolution was anything but routine from where young Damon was seeing it. Beams of reflected light flashed from sail to sail, were split by gleaming stays and braces, and all the while the skylar fabric reflected a strangely different vision of the stars around the ship.

Damon fed tiny increments of delta-V to his reaction controls, forcing himself to face outward, toward the universe. His hands clenched and he sucked great gasps of pure oxygen into his lungs as he looked at the dusted scatter of stars that was the edge of the Milky Way galaxy—a river of light from this position, a river that surely contained a billion billion stars. How close to home we have remained, Damon thought. It was a very un-Damon-like response to the open universe. *Perhaps,* he thought as his fear closed in again, *I will learn to look outward and upward as Duncan and the others do.* It was the thing he wanted most in life. To live unafraid.

He perceived the pattern of the universe in its immensity and then, perhaps because the vision was too vast to contain, he saw it closer too, on a human scale. Suddenly it seemed that he had only to reach out and scoop up a handful of stars from that living, glowing carpet of gems on black velvet.

He tried to recall some lines of the Earth poet Thomas Gray that Duncan had once used: "'Full many a gem of purest ray serene/The dark unfathomed caves of ocean bear—'"

Duncan was a man of so many, and so varied, tastes.

"Take one," a mocking voice said in his headphones. *"Pick one*

and give it to some Trekker whore. I have heard they'll spread their fat legs for a half-rand. Think what they would do for one of those beauties."

Marq, Damon thought. Probing with a dirty finger. What a terrible man the mathematician was.

"Privilege of rank, mon ami. Mathematician ranks Rigger. You are merely tolerated, but I am beloved for my dirty mind."

Damon pictured him, lying in his pod, using *Glory* to broadcast his nastiness. Yet Duncan tolerated him, and so did Anya. Krieg didn't matter. He had no feelings.

"Don't be so sure, young Damon," Marq said clearly. *"The Boche has unexplored depths. I have seen him get drunk and weep when Rhine Maidens sing 'Die Lorelei.'"*

Damon had no idea what the crazy Frenchman was talking about. The notion of Krieg weeping was absurd. Though it was strictly against orders, and though the isolation it created made him even more fearful, Damon turned off his suit communications.

With a prod from his thrusters he began the long, slow slide down the stay toward *Glory*'s whalebacked hull. He descended through the web of rigging and the labyrinth of golden skylar. The descent took him twenty long minutes, but presently he hung just over the transparent dome of the observatory.

He looked inside and there, in the shifting light reflected from the sails, he could see Duncan and Anya making love in zero gravity, slowly spinning and tumbling like dancers, their naked bodies intertwined.

He watched, breathless. It was beautiful to see, even for a young man raised among the Puritans of Grissom who had reduced sex to a genetic exercise.

Presently he became aware that Anya's eyes were open and fixed on him. He felt a flush touch his cheek, but the girl from New Earth only smiled languorously and lifted a hand from Duncan's broad shoulder to wave a greeting.

With a start Duncan realized his radio was still off. He tongued it back to life in time to hear Duncan say softly:

———

"'Just such disparity
As is 'twixt air and Angel's purity
'Twixt women's love, and men's will ever be.'"

What poet spoke *those* words? Damon wondered. He only
knew that given the setting and circumstance, Anya Amaya must
be finding them beautiful.

———

6

A HEALER AT VOERTREKKERHOEM

Deeply troubled, Healer Tiegen Roark, the Voertrekker-Praesident's family physician, turned away from the girl in the large bed. He walked across the room to stand at a window looking out over the vast, starlit grounds of Voertrekkerhoem.

Roark had fought several duels at the Healer's Faculty, in Pretoria, and he wore a scar on one cheek. The upper-class women of Voerster found the marks of manhood irresistible.

He stood with hands clasped behind his back, a stance taught to all physicians at the Faculty. Roark, over the course of a long medical career, questioned the value of such teachings. He had often argued with the board of governors that the entire curriculum of medicine at the school was in desperate need of revision. He contended that much less time should be spent on teaching young physicians their social responsibilities and more on actually working with sick patients.

Historically, on Earth, armed conflict had stimulated medicine to superhuman achievements. But the Great Kaffir Rebellion on Voerster had done no such thing. Instead it had wiped out the laboriously won advances of the first three centuries on Voerster and made the next thousand years a medical purgatory. To recognize diseases from the old texts and yet lack the means to combat them was hell for a physician. It was, Tiegen Roark thought bitterly, like blundering through life blindfolded and handcuffed.

He turned back to look again at the sleeping Broni Ehrengraf Voerster. The girl had passed her twelfth birthday in the month of Trinity. She was now past the age of marriage and marriage was clearly impossible unless her health improved.

A touch of tuberculosis, the Voertrekker-Praesident said, of no matter. Tuberculosis was indigenous to Voerster. Well, *perhaps,* the Healer thought. But Broni's illness was like no tuberculosis Tiegen Roark had ever seen.

Women of the ruling class on Voerster married for political reasons and no other. There were already whispers of a political union for the Voertrekkersdatter.

Roark studied Broni's face broodingly. On Voerster tuberculosis ran a slower course than it had on Earth. It was a wasting disease, to be sure, and unfortunately common among the mynheeren. The progress of the illness ran to early feverishness, followed by loss of weight, a weakness of the respiratory system, and chest pains. Then came the expectoration of blood and the occasional hemorrhage. Women, more often than men, tended to acquire the disease. Most bore its ravages all their lives, and still managed to bear several children before the lung-fever killed them.

The Voerster demanded to know why his daughter was in a stage of the disease usually found in females of middle age.

The difficulty was, Roark thought, rubbing his scarred cheek, that he dare not say to Ian Voerster that his daughter suffered from an ailment Tiegen Roark could not treat. True, the symptoms *appeared* to indicate that it was the tubercle bacillus at work in Broni's lungs. But neither Tiegen Roark nor any of the diagnostic specialists with whom he had conferred had been able to find the bacterium in any specimen of Broni's sputum. *We are no better than tea-leaf readers,* Roark thought. *If only the Faculty had taught us real virology and neurology, it might not have been necessary for them to work so hard showing us how to stand, hands clasped behind, bellies outthrust, looking like physicians.*

Roark, though he had a deep and passionate love of the world on which he had been born, felt its failings deeply. Somehow, the science of optics had never developed as it should have subsequent to the Rebellion. Even after many years, the native lens grinders were capable of producing only mediocre microscopes. Much of the planetary pharmacopoeia was holistic, borrowed from the kaffirs who, denied proper medical care after the Rebellion, turned to the native plants and minerals for healing potions. But the sad truth was that, contrary to legend, kaffir medicine was no better than that practiced by the Voertrekker Healers. The kaffirs were sturdy, Roark was certain, because they lived stringent, severe lives. There was a Voertrekker saying: *"Arbeit macht Gesund"*—work makes one healthy. That was, Mynheer Healer Roark thought, a convenient assurance, to be sure. But it was useless in the case of Broni Ehrengraf Voerster, the Voertrekkersdatter of Voerster. She could scarcely be put to stoop labor in the fields to cure what Tiegen believed was heart damage caused by rheumatic fever in infancy.

And while I ponder and theorize, Tiegen Roark thought bitterly, *this lovely child gasps for breath and appears to be slowly, inexorably dying.*

Through the open window, and across thirty flat kilometers of grass sea, Roark could see Voersterstaad. He could easily make out the yellow sky-glow of the municipal system of gas mantle street lighting. The gaslights were new, as things were reckoned on Voerster. They had been ignited for the first time ten years ago, in the month of Trinity, when three of the gas giants in the sky formed their rare conjunction—as they had done again three nights ago.

The city underclass of Voerster, *lumpen* and Voertrekkers fallen on bad times—totally a disreputable lot—had staged an all-night drunken jamboree, dancing and sopping up liquor in the gas-lit streets because the astronomical event coincided with Deorbit Day and with the totally unrelated news that a Golden-wing was approaching Voerster.

The Trekkerpolizei had been pressed to keep order, but to his credit, the Voertrekker-Praesident had enjoined moderation. No broken skulls for drunkenness, no strict enforcement of the blue laws. His restraint had earned him small thanks from the *lumpen*, and no more from the kaffirs. Gratitude, Mynheer Voertrekker Tiegen Roark thought, was not a kaffir virtue.

*

The Healer walked around the room, looking without affection at the dressed stone walls. Austere. Barren. Like a fortress. The entire house was like this. Built to be defended. It had been built on the remnants of an earlier, and even grimmer fortress. There were catacombs below where the Voertrekkers of the Rebellion era had punished kaffirs who had the misfortune to be taken alive by the Voertrekker commandos.

The seeds of the tragedy, Tiegen thought rebelliously, had begun on the day of First Landing, when Bol-Derek Voerster died coming out of cold-sleep. He died, and his promises were forgotten. And thirteen hundred years later a physician has to watch a young girl die on a planet of arrogance and ignorance, he thought. How bitter it was. But Voertrekkerhoem had seen worse. This was a house steeped in the history of the world of Voerster, and of the family who resided here. Not a happy world and family, the physican mused. Not at all.

Roark, as family physician, had personal knowledge of the way in which the first couple of Voerster lived. He wondered if The Voerster and the beautiful Eliana had had intercourse since Broni was conceived, these twelve years gone. He doubted it. Eliana would have submitted, of course, for she was an Ehrengraf, a mynheera of Voerster. He had been about to indulge himself in a cliché: *"A Voertrekker to her fingertips."* But was that really so? Most Voertrekker women had eyes blue as saucers, shallow as porcelain platters. To look into Eliana's dark and melancholy eyes was to see great depths.

Roark was a heavyset man with receding gray-blond hair and the pale eyes of the prototypical mynheer. He was younger than he appeared to be. Another of the "social" skills taught at Healer's Faculty was how to look older than one actually was. Somewhere in the racial psyche there was a memory of Old Earth, a memory that insisted that one's worth was calculated by totting up the number of years one had spent ingesting one's professional qualifications.

The curriculum at Healer's Faculty could be mastered by any bright young man (there were no Healer's degrees for women on

Voerster) in two years. Roark had chafed at Healer's for five, constantly being admonished by the Chancellor of Medicine that patience was a prime virtue in a physician. The old idiot, Roark remembered sourly, would then burst into foolish laughter at the brilliance of his soggy pun.

The Roark Kraal had bordered the lands of the Ehrengrafs, and Tiegen had known Eliana since they were children. Had he been other than a mynheer he would have acknowledged that he had loved her hopelessly as a child, as an adolescent, and as a man. But no Roark could aspire to an Ehrengraf, and over the years Tiegen had learned to deal with his attachment for Eliana in a civilized, Voertrekker manner. As far as Roark—or anyone— knew, Eliana had never been in love with any man. She had always stood apart from life, even from love (or its lack), by choice. She was civil to all, even to her social inferiors. She displayed courtesy to everyone with whom she dealt. But love? The female love of a woman for a man? That, Roark thought, was fated not to be part of Eliana Ehrengraf's life.

The physician bent over the sleeping girl and let Broni's gentle breath play across his cheek. Her respiration was shallow, her lips tinged with blue. The lace handkerchief she held in one delicate hand was bloodstained. Her other hand rested on her small breasts under the thickly embroidered nightdress. Rheumatic heart failure, yes, Tiegen thought. Compounded with the common touch of tuberculosis. The child will probably die. *And I can do nothing about it,* he thought bitterly.

The house kaffirs and the *lumpen* in the city all called her "The Golden Broni." In a society in which the approval of the lower orders was not sought, it seemed every Voertrekker found it easy to love the Voertrekkersdatter. When Broni was abroad the people called her name with affection. The local congregation of the Cult of Elmi offered daily prayers for her recovery, as did all the Voersterstaad parishes of the Church of Voerster. It was all very sad. Because though Healer Roark was only as good a scientist as backward Voerster could produce, he was physician enough to know the prognosis was very poor. It was an unpleasant truth, which for different reasons, neither of her parents would accept.

Broni's pulse was light and slow. Roark could see the depression of the flesh above her larynx as she labored to draw breath. He produced his stethoscopic tube and listened to the faint, uneven beating of her heart. *God curse our ignorance*, he thought. He had heard that particular sound only once before, coming through the tube from a heart of a very old man.

Her problem lay there, but The Voertrekker would not have it. The daughter of Ian Voerster could not be incapable of marriage and childbearing.

Carved into the insanely expensive wooden planks of the headboard of Broni's bed was a quotation from the Earth Bible:

WHAT IS MAN THAT THOU ART MINDFUL OF HIM?

The line was heavily embellished with the sculptured figures of imps and demons and necrogenes and remembered mythic animals of Old Earth. How like the Voersters to have a sick child sleep under that grimly decorated admonition every night. For that matter, how like them to take what was clearly a celebration of Man and his relationship to God and turn it into a warning of dire mortality.

Roark was not a religious man, but Earth Bible reading was a part of the curriculum at the Healer's Faculty, and the physician had developed an affection for the verses of the Psalmist.

"Do those words trouble you, Tiegen? They trouble me." Eliana stood behind him. She had come in soundlessly. As he turned he could smell the faint flower scent in her glossy black hair.

Roark bowed as protocol demanded. "Mynheera," he said.

Eliana was dressed, as always, in dark colors. A deep maroon dress of velvet, and a surcoat of heavy quilted fabric, unadorned but for a black-and-silver sash and a wooden pin to match the wooden comb in her hair. Her complexion was pale. She never darkened. And her black brows arched like the wings of a bird over luminous brown eyes. If ever there was a denial of the Voertrekker genotype, the mynheera Eliana Ehrengraf Voerster was it.

She was not tall, but her slenderness made her seem so. Her gown reached to her ankles in the modest fashion approved for married Voertrekker women, and she wore black leather-thonged sandals on her long, graceful feet.

On the bed Broni opened her eyes and smiled at her mother. Eliana took her hand and held it. "Did you sleep, child?" she asked.

"Very well, mynheera," Broni said. Her smile, despite all, was brilliant, sunny. "Marvelous dreams. About the Goldenwing coming."

"We will have to have you up and around by the time it arrives," Eliana said.

Never, Tiegen Roark thought, without enormous luck and the help of an unfeeling God. The Goldenwing that was the topic of everyone's conversation these days would not arrive for more than a month, almost two. Who on this benighted world, the physician wondered, knew enough medicine to keep this beautiful child alive that long?

Eliana Voerster appeared to have sensed his doubt. She released Broni's hand and covered it with the counterpane. "I must speak with Healer Roark, Broni," she said.

"Secrets?"

"Small secrets, my love."

With the physician following, Eliana crossed the room to stand in a prayer bay, surrounded on three sides by stained-glass windows. She turned and regarded Roark intently.

"I have sent for the Starman," she said.

In spite of what he had heard about Eliana's regard for the offworlder, it came as a jolt to hear it from her. "The kaffir?" he said.

"Are you shocked, Tiegen?"

"No, mynheera. No," he lied. "It is only that—" He found

the statement impossible to finish. He himself had occasionally encountered the black Starman, had heard him preach and sing. But he had never seen him heal. "Such things are for the *lumpen* and the kaffirs," he said.

There was a flash of anger in Eliana's dark eyes. "I expected better from you, Healer," she said.

Roark flushed. All his life he had prided himself on his liberality, his freedom from prejudice. Yet the idea of Eliana turning to township jujus revolted him.

"He is from *Earth*," Eliana said.

"Yes, he probably has knowledge I lack, But he is not a physician. He is only an adventurer, a wanderer."

"And a kaffir?"

"Since you say it. Yes, a kaffir," Tiegen said defiantly.

"And can *you* cure Broni?"

I would discard my birthright, give my life, endanger my soul to say yes, Tiegen Roark thought. *But I cannot.* He shook his head slowly.

Eliana's hand rested for a moment on his sleeve, a touch as gentle as a falling leaf. "Forgive me, Tiegen. But Broni is my only child."

"And most beloved, mynheera," Roark said heavily. "I know, I know."

"It is not tuberculosis," Eliana said.

"No. It is not."

"The Voerterkker-Praesident insists."

"I am sorry. But the ills of the universe do not obey the commands of The Voerster of Voerster," Roark said.

"He plans a marriage soon."

"That is absurd, Eliana. It is impossible." In fifteen years, Tiegen Roark had not called Eliana Ehrengraf by her given name. The breach of etiquette was enormous. But the statement had been so blunt, so harsh, that it took him a moment to recover himself enough to say, "Forgive me, mynheera. They taught me better than that at Healer's."

Eliana said, "In the hall, if you please?"

———

They left Broni's great room and stood in the stone hallway decorated with the mounted heads of every sort of ancient necrogene in the Sea of Grass. Eliana said, "Believe me, Healer. The Voerster intends to marry Broni to a Highlander."

"*A Highlander?* Who, mynheera?'

"I don't know yet. There are at least three Planetian Kraalheeren that The Voerster needs to hold the highlands. Every one of them is a savage."

Tiegen was shocked at the cold hatred in her voice. "That is out of the question, mynheera."

"I agree," Eliana said in a voice Tiegen had never heard her use. "I will never allow it."

"The Voerster would not send her to live in the highlands."

"There are the Hurtsiks. They hold three quarters of a million hectares above Blomfontein." Eliana's eyes seemed to have hardened to chips of brown obsidian. "Hurtsik has six sons. Not one of them yet married. There are others."

"No, mynheera. It could not possibly be," Roark protested.

"I wish that were so, Tiegen. But I know The Voerster. So do you. If not the Hurtsiks, then some other. Perhaps the Fonteins, who are even worse. Wild animals."

Tiegen Roark drew a deep breath. Having been physician to the Voersters all these years had been a great windfall. He was now, by any normal standard, a rich man. He could even retire and devote himself to research on necrogene physiology, a subject that had fascinated him since Healer's Faculty. *But, Lord God,* he thought, *how I shall miss seeing Eliana . . .*

He suddenly realized that despite his denials, he had quickly accepted the future Eliana Ehrengraf described. Why else would his thoughts turn suddenly to retirement?

But viewed realistically, a highland marriage for Broni Ehrengraf Voerster was out of the question. She could not possibly survive on the Planetia. The rest of it—that virginal girl a bride of some barbarian kraalmeister's six-fingered son—was revolting.

"Well, Tiegen? I am waiting."

"With respect, mynheera ..." Tiegen felt a flash of fear. Eliana clearly expected him to say that he would prevent The Voerster doing anything so harsh as giving Broni over to a matrimonial rape in an environment that would tax even a healthy woman beyond endurance. Eliana Ehrengraf Voerster was asking for an ally. No, for a coconspirator. And on Voerster, the Voetrekker-Praesident had the power to condemn. By simple fiat, if he chose.

"Please, mynheera," Roark said. "Be very careful what you say." *What you say* to me, he thought.

"I intend to stop him," she said. "My husband is not God."

Tiegen Roark sucked in a shallow breath, "I cannot *listen* to you, mynheera."

Eliana's face showed the emotion she was feeling. "Are you so very much afraid, Tiegen?" she asked bitterly.

"Her illness will dissuade him, mynheera," Roark said. "But if he persists—it is his right to choose the time and circumstances of the Voertrekkersdatter's marriage. It is the *law*, mynheera."

Eliana Voerster seemed to withdraw into some stratospheric, icy height. "I thank you for telling me that, Healer."

"When the Voerster returns from the Convocation, perhaps we could suggest a stay at Einsamberg for the Voertrekkersdatter," Roark said. "The mountain air—"

"Thank you," Eliana Voerster said. "I will take it up with my husband."

Tiegen Roark felt as though his heart had turned to stone. Eliana's withdrawal was near to complete.

"I hope," he said, with what dignity he could muster, "that the black Starman is able to amuse mynheera Broni. I am told he is very clever."

"Good morning to you, Healer," Eliana said. "I will watch with my daughter now until morning."

In the great bed, Broni lay half-sleeping. She could hear the murmuring voices of her mother and the Healer in the passageway. She could feel the emotions they were experiencing as a kind of milky star stream, rather like the currents of stars in the moonless skies of Voerster. She often used night images and star visions to explain to herself what it was she had seen and felt since she was a small child. Once her mother had told her that she, too, had experienced the same things when she was a very young girl at Ehrengraf Kraal at Einsamberg. But Eliana no longer had the gift. Broni could tell.

Before Tiegen and her mother had awakened her, Broni had been having such lovely dreams. Familiar dreams of warm summer skies and fields of flowers such as never were on Planet Voerster. The fact was, Broni thought, that God was showing her the place in heaven where she would breathe the scents of spring and run, as she had never been able to do, through fields of real grass ablaze with true wildflowers.

Her mother's sharp, imperious anger with the Healer flashed through Broni and she shut her eyes tight and buried her face in the deep pillows, saddened by the conflict between the two outside her door. Didn't they understand that everything was already decided? That before year's end Broni Ehrengraf Voerster would be gone from this life?

7

A LATE NIGHT MEETING IN VOERSTERSTAAD

I cannot do it, thought Ian Voerster. *I simply cannot bring myself to do this thing.*

He stared across the table at the Kraalheer of the Fontein Kraal—known to everyone as *Winter* Kraal, for the spirit of the place. *By the Lord God,* the Voertrekker-Praesident thought, *what would our mutual ancestors have thought of such a creature?* The dark gossip of early experiments by the ruthless biogeneticists among the First Landers always came to mind when one faced a Highlander at close range.

Vikter Fontein was but 152 centimeters tall. In the old English measure used by the First Landers, five feet and one inch. He massed 144 kilos, half again what a normal man might, and this bulk was strangely apportioned over his barrel-like frame. His waist and midriff were large, but made to seem small by the vast expansion of his chest and lungs. His skin, as much of it as could be seen under the mat of facial hair Planetians favored, was tinged with gray-blue. His eyes were hooded by the heavy epicanthic fold of the Highlander. An occasional Planetian displayed the rudiment of a nictitating membrane, another legacy of the genetic engineers who dominated the first three hundred years of medical science on Voerster. Vikter Fontein was not so favored, but it was said that his third wife (who had died like the others) had been.

The Planetians had been put on an evolutionary fast track. But even the most charitable observer would be tempted to say that they were now a biological dead end. Kraalheeren from the high plains now valued lowland women as the means of breeding themselves back into the biological mainstream of Voerster.

The Kraalheer sat with one hand spread before him on the table, displaying six long fingers. His chest expanded and contracted with a hollow, rushing sound in the high air pressure at sea level.

The total effect of these physical differences was daunting, Ian Voerster thought, and repulsive.

"I can deliver the Highlanders," Fontein said in his deep, reverberating voice. "Or I can take them for my own. It is for you to decide, Voertrekker."

"We have been one nation for thirteen hundred years," Ian Voerster said. "Do not threaten me, Mynheer Fontein." What he said was only conditionally true. The Rebellion had bifurcated the colony long ago, and the rift remained. But the people of the lowlands and the Planetians had always pretended they were one people. Without the kaffir enemy, Ian Voerster thought, matters could be quite different.

The Fontein leaned forward across the polished graystone table. As he did, Voerster was struck by how much he resembled the pictures of terrestrial Japanese *sumitori* in the *hohere shule* texts: thick, broad shoulders, huge chest, outthrust head with almost no neck, staring eyes, and a broad, hooked beak of a nose.

"I don't threaten, Ian Voerster. I say what is obvious. You are frightened of the independence movement on the Planetia. You have cause to be. I organized it."

The Voerster glanced swiftly at the closed door behind which stood Han Ryndik and a dozen members of the Trekkerpolizei's Special Branch. A touch on a hidden buzzer and there would be a stampede of armed men through the door to arrest the Kraalheer of Winter. He had just admitted treason and subversion of the Voertrekker State.

But then what?

To break the independence movement on the Planetia was impossible as long as Lowlanders could not fight and dirigibles could not effectively fly there. If Fontein were gone, the leadership would fall to the Hurtsiks. If they went down, another of the highland tribes would rule. The movement could not be defeated, only co-opted. *Which is why I am here, meeting in secret with this barbarian,* Ian thought.

"Don't talk to me about Voertrekker unity and racial purity," The Fontein said, staring. "If that's what you intend."

"That was not my intention," the Voertrekker-Praesident said heavily. He thought: *The truth is that we have more in common with our Grassersee kaffirs than with this Voertrekker-descended human variant.* But the widening gap between white and white on Voerster had to be stopped. It was too late to annul the physical changes taking place among the people of the Planetia. The medical skills that had created them were lost a thousand years ago. But the men of Voertrekker blood on Voerster dared not break the fragile social compact they had made with one another long, long ago when they decided to flee Earth for the sake of the chimera of racial purity. *Not while we still send kaffirs to the Friendly Islands for infractions of the racial laws,* The Voerster thought. *They are more civilized than* that *in the high country.*

Ian Voerster tried to regard Vikter Fontein calmly and dispassionately, as a ruler and politician should. It was obvious that Fontein Kraal was prospering. Fontein's clothes had been made by a skilled tailor, probably in Pretoria, where the people of the Planetia customarily conducted their business. His tunic was made of deep green felt and velvet flashed with gold. There were gold chains around his bulging neck, a small fortune's worth of them. On his head, in the highland manner, he wore a green tam on which the Fontein badge was worked with more gold and several quite respectable stones.

The diamond mines of Fontein Kraal were productive, that was obvious. If Broni goes to Georg or Eigen Fontein, Voerster thought, she will never want for anything tangible.

Only for air to breathe and a human being to love her. His own sense of honor mocked him cruelly.

"Will you say what you brought me here to say?" The

Fontein said. "I feel confined in this stone box of a house. The walls are too near. The air is too thick. How do you breathe this soup?"

There was actually a sheen of sweaty moisture on The Fontein's bluish brow. As a courtesy to the Kraalheer of Winter, the temperature in the room stood at fourteen degrees Celsius, five degrees less than Ian Voerster found comfortable, even wrapped in his customary furs. Yet the dour Highlander from the northeastern edge of the continent found it too warm. Clearly, very special arrangements would have to be made for Broni's comfort if she were to live on the high plain.

"It would be a tragedy if, after all these hard years, the Voertrekkers on Voerster should fall into white-on-white strife," Ian Voerster said. "Do we agree on that?"

"There are worse things, Voerster."

Being a Highlander he would think so, the Voertrekker-Praesident thought. But civil war would not be like the tribal skirmishes of the high plateau. What technology existed on Voerster was centered in the Sea of Grass.

"I have no experience of war," Voerster said. "I have no wish to acquire any. There are better ways."

The pale gray eyes narrowed. Fontein was not so confident as he wished to appear. That was worth remembering. Once an alliance was made, it had to be clear who was the dominating partner.

"I thought you would never get to the point," Fontein said.

"I am not there yet," Voerster said, controlling a flash of anger. To have one of this creature's get as son-in-law would be taxing, he thought.

But necessary. The Trekkerpolizei Domestic Intelligence Unit warned that the highland tribes were ready to start raiding the towns and villages of the Grassersee. "I am prepared to offer you a post in the government."

Fontein placed another hand on the table. Twelve fingers. *Angatch!* (The Voertrekker, as he often did, fell back on naming the kaffir gods of the nanny who had raised him.) He really must stop reacting with such revulsion to the Planetian's physical deformities. But those hands were disgusting.

"I would never live in Voersterstaad. Not if you made me Voertrekker-Praesident."

Ian Voerster flushed. "The post could be honorary. Most government posts are, Vikter," Voerster said with controlled mildness.

"What else are you offering? How badly do you want the Highlanders to stay in the high country?"

Voerster regarded The Fontein speculatively. So even after years of separate development, even separate evolution, a Voertrekker was still a Voertrekker. Cupidity had been a Voertrekker trait when the first Boer commando left the Cape Colony for the north. Nothing had changed, not really. For some reason the realization made him feel far more confident about what he must do.

"I propose an alliance, Kraalheer. I propose linking our two ancient families by marriage."

The heavy face betrayed cupidity. "I have two sons," Vikter Fontein said. "Georg and Eigen."

The Voerster said, "To me one Fontein is like another. I have only one daughter."

"They say she is sickly."

"It is a lie."

"Could she live on the Planetia?"

"Arrangements would have to be made."

"And she could bear sons?" The eyes were cavernous now and the strange hands had vanished to fondle the holsters where his customary weapons had rested before being surrendered to Colonel Ryndik.

"Yes." *May the Lord God of Hosts forgive me*, Ian Voerster thought. *He knows about Broni's frailty*. "There is more."

"Offer, Voertrekker-Praesident. What more?" Not nearly so scornful now.

Cupidity runs our world, Ian Voerster thought. *You are a shopkeeper, after all, Fontein.*

———

"The estate of Einsamberg. The ancient Ehrengraf Kraal. It is part of Broni's inheritance. To be yours when the banns are read."

"And the town of Grimsel, on the Shieldwall. And the funicular railroad through the Pass."

He might be a great Kraalheer in the highlands, Voerster thought coldly. *But he bargains like a* lumpen *shopkeeper.*

"A plebiscite in Grimsel." Most of the inhabitants of the Shieldwall town were Highlanders in any case and were already Fontein partisans. "But not the railway." That was the only access from the Grassersee to the Planetia. It could not be exclusively in Vikter Fontein's hands.

The Kraalheer of Winter stared at Ian Voerster. Purple-red lips within the mat of beard slowly formed a grimace that among Highlanders passed for a smile.

"Done," he said. "With one alteration."

"Which is?"

"I have been a widower for ten years. I see no reason for wasting a young lowland beauty on either of my brutes."

For a moment the Voertrekker-Praesident was nonplussed.

The matted smile broadened and the eyes grew cold as sea-ice. "As you said yourself, Cousin. One Fontein is like any other. I will marry the girl myself."

8

AN EBRAY ON THE SEA
OF GRASS

The vehicle, commonly called "a steamer," was a massive cart that rode on six unshod steel wheels. The seven-meter-long machine, which surrendered its rear deck to a cast-iron boiler and several polished brass pistons and rocker arms, was controlled from an open cockpit in front—furnished with three small seats upholstered in leather, two forward and one behind beside the luggage bay.

Mynheer Osbertus Kloster sat in the right-hand front seat before the tiller and drove the clattering, wheezing car swiftly southward and across wind through the Sea of Grass toward Voertrekkerhoem.

The steamer progressed at good speed across the flat ground with an assortment of clangs and hisses, leaving astern a cloud of dust, steam, and flying grass. Beside the Astronomer-Select sat Black Clavius, knapsack and balichord clutched protectively in his lap. He peered ahead into the near distance lighted by the three focussed gas lanterns on the bow of the steamer, and to the sides where the tall grass lashed and whipped as the vehicle stormed by.

Electric carriages were fairly common on Voerster, but they were limited by the primitive batteries Voertrekker industry was able to produce. The planet supplied the lead and acid used, but lacked the more sophisticated materials of which the old science texts spoke. The technology of the First Landers and their descendants for the first three hundred years had been handicapped by the limitations imposed on specialization by the colonization plan. By the time of the Rebellion, science and industry had become well established on Voerster. But all advancement was stifled and techniques were lost as the war against the kaffirs became a Voertrekker priority. And in the dark ages that followed the Rebellion there had been a revulsion against the technology producing the weapons that had so nearly depopulated the planet. Scientific knowledge became a swift ticket to the gallows as Luddite moralists did their best to reduce Voerster to the presumed safety of a primitive, agricultural world. Scientists and inventors were no longer lynched on Voerster, but thirteen hundred years since First Landing, the Astronomer-Select Kloster's steam car was a "state-of-the-art" device.

Both Clavius and Osbertus wore white-cloth dusters to save their clothing and protective goggles over their eyes against the flying grasses and the lash of the Nachtebrise.

"Mynheer, this is breathtaking," Clavius said. "How fast are we going?"

Osbertus glanced at the relative wind gauge fixed to the double-monocle windshield and said proudly, "We are making fifty-four kilometers an hour. Do you know that style of measurement, Clavius?"

The black man smiled broadly into the wind. "For some years now, Mynheer Osbertus, I have moved only on my two feet, and somewhat more slowly. But yes, I do remember something about kilometers and hours."

The astronomer squinted into the wind and chided himself for asking so foolish a question of a man who had journeyed among the stars. But Black Clavius, with that strange sensitivity he so often displayed, said, "This mode of travel is most exciting, Mynheer."

Osbertus risked a quick glance to see if the big man was ridiculing him. But Clavius was plainly enjoying the charge of the steamer through the Sea of Grass, with all of its noise and bumps and attendant discomforts.

Clavius said, "Between the stars, there is great beauty, but no excitement. One floats in eternity, seldom near enough to anything to experience speed. Here the sensation of motion is irresistible. Can we go faster?"

"Faster than this?" Osbertus was a trifle breathless from the steamer's rush through the Grassersee. The mech who had assembled the steamer, from parts ordered by dirigible from Pretoria, was a brash journeyman. He had boasted to the Astronomer-Select that the steamer's speed was limited only by the terrain under the wheels and the courage of the tillerman. But he soberly suggested that given the Mynheer's age and eyesight, speeds in excess of sixty kilometers per hour were unwise.

Eliana, after riding with Osbertus (How she had smiled and laughed with delight!), had admonished him. "I enjoyed it tremendously, Cousin," she said. "But you must drive carefully. Who shall be my friend if you crack your skull?"

Osbertus took a deep breath and made the ultimate gesture of trust. "Would you like to drive, Clavius?"

For an unlicensed kaffir to drive any powered vehicle on Voerster was discouraged. Once it had been a punishable offense. Now it was only custom.

"I thank you for the offer, Mynheer. But I had best remain in the hands of one who knows how to handle this powerful machine."

Osbertus Kloster sat up a trifle straighter and flexed his cramped knees. There was very little room between the thin steel floorboards and the tiller. But despite his discomfort, he was compelled to reply to the Starman's graciousness in kind. He advanced the throttle, valving steam until the steamer's speed reached a full seventy kilometers per hour. Behind, the rooster-tail of grass and immature spore pods rose even higher.

"Marvelous, Mynheer Osbertus, marvelous," Black Clavius said over the sounds of passage. His great hands encircled the neck of the balichord, and as the steamer's speed increased he looked skyward at the star-river of the Milky Way. "'Look now toward heaven, and tell the stars, if thou be able to number them.'"

"You astonish me, Clavius," Osbertus said. "That was from

the Book of Genesis, wasn't it? We have so few eidetics on Voerster. Do you remember everything?"

"Yes, Mynheer."

"Remarkable."

"It is not always a blessing, Mynheer."

"Yes. I can understand how that might be. One seldom imagines a Starman suffering the ordinary problems of life."

"We do, Mynheer." His teeth showed white again in that dazzling smile. "And some not so ordinary." He paused; he seemed suddenly to be listening to something only he could hear above the clangor of the racing steamer. "Mynheer. Stop."

"The Mynheera Eliana summoned us posthaste to Broni, Clavius."

"Nevertheless. Please stop now."

Perplexed, Osbertus Kloster reduced the throttle and hauled on the brake lever. It took the steamer almost a full kilometer to come to a halt. It stood wheezing and emitting vapor on the dark grassland.

Quite suddenly an ebray, a gravid female, lurched to her feet and stood spraddle-legged, regarding the lamps of the steamer with huge, gleaming black eyes. The animal was a meter high at the withers and stood on legs as delicate as grass-stems. In full, leaping flight—what the Voertrekkers called "pronking"—the ebray was capable of outrunning the steamer. But this one was about to give birth. She had the ravaged look of a beast being consumed from within, as indeed she was. A necrogene, she could expect her voracious offspring to gnaw and rip its way into the world through the soft velvety hide of her belly. The ebray would then die and the young ebray would stay with the maternal corpse until the edible flesh was consumed before trotting away from the remains of the creature who had, in effect, transferred her future to him.

"Go around her," Clavius whispered. "She is close to her time."

Osbertus, not an unkind man, was strangely moved by the

Wired Man's obvious concern for the doomed ebray. He advanced the throttle slowly and drove a wide circle around the expectant necrogene, who turned to keep facing the steamer, tottering weakly on legs that would no longer firmly sustain her.

When Osbertus had consulted his compass and resumed his course through the grass for Voertrekkerhoem at a somewhat slower pace, he asked. "How did you know?"

Clavius said only, "I knew, Mynheer. I knew."

Osbertus turned to look at his passenger. Clavius' goggles were pushed high on his forehead, and the Voertrekker was astonished and touched to see tears running down the Starman's black cheeks.

As the steamer moved majestically out of the savannah and onto the curving, cobblestoned esplanade leading to the Great Gate at Voertrekkerhoem, Osbertus Kloster pondered the Starman's behavior out on the Grassersee.

The Astronomer-Select was a compassionate man. For all that he was a mynheer and had lived all his life in circumstances that made liberalism and consideration for his inferiors relatively easy, Osbertus could not be faulted for the genuineness of his feelings. He did his best to uplift the benighted kaffirs, he contributed regularly to the collections of alms for the indigent *lumpen* in the cities of Voersterstaad and Pretoria, to the simple preachers of the Cult of Elmi, and to the Society for the Respect for Native Life. In a nation of hunters, Osbertus Kloster had fired a gun only a dozen times in his life, and had always (to his stern father's disgust) managed to miss his targets. He regarded his fortunate birth as a burden requiring him to display kindness and consideration to all the creatures of Voerster, human and otherwise.

But the Starman's reaction to the encounter with the gravid ebray fascinated and disturbed him. Not because he regarded Clavius' tears for the poor creature weak or demeaning, but because had he been alone on the Sea of Grass at the time of the encounter, he, the softhearted Osbertus Kloster, would have driven past the ebray, or even over her, without a second thought.

This, he understood, was because he had been born and raised on a planet where all native life was necrogenic. It was very sad, but he (and, indeed, nine hundred Voertrekkers out of a thousand) would have been quite unmoved by the fragile creature about to give terrible birth alone on the Sea of Grass.

Before driving through the sally port to the Trekkerpolizei station just inside the walls of the Voertrekker-Praesident's residence, he slowed to a crawl along the cobblestoned way and said to Black Clavius: "Is Voerster very different from the other worlds you have seen?"

"Different," Clavius said. "And much the same."

"I don't understand you, Clavius."

"The worlds of near space are human worlds. To the limit of our reach, Mynheer, it seems our species found worlds waiting. Some fallow, some possessed of native life, but only of a low order. It is as the Psalmist wrote, these many millennia ago: 'Thou madest him to have dominion over the works of thy hands; thou hast put all things under his feet.'"

"Yet you wept for the ebray."

Clavius regarded the Voertrekker steadily. "The beautiful creature was dying, Mynheer Osbertus."

"Yes, of course. But ebray are necrogenes, it is the way of things on Voerster." Never in a long life had he ever considered a challenge to the way things were on Voerster. It would be as sensible as regretting the color of the sky or the way the Six Giants moved about the heavens. How could the natural order of things be challenged, even by human grief?

"Of course, Mynheer. I should not criticize merely because I feel deeply." Black Clavius smiled sadly at the Astronomer-Select. "You see, I am an empath. To a degree, all Wired Ones are. It derives from our 'enhancement.'" He touched the socket hidden in his hair. "But perhaps you can understand better if I tell you that as we watched the little ebray, I *felt* some of her pain, her perplexity, her sadness."

Osbertus slowly advanced the throttle and let the steamer roll forward toward the police post. "Why do I think, Clavius, that you find Voerster a melancholy world?"

The Starman did not reply. His eyes were fixed on the towering, ugly structure ahead. There were armed sentries on the roof walks. *Lord,* Clavius silently addressed his Friend and Creator, *I cannot understand why you made us as we are. For that matter, why did you populate this world with necrogenes? Perhaps just to hold it until we humans arrived? If so, I thank you, but wasn't it a bit extreme? The ebray was beautiful. Must beauty live briefly and perish young? Then why is the glorious whirlpool of M-31 in Andromeda so breathtaking, and so nearly eternal? You perplex me, Lord, indeed you do.*

The Trekkerpolizeikapitan was acquainted with the Astronomer-Select and his crazy land-yacht. Everyone in the west of the Grassersee was. Even the *lumpen* took a perverse pride in Osbertus and his ideosyncrasies. Heat radiating from the boiler on the steamer smelled of coal gas and hot metal. The policeman, a young man, could scarcely restrain his curiosity about the vehicle. There were only a dozen such machines on Planet Voerster, and one was in the Voersterstaad Museum of Contemporary Science and Industry. They were stunningly expensive and available only to members of the mynheeren class. The officer forced his attention from the steamer to its passengers.

To Clavius he said, "Your passbook, kaffir." He knew that the black man had been summoned by the mynheera Eliana Ehrengraf and so must be admitted to Voertrekkerhoem, passbook or no, but the strictures of Voertrekker society had been established very long ago, far away, and reinforced by the memory of the Rebellion. Kaffirs wcrc *always* challenged entering the home of the Voertrekker-Praesident of Voerster.

Clavius, understanding exactly the thoughts that were in the young policeman's mind, produced a tattered passbook issued to him many years ago, when The Voerster had been young in his office.

The policeman inspected and returned it. He stepped back and saluted the Astronomer-Select to indicate that the road to the Grand Portico—the narrow stone porch facing the front of the great house—was clear.

He watched the steamer proceed around the long curve of the drive—an avenue lined with a few of the Earth trees that had managed to take root in the alien soil, and a great many native plants, pulpy, flowerless, and ugly. They grew to thirty meters and more in the protected environment of Voertrekkerhoem's garden.

The Nachtebrise was still blowing toward the slowly lightening horizon. Clavius dismounted from the steamer and stood while Osbertus moved it into the paddock where the mounts of visitors were confined. None of the beasts were to be seen in the paddock and Osbertus was glad of it. The mock horses of Voerster, toothed necrogenes distantly related to the ebray, had an insatiable taste for the gum used for the steamer's water hoses.

Clavius stood looking up at the lighted tower window at the end of the long hall off which would be found the Voertrekkersdatter's room. He had never been inside Voertrekkerhoem, but he had encountered Broni and her mother on the mynheera Eliana's excursions into the townships with help for the kaffirs who labored on the Voerster and Ehrengraf lands. Broni had been enchanted with Clavius' balichord and with the ancient songs of Earth he knew.

To the Starman she had described in minute detail the establishment in which she lived, down to the colors of the stained glass in the prayer bays and the weave of the tapestries on the walls. Clavius had suspected then, when Broni was still prepubescent, that the girl was a potential eidetic and almost certainly a developing empath.

He had never mentioned it, not even to the mynheera Eliana.

It had seemed best, considering the precarious state of the girl's health.

But Voertrekkerhoem was precisly as Broni Ehrengraf Voerster had described it. As a lark she had even given Clavius the exact number of slate slabs in the broad stairs leading to the Portico. He did not count them because he knew that Broni's tally was correct. It was characteristic of eidetics *not* to make mistakes with numbers or with any physical facts. Clavius wondered if Broni had ever sat at an open window here at Voertrekkerhoem, counting the number of stars she could see at one given hour of the night. He had done that himself, many, many years ago, by a slow river in a place called South Carolina on Old Earth.

"Clavius?"

"Mynheer."

"Do you find it impressive?"

"I find it—unique, Mynheer."

"I am far not sure what you mean by that, Clavius," Osbertus Kloster said dubiously. "But follow me. I will take you to the Voertrekkerschatz Eliana."

9

A TRANSIT OF DRACHE

The brilliance reflecting from the nitrogen ice clouds of Drache was so dazzling it was painful to look upon the white giant with unprotected eyes. The light struck the skylar surfaces of *Glory*'s sails and was flung like a million arrows in all directions so that the great Goldenwing appeared to be flying through a sparkling shower of liquid diamonds.

By now *Glory* was moving at a significant percentage of the speed of light. The process of bleeding off interstellar velocity continued. The time dilation between *Glory* and her destination had dropped to a small fraction. The blue shift of stars ahead was all but gone. The red behind *Glory* had faded to a dusty rose.

Under Anya Amaya's guidance the deck crew of four had assembled in the bridge to begin the long, slow process of furling the speed sails: stuns'ls, t'gallants, flying jibs, and spankers. In *Glory*'s sail plan these numbered over one thousand and each had to be furled with great care in order to prevent damage to the whisper-thin skylar.

The observation dome of the bridge was uncovered, making it possible to observe almost the entire, vast spread of skylar. Among the sails, swarming along the monofilament stays and braces, monkeys raced from hull to tops and back again as each bit of skylar was carefully gasketted to its yard.

This was Damon Ng's first participation in this complex evolution. He was terrified that he would commit a gross error, but elated that so far he had not. Only Marq was in a pod. Anya, Damon, and Duncan were Wired, but floating free in the bridge.

Damon did not completely understand why the Master and

the Sailing Master wished to sail the ship "hands on" at these times, but they did. And it seemed to Damon that *Glory* responded to their personal touch. *"She becomes sweeter, easier to sail,"* Duncan explained. His quiet smile made Damon wonder if he was being hazed in Duncan's low-key way. He doubted it. *Glory* did seem most particularly *yare* at these times.

He loved that Old Earth word borrowed from the sailors who sailed wooden ships on a blue-and-white ocean. When first Damon essayed to use the expression, Anya had said with serious mien: "It is pronounced *yar*, Damon. *Yar*. Remember. The others will laugh at you if you say *yair*."

The young man from Grissom finished the remote furling of the starboard mainyard stuns'l with a genuine flourish. *Glory* reported the task complete through his drogue and Damon allowed himself to enjoy the moment.

"So take a bow, sailor. You have accomplished the simple."

That was Jean, who was never pleased or satisfied with anything Damon did. He glanced over at Marq's pod. The Frenchman lay deep in the glyceroid, to all appearances in a deep operational coma. Damon knew better. Jean Marq never surrendered completely to *Glory*.

He felt a firm grip on his shoulder. It was Duncan floating in midair above the manual control panels for the starboard side of the rig: the starboard main, mizzen, and foremasts.

"That was well done, Damon," Duncan said aloud. His drogue cable curled about him. Today he was wearing the bottom half of a skinsuit because he had earlier been EVA. "Don't let Jean trouble you. He knows good work when he sees it."

Anya floated high, near the crystal dome of the bridge. She was naked, as she customarily was when working the ship from inboard. Damon was young enough to find her nudity and availability fascinating. Anya was far more provocative than any of the girls he had known on Grissom.

She was silhouetted against the brilliant light of Drache. The photons were penetrating her slim arms and legs. Damon could see the shadows of the slender bones within.

———

"Give me a hand with the port foretops'l, Damon," she said through the drogue. *"The silly monkeys are trying to furl it wrinkled."*

Damon launched himself upward to join her. Near Anya, and inside the dome, he could almost ignore his acrophobia.

Through the drogue Anya sent a series of sharp commands to the monkeys. *"Damn,"* she said. *"They aren't responding. How long since they recharged, Damon?"*

"Twenty-one hours, Sailing Master."

"Shit. They aren't holding a charge. The cybercells need replacing, Duncan?"

Duncan appeared at her side.

"Take over? Send the foretop team to the Monkey House. I'll go out. I don't want to lose that sail."

She released her drogue and made for the transit tube. As she floated over Marq's pod, the Frenchman's eyes opened and stared at her.

Three decks down, in the vast empty spaces of what was once the hospital, Dietr Krieg received a series of signals from the computer and frowned.

He removed his drogue and stared perplexedly at the graphical interface. The life-signals of the crew—including his own—were represented there in light-bars. It was a visual approximation of the information that customarily came to him in a far more refined form through the drogue.

He reset the drogue in his socket and said, *"Duncan?"*

"What is it, Dietr?"

"Take a look at Jean, will you?"

There was a long pause during which the light-bar representing Jean Marq's life-signals twitched and waved across a cathode-ray plate.

Duncan replied, *"Jean says to fuck off, Dietr."*

The neurocybersurgeon sensed the impatience in both Duncan and Marq. Sailors tended to be edgy when a complicated maneuver was being performed. Krieg was not interested in spacemanship. He had no interest whatever in ship-handling. He understood that today's evolution entailed much furling of sails, resetting of yards, and eventually a tack and a close pass by Drache followed by a new course and a long fall to the inner system. All of which meant orbit at Voerster in a week and a month of solitude while the rest of the crew went downworld. Dietr Krieg avoided going down to the planets *Glory* visited. It was foolish, he knew, but he had the illogical impression that spending time downworld would steal from his allotted uptime. It was a ridiculous notion. Time dilation did not work that way. Time was time and objective reality was what one experienced. No more than that. But he felt it nonetheless, and usually stayed aboard, Wired to the medical banks of *Glory*'s computer.

Unlike Duncan, Anya, and Damon, the physician never thought of the time he spent Wired in terms of being at one with *Glory*. To Krieg the *Gloria Coelis* was only a construct, a thing of titanium and skylar and monofilament fabrics. The *computer* was the wonder, and it, according to Dietr Krieg, was only a machine.

"What's troubling you, Dietr?" Duncan asked.

"It can wait. Go on about your business." But he opened his personal medical file and made an entry:

> *Strange readings on Marq. Supposition: He begins to show signs of fugue. Data as yet incomplete, but he has all the prerequisites for serious mental incapacity.*

He leaned back in his chair and considered the graphical interface. Marq's line steadied. A less experienced physician would have been reassured. Krieg was not. "Fugue" was a swift flight from reality during which the subject could act with perfect normality. When the fugue terminated, the subject would remember nothing of what had transpired during the affected time. Jean Marq was a prime candidate for a swift progression from neurosis to psychosis and a flash into fugue. Dietr Krieg knew his history. It was in the database.

He closed his eyes. *"Jean?"*

"What the fuck do you want, Dietr? I'm busy now."

The response was more violent than the occasion called for.

———

Jean Marq was hardly sailing the ship alone. Duncan and Damon Ng were on the bridge with him, and Anya Amaya was just now stepping through a valve onto *Glory's* carapace, about to do some mysterious sailor thing or other outside the ship.

"When your watch ends I want you to come to sick bay for some tests."

There was no reply through the drogue.

"I mean it, Jean. Or no more gifts." It was far better to suggest that he would cut off his ration of Dust than to threaten him with Duncan. Duncan was no martinet, but he could be fierce where the safety of the ship was involved.

"Of course, Dietr." Jean Marq's weirdly acquiescent reply sent a shock wave through the physician. Immediately he changed computer protocol and entered the medical directory section. Here were contained volumes of medical lore, every bit of medical technology gleaned from the worlds *Glory* had visited, every anecdotal case study logged by each of the neurocybersurgeons who had ever worn *Glory's* drogue. Here, too, was the complete medical history of everyone who had ever belonged to a *Glory* syndicate, back to the ancients who had sailed her for the Holy Brothers on her first journey. Viewing from this perspective, another man would have thought of *Glory* as an immortal being, learning, saving, guarding, being served. But to Krieg the medical archives were only data. The physician had ample intelligence. What he lacked was imagination and a sense of wonder.

"Glory?"

"Yes, Dietr."

"Give me Jean Marq's indices."

The computer complied. The data was indicative, but incomplete. Dietr scowled. Psychiatry was still witchcraft, he thought. It was possible to observe, test, assume, and consider. But no psychiatrist born had ever discovered a way accurately *to predict*.

Jean would bear watching. An insane man in deep space could be deadly to everyone around him.

*

Anya Amaya, armored for space and carrying a small reaction motor, launched herself straight into the forest of titanium yards projecting from the foremast. With the skill of an acrobat she avoided the stays and braces, swung by and over the yards until she paused, balanced precariously on a furled stuns'l three quarters of the way to the foretop.

She looked about her with real delight. She enjoyed being EVA but as Sailing Master she felt it unseemly to indulge herself overmuch. Serving with Duncan had a tendency to make one aware of one's responsibility to *Glory* and the syndicate. There was an ancient mariner's saying: "One hand for the ship, one hand for the sailor." But the truth was that the ship could be more demanding even than that. *Glory* was a sweet ship, but she had killed sailors as any ship might do. A mistake, a slip, a moment of bad judgment could snuff out a life. The ship would go on, but the syndicate always required regeneration.

She floated off the spar and held herself in place with a hand. She tried to imagine what it would be like to see *Glory* vanishing into the infinite distance while one hung alone in emptiness. That would be loneliness. She shivered a bit and dismissed the thought. She was at home in deep space, at home on *Glory*'s bridge, at home kilometers high in the winged rig. Her former life on New Earth grew more vague as uptime passed. She now found it sad that on her homeworld the men and women who had found her flawed and worthy only of being sold to a Goldenwing syndicate were now old, or dust.

While I, she thought, *fly among the stars.*

She released her hold on the spar and turned a slow, deliberate pirouette in the maze of rigging around her. The blinding white disk of Drache seemed to rotate around her, as though she were a sun. The starfields rose and set, reflected in golden light. How absolutely, incredibly beautiful, she thought. The hard inner surfaces of her space armor sent shivers of sensation through her body. She had not bothered to don a skinsuit. She was naked under the armor.

Using the reaction motor she added a touch of delta-V and flew slowly away from the towering foremast. To her right the even higher, more intricate starboard mainmast loomed like a castle of light against the black of space. Everywhere she looked she could see reflected images of Drache, all made magical by the curved surfaces of skylar.

In the brilliant lighted bridge, under the loom of Drache, Duncan said, *"Jean. What's wrong with the cameras on the foremast?"*

Dreamily. *"A small malfunction, Master. I'm working on it."*

Duncan frowned. A Starman hated anomalies when performing a maneuver. He most particularly disliked it when shipmates behaved peculiarly. There was something odd about Jean. Krieg must have sensed it earlier.

"Anya. Forget the sail. Let the monkeys handle it. Get back inside. We can't see you."

"Yes, Duncan."

She was feeling slightly put upon. As Sailing Master she seldom went EVA and now Duncan was cutting short her lark. But she twisted about and pointed the reaction engine at the stars. Her delta-V increased and she seemed to be sliding down an invisible slope toward the golden wings of the foremast.

As she made ready to alight on a spar there was a sudden movement of the braces and the spar that had been her destination jerked violently in her direction.

It struck her across the lower abdomen and drove the breath from her body. Only the armor saved her from crippling injury. The impact doubled her over and sent her tumbling out into space. Within seconds, she was a hundred meters from the ship and the distance was increasing. She saw the reaction engine she had been carrying spin away, its polished surfaces sending out flashes of reflected light.

With enormous effort, she controlled her voice as she called for help. *"Duncan! Mayday!"*

Already *Glory* had moved a thousand meters away.

*

Duncan was unsure what had happened to send Anya tumbling off into space. But he had a strong suspicion. For one single moment of agonizing indecision he resisted what he knew must be done and then he gave the order. *"Krieg, to the bridge! Damon, get suited and go after her. Use one of the Donkeys. Move!"*

Damon floated, staring in horror at Jean Marq's still form in the pod. "What did he *do?*"

"We don't know that he did anything, boy. *Go! Now!*"

Damon flung away his drogue and felt the slurring diminishment before flying into the transit tube. It was like a nightmare. He found his mind trying desperately not to see what Anya must now be seeing: The distance increasing between herself and *Glory*. The ship fading like a spark in the ghastly white glare of Drache. . . .

Damon had never made so swift a transfer into space armor. There was cold sweat on his flanks and face as he closed the ziplocks. He kicked off through the hangar deck valve. In the gloom he could make out *Glory*'s arrowhead shuttles and the row of Donkeys—no more than sleds with reacton motors fore and aft together with maneuvering thrusters. Their best speed was no more than a dozen meters a second, but they were already moving with *Glory* at thirty-five percent of the speed of light.

The hangar deck was open to space and seldom visited when not in planetary orbit. Through the open bay Damon saw the stars, bright and distant, and Drache, immense and vertigo-inducing. He straddled the Donkey and lighted off the after motor. Liquid hydrogen was converted to vapor by the instantaneous pressure drop, and the Donkey skidded along the deck to the open bay and out through it into space.

Immediately terror surged in Damon, threatening to suffocate him. He felt himself leak urine and felt his armor suck the moisture out of his suit air.

"Anya! Signal! Do you hear me? Light your rescue torch and signal!" That was Duncan on the ordinary radio. Drogues were useless in open space; there was not room for the supporting technology in the space armor.

———

Damon heard a breathless voice in his headphones: "I am at about seven o'clock. Eight hundred meters, I think." Anya speaking. "My strobe light is broken. Oh, God, Duncan, I'm frightened."

Damon tongued his transmitter. "I am out with a Donkey, Anya. I'm coming. Keep transmitting so I can home on you."

Behind him *Glory* was like a sunburst of golden light. Growing smaller as the distance increased. Overhead the huge sphere of Drache dominated the sky. *Glory* was close enough now so that Damon could see the swirling movement of the frozen gasses in Drache's atmosphere. The stratospheric winds on Drache reached speeds of ten thousand kilometers per hour. At lesser altitudes, where the ice crystals blew, the wind velocity was far higher. Drache and the other gas giants in the Luyten system were failed stars, just under the mass needed for thermonuclear ignition. If any one of the six had succeeded in consuming even one of its siblings, Luyten 726 would have been a multiple system, with a close companion in addition to the distant dark dwarf brothers far beyond the Oort Cloud. And Voerster would never have been. Instead there would have been a cinder following an eccentric orbit between a fiery pair.

"Damon, where are you?"

Duncan, Damon thought, thank God for Duncan. He sounded as though he were calling from inside a suit. Krieg must have taken over the task of monitoring Jean Marq, and Duncan was coming out to help find Anya.

"I am at six o'clock, Master. About five hundred meters from the ship. I have my strobe alight."

"Turn forty-five degrees right and then resume course. I will bracket on the other side." Then, "Anya. Keep sending, damn it!"

"I can still see *Glory*." Anya's voice was strained to the breaking point, but she kept on. "I can see all of her starboard rig and some of the port. But she's transiting Drache now and the glare is too great. Duncan, Damon, she's so beautiful. She is like a golden bird, a flower, a butterfly. Did you know we had butterflies on New Earth, Duncan? We did. Our First Landers brought them. Some fool thought they made honey. Can you believe that? Oh, God, Duncan, I am so *scared*—"

"We'll find you, Anya."

"We won't leave you," Damon said.

There was a long empty space and then, "I think I see one of you. Who has the blue Donkey? Is that you, Duncan?"

"No, Anya. I'm on the blue," Damon said, refusing to look up at the enormity of gas and storm that filled two-thirds of the sky. "Guide me. Talk me in." *Oh, God, hurry,* Damon thought. *The panic is trying to grab me by the throat. Resist. Resist!*

"It *is* you, Damon. Oh, good boy. Good boy. Bear right and up a little. There, can you see me? Look for me at eleven o'clock."

Damon forced himself to look away from the Donkey's rudimentary instrument panel and into the sky. Instantly he felt as though he were falling.

Resist!

He caught sight of a slowly tumbling figure. Over and over and over again. He said, "Anya, spread your arms. It will make you stop tumbling."

The tumbling slowed. He drew nearer. "More, Anya. Spread your legs. Spread them."

Shakily: "Duncan, do you hear that? The boy thinks of nothing but sex."

Damon heard Duncan's short laugh.

He brought the Donkey to a stop relative to Anya and put out a hand. She caught it and held on. The delta-V was transmitted to the combined mass of girl, Damon, and Donkey and set it all to tumbling very slowly.

"I am behind you," Duncan said. Damon looked to see the Master astride a red Donkey. He matched velocities and came to a stop. Through her fogged faceplate, Anya was looking at first one then the other. Damon could see that her cheeks were wet.

"Don't do that, Anya. The suit can't handle much moisture. I know," Duncan said.

Duncan locked his Donkey to Damon's and turned them around. *Glory* was already a half dozen kilometers away. The immense span of her triple rig filled the sky with flashing light. She was like something to be seen only in the dew of an early morning on Grissom, something woven by the crystal spiders who spanned their own version of the universe—the space between the great trees—with their reflective webs. For just an instant, Damon Ng felt a blue spear of homesickness. Then he no longer did. He was at home now, as much at home as he would ever be.

With Anya secure between them, Damon Ng and Duncan Kr advanced the reaction engines and closed the distance between themselves and the golden apparition of *Glory*.

"I'll kill him," Duncan said.

Krieg shook his head, looking down into Jean Marq's pod. "He is in fugue, Duncan. I have no doubt he did it to Anya, but it is probable we will never really know why. One is able to behave quite rationally in fugue, but when the state passes, there is no memory of what happened during the seizure. None. He will be aware that time has passed, but knowing Jean, he will try to cover the time discrepancy."

"Will we have to put him ashore?" Duncan asked, frowning.

"He can recover. Perhaps."

"But *why* did he do it? To *Anya?*" Damon demanded. He was sweat-drenched, with the stink of his phobia still on him. But inwardly he was angry—and proud. Anya Amaya had retired to her quarters without a comment.

"You would have to know more about Jean than you do, boy."

"Don't call me that."

Krieg's narrow eyebrows arched. "Very well. Damon."

Duncan regarded the man in the pod. Krieg had surreptitiously tranquilized him on coming to the bridge. "What do we tell him, Dietr?"

"I have an idea. It may be worthless. But we can see. It might make a difference."

"Anything. We have lost Han Soo; I don't want to lose Jean too."

"All right. Damon. Go to his compartment and look in the drawer under his quarterberth. Bring the thing you find there."

Mystified, Damon Ng floated into the transit tunnel. He was back almost immediately with the paracoita.

"He has a *doll?*"

"It is a bit more than that, youngster. A little tolerance is in order," Krieg said. He looked at Duncan. "Well, you are the Master and Commander. She's his property, after all."

"My name is Amalie. Fuck me, please," the paracoita said seductively.

Startled, Damon dropped it. It struck the deck, sensed its position, reclined, opened its thighs.

"Yes," Duncan said. "That may have been what he was trying to do. We will do it for him."

"I don't understand any of this, Duncan," Damon Ng protested.

"Put her through the port."

"Out? Out there?"

"Yes."

Damon did as he was told. Soon the paracoita was drifting free in space, a few meters from the bridge dome. She looked pathetic, her xylon hair floating in a yellow cloud about her smiling, stupid face.

"She'll stay there for hours," Damon protested.

"Yes," Duncan said, turning away.

Krieg regarded Damon with more melancholy than the young man had believed him capable of showing. "When he asks you—if he does—tell him he did it himself. As a joke. Tell him you find it very funny." The neurocybersurgeon turned for the transit tubes. "But of course, he may prefer not to ask. A man like Jean may prefer to make up his own lost memories."

Perplexed, Damon left the bridge and floated slowly toward his own compartment. At the valve to Anya's he paused, wondering. When he looked in she seemed asleep. But the girl was not asleep. She was lying in her bunk reliving the terror of her ordeal. She had been hoping that Duncan would come to her, but he had not.

When Damon turned to go, she said quietly, "Come in, Damon. I would rather not be alone just now."

10

BRONI

A small fire burned in the raised hearth of Broni's sitting room, but the chill of early morning remained deep when Clavius and Osbertus entered. The girl was propped up on a massive, opulent chair, dwarfing her slender figure. Her hair had been dressed in the formal Voertrekker triple tiara of golden braids. Her cheeks had been pinched for color, and under a jumper of softly tanned ebray leather she wore a nightdress of sea green, long-sleeved and fitted to her delicate wrists.

Her silver cheet lay curled in her lap, deliberately grooming its long, slender forelegs and emitting the occasional soft growl that indicated contentment. Cheet, like the Earth cats for which they were named, were uncommonly aloof and difficult to domesticate and they were prone to vanish and take up with their feral brethren in the grass sea or on the mountainsides. But Broni had a way with animals.

Clavius was touched to see her arrayed with such care. It was a measure of how she regarded him, and for that he was grateful. But if the Voertrekker-Praesident were to see her it would mean trouble. To Ian Voerster, a kaffir was a kaffir. No more, no less.

The sky beyond the tall windows was turning slowly to a dusty powdered blue. Five of the Six Giants were setting, one after another. Smuts was gone, as were Thor and Drache. Wallenberg shone low in the west. And Erde, called Mandela in the townships, had dipped close to the western horizon and was rising again in the north, as was her habit at this time of year. The kaffirs claimed red Chaka—the giant the Voertrekkers called

Thor—as their tutelary star, but the women chose Mandela, far
north of the ecliptic plane and always in the sky. "That is *our*
mother, never setting," they said in their women's songs. The
kaffirs did not even use the Voertrekker name for Voerster. In
the townships it was *Afrika*, the mythic parent of the kaffir race.

Eliana said, regarding her daughter protectively, "She would
not meet with you, Starman, unless we allowed her to prepare."

"I understand, mynheera," Clavius said.

Osbertus whispered, "When does she sleep?"

"When she can," Eliana said quietly.

Tiegen Roark, the Healer, stood by the door looking
uncomfortably at Black Clavius. The Starman made him
uncomfortable. He was unaccustomed to kaffirs with such *presence*. The pedagogues at the Healer's Faculty would be outraged
by this black offworlder, Roark thought. Kaffirs were not supposed to look like Clavius, were not to carry themselves with
such authority. They were not nearly so dark of skin, either.
Voerster's kaffirs were far distant from their purebred black
ancestors, though no one in either kraal or township spoke of it.

Tiegen was still shaken by the conversation earlier with the
Voertrekkerschatz. Eliana was speaking marital insubordination
at the very least—a serious infraction of Voertrekker custom and
legal code. Viewed disapassionately, she was hinting at treason
and betrayal. If there was one man on Planet Voerster capable of
surrendering Eliana Ehrengraf Voerster to the Trekkerpolizei,
that man was Ian Voerster.

Tiegen watched Clavius walk across the bare, polished stone
floor and bow formally to the Voertrekkersdatter. "I am delighted
to see you again, mynheera."

Broni regarded him with open pleasure, and with more
animation than Eliana or Tiegen Roark had seen her display for
many days.

"Welcome to Voertrekkerhoem, Clavius. I am glad you
finally came. It's very large, isn't it? Too large, I think. There are
dozens of rooms we never use." She spied the balichord and sat

up straighter in the great chair. "Oh, I was hoping you would bring it. The plans you made for my artificer mustn't have been quite right, Clavius, because my balichord doesn't sound at all like yours."

Clavius took his instrument from his shoulder and caressed the inlaid offworld woods of the keyboard and tambour. "That is because it is a young instrument, mynheera. It takes many years for a balichord to mature."

Broni regarded the Starman and said, without self-pity, "I haven't got a lifetime, Clavius."

Clavius struck a chord that was like a labyrinth of sound. "That is a matter of definition, mynheera," he said.

The cheet reacted to the sound by arching its back and baring its teeth at the balichord. Then it jumped down and stalked across the floor to arrange itself on the hearth, still regarding Clavius as though he were dinner.

Broni laughed and said, "Ylla is jealous, Clavius. Can you feel it?" She made the clicking sound with which Voertrekkers caught the attention of their cheets and other domestic animals and murmured to the small beast, "It is all right, Ylla. He is our friend."

The cheet stretched itself carefully before the fire and settled down to watch. Broni said, "You see, Clavius? He is thinking it over."

Clavius smiled. The child was right, of course; the jealous pet was considering his mistress' judgment. One more bit of evidence that Broni was a natural empath.

He said to Eliana, "Tell me how she fares, mynheera."

Eliana turned to Roark. "Tiegen?"

Roark inclined his head toward the door.

Clavius placed the priceless balichord in Broni's lap and said, "Play it if you can."

"I will," Broni said.

Clavius followed the Healer from the room, and Osbertus said to Eliana, "Has there been any more nonsense about a husband for Broni?"

"None The Voerster has shared with me, Cousin," Eliana said.

Osbertus watched as Broni applied herself to the balichord's keyboard and strings. Talk of marriage was something she had heard all her life. As the daughter of generations of Voersters, she knew her duty. What she *felt*, Osbertus Kloster could only surmise.

"He wouldn't force that fragile child into marriage. How could he even consider such a thing?" he protested. Eliana's eyes showed her distress. But she spoke with the controlled calm of a woman of her class. "We have discussed it, Osbertus."

"I don't mean to pry, mynheera."

"So let's not talk about it." Eliana Ehrengraf's expression changed from shut to open in an instant, a typical shift for the Voertrekkerschatz. Under the calm, dark beauty lay a personality both volatile and fiery. Her sudden smile warmed Osbertus as she said, "It was good of you to bring The Kaffir, Cousin." Only Clavius, of all the blacks on Voerster, commanded that clearly upper-case honorific.

The Astronomer-Select knew her well enough to know that she was sick with worry over Broni. What had Ian Voerster been saying to her? he wondered. And what advice was she receiving from that so-called physician who spent his days at Voertrekker-hoem, mooning after what he dare not touch? Infidelity among the mynheeren was no small sin, it was a capital crime. He hoped that Eliana kept that always in mind. Not that any man alive could corrupt the heiress of Ehrengraf against her will.

It was likely, however, that Tiegen had been making himself important by telling her dire things about Broni's chances of seeing another season. It would be just like him. He would do it because it was *right* to be *honest*, and he was a man who *relished* being right.

How could any man who loved her take such satisfaction in saying things that pierced her heart? Perhaps they taught self-righteousness as a specialty at the Healer's Faculty.

Osbertus Kloster wondered if he were pinning too many hopes on the Starman, who was, after all, only a kaffir. Osbertus' grasshopper mind leaped and danced from one idea to another with a speed that often made him seem giddy. But he was far from that. *I, of all people on Voerster,* the Astronomer-Select thought, *should understand how backward our science is. Clavius comes from a different sort of world. And,* he added with a touch of superstitious awe, *Starmen live—if not forever, then nearly forever.* Black Clavius might well have been slightly mad, but at one time he had performed mysterious duties aboard the *Nepenthe.* He came from a Goldenwing syndicate. *I wish I had the capacity to know what Black Clavius knows,* Osbertus thought. But there was no chance of that, not even if he, like a Wired Starman, were to live a thousand years.

The thought depressed him enormously.

He raised his bowed head to speak again with Eliana when he heard a chord of music. It was far simpler than any chord Black Clavius might have struck, but it nevertheless brought a shiver of pleasure as it hung in the cold air of the vast room. Broni laughed with delight and struck another and still another. "Isn't it a *beautiful* balichord, mynheera?" she asked her mother. "It *sings.*"

"And you, Broni love, would you sing for your old Cousin Osbertus?" The astronomer regarded the girl tenderly, and thought: *This will be a darker life without Broni.*

Eliana studied Osbertus and he knew that she was reading his thoughts as clearly as if he had stated them. He felt constrained to say, "Clavius *will* help, Cousin. I promise you."

But he knew that he had just done what he often admonished himself never to do in his dealings with Eliana Ehrengraf. He had promised the undeliverable, lying to her out of love and concern.

From the doorway, Clavius said, "Play, Broni. One of the old songs."

Broni, with that way she had of anticipating, struck up an ancient melody.

Tiegen Roark, standing behind the Starman, knew how carefully and diligently she had practiced this piece. And he realized now why the girl had insisted on dressing as she had. He felt a dampness in his eyes. He was not a sentimental man, but Broni had a way of affecting everyone around her. There was an old and very foolish saying about certain people: "To know her is to love her." In Broni's case it was not foolish.

Clavius recognized the tune and nodded approval. It was a song he had taught her during one of his encounters with Eliana and her daughter in a township belonging to the Ehrengraf Kraal.

The Starman walked to the raised hearth and sat down beside the cheet. The animal came to him and settled trustingly in his lap. He ran his pink-palmed hand over the silvery fur and began to sing:

> *"Alas, my love, ye do me wrong*
> *To cast me off discourteously*
> *And I have lov-ed you so long*
> *Delighting in your company."*

Broni joined him, singing with a sweet, pure voice:

> *"Greensleeves was all my joy,*
> *Greensleeves was my delight;*
> *Greensleeves was my heart of gold,*
> *And who but my Lady Greensleeves?"*

Osbertus listened, blushing, to the verse that followed, so intimate, so improper for a mynheera and a kaffir to be singing together:

> *"Thy gown was all of grassy green*
> *Thy sleeves of satin hanging by,*
> *Which made thee be our harvest queen,*
> *And yet thou wouldst not love me . . ."*

"Clavius," the old man protested. "I hardly think—"
Eliana touched his arm in restraint. "Let be, Cousin. How

long has it been since you have seen her so animated? She is flirting with the Starman and he with her. Let be."

Osbertus subsided and listened until Black Clavius and the Voertrekkersdatter finished the song. When the last notes of the balichord had died away, Broni said, "Cousin, Tiegen. Do you know how old that song is?"

"Very old, I am sure," Osbertus said uncomfortably.

"Even older," Broni said with a flashing smile. "It is said that it was written by a wicked Brit king of Earth to woo a beautiful mistress. Oh, thousands of years ago."

"That is very interesting, I'm sure," Osbertus said primly.

"It is a lovely song, mynheera," Tiegen Roark said. "I thank you for it."

"You are welcome, Healer," Broni said formally.

Clavius said to Eliana, "I should like to examine her, mynheera."

"Of course, Starman."

"I will retire," Osbertus said. Despite the fact that he had brought Clavius to Voertrekkerhoem for this precise purpose, he could not imagine remaining while the offworlder examined the Voertrekkersdatter. He looked expectantly at Tiegen, but the Healer clearly had no intention of leaving.

Osbertus said to Eliana, "I know my rooms, Cousin. I will make my own way."

Eliana offered her hand and he kissed it with great formality. He left the room troubled and wondering if he had done the right thing this early morning. Yet what else could he have done after Eliana had asked him?

In the space of a quarter hour, during which the sky beyond the windows of Voertrekkerhoem grew steadily lighter until Luyten 726's rising chased the last Giant from the sky, Clavius counted Broni's heartbeats, listened to her chest with Tiegen's listening tube, pricked her fingers and tasted her blood, and held her narrow naked feet between his hands and judged the pressure of the pulse above her heels.

———

"It is almost certainly rheumatic fever, mynheera," he said to Eliana. Tiegen Roark stood listening in stolid silence. He had made that diagnosis weeks ago. The problem was: What to do about it? The pharmacopoeia contained no remedy.

Broni had begun to look very worn. The Wired One placed a hand over her eyes and uttered a soft, crooning chant. Eliana recognized it as similar to the chant kaffir mothers used to lull their children to sleep when they were cold or hungry. In the townships, sometimes sleep was preferable—the only anodyne for deprivation.

Immediately Broni began to breathe more deeply and easily. Within moments, the girl was asleep. Her cheet, Ylla, climbed once again into her lap and took up a position of guardianship.

Clavius indicated that they should leave the girl's bedside. At the dark far end of the long room, the Starman said softly, "The fever has damaged her heart, mynheera. There is leakage through the valves. It is the cause of all her difficulties."

"You have some knowledge, kaffir," Tiegen said. "But what's to be done?"

"As you know," Clavius said tactfully, "rheumatic fever is an illness of the very young, Healer. Many times a child can contract the disease and suffer little or no damage. At other times the heart can be fatally damaged." He felt the turmoil in Tiegen Roark's mind. The man knew that Clavius' knowledge was superior to his own, but he hated to know it. *Understandable,* Clavius thought.

Tiegen was thinking: How many children like Broni would die because medicine on Voerster was little better than witchcraft? Tiegen Roark felt suffocated by his own ignorance.

All this the empath in Clavius detected. he said, "Of course, Healer, remember that I am not a qualified physician—"

"Nor am I." Bitterly.

"What can be done, Clavius?" Eliana asked.

"By us? By me? Nothing, mynheera. There is a surgical procedure, but it is impossible here."

Tiegen Roark flashed, "A surgical procedure? To work *inside the heart?*"

Clavius nodded. "Heart-valve repair was common practice long before *Milagro* left Earth, Mynheer Healer. My guess is that the Voertrekker physicians practiced it routinely before the Rebellion."

"A thousand years ago?"

"Downtime, Mynheer. Yes."

Roark looked ill. "How did we fall so far behind?" The question was rhetorical. Everyone knew what the Kaffir Rebellion had cost. The textbooks blamed the kaffirs, of course. But what did it really matter who was responsible, Tiegen thought desperately. *We are bound for the Pit, all of us,* he thought.

Clavius regarded the Healer sympathetically. "It is not your fault, Healer."

Eliana interrupted fiercely. "What can you *do*, Clavius?"

"I haven't the skill, mynheera," the black Starman said.

"There is a Goldenwing coming," she said. "Goldenwings carry physicians, surely?"

"Yes."

"Will the syndics help us?"

"I don't know, mynheera," Clavius said. "Goldenwing syndics are not saints. They are ordinary men."

Eliana gripped his forearm. "This is *Broni*, Clavius. This is my only child."

"She is right, kaffir," Tiegen said roughly. "If there is a physician aboard the *Gloria Coelis* who can perform the surgery, they must allow it."

Clavius raised his eyes to heaven. These folks expected unbounded altruism from the Starmen. From the living myths who brought them from the distant Earth. But what he said was true. Syndics were ordinary men—with extraordinary skills, perhaps—but still ordinary men. *The people of* Nepenthe *marooned me because they thought me mad,* he thought. Was that the act of mythic demi-gods?

His deliverance came from an unexpected and unwelcome source.

A female house kaffir came running through the door

breathlessly. *"Mynheera, mynheera—the Voerster has returned from Voersterstaad. He is very angry about the Starman's visit, mynheera—"*

Eliana stood in the doorway, backed by Clavius and the Astronomer-Select. Down the hall marched a detachment of four Trekkerpolizei. One saluted Eliana and presented himself to Clavius. "I am Trekkerpolizeioberst Transkei, kaffir. By order of the Voertrekker-Praesident, I place you under arrest."

Six hours later, as the halfday bells tolled, Eliana Vorster stood on a widow's walk overlooking the Voertrekkerhoem landing ground, despairing as a detachment of the Trekkerpolizei marched Black Clavius into the police dirigible for the flight to Hellsgate.

She was livid with anger and fear for the black man. It was she, after all, who had put him in the position of so outraging the Voertrekker-Praesident by his "uninvited" presence at Voertrekkerhoem.

Eliana had presented herself like an avenging Valkyrie in her husband's suite of offices and she had flamed, threatened, and finally pleaded. But Ian Voerster was rockbound when he had made a decision.

"The kaffir will go to the Friendly Islands and there is an end to it, Eliana. In a week's time or a month we may reconsider the matter. That finishes it, mynheera. Do not vex me further about this."

Eliana Ehrengraf Voerster stared at her husband with loathing. But for the moment—perhaps for all the foreseeable moments in the future—she was helpless in this affair.

Now she stood in the wind, unmindful of the cold, and watched the police airship lift off into the icy blue sky and whir away toward Hellsgate, the prison town at the southern end of the Isthmus of Sorrow which was the portal to Voerster's gulag archipelago.

11

BLACK CLAVIUS

The bone-skinny *lumpe* calling himself Fencik leaned against the bare wall of the Common Room and said condescendingly, "The truth is, kaffir, that you don't know a damned thing about clangs. This paradise is no clang, it's a camp for nasty boys." He made a sweeping gesture encompassing the Common Room and the covered walkways separating it from the Refectory and the barracks. There were some rather feeble flowerbeds and areas of dry grass where the detainees could play at soccer. The effect was sere and depressing, but Detention One was not nearly as severe as Clavius had expected it to be when the police dirigible transport had deposited him here.

Detention Two (a generic term to identify the several camps on the Friendly Islands a thousand kilometers southwest of Detention One) was a far different matter. The Friendlies were situated in the Walvis Strait between the Sabercut Peninsula's south cape and the Icewall of the antarctic island. The currents of the Great Southern Ocean flowed through the strait at forty kilometers per hour, frothing and surging against the ice-clad rocks of the Friendlies. Prisoners had occasionally escaped from Hellsgate on the Isthmus of Sorrow, and from Detention One at the northeastern end of the elongated anvil of the Sabercut Peninsula. But from Detention Two, a camp "of the strict routine," never.

"This part of Voerster is something you did not show me before, Lord," Clavius murmured to God. But it appeared that God was not much interested in carrying on a conversation with a fool who got himself confined among the white *lumpen* and foolish kaffirs who inhabited Detention One.

Beyond the fence topped with razor wire lay nothing whatever but open savannah. The Sabercut Mountains, from which the peninsula took its name, rose precipitously south of the settlement of Hellsgate, where detainees were inducted into the prison system. Though escape was possible, at night the wild cheet came to the perimeter to warn the camp inmates that life outside the wire was dangerous and could be very short.

It was a matter of some interest to Clavius not only that he was the only kaffir in this section of Detention One, but that the *lumpen* of the section were shocked—and some even angered—by his presence among them. The fences were patrolled by armed *lumpen* officered by men of the mynheeren class. The staff had a military look, though all wore the uniform of the Trekkerpolizei, which strictly speaking, was not a military organization. Quite obviously this part of Detention One was a very special sort of prison. No cruelty was practiced, but the place had the feel of an *oubliette*. There were old men here—and, Clavius supposed, old women in the female barracks twenty kilometers farther east, in Vanity, the small camp at Skull Key. Some of the inmates of One claimed to have visited the women of Vanity, but judging from the disgusting sexual practices of the prisoners, Clavius seriously doubted it.

Inmates held at One were in stasis, their cases forever unresolved. "From here," Fencik said, "they send us God-knows-where, but never back. We'll never see Voersterstaad or Pretoria again." It was the sort of thing prisoners said, but Clavius had begun to think it was true. He had been at One for forty days, nearly a Voersterian month. And it seemed he might be here forever.

Fencik (the *lumpe* seemed to have no other name) was the the only inmate willing to have close contact with the Starman. That opened up the possibility that Fencik was a police spy. Black Clavius was still not certain what his offense had been. Obviously he had infuriated The Voerster by responding to the mynheera Eliana's summons, and on Voerster that was offense enough to land a man "South of Hellsgate," as the *lumpen* lawbreakers said. Or "in clang," as the attenuated Fencik described their situation. It did, however, give Clavius some indication of how bitter the personal war between the Voertrekker-Praesident and his consort had become.

Clavius pursed his lips at the empty blue sky of midday and addressed himself to the Almighty. "Fencik is right, isn't he, Lord? For me this place is not just a prison, it's a tenderizer and I am the meat."

God remained stubbornly silent. Clavius sighed.

"The truth of the matter is," the skeletal *lumpe* declared in a pedantic manner Clavius had learned to disesteem in the month he had been detained, "that I was told personally by the Oberst that you were coming, and that it was up to me to see to it that there was no touble with the other fish."

Clavius had learned a whole new vocabulary. A prison was a *clang*. Detainees were *fish*. A woman on the outside was a *squeeze*, and a woman of Vanity willing to indulge in intercourse with a fellow fish was a *randy*, for the denomination of the coin such services were said to command. Clavius had on occasion run afoul of the Trekkerpolizei in the townships, but never seriously enough to earn detention. In the townships the police kept a deliberately low profile. The only really serious crime for kaffirs was rebellion, and there had been no organized rebellion on Voerster for a thousand years.

That caused the philosophical Clavius to consider the relativity of time. As a Starman he was well aware of the physical relativity of time and space. Like all Wired Ones he had learned to accept the notion that time was not necessarily *time*. That was a troubling concept but one with which every Goldenwing sailor was familiar.

But there was another sort of relativity. Clavius thought of it as *social* relativity. Some societies—many on Earth at different times in history—moved so swiftly that vast changes were wrought in a century, a decade, a year. Other societies moved far more slowly. The ancient Egyptians of Earth had once fascinated

Clavius. It was difficult to imagine a society so unchanging that centuries passed without alteration. But Voerster was such a society. In the millennium since the Rebellion, the Luyten sun had risen and set on an immutable world. To the Voertrekkers and kaffirs of Voerster, the Great Rebellion might have happened yesterday. Fear of one another had stopped time, had cast the people of Voerster in amber.

Clavius had sought to speak of these things with Fencik. But the old fish was not interested in offworld philosophy. He spoke only of prison matters.

Fencik could be an informer, Clavius thought. But if that were the case, then the Trekkerpolizei were wasting an agent because Clavius had no information to give or withhold. Rebellion, treason, or general criminality were impossible for a true empath. Only an insane Starman could engage in such pursuits.

Clavius worried more about Broni every day. The girl's time was limited at best, but he knew that if permitted, he could make her last weeks comfortable, which, sadly, was more than Healer Roark was able to do.

And there was the secret hope in Black Clavius that the syndicate of the approaching Goldenwing might have a physician skilled enough to make Broni whole. It was, after all, possible. Heart-valve surgery was unknown on Voerster, but it was routine and had been for centuries elsewhere in near space. And who knew what other medical miracles a starship surgeon might have discovered in his travels?

What Clavius did not give voice to, was the aching fear that the Goldenwing—Osbertus Kloster had identified it as the *Gloria Coelis*—would come and go, and he, Black Clavius, would never see it. The image of a tachyon-sailing ship was ever in his mind, like a lovely, unattainable glory in the sky.

Fencik took a rolled cigarette from the pocket of his prison shirt and offered it to Clavius. "Five rand, kaffir? That's fair. It's first-class weed."

Clavius spread his empty hands and let his deep voice take on the singsong cadences of a native township kaffir. "Where would a poor black kaffir come by five rand, Zor?"

Fencik slapped his thigh and laughed aloud, "Oh, good. Very good, Clavius-kaffir. You have the black lingo down perfectly." He put the weed between his lips and lighted it. As he exhaled luxuriously, he said, "You don't know what you're missing."

Clavius sat on the stoop and watched a gang of fish fitfully kicking at a ball. The game was ancient. He had seen it played on worlds light-years from Voerster. He took a deep breath and bared his great chest to the white light of the low Luyten sun. Odd how the melanin that had brought the kaffirs to Voerster as an underclass protected them so well from the high ultraviolet in Luyten 726's radiation. By contrast, Voertrekkers of every social class, those who had kept themselves racially unmixed, were uniformly pale of skin and likely to remain so. The incidence of skin cancer among the whites of Voerster was—he apologized to the Lord for the terrible pun—astronomical.

Clavius was a patient man, but he disliked inactivity and he missed his balichord. He wondered if Broni still had it, or if it had been taken from her. Knowing the Mynheera Eliana Ehrengraf, it was unlikely that anyone would try to confiscate anything Mynheera Broni wished to keep.

He let the pallid sun caress his torso and began to sing.

> "Is it so?
> Really so?
> A Bible story
> Can be gory,
> And not necessarily so!"

"That will get you in trouble with the Unter Oberst damn quick, kaffir," Fencik said. "He's a great believer in Scripture, our Oberst."

"'And he spake three thousand proverbs: and his songs were a thousand and five,'" Clavius said.

"You're a wild one, kaffir. Where did you learn such things?"

Clavius, still smiling, said, "'So the number of them, with their brethren that were instructed in the songs of the Lord, even all that were cunning, was two hundred fourscore and eight.'"

"Is that the number of Starmen? Tell the truth, Clavius-kaffir. And don't exaggerate. Of Starmen I have seen one. You."

"'Thou art my hiding place; thou shalt preserve me from trouble; thou shalt encompass me about with songs of deliverance. Selah.'"

"What an exasperating creature you are," Fencik declared, flipping his weed in a high arc to the stubbled grass. "I often wonder why kaffirs were brought to Voerster. Knowing you, I wonder even harder."

Clavius showed his pink palms in a gesture of innocence. "'For there they that carried us away captive required of us a song; and they that wasted us required of us mirth, saying, sing us one of the songs of Zion.'"

"Enough, enough, y'bloody black man. I stagger under the weight of your knowledge of Scripture. Pity, Clavius, have pity."

"Most Starmen are eidetics, Fencik," Clavius said.

"Which means?"

"That we can't forget."

"Anything?"

"Anything."

"Poor bugger. Forgetting is no bad thing unless you are an angel."

Fencik jumped to his feet with surprising agility. "Listen!"

"A dirigible. I hear it."

"There." A silvery shape glistened in the sunlight. The drone of hydrogen motors grew. Since from this place men only went south to the Friendlies, inmates were frightened when an airship appeared in the sky. Police dirigibles were "balloons to nowhere."

In a hushed voice, Fencik said, "Are they coming for you, Clavius?"

"Perhaps." Clavius was thinking of Broni.

———

"Better you than me, kaffir." The thin prisoner was undergoing a transformation. He appeared to be withdrawing himself from any personal contact. It was as though *if* the airship had, indeed, come for Clavius, it initiated a process of disengagement so complete that by the time the ship lifted off again with the Starman aboard, Fencik would have forgotten he ever knew anyone name Clavius.

It happened that way.

"I am Trekkerpolizeioberst Transkei, kaffir. Do you remember me?"

"Indeed I do, Mynheer Oberst. You arrested me," Clavius said.

He sat, unshackled, on the hard metal bench that ran down the centerline of the gondola of the police dirigible. Close to the glass of the outward-slanting window, he could see the disk of the craft's starboard propeller. The carefully burnished bronze blades glittered in the white sunlight.

Clavius found himself the only prisoner aboard the airship. The benches were empty and through the open door to the pilots' deck he could see only the men flying the machine and three heavily armed policeman. Clavius wondered wryly at the precautions taken for the transport of one peace-loving kaffir.

"I have been instructed to treat you with consideration, kaffir. Have I your assurance that you will not attempt to escape?"

Clavius regarded the jagged mountains a thousand meters below the dirigible. "I have no wings, Mynheer Oberst," he said mildly.

The police officer was gray, thin-lipped as a lizard, and totally uninterested in any discussion of capabilities with his prisoner. "You can be cuffed or not," he said. "It is up to you, kaffir."

"I will not attempt to leave this dirigible without your permission, Mynheer Oberst," Clavius said solemnly.

"Very well." The officer signalled for one of the *lumpen*

constables to enter the compartment. "Bring the prisoner his meal." At Detention One the detainees ate twice a day, both meals exactly the same: grain porridge, a two-hundred-gram portion of boiled faux-goat meat, a tangeroon, and a mug of hot kava. On the police airship the meal was the same, save that it was cold. The lifting gas used on Voerster was helium, but the motors were powered by volatile hydrogen and Voertrekker airshipmen did not light fires aloft.

The constable brought in a tray. The police colonel withdrew to the flight deck. Clavius was mildly surprised to discover that he was hungry. He ate in silence under the somber gaze of the *lumpe*. Young, Clavius thought, barely out of adolescence. But probably sensible, as most of the Voertrekkers were sensible. In a static society that did not permit the commons access to political power, it made a certain sense to seek advancement in the police. Clearly the Trekkerpolizeioberst thought so. Under that desiccated exterior lived a man certain that he had made only sensible choices in life.

How wonderful, Black Clavius thought, to be so certain. He closed his eyes and addressed himself again to the Almighty. *Why did you make us all so different, Lord? Between the Oberst and me there is a gulf that has nothing to do with light-years or uptime-downtime. I am never as sure Monday is the first day of the week as he is that Voerster is the Universe and that he stands at the center of it. How come, Lord? Answer me that? Thus saith the Preacher: "For in much wisdom is much grief: and he that increaseth knowledge increaseth sorrow."*

"Kaffir? Are you asleep?"

Clavius opened his eyes and regarded the young policeman. He was leaning forward so that he could speak without being heard by the Oberst on the flight deck.

"Is it true you came from the stars?"

"It is true, Mynheer." The use of the honorific appeared to make the boy uncomfortable. It wasn't surprising. The *lumpen* lived even bleaker lives than did the township kaffirs. "But I have been on Voerster for many years."

―――――

"Voerster is a long way from the stars," the policeman said. He lowered his voice even more. "I bear you no ill will, kaffir."

"I am glad of that, constable."

"Elmi taught that all men were equal. So our preachers say."

Unlikely, that, Clavius thought. But it was a pleasant fantasy. One that could do no harm to a world set in amber. It was interesting to know that the Cult of Elmi had reached even into police ranks. The mynheeren discounted it, and probably they should. There was not enough of anything, even anger, on Voerster to start another Rebellion. But a gentle cult might comfort the people as the days dwindled down.

"They say a Goldenwing is coming for you." The youngster had pale eyes and they were fixed on Clavius with what appeared to be envy, mingled with fear. *My reputation as shaman, sorcerer and witch appears to have reached the airborne Trekkerpolizei,* Clavius thought. *I would have preferred less notoriety, but one could not roam downworld with a computer drogue socket in one's hair without arousing a certain awe.*

"Is that true, kaffir?"

"I have heard that a Goldenwing is coming, but not for me, I assure you."

"That's too bad. Look down there."

Clavius did as he was bid. To the south, white against a pale blue sky and a ribbon of almost purple sea, there were sheer frozen cliffs.

"The Southern Ice," the *lumpe* said.

Clavius felt a chill that was not from the open cabin window.

"And there, ahead." The peninsula over which they had been flying ended in a jumbled archipelago of tiny, rocky islands.

"The Friendlies?"

The constable nodded. "Detention Two admin is on the tip of the peninsula and the compounds are spread over a dozen islands between here and the edge of the Southern Ice."

Clavius accepted that gloomy news in silence.

The dirigible droned on through a clear, cold sky. Forty minutes passed. Fifty. The Oberst appeared again.

———

"Get up, kaffir. Look below."

The dirigible was swinging over a bleak settlement on the largest of the islands in sight. Row after row of stone-and-sod barracks covered the great stone in the sea. The shorelines of Detention Two and the neighboring islets were white with seafoam as the current of the Walvis Strait flowed in a torrent from west to east. Without large satellites to make tides on Voerster, the Great Southern Ocean was powered by the vast Coriolis force of the planet's rapid spin.

"Take a good look, kaffir."

Clavius could see tiny, antlike figures moving far below. What did the passage of a dirigible at this height mean to them? God help the poor souls, he thought. Probably nothing at all.

The dirigible made a long, slow circle. Another. Then the pilots pointed the nose to the north across the Sea of Lions. Soon nothing was in sight but ocean, whitecapped and frigid, between the Walvis Strait and the south coast of the Grassersee a thousand kilometers to the north.

"'And they showed Galileo the instruments,'" Clavius whispered, "'and said to him: "recant."'"

"What did you say, kaffir?" the Oberst asked.

"Nothing, Mynheer," Clavius said. "It was something that happened very long ago and very far away."

For hours they flew over the Sea of Lions. The Luyten sun was sinking off the port quarter when the constable, who had returned to guard the prisoner, asked, "Is it true, kaffir, that you were born on Earth?"

"It is, young man."

"Don't call me that. I am a constable of the Trekkerpolizei."

"My apologies, Mynheer," said Clavius.

"Where did you learn to sound like that? Our kaffirs don't talk that way."

"No, your kaffirs sound like what they are, Mynheer. Natives of Voerster."

Searching, thought Clavius, watching the constable's face

grow even paler, his lips grow thin. Like any human being. Searching for himself. For others. For his world and what it means. *He also suspects I am being insolent, and that is still forbidden on Voerster.* On any planet, the *lumpen* or equivalent were more protective of status than were the aristocrats. *Lord,* he told God, *your designs do not vary much.*

The Oberst appeared in the door and spoke sharply to the constable. "Your orders are to watch, not to fraternize."

"Sir."

The Oberst looked at Clavius. "Have you thought about what you saw back there near the Ice?"

"Yes, Mynheer."

"Remove yourself to the flight deck, constable. I wish to interrogate the prisoner."

"Sir!" The constable stamped his foot, making the deck tremble. He withdrew. And the Oberst, who slid closed the door to the flight deck, stationed himself between Clavius and the starboard windows.

"You are traveling at the express command of the Voertrekker-Praesident," he declared.

"I thought perhaps I might be," Clavius said.

"Mynheer Oberst."

"Mynheer Oberst."

"You expected to be reprieved, then."

"I did not know I had been convicted of anything, Mynheer Oberst. Have I been?"

"In absentia. Of persistent vagrancy."

"Ah. I see."

"On Voerster that is a serious charge, kaffir."

"I am sure it is, Mynheer."

To break the taut silence, Clavius asked, "Where are you taking me?"

"That's not your concern, kaffir," the Oberst said.

Did the man have any idea how absurd that statement was? *Lord, doesn't he think I have the right to be "concerned" about where I am taken, and to whom?*

———

"I have heard that you converse with God," the Voertrekker said. "That is blasphemous."

Ah, Clavius thought. A believer. New Luth or even Babst. Not Cult of Elmi. "I speak to Jehovah, Oberst. But I have never claimed he spoke to me."

"Once you would have been whipped and put in the stocks, kaffir."

Clavius sighed heavily. Most of his conversations with Voertrekker policemen seemed to end up this way. "Yes, Mynheer," he said. "Very likely."

He directed his gaze beyond the standing police colonel to what could be seen through the broad windows of the dirigible's gondola. The airship had made its landfall. Ahead lay a low shoreline and beyond that the broad plains of the Sea of Grass, blue-green now as the time for spore-flight came near. The savannah winds made quite lovely patterns in the tall grasses. It seemed invisible dancers spun and whirled from the sea to the land, making circling, curving patterns that transformed both sea and grass into a dancing floor.

The course was north by northwest. The white sun touched the horizon and prepared for its plunge into the Voerster Sea.

"What do you see, kaffir?"

"Nothing you cannot, Mynheer," Clavius said. "The Sea of Grass, the Southern Ocean, the sky. It is a beautiful world."

"Yes?"

Clavius looked inquiringly at the policeman.

"You think it cold and barren, kaffir?"

"No, Mynheer Oberst. I have seen much worse."

"You are arrogant, kaffir. You make judgments," the Oberst said heavily.

For a moment, Lord, Clavius thought, *I was one with the sky and land, one with white Luyten, and almost a free man. But this dour man has drawn me back here, like a fetus in the belly of a necrogene. . . .*

The dirigible droned on over the darkening Grassersee. In the long twilight, the night seemed to rise from the heart of the land. The last of the daylight stayed in the sky until the stars began to appear.

The policeman marched to the door of the flight deck before he turned to say, "Get some rest if you can, kaffir. I am to deliver you directly to the Voertrekker-Praesident when we reach Voertrekkerhoem. You'll get little rest after that."

———

12

IN THE GAP

*W*ith Mira on his naked shoulder Duncan Kr swam in a black sea
bounded by distant stars and dominated by the swiftly diminishing
ringed disk of Wallenberg. Hard-wired to Glory, Duncan was the ship.
The golden wings he spread were his own, the rain of tachyon impacts
on the square kilometers of skylar felt like rain on naked flesh.

In near space there was not an object bigger than a micrometeoroid
within two hundred million kilometers. Still decelerating, Duncan's
speed was now down to sixteen percent of the speed of light. Brighter
than Wallenberg, and growing with each passing minute of time, was
Luyten 726—white, featureless, showering Duncan with photons that,
unlike the tachyons streaming out of the galactic center, were short-lived,
ardent, burning.

Glory experienced her environment like a living thing and every
sensation centered in the brain of the man supine in the glyceroid
medium inside his pod.

Duncan could also capture some of the rich sensations Mira was
experiencing. She saw space as a great empty room into which she had
leapt with feral joy. There were creatures in the dark, things too subtle
for the man (who Mira thought of as "the dominant tom") to detect, but
the cat sensed them and arched her back and bared her teeth to warn
them not to come near. She had sensed these creatures before, usually
when teamed with this tom, who was more alert than the others. Far
off, well beyond pouncing range, floated a great white-hot ball of light.
She could see with her inner eye the streams of hot droplets that streaked
the black emptiness with a suggestion of light. Behind lay another ball,
this one ringed, but it was receding swiftly and Mira's attention span
was short. She, too, was the ship (who was the "queen-who-was-not-

alive"), and what were wings to the man were claws to the cat. Come to me, she mewed, clicking at the creatures watching her and the tom. But they never came. Instead, when they sensed her they slipped away into a deeper darkness, vanishing into a geometry without light, time, or space. Mira preened herself on her victory, clung to Duncan's shoulder and, catlike, fell into a drowsing dream.

From the drogue in the medical computer came Dietr Krieg's cold thought: *"She never stays awake long enough for me to identify what she sees, Duncan."*

Jarred out of his own spatial dream, Duncan let the Universe contract to the interior of *Glory's* crew spaces. *"They are the spirits of the dead, Dietr. Or they are the angels who dance on the heads of pins. What difference does it make? Mira will always be able to see ghosts that evade us. The secret is that she doesn't care. Let her rest."*

"Yes, Master and Commander. I hear and obey. May I come to the bridge?"

That meant, Duncan thought, that Krieg wanted to convey information that he preferred to keep from *Glory's* computer where it could be accessed by others in the crew.

"Come," he said.

Reluctantly he sat up in the pod and disconnected his drogue. He had, in fact, been indulging himself. *Glory* was traversing the Gap, the region of the Luyten 726 system that corresponded roughly to Sol's so-called "asteroid belt" between the orbits of Mars and Jupiter. Here, however, the space between the outermost inner planet, Voerster, and the innermost of the Six Giants, Wallenberg, was far more vast. It differed, too, in the almost sterile quality of the region. Aeons ago the gravity of six great gas giants had swept the rubble from the Gap, and for a radial distance of five hundred million kilometers *Glory* would encounter nothing more substantial than grains of dust.

Duncan lifted Mira from his shoulder and set her down on the curve of the pilot pod's lid. She stretched and regarded him reproachfully. With a soft trill she rotated several times in a genetically programmed sketch of making a nest and arranged herself in a furry disk, one paw covering her eyes.

Duncan ran a hand over her head, avoiding the cerebral antenna. He scratched her briefly behind the ears and turned to the control panel. With his drogue withdrawn into the console he was, as he sometimes secretly described himself, merely a man again. *Glory* sailed herself inward, making what use she chose of the tachyon-rich Coriolis wind. Even at twice the speed of light, a single tachyon might take ten thousand downtime years to reach this far from the great black hole at galactic center. From time to time Duncan was near to overwhelmed at the sheer size of the universe. It was a feeling very like that he had known as a child, alone in a skiff, contemplating the vastness of the Thalassa Sea.

In a curious way, he thought, *we are always prepared for what we experience*. Did that postulate the existence of a God? Perhaps so, but if it did it would take a far more believing man than himself to *know* it. Duncan accepted that there was life in the universe: He could be certain only of Earth and her colonial children, and perhaps the strange things Mira seemed to see when she was "in space." But if they really existed they were denizens of some strange dimension that Man would not penetrate for another million, or perhaps twenty million years or more. For now, Duncan thought, if Earth's children were alone, why then, amen.

He opened the dome of the bridge and studied the rig. Half the sails were furled, but *Glory* still spread a half million hectares of skylar. It was arranged in an intricate pattern that caught both the tachyons and the hot photons streaming away from the Luyten sun. He recalled how they had felt only a moment before, savoring the memory of an incredibly sensual experience. There was nothing like that now. Data came to him through purely human senses. Adequate, but nothing more.

Dietr Krieg, dressed in a silver skinsuit, flowed out of the transit tube from below. Duncan glanced at the locator and saw that Damon was working out in the gravity-spin section, Jean Marq appeared to be sleeping peacefully in his bunk, free of nightmares as he had been ever since he had come to believe that he had "murdered" his paracoita. Anya Amaya was in her quarters, drogue-connected to a Zen program she had asked *Glory* to run for her.

The girl had been badly frightened in the incident near Drache, but she had vast reserves of strength upon which she could call. It had taken courage to survive as a sterile female on New Earth. The taste for Zen was something new. But if it helped her cope with the knowledge that while in fugue Jean had tried to murder her, so be it. Anya had ethnic roots going back to the Hispanics and Slavs of Old Earth. Both strains, according to Krieg, were susceptible to melancholia after events of great emotional impact.

Dietr looked at the sleeping cat. "Willful little beast. Sometimes I think she thwarts me just to be contrary. I may have to do another and train it to be more responsive to orders."

"You know a great deal about cybersurgery and not very much about cats," Duncan said.

"Probably," Dietr Krieg said. He anchored himself to a wall with his Velcro slippers. "I am still concerned about Marq," he said.

"I thought you did very well by him with that trick with the paracoita."

"I only gave him a logical substitution for the memory he carries with him. I am afraid he will wake up one fine moment and realize that he tried to kill a real woman a second time. His hatred of females is vast, Duncan. He even hates that one."

Mira moved her paw and regarded the neurocybersurgeon with unblinking eyes.

"She knows. Don't you, small beast?" Krieg made as if to pet the animal and she retreated just out of his reach, hissed softly and leaped across the bridge to the tunnel.

"Arrogant little monster," Krieg said. "By rights she should treat me like God. I gave her her enhancements."

"What can be done about Jean?" Duncan asked.

"For now, nothing. But he needs time ashore. How long will we stay at Voerster?"

"Long enough to deliver the cargo. Very little more. We have commitments to Aldrin and Gagarin on this voyage."

"You are Master. But I recommend a longer stay. Jean needs to get away from *Glory*. The computer has pumped up *his* enhancements so that he is afraid to sleep without Dust."

"I thought that was before the— What should I call it? The incident?"

Krieg said, "I am a surgeon, not a psychiatrist. I call things by their names. Before he tried to murder Amaya."

"Then his improvement is only temporary," Duncan said.

"I don't *know*, Duncan. The business with the doll was a snatch at a straw, an experiment."

"You don't snatch at straws, Dietr."

"Well, it seemed expedient to let him think he abandoned the paracoita while he was in fugue. If he hungers for woman-killing, the silly doll was a surrogate. If nothing else it has bought him some time."

"Will he try again to attack Anya?"

Krieg shrugged, a strangely fluid gesture in free-fall. "It's possible. Jean Marq is a very sick man. As far as I am concerned, he remains dangerous."

"Anya knows how to be careful," Duncan said. "And don't mention it to Damon. He has appointed himself Anya's protector."

Krieg's pale eyebrows arched. "Since you have delegated your duty."

Duncan stared at the physician. "Is that what you believe, Dietr?"

Krieg could not meet Duncan Kr's eyes. "No, of course not. That was a stupid thing to say."

"Yes," Duncan said, turning away. "It was."

"The fact is that you are a better practical psychologist than I am," Dietr Krieg said. "Have you stopped sexual contact with Anya as well?"

"Yes," Duncan said. "For a time it is better that Damon be her man."

———

"I will log that in my diary," Krieg said. "I hope there are substitutes on Voerster."

Duncan regarded the physician with a thin, wry smile. "I doubt it, Dietr. But you can do without. Devote your time to learning ship-handling."

"Shipmaster, you have ruined my day," Dietr Krieg said. "Where is the challenge in becoming half-computer, half-starship?"

In her compartment Anya Amaya floated naked in the Lotus, eyes closed. For the last thirteen minutes she had been repeating a mantra. Repeated injunctions from *Glory*'s computer to concentrate on the sound of one hand clapping had so exasperated her that she had disconnected her drogue. On New Earth she had been caught up in Eastern Terrestrial religions as had all the young people of her population cohort. But the truth was that mysticism as a credo was unsuited to the pressures of life in a Twenty-second Century colonial society. It was all very well, her professor of spatial integers had once remarked, for nontechnical beings living in a nourishment-poor environment to sit in odd positions and try to recite the One Thousand and One Names of God. It was quite another—and time-wasting—for the children of a society whose technology was surpassing that of the home planet to do the same.

Anya opened her eyes and floated, breathing deeply, in an effort to become one with the Cosmic Self. Regardless of *Glory*'s excellent program library, Anya remained too decidedly Caucasian to meld with the Cosmos in the manner of a Dravidian beggar.

It was quite impossible, she told herself. She would simply have to learn, in the way of a Wired Starman, how to deal with her new fears. It was not, she told herself, the same terror that Damon felt when floating in space twenty kilometers above the deck. *Of that sort of thing,* she thought, *I have no more fear than a monkey. I revel in extravehicular activity.* No, what terrified her— what no Zen program or breathing exercise would ever make her forget—was that a shipmate, Jean Marq, had deliberately tried to destroy her, tried to send her spinning off into deep space to die a death so cold and lonely that it defied description. Krieg had explained that the Frenchman was in fugue when he had swung the yard at her. The explanation did not help. In fact it made matters worse. If Jean was unaware of what he had done, what assurance was there that he would not do it over and over again until he succeeded?

It had been young Damon who had come to her aid, young Damon who held her, comforted her, confessed to her his own personal dreads, offered to share hers.

The boy's attention had been a healing influence. She was still not willing to go EVA when Jean was in a pod on the bridge, but Damon's sweet concern strengthened her.

It was strange, she thought. She had expected all of that from Duncan, who was the rock upon which the *Glory* syndicate was anchored. But he had remained oddly aloof, looking at her new relationship with Damon Ng with benign indifference.

She thought about Damon's youthful, quasi-Asiatic body, smooth, with undefined yet strong musculature, small but efficient sex, and almond-shaped, innocent eyes. *Damon was not who I had expected to cling to in extremis,* she told herself, releasing her legs from the Lotus. But he served. He was a shipmate. She stretched her cramped muscles, then rolled into a ball, arms around her knees. With a small change of inertia, she started to spin, her hair flying. When she began to feel disoriented she snapped out to full length and bent into the pike position. Again she extended to her full body length, spinning like a baton, feeling the centrifugal force expand and lift her breasts.

"How beautiful," Jean Marq said. He rested in the mouth of the transit tunnel. He had shaved off his several weeks' growth of beard, trimmed his guerilla-style moustache, dressed himself in a green-and-red skinsuit.

Anya stopped herself with a hand and knee against the fabric wall. Her heart was suddenly pounding.

"Why are you here, Jean?" she asked.

———

He seemed puzzled. "Is there any reason why I should not be, Anya?"

She was too terrified to answer, but she kept herself calm. She opened a wall pocket, withdrew a skinsuit and pulled it on over her nakedness.

"Are you angry with me, *chérie?*"

"No," Anya said tensely, ready to flee.

The Frenchman frowned. "But you are. I can feel it. Was it because of that foolish doll of mine?"

Anya stared in silence. Jean Marq turned thoughtful. "I am sorry you feel like that," he said. "I only bought the creature as a prank. I had no idea it disgusted you so."

Anya's silence remained unbroken, but Jean Marq seemed not to notice.

"It embarrasses me, *chère* Anya. I hope you don't think I indulge in perversions. Quite the reverse, I assure you. Even in my student days I was considered one of the most moral of men when it came to sexual practices."

"Were you," whispered Anya.

"Believe me, when Duncan suggested I space the paracoita I didn't protest. I put her through the airlock without a moment's hesitation. And do you know, Anya? Ever since I did, I have been feeling very much better. I can sleep. How do you account for something like that?" He essayed a roguish smile. "Perhaps the mystics are correct. Perhaps we must make sacrifices to the ghosts and spirits."

God, the girl thought. Does he really believe *he* put the paracoita out the airlock? Was that what Dietr intended? Anya heard Duncan's voice in the transit tunnel and relief flooded over her like cool water.

"Jean," Duncan said. "I am pleased to see you up."

"Duncan." Jean embraced Duncan Kr warmly. "I have been explaining to Anya about the paracoita."

Duncan looked at Anya reassuringly. "She understands, Jean. We all do."

———

"Thank you, Duncan." Jean hesitated. "Now where was I going when I stopped to watch Anya?"

"Spin section? If so, I'll go with you," Duncan said.

"Perhaps that was it." Marq turned to Anya in farewell. "I hope you understand, *ma chère,*" he said. "The doll was only a joke."

Anya could hear Duncan and Jean Marq laughing as they made their way down the transit tube. The girl floated motionless in the air of her quarters, listening.

Mira appeared, clung spread-legged to a wall, and looked at Anya.

Anya extended her arms and Mira released her hold and leaped, slowly, into her arms. Anya buried her face in the cat's silky fur and said, "He's a killing madman, beautiful Mira. You have always known, haven't you? The question is, what do we do about it?"

13

NOT A QUESTION OF ETHICS

Nothing in his brief earlier visit to Voertrekkerhoem had prepared Black Clavius for the complexity of The Voerster's kraal. What he now saw was a formidable fortress housing and sustaining not only the Voertrekker-Praesident and his family and staff, but also a brigade of Trekkerpolizei and hundreds of servants and bureaucrats.

At the conclusion of his long flight from the south, Black Clavius had been deposited at the landing ground known as Lufthavan, the police airship base at Voertrekkerhoem. Ordinary flights from the southwest coast to the cities and towns of the north and east did not depart from Lufthavan. Civilian travelers used the much larger airship ground north of the capital.

When Clavius debarked from the police dirigible, he was immediately taken into custody by a detachment of the Voertrekker-Praesident's personal police-guard detachment, known as the Wache, of whom there were said to be one thousand. Within this *corps d'elite* was secreted a clandestine, almost furtive element of Voertrekker society. The enlisted ranks of the Wache were filled entirely by children of Voertrekker-kaffir sexual unions. These relationships, though illegal, were tacitly accepted. The practice of black-white cohabitation had been anathema in the pre-Rebellion period. But after the end of hostilities it became a necessity. The casualities of the Rebellion had mostly been men—men of both races. Kaffir men had come close to extermination and were still, even after a thousand years, heavily outnumbered by kaffir women. The population had dwindled almost to the point of extinction three hundred years after the Rebellion, and at that point a desperate Deliberative Assembly had made the decision to accept children of Voertrekker-kaffir unions as *potential* Voertrekkers—the status to be won by public service.

As a means of repopulating Voerster, the scheme was never more than a minimal success. Social pressure to maintain apartheid remained a powerful influence in the politics of Voerster. But like the Anglo-Indians of Old Earth, the half-breed children of Voertrekker fathers and kaffir mothers tended to be fiercely patriotic, dedicated to the State and the Voertrekker ethos, and protective of their slightly elevated status. As the popular saying put it, "Better the Wache than exposure on the Grassersee." Meaning that the children who might once have been left to die in the grassland could now hope for a post in the Wache.

Children of Voertrekker mothers by kaffir men were, in theory, entitled to straightforward mixed-blood status. In practice they were discriminated against even by their peers.

But it was a fact that the Wache was considered a prime assignment for the Trekkerpolizei officer corps, many of whom were the partially kaffir second and third sons of Kraalheeren.

Within the first hour after being landed at the detention barracks attached to Lufthavan, Black Clavius was guilty of a social solecism. He quite naturally assumed that the coffee-skinned Wache noncommissioned officer commanding the detachment escorting him was a kaffir and addressed him in the cadences of the townships.

After the swift tongue-lashing, the Starman found himself in solitary confinement with a single meal a day. *Well, Lord,* he murmured, *I am still on boiled goat and one tangeroon. And I get one meal now instead of the two they gave me south of the Isthmus. I am not making much progress, Lord.*

At dawn of Black Clavius' third day of solitary in the Lufthavan cells, the warder who brought him his goat and tangeroon said, "Eat and then stand by the door."

"Yes, Mynheer. May I ask why?"

The warder, a young man with broad features, glared at Clavius. "You may not, kaffir," he said. "They say you are a Starman. Well, you will get no special treatment here."

"Quite so," murmured Clavius.

"Stand and wait."

Clavius did. For three hours. *Lord, we agreed I should stay downworld on Voerster for a time,* Clavius said to no one visible. *You didn't promise me a flower garden. But it would be much easier if you would make the Voertrekkers into clock-watchers.*

By noon, a commissioned officer of the Wache appeared and said, "Follow me, kaffir."

Clavius did as he was told. He was led from the barracks, across the leveled dirt plain of the airship field, and across a steeply banked ditch into the great house.

The officer, a subleutnant, was erect and very correct. He wore the red-striped trousers of the presidential detachment.

Inside the house Clavius surreptitiously tried to orient himself and failed. He was far from the suite of rooms where he had seen Broni and Eliana Ehrengraf so many weeks ago. Instead he was marched through echoing stone corridors, out and through covered walkways atop crenelated walls, again into dark buildings and up broad, empty staircases, until he found himself in a populated anteroom filled with stiff and anxious Voertrekkers, all hanging on each word spoken by the young woman sitting at a desk which guarded a tall door. She wore the Wache stripes of a lance corporal. She was tall, with light eyes. Brown skin and nappy black ahir showed her ancestry.

"Kaffir Clavius," the subleutnant said, surrendering a paper slip.

The corporal, who looked still in her teens, stared at Clavius. Clavius stared back. He had never seen a blue-eyed kaffir.

"Kaffir, what are you gawking at? Mind your manners."

"I will, mynheera."

"Don't mock me, kaffir, or you will regret it. I am addressed as lance corporal. You may be with us for a long time. Learn."

———

"Yes, lance corporal."

"Sit down there." She indicated an empty chair. "I will call you when it is time."

"Excuse me, lance corporal, but I am a stranger here. When it is time to do what?"

The girl looked at him in amazement. "Why, to see the Voertrekker-Praesident, you foolish kaffir," she said. "Didn't you know that is why you were brought here?"

It was purely the hand of Fate and the teeth of a hungry giant cheet that had brought Ian Voerster to the Machtstuhl. Heinrich Voerster, son of Alfried Vorster—Ian's great-uncle—had been destined to rule Planet Voerster from Voertrekkerhoem.

But Heinrich lived only to the age of seventeen. During the high hunting season (that time of year when upper-class Voertrekkers devoted themselves to murdering the indigenous life of Planet Voerster), while stalking a large wild cheet alone, the heir to the title of The Voerster and the Machtstuhl was killed and eaten.

In the Alfried Voerster Kraal near the south coast city of Durban there stood a stone mausoleum, on the lintel of which was carved the Alfried Voerster motto: *To Rule is to Serve; to Serve is to Live.* Within the mausoleum, next to the crypts containing the bones of Alfried and his wife Brigidda, there was a sarcophagus containing only a human femur, some ribs, and parts of a human skull, all of Heinrich Voerster that the irritated giant cheet had not consumed.

Ian Voerster was not a hunter, nor a sportsman of any sort. A few academic critics said that Heinrich would have been a better Head of State, would have done a better job of maintaining "the Voertrekker ethos." But among the Kraalheeren and the members of the mynheeren class there was no dissatisfaction with the performance in office of Ian Voerster.

Ian's short, muscular frame and large head and features projected an image of vigor. He was ruddy, blue-eyed, and white-blond enough to have been one of the storybook Boers of ancient African legend.

Among the Kraalheeren of the Grassersee, he was recognized as a man of furious temper, dangerous and shrewd. He cultivated that image. It had served him well over the years. He let it be known often that as The Voerster he had no reluctance to exercise the enormous power the covenant of the Voertrekker State bestowed upon him.

Ian had married young, as all Voertrekkers did. He had been bereaved almost at once. His consort, Ulfrieda Klawiter Voerster, died in childbirth. She had had three bloody miscarriages. Her fourth attempt to deliver a child killed her.

What followed was Ian Voerster's most shrewd political act. He betrothed himself to Eliana Ehrengraf, heiress and kraalheera of the one Voertrekker family disenfranchised for one hundred years after the Rebellion for sympathizing with the kaffirs, but a house with a vast political following among all classes of society.

The union of Ian and Eliana, too, was troubled by repeated infant deaths and miscarriages. Voertrekker bloodlines were attenuating. Ian Voerster began to wonder secretly if he had not somehow offended the Almighty. He was, in his private way, a religious man.

Then sixteen years ago, Eliana had carried to term the Voerster family's only living child, Broni Ehrengraf. Golden Broni. In a nation where members of the ruling class were not customarily greeted with hosannas and paeans, Eliana Ehrengraf Voerster and her daughter, the Golden Broni, were beloved by Voertrekker and kaffir alike. But as Broni approached puberty, she sickened. Now she lived day by day. Ian Voerster privately believed that she managed this by the grace of some *Greater Power*, a Power aware of the needs of the Voertrekker State.

The Voerster looked up from his work and saw the large black man standing in the doorway. "Come in, kaffir Clavius," he said.

The Voertrekker-Praesident's office was as narrow and dark

as most of the rooms in Voertrekkerhoem. Late-afternoon day-light came through an arrow-slit of a window high between the stone groins of the western wall. An electric lamp cast a pond of light on the slab that served Ian Voerster as a desk. A second lamp illuminated a Mercator projection of the continent of Voerster on the wall. The map was cluttered with colored pins marking projects of interest to the Voertrekker-Praesident.

Voerster looked past Clavius at the lance corporal. "Thank you, Klara. Close the door behind you."

When she had done as she was told, Ian Voerster addressed himself to Clavius. "I am curious. Are there still kaffirs on Earth?"

"I believe so, Mynheer."

"And mixed bloods like Klara?"

"It has been many years since I was on Earth, Voertrekker-Praesident. But I would be surprised if there were not."

The Voerster used a stiletto-like letter-opener to point at an ornately carved straight stool without cushions. "Good, you are a plain speaker. Sit there."

Clavius lowered himself carefully. The stool was more sub-stantial than he thought, but low. The "kaffir seat," Clavius thought wryly. He allowed himself to relax a trifle.

Ian Voerster regarded him silently over steepled fingers. Presently, he said, "You saw Walvis Strait, kaffir Clavius?"

"Yes, Mynheer."

"And Detention Two?"

"Yes, Mynheer."

The Voerster locked his hands and rested them on the surface of his stone tabletop. "I understand from Oberst Transkei that the weather was benign."

"It was clear and bright. Cold."

The Voerster essayed an icy smile. "It gets much, much colder than that. Detainees die of the cold in the sunshine there, kaffir. Detention Two is the last place in the world."

Clavius said nothing. The Voerster's point was made. The Friendly Islands, straddling the freezing Walvis Strait between the Sabercut Peninsula and the Southern Ice were like the Ninth Circle of Dante Alighieri's *Inferno.* Hell on a clear day.

The Voerster said, "Transkei told me what you said there. *'And they showed Galileo the instruments.'* You are learned."

Clavius fixed Ian Voerster with a look of infinite sadness. "For a kaffir?" he said.

"Yes," Ian said. "For a kaffir."

On the wall behind the Voertrekker-Praesident was mounted a Zulu *impee*-leader's *assegai* and shield. *They must be two thousand Earth-years old,* Black Clavius thought. The painted bars of the long-dead warrior's rank were still sharply limned on the desiccated cowhide.

"An anchestor of mine was a Boer scout at Rorke's Drift. He took that shield and assegai that day," Ian Voerster said.

"Long, long ago," Clavius said.

"We have long, long memories on Planet Voerster."

"I have come to understand that, Voertrekker," Clavius said.

"Good. We may begin to understand one another."

"I hope so, Mynheer."

Ian Voerster leaned back in his large chair. "What a kaffir you are, Black Clavius. Looking at you—one might take you for a Zulu." It was a compliment, of sorts. The ancient Zulu of Africa on Planet Earth were the only kaffirs Voertrekkers respected.

"I fear not, Voertrekker," Clavius said. "I was born in a place called South Carolina. There are no Zulus there. Long ago."

"That phrase keeps coming up when kaffir Clavius is the subject of discussion," Ian said. "How old are you really?"

"I am sixty."

"On Earth, how many years have passed since you were born?"

"Ah, that is a different matter, Mynheer. Many years have passed on Earth. You asked me how old *I* was. I took that to mean how many years of life have I experienced. The answer to that is sixty."

———

Ian Voerster's light eyes transfixed Clavius. "Give or take a few."

"Yes, Voertrekker."

"The men of the Goldenwing that is coming. The syndicate. How old are they?"

"I cannot be sure. But I would imagine they are in their thirties, forties. Perhaps older than that. There are Starmen of all ages," Clavius said. *Lord,* he wondered, *is he going to fall into the immortality game with me now?* It almost always happened. Landsmen thought the Wired Ones lived forever. "The question is almost meaningless."

"It is far from meaningless, kaffir Clavius. It means a great deal. It always will."

"On Voerster," Clavius said quietly.

"You are *on* Voerster, Starman."

"So I am, Voertrekker," Clavius admitted.

Ian Voerster stood abruptly and began pacing the narrow room. He wore a dashiki. The warm-weather quasi caftan designed for the climate of Africa on Earth had been modified with cheet-skin and ebray leather to serve as an overgarment in this chilly climate. *But what a strange lot we humans are,* Clavius thought. *We adopt what we like from those we despise.* He refrained from sharing that observation with the Lord. Lately the Lord seemed bored with Black Clavius.

"You saw my daughter," Ian Voerster said abruptly.

"Yes." Clavius could not help but add: "Before my unexpected trip south."

Voerster ignored the tiny insolence. "Well?" Impatiently.

Clavius said carefully, "She does not have tuberculosis, Voertrekker."

"Of course she hasn't. Do you take me for a fool?" The Voerster returned to his desk and sat down, spreading his well-kept hands on the polished rock surface. "According to my cousin, the Astronomer-Select, the Goldenwing should be achieving orbit within thirty days. Always assuming that Osbertus has not made some gross error, Voerster is in store for some remarkable changes." He fixed his pale eyes on Black Clavius. "Goldenwings change things simply by appearing, kaffir. Seen from another perspective—yours, for example—the changes may appear to be small. But I assure you that they are profound."

"Yes, Mynheer," Clavius said. "I can accept that."

"Thank you, Clavius," The Voerster said drily. "I do not refer, in case you are wondering, to the cargoes the Goldenwing will bring. Though I do not underestimate the impact of the goods my great-uncle Alfried ordered. By no means." He held an index finger to his thin lips in what was a characteristic gesture. "There are those at Pretoria University's Faculty of Husbandry who are concerned about the effect a large invasion of Terrestrial genotypes will have on Planet Voerster's ecology—

"But that won't be my concern, will it, kaffir? I will be long buried before that kind of problem becomes acute." He looked at Clavius with an expression of such speculation that it was almost an expression of cupidity. "You and yours, kaffir, take a different view. It is quite possible that *you* will still be alive in that far-off time."

"Not unless I am taken once more aboard a starship, Mynheer, and then returned here on some future voyage," Clavius said.

"Ah, of course. The paradoxes of time dilation," Ian Voerster said. "So difficult for a mere downworlder to grasp with any true understanding." The pallid eyes grew suddenly as cold as the sky over the Southern Ice. "Tell me, kaffir. Is there any possibility that the syndicate now aboard the *Gloria Coelis* is the same as the *Nostromo* syndicate with whom my great uncle Alfried dealt?"

"No, Mynheer. Time has passed uptime. Perhaps a great deal of it," Black Clavius said cautiously. "Until I came to Voerster, I had never heard of Goldenwing *Nostromo*. It is that way in space, Mynheer. There are probably fewer than a dozen Goldenwings still sailing, but they learn of one another only if and when word is circulated by downworlders during a port call. *Nostromo's* syndicate quite probably sold your great-uncle's contract to another syndicate, and that to still another until it became the property of the *Glory*, hers to fulfill. As to how long ago all this took place uptime—well, Mynheer, if you will forgive me, the question is meaningless. The answer could depend on where the winds of space have carried the *Glory*, for how long, and at what speeds."

Ian Voerster leaned forward slightly, betraying an intensity that disturbed Black Clavius deeply. On Voerster *any* anxious Voertrekker could mean trouble. And when the Voertrekker in question was the hereditary leader of this benighted society, the trouble could be bitter. "The Rebellion set our sciences back by centuries, kaffir. Am I correct in assuming that technological progress on Earth and the other colony worlds has not suffered such setbacks?"

"Probably not, Mynheer. But the march of technology is a sporadic thing. No two worlds live at the same pace."

"I understand. But medical technology?"

"The same assumptions apply, Mynheer."

"But they will have a physician aboard the Goldenwing."

"Almost certainly."

"A wiser, better educated man—a more *able* man than our Tiegen Roark. That surely."

Clavius saw the danger signals flying, but knew not how to avoid the pitfalls ahead.

"I want an answer, kaffir."

"A Goldenwing surgeon would be more skilled than a Healer of Voerster," Clavius said carefully. "But if you are thinking of Broni, Mynheer, do not expect too much. One would have to do a proper diagnosis, and that would almost certainly have to be performed aboard. And a voyage to orbit for someone as ill as the mynheera Broni could be extremely dangerous. The syndicate might simply refuse to take such a chance. I cannot say."

"They will do what I say must be done, kaffir Clavius. I am not easily dissuaded." He pressed a buzzer on his desk and stood again. "I want you to think about it. And to consider how you might best serve me—and mynheera the Voertrekkersdatter."

He walked around the desk as Clavius rose from the stool on

which he had been sitting. "You shall be my guest here at Voertrekkerhoem, Clavius, while you devote yourself to the pursuit I suggest. You will do this, of course—"

"Because, like Galileo," Clavius said with deep melancholy, "I have seen the instruments."

"Exactly, kaffir. And because a starship is coming and when it departs you want most desperately to be on it. We both understand your situation to perfection. Rest assured that I shall be protective of your Starman's ethics." The Voerster was heavily ironic.

The door opened and the lance corporal stood ready for orders.

"Take my special guest, the Starman Black Clavius, to Leutnant Bostik in the visitor's quarters," The Voerster said. "Instruct the leutnant that Starman Clavius is to want for nothing."

Except my freedom, though Clavius. *So I do what I must do. It is not a question of ethics, Lord, but one of survival.*

14

APPROACH—AND TREASON AT STERNBERG

*C*linging to the fabric bulkhead of the bridge, Mira regarded the large *ones. All were lying in their nests, thinking together with the queen-who-was-not-alive. The great queen had her paws on their heads. One of Mira's kittens who had followed her through the tunnel to the bridge mewed his hunger call and she trilled impatiently at him to be silent.*

Overhead, the ceiling had been opened to that great room she so loved to prowl, but now there was a vast, mottled ball nearby that Mira understood the large ones thought of as another room that they were anxious to enter. The nearness of the lighted ball drove away the creatures she often challenged when she and the dominant tom were alone in the emptiness.

There was no chance of a hunt here. The tom was involved in some big, clumsy way with the other large ones. The small queen had done something clever, but nothing that interested Mira. The tom-who-cut was exchanging thoughts with the great-queen-who-was-not-alive; the young tom was watching and learning; the mad tom was unreadable but the aura surrounding him made Mira's fur rise.

The kitten mewed again, complaining. Mira cuffed him with retracted claws. She looked once more at the large white ball beyond the roof. The face of it, seen through the maze of lines and colors where the monkey things lived, was colored blue and green.

She looked away and forgot it, attention withdrawn. What the large ones were doing did not interest her. She imagined the taste of freshly killed fish. With a warning trill to her kitten she launched herself into the transit tube toward the compartment containing the terminals for the food synthesizer, which the great-queen-who-was-not-alive had taught her to operate.

"Du lieber, *that damned cat. I can taste the fish,*" Dietr Krieg
complained.

"*You are her godfather, Dietr,*" Damon said. "*You made her what
she is.*"

Duncan was pleased that young Ng had found enough confidence
to jab at the neurocybersurgeon. "*Pay attention, all,*" he said.

The others fell silent.

Duncan said, "*How long to orbit, Anya?*" Ordinarily it was a
question that would have been addressed to Glory's computer, but
Duncan knew his people. Anya needed to be busy.

"*Six days, ten hours uptime, Duncan.*"

"*Are we time-conformed?*"

"*Within two decimal places,*" Damon said.

"*Sail trim?*"

With blind eyes they could all see the newly configured sail plan.
All jibs, spankers, tops'ls, and t'gallants tightly furled. Courses on the
mains and foremasts braced around to catch the torrent of photons from
white Luyten. Tachyons were forgotten now, their influence too subtle to
affect the course Anya Amaya had set for Glory, bringing her into low
planetary orbit around the luminous, glowing blue-green planet. And it
was overhead now; they were within seven hundred thousand kilometers
of the surface, carefully bleeding off the last of their interstellar speed.

In all, it was a magnificent job of sailing. Duncan told Anya so and
felt the warmth of her response permeating the entire pre-planetary orbit
injection gathering. Only Jean Marq made no response. Ordinarily he
would be swarming over Anya's calculations, making dozens of tiny
changes. But nothing. Duncan probed and found that the Frenchman
was daydreaming. Duncan felt the soft breath of a warm wind, the smell
of growing things. Provence? God, he hoped not that again. But Dietr
had warned that Jean could break open. Still, as a member of Glory's
crew, he was here on the bridge. What alternative was there? To open
an airlock and send him after his paracoita?

"*Any messages from Voerster?*" Duncan asked.

"*Damon has taken that over,*" Anya said.

"*Well, boy?*" Dietr Krieg asked.

"*I have been getting voice from their observatory at Sternberg.*

Osbertus Kloster sends gigabits of anything and everything. He is eager to please, Duncan. I put most of it through the demographics program. We have the landing coordinates for the cargo shuttles, though, and something else. I may have misunderstood the meaning—they still speak a kind of weird Afrikaans—but they asked several times if we had a physician aboard. A 'healer' they said. I gather someone important is sick."

"Downtimers expect immortality," Dietr said scornfully.

Duncan said, "Keep guarding their frequency, Damon."

"Yes, Duncan."

"Jean," Duncan probed gently. "Jean Marq?"

A long pause. Then: "Yes? What is it, Duncan?"

"Can you take the cargo pallets down?"

"Why, yes. If you want me to."

Dietr asked, "Have they the proper facilities for keeping the embryos frozen?"

"They did when they ordered them," Duncan said.

"That was two hundred years ago, down there." Krieg had little faith in colonists. None at all in their ability to advance their technology. Krieg had examined all that Anya had put into the data bank—data derived from the man called Kloster—and he was not impressed. Societies that suffered major shocks tended to remain low-tech. If they recovered at all.

"The Voertrekker Minister of Husbandry said they are ready to receive the beasties," Anya said.

"Maybe they think they are getting grown animals," Krieg said.

"Even folk of Germanic stock could not be so badly informed, could they, Dietr?" Damon asked wickedly.

"Mind your manners, boy," Krieg said, "or I'll cut out your liver for Mira and her kindle."

"Anya," Duncan said, "I'll conn her for a time. You get some sleep. Damon, collect the monkeys in the Monkey House." The tiny cyborgs tended to become confused when Glory was in low orbit, unable to decide which was up, which down. "And Dietr, as soon as we make orbit, start the mapping cameras. Colonists are always in need of new maps." Ordinarily this would have been the task for either Jean Marq *or Han Soo. But Dietr was capable and it would keep him occupied while* Glory *was at Voerster.*

Overhead, the planet turned. Now under a swirling patchwork of cloud, the single continent showed green in the heartland, gray-brown in the high plains. The ice caps were enormous, reaching from the poles to latitude 49 degrees. Duncan was reminded of Thalassa. But his homeworld was a planet of rock and lichen and sea. On Voerster there were grass and growing things. Thalassa was winter, Duncan thought. Voerster was early spring or late autumn.

Glory's *sailing directions, available through the computer drogue, informed Duncan that though Voerster was eleven-twelfths ocean, the land received little rain.*

He could see a great cyclonic storm building in the empty ocean of the water hemisphere. By the time it reached the continent of Voerster, it would soar into the stratosphere in great upwellings along the Shieldwall of the Planetia, or it would blow itself out on the vast, level Grassersee.

The southern ice cap was reflecting the light of Luyten 726. But Glory *informed Duncan that the surface temperature there was 210 degrees Kelvin—62 degrees below zero Centigrade. Survivable, but only just.*

Snow was falling on the eastern edge of the stratospheric Planetia where the Blue Glacier joined the Northern Ice. Not an easy world to live on, Duncan thought. But beautiful. Duncan Kr had been shipfast for two dozen months of uptime. The sight of Voerster made him restless and anxious to feel ground beneath his feet again.

In the hold the brain of Han Soo, still and empty at last, said nothing.

The old refractor was a fine instrument. It had been centuries out-of-date on Earth when it had been built as a rich man's plaything. And it had been loaded on *Milagro* because the then-selected astronomer had held a fixation about the durability and usefulness of refractors in planetary work. Now, Osbertus thought with wry amusement, it was state-of-the-art on Voerster. For broad field observation it had no equal on Voerster. Osbertus had focussed it so that Eliana could see the dust of tiny diamonds that was the stuff of the Galactic lens' edge. In the field as well shone Smuts, smallest of the Six Giants. And—like a fragile butterfly, small, yet the brightest object in the field—the Goldenwing *Gloria Coelis*.

Eliana drew in a startled breath. She had heard tales of the Goldenwings all her life, had seen numberless artists' renderings, but this was something very different from all that. No living artist had ever seen a Goldenwing until *Nepenthe* had materialized without warning in orbit around Voerster. So unexpectedly had the vessel arrived, and so swiftly did it depart that no artist had had the opportunity to study it through the telescope atop the Sternberg. On Voerster there was no means of capturing and preserving an image in color. Photography was an art limited to the observatory's glass-and-silver-nitrate, black-and-white technology. Astronomer-Select Kloster had found it impossible to produce more than a half dozen badly blurred images as he tried desperately to adjust the telescope to the low orbit *Nepenthe* had assumed to put Clavius downworld.

The telescope's rather clumsy mounting made observing anything in such an orbit difficult. The Astronomer-Select was of the private opinion that close-orbit observing techniques had never been developed by his predecessors because Voerster lacked a proper satellite. Osbertus had studied the Oral Histories of the First Landers. They had remarkable things to say about the "Moon" circling the homeworld. It was a heavenly body laden with an enormous baggage of legend: the home of the Hunt Goddess, the origin of female menses, the subject of an infinite number of verses, songs, and apothegms worthy of Black Clavius: *"Now Cynthia, nam'd fair regent of the night—" "Fear may force a man to cast before the Moon—" "By the light of the silvery Moon—" "Moon over Miami—" "That gentle Moon, the lesser light, the Lover's leap, the Swain's delight—"*

Clearly, without such a satellite, both love and astronomy languished. Even the dour Board of Censors acknowledged the *nuda veritas* that space travel began in the year Anno Domini 1969 with a flight from Earth to the Moon. Without a moon the first leap into space would never have happened and half mankind's lovers would have died celibate.

Now nearing Voerster, the approaching Goldenwing displayed itself as an object so intricate and brilliant that it resembled an example of the jeweler's art displayed on black velvet.

Eliana Ehrengraf had not come to Sternberg with her escort of two female Trekkerpolizei and a dour Wache captain just to peer through the telescope. She arrived at the observatory in an aristocratic fury—a mood that had darkened as her suspicions grew. She was at Sternberg for a purpose, and the purpose was not sightseeing.

But the object in the field of the telescope commanded her attention. For a few moments she appeared to have forgotten the uniformed trio standing uncomfortably with Buele on the floor of the observatory dome below the observing scaffold.

The distant Goldenwing was the most beautiful object she had ever seen. It was more than a *thing*. That it was made by people like herself made it even more remarkable. There in the sky was a visible symbol of the accompishments of *her* species, one willing to challenge the grandeur of heaven.

The vision tempered her anger and made her wish that Broni were here to share the wonder of it.

"Isn't it fine, Cousin?" She heard the voice of Osbertus Kloster in her ear. He had climbed the scaffolding to the eyepiece and was puffing with the effort. As it was with Broni, though to a lesser degree, strong emotions in Eliana Ehrengraf affected those nearby. Customarily she maintained a reserved stillness about her for propriety's sake, but the sight of *Glory* in the telescope affected her disciplined emotional control.

"More than fine, Osbertus," she murmured.

"They've passed Wallenberg and are inbound through the Gap." Osbertus was tempted to boast to his beautiful cousin, the Voertrekkerschatz, that *this time* he had established contact with the syndics aboard, and that this time the Goldenwing carried cargo for Voerster. It would not be, he thought, like the humiliating experience of nineteen years ago with *Nepenthe.* "They estimate arriving in six days. Six, Mynheera. Think of it."

Reluctantly, Eliana moved away from the eyepiece. "But I didn't come here to stargaze, Cousin. I came to ask your help."

Osbertus Kloster, distressed both by Eliana's tightly reined demeanor and by the police escort that appeared to provoke it, was the last man on Voerster wishing to become involved in a family quarrel—most particularly when the family was that of The Voerster and Voertrekker-Praesident. Cousin Ian was not a man to be trifled with. But for Eliana Ehrengraf, Osbertus Kloster would do anything.

Eliana moved away from the telescope eyepiece. "We must speak about Clavius," she said in a low voice. "Privately. Without my husband's snoops."

"Well, let us see if they have any imagination," Osbertus said. "Maybe heaven can immobilize them." He leaned over the railing of the observing scaffold. "Buele— Bring the police ladies and the Wachekapitan up here. I am sure they would enjoy seeing the Goldenwing."

"Yes, Brother." The boy's reedy voice seemed to rise from the darkness below.

"Brother?" Eliana regarded the old man quizzically.

"Yes, well—" Osbertus flushed and said, "Some time ago he asked me to explain why Black Clavius so resembled our kaffirs on Voerster when he came from the stars. I told him that all men are brothers. He asked me if that included Voertrekkers, and I said yes, that it did. Then he asked: 'Mynheeren, as well?' What could I say? I replied yes, that it included black and white, mynheeren, and *lumpen.* From that time on he has called me 'Brother.' He has a very literal mind, mynheera. Does it offend you?"

"Of course not, Osbertus. You believe what you told him, don't you?"

"I hope I do, mynheera."

"Then there is nothing to resent."

———

It was the answer Osbertus expected from Eliana Ehrengraf. The Ehrengraf humanitarianism was part of Voerster's history. It had got them into trouble during the Kaffir Rebellion, as a surfeit of humanitarianism and courage often did.

As the police people and Buele carefully climbed the badly illuminated ladder to the observing platform, Eliana returned to the telescope and touched the polished brass of the eyepiece tube with her fingertips. It was an almost religious gesture. She lowered her face and looked again. Osbertus could see the golden light from the *Glory* shining out of the tube and into Eliana's eye.

"It has moved," she said.

"Indeed it has," Osbertus said. "According to the wireless messages we have been receiving, *Glory* is still moving at nearly two tenths of a percent of the speed of light."

"How fast is that?"

"If we had a dirigible that could fly so fast, it could circumnavigate Voerster in three minutes, mynheera."

"Surely that's ridiculous, Mynheer Osbertus," the Wache captain said, breathing heavily. Dietegen Kreiske was a man with a pedestrian mind—what the Voertrekker-Praesident called "a bean counter." Perfect for his present task, Osbertus Kloster thought: To spy on Eliana Ehrengraf and remain unmoved by her elegance and beauty.

"Look and wonder," Osbertus said loftily. "Then tell me what is ridiculous and what is possible, Kapitan Kreiske."

The two policewomen were typical *lumpen* females, not of the Wache, thick-bodied and plain of feature with straw-blonde hair and the blue porcelain eyes of the true Voertrekker underclass. Buele followed them up the ladder and joined the group on the scaffold.

Osbertus said, "It is crowded up here. We will go down, mynheera. Buele, see to it that the ladies and the captain get a fine view."

The police contingent's attention focussed on the telescope. None objected to the retreat of Eliana and the Astronomer-Select.

Osbertus had a puckish impulse to remove the ladder and leave them stranded ten meters above the observatory floor, but he denied himself.

Eliana followed Osbertus to an open balcony overlooking the steep, regular slopes of the Sternberg. The night was so clear and the stars so bright that the patterns of the Nachtebrise in the Sea of Grass were visible. From the paddock behind Osbertus' living quarters and in front of the barracoon where the domestic kaffirs lived, they could hear the squabbling of the ferden—the Voersterian cognate for meat animals. The beasts had to be kept segregated by sex since they were always in estrus and a pregnancy meant the certain and untimely loss of a breeder.

Eliana listened and said, "We live in a strange, unfinished world, Cousin Osbertus. Are there necrogenes on Earth, I wonder?"

"There were none when the First Landers departed. At least none that I know of. There were egg-layers and placental mammals, of course, and all sorts of other untidy ways of propagating, but none quite so brutal as the way of Voerster."

Eliana said, "The beasts of Voerster die so that their young can live. I live and my children have died."

Osbertus impulsively took her hand. "Do not blame yourself, Cousin. And there is Broni," he said.

"For how long?" Eliana said desperately. "Tell me how long."

Far out in the Sea of Grass a hunting cheet roared at the stars. On nights this bright with starlight, hunting was poor on the open savannah. Overhead the constellations performed their slow, majestic dance: The Ploughman followed the Maiden and the Serpent followed the Hanged Man. There was an eotemporal grandeur to the nocturnal rotation of the heavens, Eliana thought. What were they like, those people aboard that glorious winged thing approaching her world? Had they mortal needs and sympathies? Were they like Black Clavius? Or were they beings of power, secretive and evolved beyond humanity?

Eliana looked back into the observatory. Her dogged escorts were still on the viewing scaffold with Buele. She shivered with resurgent anger. "Ever since he arrested Clavius, I have had those three or others like them with me night and day. What is he thinking of?"

"Perhaps he is asking the question: 'What are *you* thinking of?'" Osbertus said.

"I intend to take Broni out of Voertrekkerhoem."

"She is very ill, mynheera," Osbertus said fearfully. He suspected what would come next, or if not next, then soon.

"Do you know Einsamberg? The house in the Grimsel mountains I had from my godfather of Ehrengraf-Rand Kraal?"

"No, Cousin. I did not know you still owned property." It was customary on Voerster for an heiress to deed all her property to her husband when she married. Only lands that were part of a First Lander's Portion were exempt from the Man Laws. A domicile protected by a First Arriver's deed was sacroscanct. It could not even be entered by the Trekkerpolizei. The kraal at Einsamberg must have been so protected.

Osbertus began to get an uneasy feeling in the pit of his ample belly. "I heard a rumor that Black Clavius is often seen in Cousin Ian's company," he said.

"He has been at Voertrekkerhoem for a month," Eliana said. "I have not been allowed to see him. But Tiegen Roark tells me that Clavius has seen Broni and that his visit cheered her. She was very depressed when Oberst Transkei took the Starman away. They had him confined south of the Isthmus, you know."

Osbertus shivered and glanced back into the darkened observatory. The police visitors were laboriously clambering down the ladder.

Eliana caught his arm and said, "I mean to take Broni to Einsamberg. I don't trust Ian. He intends something he knows I will oppose. I intend to take the Starman, too. And I will have a promise from Clavius that when the Goldenwing and its syndicate arrive, he will assist me to demand their help for Broni. I came here tonight to ask you for your loyalty, Cousin. Will you give it?"

Osbertus felt as though he were suffocating. He could feel

the manacles locking on his wrists, hear the whir of the airship motors transporting him to the Southern Ice. "But what about The Voerster, mynheera? What about Ian?"

"Ian now allows me a single visit with Broni each day. It will be enough." She paused, drew a breath. "If he tries to stop me I will kill him, Cousin."

"*Eliana! My God, be careful what you say!*"

"The Ehrengrafs were not always so docile as now, Osbertus. In the Rebellion they fought with the kaffirs."

"And lost their Civil Rights for a hundred years. Remember who you are. You are the *wife* of *The Voerster*. You terrify me when you talk of killing."

"Let Ian beware, Cousin."

"And Broni?"

"What Clavius said is so, Cousin. Broni's heart is damaged. Without help from the men of the Goldenwing, she will surely die."

In the bright starlight, Osbertus could see that Eliana's cheeks glistened with tears.

"Ian has always known that Broni's sickness is not tuberculosis. He is convincing himself—or the public. Ian Voerster is like that. What he thinks he must do, he *will* do. He is bred for it," Eliana said.

"As you are, mynheera," Osbertus Kloster said.

"As I am," Eliana whispered in agreement.

In the starlight the aging man could see the winglike arch of Eliana's dark brows, the reflective depth of her eyes. She had more than beauty, he thought. She had the strength of a fine blade. *If I had been better born, if I were thirty years younger, if— But what did it matter, after all? She needs me, my beautiful, treasonous cousin.* And with a single word the Astronomer-Select sighed and threw his career, his comfort, and very possibly his life into the balance. "Yes," he said. "Whatever I can do for you, I will do, Cousin." *I may end my days nobly alone,* Osbertus Kloster thought fearfully, *in a very cold place.*

———

15

A FLIGHT TO EINSAMBERG

Luftkapitan Otto Klemmer was a man with a well-developed sense of his position in life. He and his family took great pride in the fact that of all the dirigible commanders of the Staadluftflot— the government air service of Voerster—it was Otto Klemmer who had been selected to fly *Volkenreiter*, the personal transport of the Voertrekker-Praesident's family.

Cloud Rider was the latest and finest of the air fleet, with a lifting body design and a length of fifty-nine meters. The gondola was furnished with the comfort of the first family of Voerster in mind, with a forward viewing salon, above which the crew operated on a flight deck equipped with the latest in magnetic navigational and wireless communication devices. The wireless had a range, under optimal conditions, of nine hundred kilometers. The navigational devices included a magnetic compass and a rather fragile and primitive directional gyroscope.

Far better devices than these were built before the Rebellion, but aviation was no longer a government priority on Voerster. Travel, except on government business, was slightly disreputable on Planet Voerster.

Carrying a nominal load the ship was capable of a nonstop flight of one thousand six hundred kilometers. For longer flights it could be refueled in midair by one of the service's tanker dirigibles. If the flight was made when the Nachtebrise blew steadily west to east across the Sea of Grass, *Volkenreiter* was capable of flying from Voersterstaad to Pretoria without refueling. Of course, Klemmer would never make such a closely measured flight with any of the first family aboard. Luftkapitan Klemmer was a careful man.

On this gusty morning, however, the airshipman who was responsible for the traveling comfort and safety of the Voertrekker-Praesident's family found himself with a problem. On the day following Allegiance Tuesday (Voerster's calendar was laden with celebration days—none of which, save First Landers' and Deorbit Days, were true holidays.), Klemmer was notified that he would be required to fly the mynheera Eliana, the Voertrekkersdatter, and a number of others from Voertrekkerhoem to Einsamberg, a distance of nine hundred kilometers.

A rest in the mountain climate of Einsamberg had been prescribed for the mynheera Broni, and a rest in the mountains she had to have, regardless of the weather or the logistical difficulty such a flight presented.

Unconfirmed orders made the Luftkapitan uneasy. And the orders for today's flight had come, not from the office of the Voertrekker-Praesident, who was away from Voertrekkerhoem on an inspection of the fisheries on Windhoek Gulf, but from the staff of the Astronomer-Select Osbertus Kloster, whom Klemmer regarded as a pompous old fool.

Early in the morning Healer Tiegen Roark presented himself at the airship shed and informed Klemmer that the *Volkenreiter* would transport not only the mynheera and the Voertrekkersdatter, but several members of her household, the Astronomer-Select and his young half-witted assistant Buele, Roark himself and the kaffir Starman, who for some time now had been at Voertrekkerhoem as a "guest" of the Voertrekker-Praesident.

It was intended, Roark said, to set up a small observatory at Einsamberg so that the mynheera Broni could observe the approach to orbit of the Goldenwing *Gloria Coelis*. All told, the traveling party would consist of twelve people and they would present themselves at Lufthavan airship field at noon.

By ten in the morning the shed was cluttered with the enormous amount of luggage the mynheera Eliana felt essential for comfort at the mountain kraal. It became immediately apparent to Klemmer that *Cloud Rider* could not carry the entire traveling party, the full crew, the baggage, and enough fuel to fly to Einsamberg and return to Voertrekkerhoem. The *Volkenreiter* was normally flown with the captain and four airmen, plus four kaffir stewards. Clearly this could not be done on this flight.

Klemmer first used the Lufthavan wireless to ask the airship sheds north of Voersterstaad for a tanker to accompany his airship. The tanker fleet was otherwise engaged. Every year at this time, the dirigible fleet made "ceremonial" overflights of kaffir townships across the Sea of Grass. It was traditional. It was also a show of force to remind the kaffirs that misbehavior would bring a rain of ordnance down on their heads from the Voertrekker-owned skies of Planet Voerster.

Klemmer next put on his best uniform and called on the Voertrekkerschatz. She was gracious, but iron-willed. He was told that neither the timing nor the load to be carried to Einsamberg could be changed. "I am confident, Luftkapitan," the mynheera Eliana said, smiling at him ingenuously, "that an airshipman of your skill and experience can devise a solution to our dilemma. Do so, Luftkapitan."

Klemmer was a willing thrall to Eliana Ehrengraf. He was married to a typically blonde and plump Voertrekker wife; Eliana Ehrengraf's dark beauty opened up fields of dreams in Otto Klemmer's subconscious.

He returned to the airship shed and sat down with navigational calculator, paper, and pencil. At an average weight of 72 kilograms per passenger (high in the case of Eliana and Broni, low for Osbertus Kloster and the Healer) and estimating all other payload, the elimination of all but one of his flight crew and the entire cabin staff would save 576 kilograms. This could be spent on 164 liters of fuel. This meant that *Volkenreiter* could carry enough hydrogen to deposit the mynheera's party at Einsamberg and, if carefully handled, return to the presidential kraal without replenishment.

A near thing, but it could be done. It was important to Otto Klemmer that he and his vessel be at Voertrekkerhoem when the

Voetrekker-Praesident returned from Windhoek. Actually, The Voerster disliked flying, but it was Klemmer's duty to have himself and *Volkenreiter* available at all times.

The news that Black Clavius would be a member of the traveling party touched a nerve. Ever since Clavius had appeared on Voerster, the presence of a kaffir who was also a Wired Starman made the airshipman uneasy. Of course, one did not attain rank as a member of the household at Voertrekkerhoem by succumbing to anti-kaffir prejudice.

The kaffirs, the Voertrekker-Praesident often said, were a vital part of the society of Voerster. "If I can accept the idea of a kaffir Starman," he once had said to the Kraalheeren in the Kongresshalle, "who are you to show prejudice?" and if Kraalheeren were not supposed to show prejudice, who was Otto Klemmer to be more exclusive than his betters?

But the fact was that Otto Klemmer, though no Kraalheer, was uncomfortable with kaffirs, foreign or native-born. For three hundred years after Landing, the Klemmers had been *lumpen*. Before the Rebellion the Klemmers had been of "uncertain ancestry." Which meant mixed *lumpen* and kaffir blood. After the Rebellion, in which they gave good service to the state, a long process of gentrification began. Early Klemmers served as commando troopers, then as commando officers. Now, after a very long and cautious testing period, Klemmers were allowed to seek university degrees, and in the case of Otto Klemmer, training at the Luftacademie.

Klemmer felt no ill will toward kaffirs; they simply reminded him that he was slightly tainted.

The Rebellion being the axiological event of Voertrekker history, most Voertrekkers believed that their color prejudice was born in that bloody cauldron of civil war. But planetary historians were well aware that Voertrekker prejudice predated the Great Trek to the Luyten system. The Exodus to Luyten had been driven by far more ancient Boer prejudices and by resentment of Earth's refusal to "understand."

In the ancient days before the uprising no Klemmer owned

anything valuable enough to be stolen by rioting kaffirs. But since the Klemmer family's elevation to mynheeren status, attitudes had changed. Voertrekker families who succeeded in escaping the bondage of class tended to regard their elevation as heaven-ordained. In the case of the Klemmers, the cause was more earthy. Otto's ancestor Erich Klemmer, who had led the family out of *lumpenheit,* managed it simply by being accommodating to a Kraalheer provincial governor when that gentleman developed a lust for Erich's quarter-kaffir wife, Mbelli.

Mbelli Klemmer was said to have been one of the great mixed-race beauties of her day. Whether or not she was that, she most certainly was the making of the Klemmers. Thanks to her, a Klemmer, in the person of the Luftkapitan Otto, was now a personal servant of the Voertrekker-Praesident. Klemmer, a rigidly righteous man, accepted slights and whispers about his ancestry with disciplined silence. But his relationships with all kaffirs, even those who served as stewards aboard *Volkenreiter,* were kept cold and formal. Otto Klemmer ran a tight ship and no one could ever say that he was slack in his dealings with kaffirs. The ghost of Mbelli Klemmer bedevilled the airshipman.

Volkenreiter lifted at thirty minutes after noon on a gusty, threatening day. Weather on the Sea of Grass was always uncertain. Seasons changed but little on Voerster. The planet's inclination from the ecliptic was a mere one-and-one-half degrees. Every season brought days of bright sunshine capable of suddenly changing to squalls and tornadoes. Airshipmen and their passengers knew that dirigible travel under the Tropic of Luyten and near the Shieldwall, at the base of which Einsamberg was located, was risky.

Under a sky filled with racing cumulus clouds growing veils of ice crystals to form the familiar anvilheads, *Volkenreiter* lifted off from Lufthaven at Voertrekkerhoem. Airships had been lost on such days, as Otto Klemmer well knew, and the airshipman was not happy at needing to fly *Volkenreiter* shorthanded. Even in good weather, the elevator control required the attention of two strong men. On this flight it had one, the mate, a *lumpe* named Blier from Joburg. The man was burly and strong enough, but the airship's new style-lifting body design tended to make it porpoise in the air even in calm weather. This had to be prevented for comfort as well as safety. Klemmer did not want his passengers frightened or made uncomfortable. He had a reputation for airmanship to uphold and he told Blier so.

As the airship rose into the gusty winds, Klemmer, standing at the helm and throttles, headed her east, away from Voetrek-kerhoem, and advanced the engine speed. Ahead, at some fifty kilometers, Klemmer could make out a pod of thunderstorms. Individuals now, they were swiftly being marshalled into a line of squalls by the winds that blew unopposed across the Sea of Grass.

Klemmer turned to a more northerly heading, hoping to flank the storm line.

"Nasty looking buggers," Blier said from his post at the elevator wheel. "Can we get 'round them, Luftkapitan?"

"Certainly. Watch your height, Blier."

Klemmer measured the distance to the parturient squall line with his practiced eye and then studied the airspeed indicator. *Volkenreiter* was making about ninety kilometers per hour and her speed was slowly rising. Her best cruise was 105 KPH, but it would take her fifteen minutes to reach it. It seemed unlikely that it was going to be possible to avoid all of the turbulence and rain ahead. As if to emphasize that point, *Volkenreiter* shouldered into several severe downdrafts that staggered captain and mate. He hoped his passengers were not frightened by the turbulence, but he could not leave the helm to make his customary tour of the main salon. This was a damnable journey in the making, Klemmer thought.

But, his *hohen schule* tutors had taught him, if there were two characteristics that set Voertrekkers apart from all other colonials, it was respect for one's betters and a dogged devotion to duty. Otto Klemmer gripped the helm with hands impeccably gloved in gray leather and drove his ship toward the distant storms. *Volkenreiter* climbed steadily into the windy, cloud-dappled sky.

In the forward salon of the gondola, Broni Ehrengraf Voerster, dressed in leather flying clothes and wrapped in a thickly woven blanket, sat as close to the windows as she could get. Black Clavius stood at the back of her chair.

"Look at the sky, Clavius. Isn't it beautiful?"

Broni turned to look up at Clavius, her pallid face alight with excitement. As if to support her contention, the white sunlight of Luyten shone through breaks in the clouds with what looked like a shower of spears. The wind kept the clouds in swift motion so that *Volkenreiter* climbed through the spearshaft rain, one moment in bright sunlight, the next in twilight. To the east, on the swirling surface of the Sea of Grass, the airship's shadow raced across the ground, appearing in the light, vanishing in the shadows of the swiftly moving clouds. Broni was fascinated by it.

"The shadow, Clavius. It keeps pace with us like a spirit. Do you suppose machines like *Volkenreiter* have souls, Clavius?"

"If God chooses, mynheera Broni," Clavius said gently.

"God?" Broni murmured.

" 'Who covereth the heavens with clouds? Who prepareth rain for the earth, who maketh grass to grow upon the mountains?' "

"That is very beautiful and I do not mean to doubt you, Clavius," Broni said, her eyes still fixed on the swift shadow far below. "But I wonder about God sometimes."

"So do I, child," the black man said. "So do I."

In the rear of the salon, where she sat in conversation with the Healer and a very nervous Osbertus Kloster, Eliana heard the exchange and felt a hand squeeze her heart. Broni's courage represented the best of the Voertrekker heritage. Just as her father's insensitive stubbornness represented the worst.

Of one thing Eliana was now certain. There was nothing she would not do, no line she would not cross, to force the creatures aboard the Goldenwing to save her daughter.

———

When Ian returned from Windhoek, weary and expecting the comforts of home, he would be furious to hear that she had taken not only Broni, but Clavius and Osbertus to sanctuary at Einsamberg.

Two of Eliana's kaffir servants, a man named Bol and a woman named Star, entered the salon and began to set a table with provisions from large wicker picnic baskets. Fruits, cheeses, pastries. Voertrekker appetites were robust because the foods of Voerster hadn't the same nutritional value as the victuals of Earth. What meat was eaten came mainly from the stock descended from the animals brought along with the colonists by the Goldenwing *Milagro*.

Bol presented the wine bottle for Eliana's inspection. She had never tasted a proper wine, and she knew it. There had been some wines of South Africa on the *Milagro*, but all that remained of them were a few bottles in museums in Pretoria and Voersterstaad. The climate of Voerster was too severe for good wine grapes. But she nodded in approval, glad of the interruption.

The two men with her were not pillars of strength, but they would have to do. *At least,* she thought, *they are loyal and they care for Broni.*

Bol poured the cold wine into thin crystal goblets which had been made before the Rebellion and were therefore priceless. Voertrekker life was filled with the reverent use of old things, the most valuable being things brought from Old Earth, from *Home*, though Voertrekkers seldom called it that any longer.

Osbertus tasted the pale red vintage and said, "An Ehrengraf Mountain. How fine, Cousin. It isn't something we get often nowadays."

"There is very little left," Eliana said sipping her own. "This is a very special occasion, Osbertus." She raised the glass and said, "To a family rebellion."

Tiegen Roark looked uneasy. He lifted his glass and drank. Buele appeared from the main cabin. His spiky hair had been pomaded by Osbertus in an effort to make him presentable. The attempt was only marginally successful. But Buele was trembling with excitement. He had never before ridden in an airship.

Osbertus asked, "Has Star given you your lunch?"

"Who can eat, Brother? We are *flying!*"

"Come look, Buele," Eliana said. "You can see the mountains very clearly from up here," and she made room for the boy near the window.

"They have *snow* on them, Sister."

"There is always snow on the Shieldwall."

"Is Winter there?" The boy regarded her intently.

"Yes, Buele," Eliana said evenly. "It is always winter there."

Tiegen Roark looked startled. Was the half-wit actually talking about a season or was he somehow speaking of Winter Kraal, and Broni's threatened future? How could he know what Eliana, herself, did not know?

"May I go up and watch the airmen, brother?" Buele looked to Osbertus Kloster.

"Yes. But don't make a nuisance of yourself. Touch nothing." Buele danced away and swarmed up the ladder to the flight deck.

"'Brother'? 'Sister'?" Tiegen Roark looked as though he had noticed a bad smell.

"It's a long story," Osbertus said. "Some other time, Healer."

Outside, and slanting away in the moist high air, a flight of lizard-birds, close cognates to the legendary archeopteryx of Earth, banked sharply away from the oncoming dirigible and vanished behind and below. The once-distant line of thunder squalls was no longer so distant. Osbertus Kloster said, "Those look ominous, mynheera. I had better recommend to the Luft-kapitan that we climb above them."

Eliana glanced at a brass altimeter fixed to the salon wall for the edification of the dirigible's passengers. "We are already at thirty-five hundred meters, Cousin," she said. "Higher might be dangerous for Broni. Tell the captain to find a way around them."

Osbertus exchanged worried glances with Tiegen Roark and stood up. As he passed Broni and Black Clavius, he heard the girl say, "But is it more beautiful than this in space?"

"The stars shine more brightly," Clavius said.

Osbertus heaved himself up the steep ladder into the flight deck. Buele was watching intently the labor of Airshipman Blier on the elevator wheel. Osbertus could see that the elevator man was perspiring with his efforts to keep the dirigible on an even keel.

Luftkapitan Klemmer stood at the helm, steering a steady course to Einsamberg, beyond the line of squalls.

"Luftkapitan," Osbertus said, holding on to the brass rail that ran the full perimeter of the flight deck under the broad windows. "The line squalls—"

Klemmer, his face flushed with the effort of flying *Cloud Rider* undermanned, said testily, "I see the storms, Mynheer Astronomer-Select. We shall climb above them."

"That is what I came to say," Osbertus said, hurt by Klemmer's impolite abruptness. "The mynheera Eliana instructs me to tell you to find a way through or around them. Any more altitude might be harmful to the Voertrekkersdatter."

Klemmer's already thin lips grew thinner. He was tempted to say, "Falling to the ground in a ripped apart airship would probably be even more harmful." But one did not speak to the mynheera Eliana Ehrengraf's messenger in that manner. "Very well, Astronomer-Select," he said. In the many fine gradations of interpersonal address among Voertrekkers, to use one's title without the honorific "Mynheer" was a slight, as though one were addressing a mere purveyor of goods or services.

Osbertus looked wounded but he retreated in good order. The captain, no less than Obertus, was clearly worried. And not mainly about the weather. Perhaps he was just now remembering that he never before had flown the Voertrekker-Praesident's women to Einsamberg or anywhere else without direct and written authorization.

Ian will be raging, Osbertus thought. And then, through his fear and misgivings shot a single bright ray of satisfaction. For once in his sedentary, ordinary, pampered life Osbertus Louis Eugen Kloster was behaving like a hero.

———

16

FIRST ORBIT

Glory, in low orbit, swept across Voerster's sky from northwest to southeast. The light of the Luyten sun reflected through and from a deck of broken clouds above the vast stretches of the Great Western Ocean. Duncan Kr regarded the vast sea with a touch of nostalgia for Thalassa. But where Thalassa's sea was ever turbulent and angry green, Voerster's Great Western Ocean was streaked with turquoise shallows and cobalt depths. From latitude 10 degrees north to 10 south the sea displayed the tops of immense underwater forests of kelplike plants that contributed to the oxygen in Voerster's atmosphere. A severe planet, Duncan thought, but not a cruel one.

Glory's rigging glowed with St. Elmo's fire as the orbital track cut the lines of Planet Voerster's magnetic field. It was a sight that never failed to awe Duncan. An incredibly beautiful aurora danced and shimmered along the monofilament stays and halyards, leaping spaces, racing up a brace to flash across to a sheet or halyard and down the slender shaft of a mast.

Duncan Kr was Wired, but sitting on the edge of his pod for a real-time view of the scintillating display. From where he sat, he could observe Anya Amaya's spacemanship with a Master and Commander's critical eye. *Glory*'s Sailing Master was the finest instinctive ship-handler Duncan had ever known. She ordinarily sailed the Goldenwing as though the vast spread of skylar were the Bermudan rig of a light-yacht.

But since her near death in space, she had grown more cautious, less free and instinctive with her helmsmanship.

Though *Glory* still responded to her touch like a lover, the computer now made allowances for her hesitations.

When Duncan discussed this with Dietr Krieg, the physician said, "How fanciful you are, Duncan. Amaya is only a woman. And *Glory* is only a ship, after all, doing what it was built to do. A machine."

True enough, Duncan thought. But if it came to that, how did one define "machine"? Did the clipper-ship captains of Earth often remind themselves that their tall ships were only wood and canvas? Duncan thought not. In his personal compartment he kept a tiny gem of a model clipper in a bottle. A tiny *Cutty Sark*. The original, named for a witch in the poet Burns' *Tam O'Shanter*, was a vessel that had made the swift passage around Cape Horn from Europe to the Pacific coast of America many downtime centuries ago. The model-maker, a septuagenarian handicapped sailor-turned-colonist on Nixon, a desert planet in the Wolf Stars, was ten uptime years dead by now, and forgotten by his fellow colonists. But Duncan remembered and honored him for the memory he had preserved so lovingly inside an ancient liquor bottle.

Were machines only objects—things? Or were they precious cells of a vast universal reality with as much claim to "life" as any other organism?

From time to time, when his mind was most alert and his natural empathy stimulated by the drogue, Duncan could intercept and interpret the emotional auras of the others aboard *Glory*. At such times he could feel what they felt, and share their view of the ship they served. Dietr Krieg was ever skeptical, but deep within his personality he, too, carried a need for the reality *Glory* represented. Damon and Anya loved *Glory* as wholeheartedly as did Duncan himself.

Mira's reality was fascinating, and the most uncomplicated. The cat experienced *Glory* as the "great-queen-cat-who-is-not-alive." That was the nearest Duncan could render the alien and immensely aware thought. He found it remarkable and humbling that Mira's cat brain did not trouble her with human-created distinctions between the living and the solely sentient—the very distinctions that Duncan's own anthropoid mind insisted upon making.

Duncan suspected that mankind had never been completely at home in the true universe. Little wonder that when humanity's australopithecine forebears finally dared to venture onto the savannahs of Gondwana, Mira's ancestors had often made a meal of them.

He looked out at the gleaming golden sails reflecting the planet below. If *Glory* was *not* alive at such moments as these, then the whole idea of life needed to be winnowed to exclude the grand, the marvelous, and the beautiful.

Anya, lying in a full sailing coma in her pod, stared at nothing (and everything) with empty eyes. She lay atop the glyceroid, rather than in it, because the changes in *Glory*'s delta-V could now be measured in millimeters per second. When Anya sailed into a low-orbit injection the resulting flight path was so secure that *Glory* could orbit the planet for ten thousand years and never graze the atmosphere. Even with her silent fear, Anya was that good.

She was clothed. It wasn't her way. But the incident with Jean Marq had chilled her ordinarily open sexuality.

Through the computer Duncan could sense Jean in the cargo bay, preparing the panniers that contained the refrigerated cargo, and the mules to move them. The inhabitants of Voerster would probably be delighted to receive what had been ordered long ago. But the computer had created a synthesis from the known history of Voerster and the torrent of information sent by Osbertus Kloster, the astronomer at Sternberg.

The Voertrekker below would be appalled, Duncan thought, if he knew what, in his babbling eagerness to acquaint the syndicate with the nature of his world, he had told *Glory*'s computer. The Voertrekker society of Planet Voerster was damned. It had lived for a thousand years without change. Its technology advanced slowly or not at all. Challenges were met with methods that had been out-of-date when Goldenwing *Milagro* left orbit around Earth's moon.

A colony based on the old and bitter ethic of apartheid would have had a difficult time surviving under Voersterian conditions. Though not a killing world, Voerster challenged men so severely that survival required an enormous altruism. A group that had carried with it from Earth all the buried hatreds and prejudices, *and* the victims of those hatreds, contained the seeds of suicide.

Some of Voerster's history was in *Glory*'s data banks, filed there when a *Glory* syndicate had scheduled the voyage purchased from *Nostromo*'s people, who had accepted the purchases made a downtime generation ago on Voerster. Duncan had studied the history files as he was tasked to do by the compact of *Glory*'s syndicate. The picture of Voerster that emerged was not an engaging one.

It may well have been true, Duncan thought, that Bol-Derek Voerster had fully intended to deal fairly with the kaffir laborers who had shared cold-sleep with the First Landers. The syndicate of the *Nostromo* had thought so, and noted its opinion in the appropriate computer files. But Bol-Derek Voerster never lived to see the Voertrekkers' promised land, and from that moment Voerster, as a human colony, was moribund.

The Voertrekkers' world wasn't in danger of collapse tomorrow or the next day, but Duncan Kr knew that when *Glory* came this way again, perhaps a hundred downtime years from now, Voerster would be a barbarian world. On Old Earth, pacifists had preached damnation for those who carried the contagion of war and racial strife to the stars. Those ancients in their sackcloth and ashes had little known how right they would turn out to be.

Duncan urged himself to think less depressing thoughts. For a time at least, the goods *Glory* brought to Voerster would raise the spirits of the colonists. After centuries without, within a Voersterian year there would again be a surfeit of Earth animals in the kraals of the single large landmass that was rising out of the east. The green-and-brown continent was a grassland, Duncan noted.

It was easy to understand how the Voertrekkers had abandoned their high-tech society after the race war to live as ranchers and farmers. There would be trout and bass in the few turbulent streams and rivers, and there would be a repetition of the natural conflicts between the imported animals and the native necrogenes. According to what Anya had been told by the downworld astronomer with the radio dishes, the Faculty of Husbandry in the single university on Voerster assumed that the Earth animals (being more biologically sophisticated) would overbear the native necrogenes. Such an outcome had been predicted before the disruption of the Rebellion, and it was the outcome expected now.

But, *Glory*'s demographic-ecological program predicted, that was unlikely to be. The necrogenes' terrible manner of reproduction kept the animals of Voerster in balance with their environment. The placental mammals from Earth would inevitably overreproduce and eat themselves out of the Voersterian ecosystem. In a hundred of the planet's long years, it would be as if the beasts from Earth had never come to Luyten 726/4.

But for now *Glory*'s cargo would gladden the hearts of Voertrekker and kaffir alike. The colonists would probably derive more benefit from the technology of the packaging protecting the frozen near-born. In addition to a thousand assorted domestic animals, each pannier contained a low-power nuclear module that, extracted from its pannier, could refrigerate food for a town, or used in another way, could generate electric power for a small city. Each embryo was protected by an individually powered capsule that could cool or warm a kraal for a year. And there were thirty panniers of animal embryos in the hold for Voerster. Such serendipitous benefits explained why the inhabitants of the planets of near space had created almost a Cargo Cult around the Goldenwings.

Anya Amaya sighed and lifted herself to float weightlessly above the glyceroid bed with a tiny pressure of her fingertips. She wore a black skinsuit which matched the glossy ebony of her hair. Since the affray in the rigging, Anya had taken to wearing it in a severe helmet-coif that she mistakenly thought reduced her sexual appeal.

Glory's computer declared: *"Orbital injection complete."* And then, almost immediately: *"Orbital parameters are 221 kilometers by 218 kilometers. Orbital period is 97 minutes 12 seconds."*

A near-perfect injection, Duncan noted. It was, actually, a maneuver comparable to docking a clipper ship by wind power alone, without smashing the pier.

"Well done," Duncan said. Overhead, through the transparency at the curve of the bridge, could be seen the last movements of the subtle evolution: The few sails still drawing were being rolled into their housings within the masts and yards. Eventually, only a few small jibs and spankers would remain flying to catch the photon streams from Luyten 726 and keep *Glory* locked in orbit.

Glory orbited upside down in relation to the bright mass of Voerster. *Glory* presently was sweeping over the vast, blue-green wasteland of saltwater known as the Sea of Storms. Cloud patterns made silver-white swirls above the empty sea. As the horizon rolled nearer, a low coastline could be seen that gradually took the shape of a continent consisting mainly of grass plains. The feature called the Planetia was a long, narrow highlands separated from the lowlands by a continent-long wall of eroded, nearly vertical cliffs. Duncan had absorbed the geography of Planet Voerster from *Glory*, but seeing the actual thing was daunting. The Shieldwall averaged slightly under ten kilometers in height.

In the north, the Planetia abutted the Northern Ice, the polar cap. At the extreme east and west, where the seas were ice-free, the Planetia rose sheer from surf to the heights. The Sea of Grass, which covered most of the continent, ended in the south at the equator in a long, empty coastline of marshes and river deltas. A barren isthmus extruded itself from the southeastern coast of the Grassersee, joining a narrow, steep, and rocky spine of land, the Sabercut Peninsula, where the Voertrekkers kept their gulag.

———

It went without saying, Duncan thought, that the colonists of Voerster would have such a place. In silence, and basking wickedly in the chill breath of the Southern Ice, it spoke volumes.

Duncan returned his attention to the planet. Cloud patterns shifted; in a number of places storms were troubling the Sea of Grass. The Planetia, Duncan estimated, had a median altitude above sea level of nine thousand five hundred meters. In the old measurement still used some places on Earth, that was 31,960 feet. The atmosphere of Voerster was more oxygen-rich than that of the homeworld, making the Planetia habitable, but only just. Could people descended from Earth colonists actually survive in such a place? Duncan wondered. Evidently they could, and did. The *Nostromo* syndics had found it fascinating that the ancestors of the high-plains dwellers, Voertrekker and kaffir alike, had been genetically engineered to live in the heights by what the *Nostromo* people thought was an intrusive society even in its best pre-Rebellion days.

The Planetia had been settled at a much later date than had the Grassersee. After First Landing, two hundred Voertrekker families had divided the grasslands among themselves. The men and women sent to the Planetia had been poor Voertrekkers, some *lumpen*, and kaffirs—all bred for the bitter environment at the roof of the world. Duncan, wise in the ways of human societies, suspected that the Highlanders were not a loveable people.

Storms swept the Sea of Grass near the Shieldwall. Accompanying one particularly violent line of thundersqualls Duncan could see a half dozen tornadoes stalking like tall giants across the empty grasslands.

The Goldenwing passed over the Shieldwall and high above the grasslands to the eastern coast in a matter of a dozen minutes. From this height, and with the sunlight vanishing, it was possible to look down and discern the two principal cities of Voerster's east coat, Port Elizabeth and Pretoria. A few smears of civilization, none of them grand, betrayed the presence of Mankind on the Grassersee.

Glory swept onward, high above the darkening eastern limb of the sea.

"It is quite a pretty world," Anya said.

Duncan, wakened from his reverie, realized that he had been watching the planet for an hour.

Anya was out of her pod, sitting on the edge of it, still Wired, but fully human now.

Duncan said, "One might imagine living in such a place, growing up on plains of grass." He smiled quietly. "Is New Earth like that?"

"Enn-Eee is a tight, nasty world." Anya's dark eyes were fixed on the sight overhead. *"That's all I can remember about it."*

Voerster was not completely dark. There was a powerful zodiacal light in the Luyten 726 system, and the stars shone in profusion. "But how odd to live without at least one visible moon," Anya said. On her homeworld, four large satellites illuminated the night sky.

Duncan turned to study the readouts crossing the computer's visual interface. *Glory* was producing a proper almanac of Voerster: Gravity 0.9981 Earth Normal, pressure at sea level 1978.436 millibars. On the high tableland mean pressure was 953.112 millibars. The average temperature in the lowlands was 291.48 degrees Kelvin; on the high plateau almost nineteen degrees less. "Life must be hell on that high plateau we crossed," Duncan said thoughtfully. "I wonder how many colonists have endured it, and how many are still there?"

Anya drifted over to Duncan's pod and steadied herself with a hand on his shoulder. "Mutants live there. Or so my old astronomer claims." Mutants was not a word Goldenwing syndics used lightly. The danger of stellar flares and radiation was never far from their minds.

Anya felt Duncan's restlessness through the drogue. *"Are you going downworld?"*

"We all should. There is Han Soo to be put to rest."

"Those racist bastards down there won't like it. I think they have forgotten that there are other races but Caucasian and black."

"Nevertheless."

She made no immediate reply. Anya was no longer completely at ease with Duncan. She missed sexual relations with him. The boy Damon was physically fine, but Duncan Kr was a man.

"You want to go ashore, don't you, Duncan?" she said. As she spoke she removed her drogue, a subconscious admission she did not want Duncan to receive her emotional emissions clearly.

He said, "I haven't been ashore since Aldrin." That had been two years ago uptime. No need to belabor the point, the girl thought. She understood. He wanted a woman. Any woman, as long as she was different from Anya Amaya. Voertrekkers were pale and blonde with great white breasts and broad hips. She turned away, frowning.

Damon called from the communications shack: "Message from Voersterstaad, Duncan."

"Put it on interphone."

"'The landing area at Voersterstaad will be clear in 100 hours. Your lighters have only to signal their approach and if needed we will supply lighting.' That comes direct from Voersterstaad, Duncan. Not from Sternberg."

"Thank you, Damon. Anything more about requesting a physician?"

"No, Duncan."

Anya said abruptly, "I'll stand the anchor watch on board." And she launched herself into a transit tube without further talk.

It was odd, but perhaps understandable, that Goldenwing syndicates laced their talk with the archaic expressions of the Age of Sail. An arrival was often a "landfall." The great Coriolis streams of tachyons swirling out of the galactic center were often spoken of as "the Trades." And, of course, downworld was "ashore." Do we do that to keep an anchor firmly fixed in the shingle of our human past? Duncan wondered. We become so nearly creatures of space, beings who live without dimensions. Perhaps we require a vivid set of memories—memories of blue water and blue skies—to keep us fully human.

He looked after Anya and smiled ruefully. The Sailing Master was human enough, he thought. We all need shoretime, Duncan thought. I will take her ashore with me.

He set the interface on standby and detached his drogue. One last glance at the orbital parameters—out of habit, not necessity—and he launched himself into the tube leading to the cargo holds, where Jean Marq was working.

17

THE FONTEINS OF WINTER

The man riding the lead animal was even larger than most men of the Planetia, where huge genotypes were the rule. He bore university duelling scars, not on one cheek, but both, as if in his student days he had developed a taste for pain and self-disfigurement.

Eigen Fontein had, in fact, killed a fellow student duellist at Pretoria, and only his Kraalheer family connections had saved him from a term of imprisonment south of the Isthmus. Eigen, the elder son of Vikter Fontein, had been formidable from the age of eight when, upon the birth of his brother Georg, he learned that primogeniture was no assurance of a heritage on the Planetia.

At nine Eigen was nearly killed on an unauthorized climb of the Blue Glacier. At eleven he raped his first kaffir girl, and at thirteen, on a pleasure jaunt to Grimsel, his first *lumpe*. And at twenty, in university at Pretoria, he killed in his first duel.

Georg, the younger Fontein, hated his brother with a passion, but the pair were inseparable. It was whispered in the deep warrens of Winter Kraal that Georg ran with his sibling hoping one day to urge him to disaster. The possibility was ever present. Eigen blustered his way through one quixotic challenge after another.

The one passion the brothers shared was hunting the giant mountain cheet. They had, almost alone, hunted the catlike carnivore to near extinction in the Grimsel Mountains, a range of jagged ridges that formed part of the eastern Shieldwall.

On Voerster a Kraalheer once had held a position similar to

the *daimyo* of Earth's ancient Japan—feudal lord at the pleasure of the serving Voertrekker-Praesident: landlord and planter, rancher and cattle baron. The folk of the highlands were well aware of their history. They had been poor relations at First Landing, then experimental animals during the high-tech years before the Rebellion. But settling them on the plateau, an act of Voertrekker expediency, saved them from many of the depredations of the Rebellion. The kaffirs delegated to form their highland labor force were genetically engineered for the Planetia in the same way as were the mynheeren. Thus when the race war began, the kaffirs of the Planetia felt very little kinship with their siblings of the Grassersee townships.

There was war in the highlands, but it was a desultory matter. The kaffirs still lived on the Voertrekkers' kraals as they had in the old days in the lowlands. They seldom accompanied their whites on incursions of the lowlands. One *Nostromo* syndic-commentator, the shipmaster, attributed this to loyalty. Another, the *Nostromo*'s surgeon, scoffed at the idea. "The highland kaffir on Voerster," he wrote into the database, "is as violent and capricious as the high country Kraalheer. Within a dozen generations Planetian society will not exist." To which *Nostromo*'s Rigger, who had apparently spent some weeks downworld during Nostromo's call, added a postscriptum: *"Nor will the convocation of bigots in the Sea of Grass."*

For a dozen generations Kraalheeren of the Planetia had tried to breed beasts known to the colonists as hornheads, a moss-and-lichen-eating ruminant resembling an Earth buffalo. The effort had failed. The hornheads being native necrogenes, no gravid female ever survived parturition. Herds multiplied slowly or not at all, and the meat was tough and unpalatable. Riding beasts were another matter. The faux horses were rodent-cognates and were born in litters, thus becoming numerous enough to make husbandry worthwhile. But the riding beasts did not thrive in the heights, thus giving the Kraalheeren of the Planetia excuse to lust after the acres of lush grassland to be found in the plains below.

With the spread across the Grassersee of homesteaders and small farmers, the age of the Kraalheer in the lowlands was ending. But on the Planetia the Kraalheeren were supreme.

It was Ian Voerster's intention to see to it that their power grew no greater. The independence movement in the high country was an intolerable threat. The instrument of his intention was to be the Fonteins.

The Fontein brothers and their troop of *lumpen* followers had descended to the village of Grimsel by way of the Grimsel Pass Funicular Railway, an engineering marvel whose completion had left Voerster financially exhausted for a generation. The railway reached almost to the Sea of Grass, but not quite. The settlement of Grimsel, in the moraine left by the retreat of the Blue Glacier, supported no more than two thousand souls, an eighth Voertrekker, a half *lumpen*, and the remainder kaffirs.

This was why Eigen Fontein, who had a well-developed taste for kaffir females, always began his hunting excursions in Grimsel.

It was rumored that there was platinum-bearing ore in the Grimsel range, but no one had ever found any. Yet the stories drew *lumpen* and impoverished, hopeful Voertrekkers from as far away as Pretoria and Voersterstaad.

It was customary for Planetians descending the Shieldwall to linger several days in Grimsel, becoming accustomed to the greater air pressure and humidity of the lowlands, before continuing their journeys to Voersterstaad or Pretoria by airship. Temperatures above freezing were rare in the highlands, and on summer days when the mean temperature of Grimsel was in the forties Celsius, Highlanders complained bitterly of the heat. They were a sullen lot, given to fighting among themselves and complaining about the differences in hardships endured by "High Voertrekkers" and flatlanders.

Airships avoided the high plateau. They were limited by their pressure altitude—the height at which the gas in the envelope expanded to the point of requiring a release of volume—in a place where no helium was available for replacement. Rarely, perhaps once in every dozen years, the Staadluftflot and the Society for Planetary Studies sponsored an aerial expedition to the Planetia, and even to the Blue Glacier and the Northern Ice. These expeditions regularly killed adventurous young Voertrek-kers and required the rescuing of others. Any lowlanders rescued from the Ice by a team of High Voertrekkers never forgot it. Were never *allowed* to forget it. Courage and bravado (as well as foolhardiness and brutality) were the stuff of life above the Shieldwall.

When the Fonteins and their hunter-marauder posse of Winter Kraal *lumpen* alighted from the funicular, they immediately did as they always did in Grimsel. They hired kaffir whores and *lumpen* whores, too, for those who favored them, and proceeded to "tree the town."

The source of the expression was Old Earth's western America and it remained in favor in towns such as Grimsel, despite the fact that most of the inhabitants had never seen a tree and others had never before seen a town.

It became immediately apparent to the people of Grimsel that the Fonteins were on hand for more than hunting and whoring. The high-country *lumpen* got drunk and made a quantity of loose talk. What they said was that Eigen had it in his mind to "take a bite of the Grassersee." Some feared that he meant Grimsel, which was technically (if not actually) a part of the Sea of Grass. Others said he meant something different. The Voerster's spies listened.

No one in Grimsel had dared ask a Fontein of Winter what sort of hunt he intended in the lowlands that required so many armed men. But the stablekeeper reported that Mynheer Fontein had been heard to say that he had descended from the plateau "to claim Einsamberg." Not from the Ehrengrafs, to whom it belonged, but from his *father*, the Kraalheer of Winter. This shocked the liveryman's listeners. The mountain lands to the west and south of Grimsel had been the holding of the Ehrengraf

clan since soon after Landing Day. The estate was seldom visited
by any member of the family, but was always kept in readiness
by a staff of kaffirs who were, by any standard shabby Grimsel
knew, uncommonly loyal to the Kraalheer family who owned
Einsamberg and the Einsamtal Valley.

The Ehrengrafs, everyone knew, were kaffir-lovers dating
from the days of the Rebellion. Whatever Eigen Fontein had in
mind for property belonging to kaffir-loving lowland aristocrats
was no concern of Grimsel's. But right was right, and no Fontein,
son *or* father, had any rightful claim to the old estate.

In stormy, near-freezing weather—it had snowed the night
before the arrival of the Fonteins, and there was still ice in the
ravines—the Winter men rode out. They were dressed in homespun shirts and trousers, hornhead leather back-and-breastplates,
ebray leather boots, broad hats with the brim pinned up with the
kraal badge (a giant cheet killing a hornhead), and great blunderbuss shotguns across their backs.

No one asked any questions. The leader's demeanor did not
encourage familiarity. The people of Grimsel saw the Fonteins
depart and were well pleased to see them go. Of course, there
were rumors. Rumors and gossip were all that made life in
Grimsel bearable.

The only man with any knowledge of the law in Grimsel was
the brewer, a quondam solicitor who had come to the hills
seeking gold many years ago and stayed to make beer. The
lawyer-turned-brewer contended that Einsamberg was protected
by a First Lander's Portion writ, and that therefore it was not
Voertrekker-Praesident Ian Voerster's to give, but the property of
his wife, the kraalheera Eliana Ehrengraf. The subject was discussed over the brewer's barrels. But it was soon forgotten. The
people of Grimsel were, for the most part, disappointed prospec-
tors, crippled miners, and unemployed funicular railroad men.
They had a short attention span. And they had little interest in
politics and none whatever in the intrigues of Voertrekkerhoem,
a quasi-legendary kraal on the shore of the Great Southern Ocean
far, far from Grimsel.

18

STORM

It was late afternoon when Luftkapitan Klemmer gave up the attempt to guide *Volkenreiter* around the now fully developed line of thundersqualls. The sun had vanished behind a low bank of clouds over the western horizon; lightning flashed angrily within the thunder cells ahead. At this stage, even without considering the risk to the Voertrekkersdatter, it was impossible to overfly the cold front. The anvilheads topping the cumulonimbus clouds reached high into the tropopause, well above *Volkenreiter*'s service ceiling.

Klemmer cursed himself for allowing pride of airmanship to overbear his natural caution. Behind the turbulence-buffeted dirigible, a fast-moving occlusion had formed still another rank of thunderheads. It was on to Einsamberg or nothing; a return was no longer possible.

The dappled afternoon sunlight through which the airship had been flying was swiftly squeezed into a narrow avenue pointed straight at the only gap Klemmer could see in the line of squalls ahead. The air darkened, the temperature dropped a dozen degrees and the slowly rising ground of the Grimsel's foothills vanished. *Volkenreiter* flew through a turbid sea of gray and black, her frames groaning complaints each time she struck turbulence.

Klemmer reached for a speaking tube and shouted to the passengers in the salon to be seated and strap down. He gave his command in the confident manner expected of a servant of the Voertrekker-Praesident's family, informing the passengers that *Volkenreiter*'s passage through "some rain showers" would be "bumpy, but quite safe and speedy."

With these assurances, he steered *Volkenreiter* into the now all-but-nonexistent gap between two thunderhead clouds. Ten minutes later, inside a fast-moving squall, Otto Klemmer grew genuinely concerned. A severe encounter with a vertical gust within the storm tore a long strip of fabric from the ventral surface of the lifting body, and it snapped and writhed in the relative wind like a giant's pennant. Hail battered the ship. The resulting noise made it sound as though *Volkenreiter* were being pelted with rocks.

Small hailstones were caught in the violent updrafts and lifted into freezing air where they accumulated layers of ice. By the time they fell and struck *Volkenreiter*'s fabric skin they had grown as large as a man's clenched fist, and they made the airship reverberate like a drum.

Volkenreiter's altitude varied with the turbulence. Klemmer could not leave the helm and Blier, on the elevator control, was sweating heavily with the exertion of holding altitude. Hidden below the undercast lay the rising terrain of the Grimsel Mountains. Within minutes the dirigible was flying blindly over the unseen first range of crags, sharp as cheet's teeth.

Luftkapitan Klemmer felt the undignified sweat of apprehension soaking through the serge of his best uniform. The cabin temperatures hovered near to eleven degrees Celsius, only a degree or two warmer than the outside air. Klemmer followed the feeble light, knowing that to allow *Volkenreiter* to penetrate to the heart of a thunderhead was to risk destruction. Klemmer had never lost a ship and he had no intention of losing this one, not ever, and most particularly while The Voerster's wife and only child were aboard.

The suggestion of an opening in the squall line showed ahead through the rime-coated glass of the control deck. But the turbulence refused to abate. Blier was swearing at the effort needed to do his job. He was glaring at Buele, who had not returned to the salon, and sat braced between the navigation table and a bulkhead. Klemmer saw, to his annoyance, that the half-wit was grinning, actually enjoying the tumult and uproar of the storm. He probably never once imagined that his worthless *lumpe* life might be in danger.

"Here, boy, Bol damn you," Blier shouted. "Come help me with this elevator wheel."

For a moment, the Luftkapitan was tempted to countermand Blier's order. It was not fitting that a child, and a half-witted one at that, be pressed into service to help fly the pride of the airship fleet. But when Klemmer measured Blier's condition, he decided against intervening. Buele might be simpleminded, but he seemed to have a knack for the way things worked, and he was certainly strong enough to help Blier, who was tiring fast.

Buele leaped to the elevator wheel, grinning like a kaffir mask. Klemmer shuddered. At home, atop the clavichord (which no one in the household could play) there stood a toothy hornhead bone carving of Oya, the kaffir god of death. Mynheera Klemmer collected kaffir art, cluttering the house with ugly, primitive images. There was the Earth Mother Mandela, a female with upraised clenched fist and enormous breasts; Nampa, Tutu, and Chaka, the warriors of Angatch, the god of all gods; and there were other, unidentifiable images as old as the colony and perhaps older. Their antiquity should have made them pricey, but Voertrekkers assigned little value to such kaffir things. Helga Klemmer was an exception. She was devoted to her hobby. The captain hated it. The figure of Oya was forever surfacing in his nightmares. Was it, he often wondered, his drop of kaffir blood that made him prey to such superstitious nonsense?

He snapped at Buele to stop his grinning. "This is serious business, boy."

Matters grew more serious by the minute. The patch of lightness ahead had vanished in the murk. It was replaced suddenly and violently by repeated blue flashes of lightning. The air became pungent with ozone. The lightning bolts, made brilliant by Voerster's oxygen-rich air, had passed perilously close to *Volkenreiter*. Blier stared at the captain in terror. Lightning was the airship killer. A strike on an aircraft carrying tanks of compressed hydrogen fuel could explode it into flaming rags and plunging bodies.

"*Turn back, Luftkapitan,*" Blier shouted hoarsely. "*We will never get through.*"

"Get hold of yourself, man. And watch our altitude," Klemmer said severely.

Volkenreiter droned deeper into the line of storm. They were staggered, like soldiers in an armored phalanx arrayed for battle. Hail clattered against the gondola windows, then strange flashes of brilliant light from the setting sun struck the cloud banks, turning them to amber. The amber alternated with periods of murky darkness.

For an instant the airship emerged into clear air in a deep ravine between two boiling, silver-white cumulus clouds rising up, up, until their tops were shredded and frozen by the five-hundred-kilometer-per-hour jetstream at the edge of the stratosphere.

It was a scene of unreal and dreadful beauty, but Otto Klemmer was aware only of the need to find a safe path between the two silver-white cliffs. His wet shirt felt cold and clammy against his chin under the heavy Luftschifflot uniform. Buele still had that foolish, skullish grin. He had remained constant while Blier had not. Otto Klemmer shivered, gripped the helm more tightly, and flew on.

In the salon below, Broni spread her hands on the glass and looked with awe at the vast canyon of cloud and sky through which *Cloud Rider* flew. She shivered with delight as repeated bolts of electric blue lightning flashed in the cloud-cliffs on either side of the dirigible.

The clouds looked as solid as the Northern Ice. It seemed to the girl that if she could reach so far, she might take a handful of silvery white light from the cliffside and hold it in her fingers.

Black Clavius, standing near her still, watched her joy with a deep pleasure of his own. Somehow he had been certain that Broni Ehrengraf Voerster would not be afraid. He knew the dirigible was in difficulty. It was such a primitive machine. But it achieved a kind of gallant grace with its soft, whirring flight through these high regions.

"'We set mountains on the earth lest it should move . . . and we made the heaven a roof strongly upholden . . .'"

"Is that from the Christian Bible, Clavius?" Broni asked.

"The Q'ran, child. It, too, is a holy book.'

"This *is* rather frightening, you know—" Broni said.

"Yes?"

"But it is so beautiful that it is hard to be afraid."

He could *feel* the emotions in her. What a strong empath she was. What a wild talent she had. What a waste to give such a spirit a damaged heart. *Lord, you should have done better by her. I am sorry to criticize, but you know it is so.* Ah, Clavius, he thought. You quote Allah's holy book, yet in the same breath you criticize Him. You like to live dangerously, old kaffir.

He glanced at the altimeter on the wall. *Volkenreiter* was flying at two thousand nine hundred meters. High, but still below the mean altitude of the Planetia. One was tempted to say something more to the Lord about poor planning and allocation of resources, but perhaps he had better choose another time to tempt Destiny.

The Wired Man turned to look back at the others in the salon. The Healer looked frightened and slightly airsick. Mynheer the Astronomer-Select simply looked exhausted. Fear did that sometimes. Instead of draining a man's courage, it drained his strength and energy. The fact was that Voertrekkers were not enthusiastic fliers. They had the Rebellion to blame for the state of Voertrekker aviation. But another society would have recovered its aerial skills much more swiftly. Without aviation as a baseline, how would the people of Voerster ever rediscover the arts of space travel? The answer, plain enough, was that they never would.

*

It seemed to the Starman that Eliana, who sat calmly looking out at the storm, was deriving much of the same fearful pleasure from the excesses of nature as Broni.

Volkenreiter, still struggling to keep above a rising floor of mist, rounded into an eastward-running cloud canyon. Luyten had nearly set, but at this height, there was still light in the sky. The interior of the gondola glowed golden. Ahead and to the left, where the mists were solid, *Volkenreiter*'s "glory"—the airship's shadow surrounded by the prismatic rainbow of Luyten's light broken into the spectrum by the moisture in the air—fled along the insubstantial cliff face. Even as they, Clavius and the two women, watched it, the glory vanished as the sun set.

As the golden light disappeared, Eliana was struck by the odd notion that the airship and its passengers were making a mortal passage. After this flight nothing would ever be quite the same again. On pure instinct she glanced at Black Clavius. *You know what I am thinking, Wired One.*

He smiled at her. Like daughter, like mother. If only a syndicate had found you years ago, mynheera The Voerster's consort. What a Starman you would have made.

Otto Klemmer studied the banked instruments before him. *Volkenreiter* was at three thousand meters. Pressure altitude. More height would expand the gas in the lifting cells, making it necessary to valve off helium. And when it came time to descend, the smaller volume of lifting gas combined with the weight of the ice the envelope had accumulated would cause the airship to plummet, and he would have to rely on the release of ballast to stop the fall. It was the eternal airshipman's dilemma. Except that on this flight, *Volkenreiter* carried no ballast.

"Blier," he commanded. "Give me ten degrees nose down."

"Luftkapitan—I don't think we should—"

"Damn you, man. Don't argue with me. We have to descend. We are at pressure altitude."

"We are near Einsamberg," Buele declared abruptly, his mouth still set in its foolish grin.

"How the hell would you know where we are?" Blier said angrily.

The boy tapped his head with a nail-bitten finger. "It is all in here, Brother."

"Don't call me 'brother,' you little *lumpenscheiss!*" Blier yelled fearfully.

"Pay attention to duty!" Otto Klemmer snapped. "Ten degrees down. *Now.*" He retarded the throttles to reduce body lift, and *Volkenreiter* settled, almost wistfully, into the world of darkness under her keel.

Light diminished on the flight deck as the outside world disappeared. Rain streaked the gondola windows and froze there in spiky white shafts. The turbulence began again, more strongly than before. *Volkenreiter* seemed to be striking a series of invisible waves, each of which made the structure creak and groan as the strain was distributed through the dirigible's light frame.

The altimeter unwound slowly through back through two thousand eight hundred meters. Klemmer estimated that the ship's keel was now probably a thousand meters above the level of the ground below. But there were uncharted peaks in the Grimsels well over two thousand five hundred meters above sea level. Tension gripped Klemmer's stomach.

The flight deck was illuminated by an intense electric blue flash as a lightning bolt crackled down nearby. Blier moaned and released the elevator wheel. But the *lumpe* Buele remained at his post, rock steady on the fore-and-aft helm. In spite of himself, Klemmer was impressed.

Volkenreiter penetrated a storm cell and paid an immediate penalty. She was buffeted, bombarded with hailstones, and almost rolled on her beam-ends before Klemmer could restore level flight. He spoke into the tube: "Is everyone all right down there?"

"Can't you find a less athletic path, Luftkapitan?" The thin voice of the Astronomer-Select trembled, but remained controlled.

"Stay belted down, please," Klemmer said. He was amazed at

the calmness of his own voice. An old senior captain had long ago said to him that flying airships was hours of boredom interrupted by moments of sheer terror. It occurred to Klemmer that fliers had probably been saying that for tens of thousands of years in tens of hundreds of places.

The turbulence eased and Klemmer caught a glimpse of what might have been snow-clad rocks below. In Einsamtal, the valley of Einsamberg Kraal, there was snow on the ground for ten months of the year. He glance at Buele. He had done no more than glance at the navigational charts. Was he some sort of navigational genius? There was a name for people like that. *Idiot savant?* One look and something in that elongated, ugly head— some cellular calculating machine kept track forever? Well, the world was filled with wonders.

But at the moment, the only wonder of interest to Otto Klemmer was the wonder of how to get his ship safely through the storm and moored in the valley of Einsamtal.

The dirigible flew through a sheeting rain mixed with large hailstones. Klemmer felt the impacts on the rudder through the helm in his hands. Gusts of wind yawed *Volkenreiter* from side to side. That meant the ground was very near. Downdrafts from thunderstorms often struck the ground and boiled away in windshears that could destroy an airframe.

Lightning illuminated the ground ahead. Patches of snow reflected the flash and burned afterimages into the eyes. There! Klemmer leaned forward and tried to wipe away the rime on the windscreens. Ahead lay a mountain valley, and at the head of the valley, nested against granite cliffs—Einsamberg Kraal. A vast, ancient stone keep. Powerful, yet strangely inviting even in these circumstances. Klemmer turned on the landing light. The facades were still alive with the glowing pastels favored by the first Kraalheer, Elias Ehrengraf, whose name Eliana was given at her christening.

The valley was called Einsamtal—Lonely Valley, a lush mountain meadowland where once great herds of hornhead had grazed. In the flash of light, Otto Klemmer saw the mooring mast in its leveled circle at the foot of the valley. Klemmer shouted to Blier to get himself under control, that landing was near.

The technique for a shorthanded mooring of a lifting body airship was to approach the mast from downwind. Then at fifty meters distance one discharged the anchor mortar, firing the hook into the ground and engaging the automatic reel under the steering surfaces, so that the ship behaved like a fish hooked by the tail. A skillful pilot was then expected to strike the mooring cup precisely so that the nose latches closed while the reel took the strain on the anchor rode and brought the ship to ground.

In calm weather it was a test of skill. In these conditions it was a test of survival.

Klemmer reduced throttle and rotated the engines so that the propellers were parallel to the ground. He used them to draw the airship down while the wind carried it toward the mast.

Another lightning flash blinded Klemmer as it struck the well-grounded manor house and coruscated into the ground.,

Blier shouted suddenly, *"Too fast, Kapitan! Too fast! We are going to crash into the mast!"* Without orders, he fired the stern mortar. Klemmer felt the anchor leave the ship, and the familiar shudder as the rode played from the reel. The anchor would strike the ground too far from the mast. The rode would run out to its limit and either snap or smash *Volkenreiter* into the ground before she could reach the mast.

"Cut the anchor line!" Klemmer shouted into the speaking tube. *"Somebody down there get aft and cut the stern anchor line!"*

Klemmer tilted the engines through a complete reversal and slammed the throttles hard against the stops. *Volkenreiter* shuddered and bridled at the rough handling. A flurry of icy rain swept across the beam of the landing light and froze on the windscreen, blinding Klemmer. Buele ran to the glass, slid it open. Freezing rain slashed into the flight deck, but Klemmer could see the mast ahead. He could feel the shock of the stern line going taut. No one had succeeded in cutting it.

It was, in fact, Tiegen Roark who found himself incomprehensibly in the stern lazaret between the mortar breach and the reel. He was sawing desperately at the hemp rode with a dinner knife.

The *Volkenreiter* slammed to a stop at the end of its misplaced stern tether. Blier was thrown forward over the guardrail and through the open windscreen. His startled shriek faded as he fell fifty feet to the ground.

The airship dropped like a stone, struck the ground on its single pneumatic wheel under the gondola. There was a crack like a pistol shot as a main longeron broke. Then *Volkenreiter* rebounded back into the air and forward again as Tiegen's efforts aft were rewarded with the separation of the stern line.

Otto Klemmer, in what was the finest bit of airmanship of his career, steered the *Volkenreiter* directly onto the cup at the tip of the mast. The mast itself was nearly uprooted, but it remained upright as the latches slammed closed, capturing the airship, which immediately castered around the mast-circle to come to a stop three feet from the ground with her nose into the wind.

Klemmer shut down the magnetos, raced down the ladder and through the salon to the lazaret. Shoving Tiegen Roark aside unceremoniously, he fired the two outward-facing small mortars. The kedge anchors struck and buried flukes in the soft ground of the Einsamtal meadow. Klemmer engaged the winches and snugged the airship down until its single wheel rested firmly on the ground. Then he helped Healer Roark to his feet with thanks and apologies for his rudeness.

"Luftkapitan," Roark said with feeling, "whenever you find it necessary to be rude in such a manner, don't stand on ceremony."

Klemmer stepped into the salon. Through the windows he could see that the Einsamberg kaffirs had gathered around the airship with carts and torches. To Eliana Ehrengraf, he said formally, "We are on the ground at Einsamberg, mynheera."

"Thank you, Luftkapitan Klemmer," the Voertrekkerschatz said formally. "You have our gratitude."

———

19

A COLD HOMECOMING FOR THE VOERSTER

Trekkerpolizeioberst Transkei stood rigidly at attention, clenched fists tight against the red stripe of his Wache uniform trousers. His ordinarily florid face was drained of color and the veins of his thick neck were made prominent by the inner pressure of his mingled fear and anger. Despite the chill in the room, the colonel was sweating.

Ian Voerster, standing behind his antique desk, still in his traveling clothes, slammed his riding crop down on the polished wooden surface. His voice was like an iron rasp. "They went *where?* Tell me again, you stupid man!"

"To the mynheera the Voertrekkerschatz's kraal at Einsamberg, Voertrekker-Praesident. The Healer said mynheera Broni needed a change." As he spoke, Transkei fixed his eyes on the Zulu shield and assegai on the stone wall behind The Voerster. Though the ancient trophies had occupied that spot on the office wall ever since Transkei came to Voertrekkerhoem, this was the first time he had ever examined them with such strained earnestness.

"Who authorized it?" the Voertrekker-Praesident demanded. "Who let them go?"

Transkei's chin actually trembled. Humiliation and apprehension griped his bowels. Gas rumbled in his gut and for a moment he feared he would physically disgrace himself.

"The mynheera Eliana Ehrengraf authorized the flight herself, sir. And I suppose I let them go," he said.

"You *suppose* you let them go? What *dreck* is in your head that you use for brains?" Ian Voerster's pale blue eyes were red-rimmed with fatigue and rage. He had arrived at Voertrekker-hoem only minutes ago, after a long and wearying ride from Windhoek.

Transkei's back and buttocks ached with the rigidity of his position. "It did not occur to me to challenge the authority of the Voertrekkerschatz, sir," he said.

"I am surrounded by incompetents," Voerster grated. "Who else was aboard the airship?"

Transkei tried to swallow the dryness in his throat and said, "Besides the Voertrekkersdatter and mynheera Eliana, there were Healer Roark, the Astronomer-Select and his assistant, some kaffirs, and the Starman Black Clavius . . ."

Ian Voerster exploded again. "Idiot. Cretin. They even took the Starman and you stood by and did nothing?"

"Mynheer The Voerster— I protest! You left me no orders—"

"I made you my Chief of Security because I thought you would not need orders to know what must be done," Ian Voerster shouted. "But you let my wife intimidate you, gull you—or did she charm you, Oberst? Is that how it was?"

"Sir!" Transkei was aghast at the accusation.

"You stood by and let them all climb aboard *Volkenreiter* and simply sail away into the blue. To Einsamberg, by all that's holy! Weren't you by my side when I signed the marriage contract with Winter? Didn't you sign as a witness?"

Transkei remembered the second meeting with Vikter Fontein and his advocate. The most secret one at the university in Pretoria. It had been a moment of enormous pride and achievement for a simple policeman (which is how Transkei liked to think of himself) to be part of so momentous and personal a transaction involving the Voersters and the most powerful family of the Planetia. He had imagined, as he affixed his signature to the documents, that the act assured him of a sinecure in the Wache until retirement. Chief of Security was only a beginning. Why, there was no limit to how far a confidant of the Voertrekker-Praesident might go. Even Minister of the Interior was not unthinkable.

———

So he had thought. Now it was a nightmare.

"Has there been any word from my wife?" Voerster demanded.

"There are heavy storms between here and Einsamberg, sir," Transkei said. The Voerster did not need to be reminded how severe the storms could be at this time of year on the Sea of Grass.

Ian Voerster said curtly, "Get Wache Kapitan Grunner to bring me the wireless log for yesterday. Next, order out a police commando and call the airship sheds at Voersterstaad for a transport. Have them stand by for orders. Now get out of my sight."

The colonel fled. He felt clammy with sweat and his cheeks burned with humiliation. How was a simple policeman to know that there had been something strange about the marriage contract between The Fontein and The Voerster? The terms had seemed straightforward enough. The Fonteins got Broni, Einsamberg, and Grimsel—a shabby town of no value. The Voertrekker-Praesident got a hard and efficient viceroy for the Planetia. He had been rather shocked that the mynheera Broni was being given to old Vikter rather than to Eigen. But that was not his business. What else was there to consider?

This was the price, Transkei thought self-pityingly, that one paid for associating too closely with the powerful. At the door to Wache Kapitan Grunner's cubicle, he paused and said harshly, "Report to the Voertrekker-Praesident with the wireless logs for yesterday." When the portly captain leaped to his feet to comply, Transkei said sharply, "Wait, idiot. I am not finished. What airships are available at the Voersterstaad sheds?"

Grunner, red-faced and asthmatic, lifted a clipboard from a rack. "There are two Hippo-class dirigibles in for new fabric. Neither is flyable, Mynheer Oberst."

Transkei shut his eyes in frustration. Now he would be blamed for that as well.

The captain eyed his superior very carefully. The colonel was in some sort of trouble and it was not Grunner's task to make it easier for him. But a little helpfulness now might be rewarded later, when it counted for more. "There is an Impala-class police cruiser en route from Pretoria to Detention One, Oberst. I could probably reach her by wireless and divert her."

Transkei considered. Not a perfect solution, but far better than having to tell Ian Voerster in his present frame of mind that there was no air transport available to move his police commando. "Do it."

"They wouldn't be able to get here before midafternoon tomorrow, Oberst. Even then, the weather—"

"Damn and blast. What's the matter with Staadluftflot? But it will have to do. Go ahead. Don't suggest anything to the Voertrekker-Praesident. He is very preoccupied. Understood?"

"Yes, Mynheer Oberst."

Transkei watched the plump Wache officer trotting away in the direction of The Voerster's cabinet. What a bitter thing a policeman's life was when he had to rely on such help as that. Then he hurried on himself to assemble the commando and inform their officer that they were on standby alert to perform a task for the Voertrekker-Praesident.

When Kapitan Grunner presented himself at the Voertrekker-Praesident's inner office, Leutnant Benno, The Voerster's personal aide-de-camp, was making notes on a pad, and the Praesident's kaffir body servant was changing Ian Voerster's travel-mussed clothes. The Voerster was running to fat as his years increased. He hated it. He liked to say that one could not do good work if one looked like a *lumpenscheiss*.

Grunner stood respectfully while the Voertrekker-Praesident, first in his underwear and then in his quilted, fur-lined dressing gown, finished dictating orders to the leutnant. Grunner was a communications and electrical devices specialist, but it sounded to him as though the Voertrekker-Praesident was planning some sort of punitive raid.

"Make certain our kaffirs know nothing about the Wache commando, Benno. There is enough unrest in this house as it is.

Now I hear that blacks in some of the townships think the Goldenwing is coming to search for future kaffir Starmen. We can thank kaffir Clavius for that," he said, scowling. "When you finish assembling the troops, report to Transkei. Inform him that he will lead the commando at Einsamberg. And God help him if he fumbles this assignment."

He brushed the old kaffir away and snapped at Grunner: "What word from the Goldenwing?"

"They are in planetary orbit now, Mynheer. There have been some troubles with language-drift, but that was to be expected. And apparently their communications are sometimes handled by a woman. I am surprised at that." Grunner pursed his lips in asthmatic disapproval.

"What surprises you, Kapitan, isn't important," Ian Voerster snapped. "What I need to know is when the Goldenwing syndicate will land the cargo."

Grunner looked uneasy. He had received his last wireless message from the *Gloria Coelis* six hours before and there had been nothing since. That might be the way Starmen conducted their affairs, but the Voertrekker-Praesident, particularly in his present cranky mood, was certain not to like it.

Something had made The Voerster tear a strip off Oberst Transkei. Grunner had not seen the *Volkenreiter* depart, but there was household gossip about its destination. The Voerster's family did not customarily depart with so little ceremony.

"I asked you a question, Grunner," Ian Voerster said, rising to his feet. He was like the carvings the kaffirs erected in the homelands. Thick, as though made of limestone, solid. All Voerster characteristics inherited from the line of Bol-Derek and Alfried and a hundred other protectors of tradition and privilege. Grunner felt a shiver of envy and resentment, but it was quickly overcome by feelings of the rightous loyalty his *volk* had given their leaders since the time of the first Great Trek and the Free State—events and values misted by, but not lost in, the millennial history of the Voertrekkers.

"I am sorry, Voerster. I do not have that information." By

calling the Voertrekker-Praesident "Voerster," Grunner was addressing him as family head. The captain had a distant claim to kinship, as many Voertrekkers had. Grunner hoped it would serve to divert Ian Voerster's anger, which had clearly already been aroused this day.

"Explain," Voerster said dangerously.

"The last message was received at four this morning. The Goldenwing was also transmitting voice to some other destination, Mynheer. Our equipment is not good enough to pick up such transmission." He paused, and then decided to risk what needed saying next. "The Astronomer-Select and his kaffirs have built more sophisticated radios than we have here. I sent in a report on this some months ago. I received no follow-up from the Trekkerpolizei office."

"Never mind that now. You say the Goldenwing was transmitting voice messages? How many and when?"

"Three, Mynheer. The last was two hours ago. As soon as it gets dark I intend to set up a sky-watch to plot the Goldenwing's orbit."

"But the Starmen made no commitment about their shuttles?"

"They acknowledge that they carry a cargo for us," Grunner said. "But nothing about a definite landing time. Not yet."

"And you have no idea to whom they are talking now by voice radio?"

"No, Mynheer." He made a show of looking into the communications log he carried, then he added, "May I speculate, Voertrekker-Praesident?"

"Wait. Kaffir Robert, get out."

The ancient house kaffir inclined his head in the submissive gesture of the Xhosa tribe and withdrew.

"You carry on, Benno. Report back to me in an hour."

"Sir."

The leutnant marched woodenly from the office.

"Now, Grunner. You may speculate."

"I think they have been speaking with the Astronomer-Select, Mynheer," Grunner said. "In Einsamberg."

———

"Are you suggesting that Osbertus Kloster is disloyal?"

The Wache officer wheezed nervously and said nothing. He was aghast at his own temerity. He was, in effect, accusing a cousin of the Voertrekker-Praesident of intriguing against the State. This was a cold homecoming for The Voerster.

"Did you know that Osbertus departed yesterday on the *Volkenreiter*?"

"Well . . . ah, sir . . . yes, I did know that." Grunner's heart was pounding heavily.

"And did you also know that Black Clavius, who was my personal guest, is with them?"

"Yes, sir."

Ian Voerster's pale eyes were cold. "Sit down, Grunner." He regarded the plump officer steadily. "You find it difficult to keep secrets, Grunner?"

"No, sir. I assure you I can be very private."

"Can you. That is rare in this house," Ian Voerster said bitterly. "The Wache may not be the best investigative force, but they are wonderfully adept at administering punishment. It is a tradition that stretches far back in our history. Do I make myself clear?"

"Very clear," Grunner whispered hoarsely. The air in the room felt cold and clammy.

"Good," Ian Voerster said. "Now stay here with me until there is some word from those strange creatures aboard the Goldenwing. The Wache may have work sooner than we could have expected."

20

A GLIMPSE OF GLORY

"*We appeal for medical assistance. A daughter of the first house is ill and requires treatment we are unable to give. Payment will be extremely generous. May your star physician descend to these coordinates as soon as orbit is established?*"

There were three more messages, sent at one-Earth-hour intervals. *They know how we keep time*, Duncan thought. *And they promise "generous payment." They think us venal. Well, perhaps, in a way, we are.*

"It needs investigating, Anya," he said. "But carefully. I won't risk Dietr."

"'A daughter of the first house.' What an inducement." Anya was unsmiling. She was actually jealous, Duncan Kr thought. Unheard of aboard a Goldenwing, where all was shared in common, even sexual satisfaction. But the experience in the rigging and Jean Marq's instability had upset Anya Amaya's balance.

"We must make special arrangements for Han Soo," Duncan said. "If we do the colonists a good turn it might simplify matters." Starmen knew that downworlders could be superstitious and difficult when it came to accepting the space dead. The Voertrekkers of Voerster would probably be more difficult than most.

"So you will go down to this Einsamberg rather than to Voersterstaad. Is that wise?"

Duncan understood her concern. It was not all vague jealousies. A shipmaster was expected to take no unnecessary personal risks. During his tenure as head of the syndicate, he *was* the ship.

"I'll be safe with my Sailing Master to handle the airsled," Duncan said.

But Anya would not be mollified. She only said, "I'll get ready," and launched herself into a transit tube without further comment. Duncan frowned at her abrupt departure.

We are all on edge, he thought. *Jean's illness has affected us all.*

Night descended on the tower at Einsamberg with a fitful series of rainshowers and buffeting winds. The clouds raced across the sky. In the clear intervals could be seen the familiar dusting of bright stars and three of the Six Giants, two low on the western horizon.

Osbertus Kloster, with the help of Buele, was putting the finishing touches on the erection of a twenty-centimeter Cassegrainian reflector next to a tall, stone-carved window open to the night.

The Astronomer-Select and the gawkish boy had spent many long nights at Sternhoem polishing and fitting out the small telescope. They were extremely proud of it.

"Are you certain you calculated the orbit properly, Buele?" Osbertus asked anxiously. He intended to give Broni and Eliana a proper view of the newly arrived Goldenwing, which passed from horizon to horizon every two hours, a gleaming-bright new star in Voerster's sky. Broni needed distraction. She was unwell, and she had been depressed by the death of Airshipman Blier, killed in the fall from *Volkenreiter* as the airship approached the mooring mast last evening.

"The numbers are exactly right, Brother," Buele said. "It is not possible for me to be wrong about numbers." He smiled foolishly and saliva glistened at the corners of his mouth. "Have you arranged for the clouds to stop hiding the sky?"

The irony startled Osbertus. He frowned at what was more likely simply a spastic impertinence by the boy. His impulse to reprimand was interrupted by the arrival, at the head of the tower ramp, of Eliana and Tiegen Roark. They pushed a wheelchair in which sat the Voertrekkersdatter. The prospect of seeing the Goldenwing had cheered her. Her blue eyes were bright. Was it excitement, Osbertus wondered, or only her fever?

It was cold in the tower with the glass removed from the high window, but Eliana had been forewarned and Broni was warmly dressed. Behind the Healer, Eliana's personal kaffir entered with a basket of earthen jars containing warm toddies. Osbertus' mouth watered at the savory, pungent smell of spiced *greena*.

"Now then," the astronomer began pedantically, "Buele has received a radio message that the *Gloria Coelis* is now well established in orbit and will begin unloading without delay."

Eliana said, "Will one of the Starmen come here, Cousin?"

"Yes. The commander informs us that he will visit us here at Einsamberg, mynheera."

"Not the physician?"

"We must deal with the Goldenwing's master, mynheera."

"Of course, Cousin," Eliana said. "Was Ian able to receive that message as well as we?"

"I fear so, mynheera," Osbertus said. He looked expectantly at the head of the ramp. "Clavius? Is he not coming?"

"Clavius is helping Klemmer with repairs to *Volkenreiter*," Tiegen Roark said.

From the sill where he stood, Osbertus could see the electric arc-lights in the field where the dirigible lay moored. Otto Klemmer and the house kaffirs, with Black Clavius' assistance, were at work on the airship. The occasional hard flurries of icy rain did nothing to discourage Klemmer, who was achingly anxious to return to Voertrekkerhoem and explain himself to The Voerster.

"Well, so be it. It is Clavius' loss," Osbertus said peckishly. "I would have imagined that after ten years he would be anxious to see a Goldenwing. But who can understand the ways of the kaffir?"

He arranged the academic robe he had chosen to wear and addressed himself to Broni. "What we shall do is this, mynheera Cousin. I have the telescope aimed at the spot on the western horizon where the Goldenwing will appear. Once that takes place, I shall start the clockwork and the telescope should track the object until it disappears in the east. The Goldenwing will be in sight for approximately twenty-one minutes. Then we must wait for an hour and some until it appears again. You might be able to see the cargo vehicles separating and beginning their descent to Voersterstaad. Am I understood, Cousin?"

"For God's sake, Osbertus. The Voertrekkersdatter is not a child," Roark said irritably.

The Healer was having serious second thoughts about his decision to come to Einsamberg with Eliana and the others. He had made a *political* decision on the basis of what he felt for the girl—and for her mother. Which had been a very stupid thing to do. Tiegen Roark had not achieved his present position in life by being rash or stupid. His second thoughts were being joined by third and fourth thoughts. All of them told him that he was in great danger, and he had put himself in this position for the sake of a woman who was far above him in the Voertrekker scheme of things. A woman he could not touch, and dare not dream of.

"She looks like a child, Brother Healer," Buele said, grinning foolishly.

The physician flushed with anger.

"Don't be impertinent, Buele," Osbertus said swiftly. To Roark, he said, "Bring Broni over here, please, Healer."

They settled Broni comfortably at the telescope. When she put her eye to the eyepiece, Buele asked, "Can you see anything, Sister?"

"Buele!" Healer Roark quivered with indignation.

"I can see stars," Broni said. "Very bright."

Osbertus craned to look up at the sky over Einsamberg. The clouds were broken, their edges gleaming with the light of the Giants Wallenberg and deKlerk. Osbertus examined his watch, a heavy gold timepiece that had come to Voerster aboard the *Milagro.* Voertrekker families tended to hoard heirlooms. Unchanging *things* reinforced their illusion of the strength of Voertrekker society.

"It is almost time, Broni," he said anxiously. "Look carefully. Tell me when you see the Goldenwing and I will set the clockwork."

Tiegen Roark whispered to Eliana, "Mynheera, I disapprove of the Voertrekkersdatter sitting in an open window in this freezing weather."

"Hush, Tiegen. Let it be."

Roark frowned and helped himself to a toddy from the tray on the table. He rubbed nervously at his duelling scar. The damned thing itched whenever he was emotionally distraught. Even the rightness of socially sanctioned, deliberate self-disfigurement was brought into question by his act of rebellion in following Eliana Ehrengraf Voerster.

From below, in the field where the damaged dirigible was moored, came the sound of Black Clavius' balichord. He was serenading the kaffirs helping Otto Klemmer repair the airship. The melody was pure and melancholy in the frigid mountain air. Blues. A kaffir lament. Eliana was listening intently. It disturbed Tiegen to see her moved by kaffir music.

He tried to imagine Eliana Ehrengraf's true life—the secret, personal life of a beautiful, passionate woman condemned to the coldness of a Voertrekker political marriage. He was overwhelmed by the wave of near grief that flooded over him. It was known that Eliana's moods affected those around her. What a dreadful power that was, Tiegen Roark thought. The more so for being unsought and unwanted.

She suddenly became aware of what she was doing and the mood in the tower room changed.

Osbertus Kloster left off frowning and began fairly to dance with excitement. "There, there it is, Broni! Can you see it?"

"Oh, Cousin! Mother! I can see it! It is so beautiful!"

Broni saw a glittering, flashing butterfly against the star-shot dark. She could hear the telescope clockwork starting and feel the instrument move to keep the golden vision in sight.

Against the starry background, *Glory* climbed into Voerster's sky, her furled sails and embracing masts and yards shimmered with light as the sun-angle changed.

Broni said excitedly, "Oh, mynheera, do look!"

Eliana took her daughter's place at the eyepiece and drew in her breath. The image was far clearer and larger than it had been through the large telescope at Sternhoem. The Goldenwing was close, so close that it seemed she could reach out and pluck the beautiful thing from the sky. She had not expected to be so deeply moved.

The *Gloria Coelis* flashed in the high brilliance of the white Luyten sun. Her spars and rigging seemed to shimmer with light. As a child, Eliana Ehrengraf had been told that the Goldenwings were the most beautiful constructs of man. She believed it now.

"Mother? Mynheera? Isn't she lovely?"

Broni's questioning voice brought Eliana back to present reality. "Yes, Broni. Lovely." She stepped away from the telescope and let Broni return.

As the girl watched, cargo sleds and mules began to slide from the *Gloria Coelis'* ventral bay. One after another they emerged from the Goldenwing's belly, flashed retrofire, and fell behind her.

Broni pushed away from the telescope, horrified.

"Mother, mynheera, she is making babies! She will die, Mother! She will die . . .!"

Eliana caught the girl in her arms.

"Broni, no, she won't die, my love. She is of *Earth*, not of Voerster, Broni, my sweet love . . ."

Osbertus Kloster cursed himself for an old fool. He might have known she would see the cargo sleds separating, and as a native of this benighted planet what else would she think but that the beautiful sky-creature was another necrogene?

"What you see are not her children, Broni. They are only landing sleds. She is a machine, Cousin, not an animal. Look again. She is much closer to us now."

What a world we live in, Osbertus thought. *A world where the giving of one life means the relinquishing of another.* "Look and see, Broni."

The girl returned to the eyepiece and stared open-mouthed. The large "children" had fallen far behind the Goldenwing. Another, smaller object separated from it and drifted across the sky beside it.

The Voertrekkersdatter had seen Duncan Kr and Anya Amaya begin the reentry that would bring them to Einsamberg.

At the crest of the ridge to the west of the valley of Einsamtal, Eigen Fontein and his brother stood in the mountain darkness and studied the activity on the floor of the valley. They could hear, faintly, the music of a balichord. From time to time figures below crossed in front of the bonfires that had been lighted at a safe distance from the crippled airship.

"A kaffir's playing," Georg Fontein said. "He's good."

Eigen spat into the brittle grass. He was far more interested in the manor house and how well defended it might be. When old Vikter had returned from Voersterstaad after Deorbit Day, there had been rumors that a lowland Ehrengraf bride might soon be coming to Winter. As the heir, Eigen had assumed the lowlander would be his.

Eigen's rudimentary nictitating membrane flashed to and fro across his pallid eyes. He was very angry. He had been angry since his father had returned, grinning like a cheet in estrus, from a second visit to the lowlands. He had been to Pretoria whence he had come with a signed marriage contract—a contract pledging himself in marriage to the daughter of Ian Voerster.

The news had enraged Eigen Fontein. A young bride might mean other heirs. It was intolerable. His reaction had been to set out on this expedition. He intended to take Einsamberg—the girl Broni's dowry—for himself and perhaps destroy the scheme his father and The Voerster had agreed upon.

Georg Fontein followed his elder brother cautiously. Eigen

was in the process of doing something very stupid, and very dangerous. There must be, he reasoned, a way in which he, Georg, could benefit from his duel-scarred brother's rashness.

Georg, the thoughtful one, had suggested a possible reason for their parent's lunacy. "The girl is frail," Georg said. "No matter what they say, she's sickly. Old Vikter intends to use the Law of Tribe to get himself something far better than Broni Voerster."

The Law of Tribe was simple and primal, designed for a colony world with a limited gene pool. It was a law out of the Dark Age immediately following the Rebellion. But like all Voertrekker laws, once written, it remained in the books as a religious canon and a part of the legal code.

Simply stated, the Law declared that once a tribe betrothed a female, the prospective groom had a right to expect a healthy and unblemished woman for his bed. If one was not forthcoming, the groom's family had the right, in his name and in the name of the Tribe, to claim from the unsuitable female's family another, more worthy conjugal mate, and to keep her until she supplied him with a healthy child. The choice was unlimited and unrestricted. A sister, wife, or even mother could be required to copulate with the disappointed groom until an heir was delivered.

"The old hornhead has seen Eliana Ehrengraf," Georg Fontein said with a leer. "The Law of Tribe will give her to him. What do you think of that? You've seen The Voerster's woman. Wouldn't you like to explore under her skirt yourself? The old man has diddled you, elder brother."

Eigen scowled at the distant balichord. He was thinking that it was an unbelievable stroke of luck to find the Voerster women here at Einsamberg. If the Law of Tribe worked for his bastard of a father, it would work as well for Eigen Fontein of Winter.

Kopje, one of the *lumpen* Eigen always brought along on hunting and whoring expeditions, was listening to the galena-powered radio. There had been feeble, hard-to-hear messages originating from Einsamberg Kraal all day. Georg said the people in the house were communicating with the syndicate in the Goldenwing that crossed the sky west to east every ninety or so minutes. If so, they were breaking the Voertrekker-Praesident's own law—the one enacted in the Kongresshalle years ago, after the *Nepenthe* had come and gone. It was written that only officials of the Voertrekker State might communicate with offworlders. It was all very interesting to Eigen. Was it possible that his hunt would net him a sled filled with who-knew-what treasures from a Goldenwing?

Another of the *lumpen* came pounding up the hill from the camp below. "Look, Eigen-sah, *look!*"

The brilliant star they had been watching was racing across the sky as before. Within minutes it transited the Plough and the Hanged Man. When Georg asked for the field glasses he was rewarded with a snarl from Eigen, who was using them.

"There, again!" the *lumpe* said. "See, it is breaking in pieces!"

Eigen watched the cargo panniers separate from the gemlike object in the binoculars' field. He watched as the smaller points of light fell behind to form a string of golden beads.

"Let me look, Brother," Georg insisted.

Eigen slammed the glasses against his brother's chest and ran back down the hill toward the camp.

Georg raised the binoculars as the racing light crossed the zenith. He could make out some details. The object in orbit around Voerster resembled a golden dragonfly. He was impressed by its jewelled beauty. As he watched, another, smaller object separated and began to descend. Across the sky now were displayed the Goldenwing, a string of golden beads, and the last object to separate, smaller than the others. All crossed the sky with distance widening among them. Georg watched until they had vanished beyond the black shadow of the Grimsel mountain crags to the east.

Georg considered, as had his brother only moments before, what of value there might be within those golden droplets in the sky. Every mynheer on Voerster had heard since childhood of the vast treasure expended when the Goldenwing *Nostromo* departed with orders to replenish Voerster's livestock and who knew what else. The Voerster must, at this very moment, be totting up the cost to the government of Voerster of the shipment that seemed about to arrive.

From the Fontein camp came Eigen's shouted order: "Make ready! We will take the manor house tonight!"

Georg shivered with an apprehension he had never before experienced. *The lights in the sky,* he thought, *will change my world.*

21

MARQ DESCENDING

The storms that had troubled the Grassersee now had moved west to the shores of Amity Bay in longitude fifteen degrees. At Voertrekkerhoem, rain fell in torrents as the line squalls swept across the flatlands between the Voertrekker-Praesident's estate and the city of Voersterstaad. The grasses lay crushed under the deluge and the land drank in the rain thirstily. When these storms were past, the grasses would grow wings and fly on the Nachtebrise, replenishing the savannah with fodder for the herds of wild ebray. And the ebray would multiply, the richness of their diet encouraging multiple births, so that the feral cheet and other predators would have a surfeit of prey animals for the approaching winter.

It troubled and angered The Voerster that certain pampered academics in Pretoria were now questioning the wisdom of accepting the long-awaited shipment of placental mammal embryos from Earth. Their argument was that the native necrogenes were perfectly attuned to the fragile ecology of Voerster, based generally on a one-for-one replacement of living animals. Mammals had shown a vast capacity to reproduce in the high-technology years before the Rebellion. Many of the native species had been forced into extinction by competition from the more biologically advanced Earth animals.

The Rebellion had shattered that pattern as it had many others. But now the question was being asked again. *I am no scientist,* Ian Voerster thought exasperatedly. *I know nothing of ecosystems and macrobiology. I only see a world sparsely populated by man and beasts. My predecessor thought it wise to restock the animals, and if he thought it so do I, and there's an end to it.* This was not the moment to worry about either the long-term effects or the cost. There were other things on Ian Voerster's plate. A disloyal wife, for one.

The weather had delayed the arrival of the Impala-class police dirigible. The special detachment of police The Voerster had ordered to prepare for a swift flight to Einsamberg stood to arms, waiting for the skies to clear. The skies did not. There were short intervals of sunshine and clear weather, but without the Impala, the troops were useless. And there was a stubborn radio silence from Einsamberg.

The intelligence wirelessed in to Voertrekkerhoem from Ian Voerster's spies in Pretoria and Grimsel was disquieting. The one thing The Voerster had not prepared for was an act of violent stupidity by one of Vikter Fontein's brutish sons. Yet the Voertrekker-Praesident was experienced enough in the statecraft of Planet Voerster to visualize what Eigen Fontein might be doing. When a professor of the Faculty of Law at Pretoria wirelessed in a long and academic dissertation on the Law of Tribe, The Voerster exploded in a fury and sent off an order that the old fool be de-tenured and banned. But the sense of the lecture was clear and Ian Voerster seethed.

And in the midst of bad news and bad weather, Ian Voerster was informed that the cargo shuttles from the orbiting Golden-wing had separated and were beginning their entry into the atmosphere.

Another delay was inevitable. The Voertrekker-Praesident dared not be absent when the spacemen descended with the *Gloria Coelis'* valuable cargo. His quarrel with Eliana and the recovery of the Voertrekkersdatter would have to wait.

Secretly, The Voerster was not only angry, he was sick with worry. It had been a mistake to tell The Fontein that Einsamberg would be his. Ian had no legal right to make such a promise and he knew it. But he had counted on Fontein's greed. Vikter's acquisitiveness was legendary even among Voertrekkers. Ian, sitting at his antique desk under the wall-mounted assegai and shield, clawed at his white-blond beard in anger. He was a man who despised the haphazard. Yet the years of planning seemed suddenly to be completely at the mercy of senseless variables: the weather, the arrival of the Goldenwing, the capriciousness of a strong woman's will. *I was not born to be The Voerster,* he thought angrily. *Why did it fall to me?*

Polizeioberst Transkei appeared at the open door to the Praesident's office. The Oberst was apprehensive. His last meeting with Ian Voerster had not been one he cared to remember.

"What is it?" Ian Voerster demanded sharply.

"The first of the shuttles is in sight, Mynheer." As if to underscore his words a sonic boom cracked across the rainswept grassland surrounding the old manor house. It rattled the glass in the high windows and seemed to shake the very stones of which the house was built.

"Any radio messages from the pilot? What rank?" It was a given on Planet Voerster that whether one's visitor came from the next kraal or from the stars, protocol had to be followed.

"Only an identification signal, Mynheer. The Starman piloting the shuttle train is called Jean Marq. He is alone. They always identify themselves as Starmen without regard for titles. It is their way, Mynheer."

Ian Voerster was well aware of all this. The ceremonials for the visit of a Goldenwing were imbedded in all colonial cultures. Man was dispersed now among all the habitable worlds of the stars within a half dozen light-years from Sol, and everywhere a port call by a Goldenwing was a rare event.

"Is there space enough for the cargo shuttles?"

"Starman Marq sees no difficulty, Mynheer. At least I believe that is what he is telling us. His Afrikaans is very bad."

"How good is your Space English, Transkei?" Voerster asked irritably. "Turn out an honor guard for this Marq person. Do the shuttles carry weapons?"

"I do not know, Mynheer Voertrekker-Praesident."

I am surrounded by fools, The Voerster thought. "Have a

company of the Wache on the landing ground. Armed. There is no point in being careless." Deep in his Voertrekker Afrikaans psyche was a strong distrust of foreigners.

The ancient histories told how the original Voertrekkers, the Boers of Earth, had been bullied and compelled by outlanders to dismantle their segregated society. Ian Voerster knew the stories very well. One of the most hated Voertrekker words—*shashon*—meant "to force and degrade." It derived from the Anglic word *sanctions*.

Ian Voerster rose from his chair and smoothed his black civilian tunic. He wore uniform when he must, but he was, he told himself, a civilian at heart. No one could ever say that the government of Voerster, unchanged for a thousand years, was a military dictatorship. "See to the guard, Oberst."

"At once, Mynheer." Transkei hurried on his way. Ian Voerster went to the door and surveyed the outer office. The clerks and male secretaries stopped work and awaited his commands. "Benno," he said to his military aide, "come with me."

The young Wache officer left his desk and stood at attention. *Everyone is playing at soldier,* Ian thought irritably. *God knows I need soldiers, but I have none. Not real ones. These are rural constables, no more than that.* Even the *ci-devant* mynheeren who came from Voerster's "best families" were, in truth, country yokels with a countryman's prejudices and bumpkin mentality. The vaunted university at Pretoria was really little more than a duelling and finishing school. Leutnant Benno was a good lad, but slow to grasp anything new or unusual.

Damn her, Ian thought. *Damn my dutiful, stiff-backed wife Eliana Ehrengraf. When I need her most where is she? Hiding at Einsamberg with my valuable daughter, and both of them intent on defying me.*

He spoke to the room. "You all heard the noise from the sky. It means that a Goldenwing's shuttle craft will be landing soon here at Voertrekkerhoem. It is an occasion you will all wish to witness. So for the time being you are all dismissed to the battlements, where you can see the proceedings." A nervous murmur of appreciation, still laced with apprehension, ran through the room. "Come with me, Benno. We still have work to do," Ian said.

Aboard the master-shuttle, Jean Marq was Wired into the shuttle-train's computer and the Local Area Network that bound the auxiliary craft to his shuttle and the lot to *Glory*'s mainframe. He was handling the varying required changes in delta-V with experienced skill. Back on *Glory*, Damon lay in his pod, Wired, monitoring the descent.

Jean Marq could see the planet below only as a virtual-reality display. Wireframe representations of reality suited Jean in his present state of mind. Virtual reality was without sexuality, without enticement. All reality would be better so, thought Jean Marq.

Still, the temptation to see the world as it really was was enormous. Perversely, Jean removed his helmet and activated a video imager.

Voerster resembled Earth. Jean had not been quite prepared for that. It was slightly smaller and more pelagic, but the chemical content of the atmosphere resulted in similar sky colors, the seas were salty and shading from deep cobalt blue to muddy green, and the continent was somewhat Earth-like. The coast of the Sea of Lions, a region kept reasonably warm by its position on the equator, reminded Jean of the Mediterranean coast of France. There were low, rocky hills behind the seacoast. Like the hills of Provence, he thought with a sudden shiver.

"What's wrong?" Damon asked through the drogue.

"Nothing is wrong, little man. Do not be so nervous. I am flying these landers, not you."

Damon subsided. The boy was edgy because Duncan and Anya were not aboard *Glory*, Jean thought. They had dropped away to make their own reentry in one of the personnel sleds. Duncan was always the altruist, Jean thought tolerantly. A colonist had only to weep for help, and *voilà!* there was the Master and Commander of the *Glory*.

The seas of Planet Voerster were, in actual fact, all parts of the same, globe-spanning ocean. The old charts showed a Sea of Storms between the North Tropic of Luyten and the Arctic circle. But the Sea of Storms became, as a circumnavigation in those high latitudes was completed, the Luyten Sea. One washed the northwest coast of the continent, the other the northeast coast. The southern sound of the Sea of Storms had been named—with considerable vainglory, Jean Marq decided—the Voerster Sea. But south of the equator, the entire planet was girdled by the Great Southern Ocean, pinched into a raging strait in one place by a nasty-looking, barren blade of land called the Sabercut Peninsula. The tip of the saber almost touched a projection of the antarctic ice cap that reached north almost to the—more Voertrekker vainglory—South Tropic of Voerster.

The old tyrant who led the migration from Earth to this half-finished world under Luyten 726 had left his name on the planet, the seas, the tropics, and the single continent. That, Jean thought sardonically, was vainglory in any reality.

But it was the Sea of Lions that attracted Jean Marq. It was narrow and several thousand kilometers long. If he allowed himself to slip into fantasy, he thought with a lump in his throat, that sea could almost *be* the Mediterranean. Tideless because Voerster had no satellites.

How strange that must be, thought Jean. Almost every world he had visited in the course of his uptime years had at least one satellite, often many. But the night sky of Voerster would display no such near neighbors. Only the stars and, of course, the six gas giants of the system's outer marches.

Still there was something about the land and sea below that evoked nostalgia. Like most men of his Gallic race, Jean was bound to his homeland by emotional ties of great strength and duration. Even after all his years in space, the appeal of a rocky coastline and a turquoise sea under a white sun was very strong. Would Duncan object to a long stay on Voerster? It was hard to say. Duncan kept his own counsel.

Along with the wave of nostalgia that shook him came other,

darker, memories. *A seminude girl lying oddly in the hot sun, blood on her head, half-open eyes glazing reproachfully in the noonday light . . .* What was it that he found so easy to remember and yet so difficult to *grasp?*

Dietr Krieg had only recently asked odd questions about the dead dream-girl in the vineyard, and about Anya Amaya and how it was that she had almost been killed while working in the rigging a dozen kilometers from *Glory.*

Each time Jean's mind seemed prepared to plunge into the black hole yawning for him, something caused him to withhold understanding in a fluttery panic.

Others panicked, he thought defensively. Young Damon. He had come from Grissom even more raw and useless than the average Starman came to his syndicate. Jean had warned Duncan that the youngster would be a burden. Fear of heights clung like the stench of *merde* to him. And yet— And yet—the boy was actually losing some of his terror. There were even times when Damon Ng reminded Jean Marq of himself.

So Duncan had been right. Again. He had said the boy would learn and become useful and it was happening just as he said it would. What a remarkable man was Duncan, Jean Marq thought. No one could command the *Glory* as well as the quiet fisherman from Thalassa. The ship and the crew all responded to him. *All,* Jean Marq thought. *Even I.*

The first shuttle in the train, the leader of the line of cargo panniers, was touching the outer fringes of the atmosphere. Odd flares of light and glowing plasmas streamed from the V-shaped nose cone. Ablative materials had long ago been abandoned. By the time *Glory's* auxiliary spacecraft were built, the metal ceramic bond needed for repeated reentries was old science.

But the curling, streaming glow of heat and fire still made a spectacular show. Jean Marq wondered if any of the primitives on the world below were watching as *Glory* sent her children into the sea of air below her. They were missing a marvelous show if they were not.

Through the thin image of the curtain of fire Marq could still see the coastline of the Sea of Lions. It really was like Provence, there was no other way to describe it. A land that cried out for vineyards, though the climate would call for very hardy grapes. With a half-smile Jean wondered if the Voertrekkers had discovered oenology. *Glory* pampered her syndicate, but the wine cellar aboard was sorely lacking in both quality and quantity. Jean Marq had, for a moment, the flashing impression that he was not thinking with his customary seriousness. The idea rather pleased him.

Dietr the Boche had been feeding him something in his Dust, Jean was certain of it. Despite all his advanced medical degrees and training, the man was a hog-butcher. Why else would one of the Boche's discernment leave the homeworld for a life of wandering among the near stars? It made no sense. And what made even less sense was that he, Jean Marq, once of the faculty of the Sorbonne, was doing precisely the same thing and, at the moment, deriving a kind of light-minded pleasure from it.

He was feeling the changes in delta-V now and he settled himself in one of the dual pilot's chairs facing the computer interface. Jean smiled vacantly. *I have let that German witch doctor rearrange things inside my head. I should not have permitted that.* But now that it was done, one felt a glorious sense of pure freedom. There had been no real nightmares for several weeks. A dream or two. But no dream Amalie. No blood. *For that, if for nothing else,* he thought, *I should thank the Boche.*

He reset the drogue in the socket in his skull. Immediately perceptions sharpened as the computer LAN reinstated the virtual-reality program and enhanced it. Ahead and below lay Voertrekkerhoem and the designated landing ground. Radar showed storms on the continental plain, line after line of them. A storm cell had only recently passed over the landing site.

Young Damon's presence suddenly came through the communications link powerfully. *"Can you handle the string?"* he asked firmly. Marq frowned. What was it that made the boy so hostile?

There was *something*. He felt it. But it was hidden behind the mental curtain Dietr Krieg had erected in Jean Marq's mind.

"*I can fly the string down your pants*, mon ami," Marq said affably. "*I was doing this when you were a smear on the sheets of your papa's bed. If I make you nervous, unplug.*"

Damon would never do such a thing when Duncan had ordered him to stand watch and monitor the descent of the cargo panniers.

Duncan and Anya had taken one of the small sleds, descending to some other mysterious destination with Han Soo's frozen corpse. Why did that trouble him, Jean wondered. *What do I care about Anya Amaya?* He was the only member of *Glory*'s syndicate with whom she had not shared her body.

But that was his own choice. Long ago he had made it plain he wished to remain celibate. Still it lessened his pleasure to think of Duncan and Anya descending together. It was not—suitable.

"*I am going to land this shuttle manually,*" he announced to Damon. "*The others can follow on program.*"

Damon had no objection. Nor any sign of acrophobia, Marq thought. But then the reality they were both experiencing was virtual, computer-generated, not actual. It made a difference.

"*I will follow you through on the controls,*" Damon said.

"*If you wish to learn,*" Jean Marq said.

In the virtual world they shared, the virtual Jean Marq raised a virtual hand and smiled a virtual smile at a virtual Damon Ng.

"*Ready to begin, boy,*" Jean Marq said. "*Nobody lives forever.*" Jean wondered how it was that thought had slipped by the mental curtain the Boche hog butcher had installed.

"*Is that what you call Dietr? Hog butcher?*"

"*Mind, now, boy,*" Jean Marq said almost airily. "*Faite attention!*"

At eighty thousand meters the ceramic surfaces of the descent vehicle glowed red. Plasmas curled away from the entering shuttle in a spectacular show of colors and light. The shuttle train was crossing the ocean side of Voerster. Beneath the fiery trail lay only rainswept, empty ocean. The fire in the sky reflected from the tideless waves unseen. As the lead shuttle approached the terminator, the first real suggestions of air began to burn, oxygen exploding into a white streak of fire against the darkening sky.

The shuttle crossed the Sea of Storms in minutes, descending from seventy thousand meters to fifty thousand. Over the northern spur of land and the lights of the Cape Colony the shuttle descended steeply to only ten thousand meters. Jean Marq instructed the computer to bank the string into a long turn to the south and Amity Bay. A series of deep, rolling sonic booms rocked the city of Joburg, bringing Voertrekkers and kaffirs into the streets.

Over the Grassersee, Jean took over from the computers and flew by wire. The lander had become a swiftly moving glider. The string crossed Sternberg at five thousand meters and leveled for Voertrekkerhoem's landing field. Jean's view of the land below was still a computer-generated wireframe sketch. The shuttle had no forward-looking windows, only a sloping carapace of red-hot ceramic. But in the virtual reality created by the computers, Jean Marq could see clearly the lights put on the field by the down-worlders. Lanes for the string of cargo panniers. One lane lay near the complex wireframe image that was the way *Glory*'s computers saw Voertrekkerhoem.

Jean skillfully banked the shuttle and lined it up with the landing ground. He armed the drag parachutes.

At five hundred meters, he leveled the ceramic arrow and lowered the skids. To celebrate his skill, he pulled the drogue from his head and made the landing blind, on analog instruments. The way Duncan might do it, he thought. The way only a veteran Starman could.

22

FEAR AND LOATHING AT THE INTERFACE

A series of terrifying booms, like the crash of thunder on doomsday, rolled across the Grassersee. The old leaded windows of Voertrekkerhoem rattled; some shattered and fell in shards to the stone floors. From where he stood surrounded by his Wache Guard of Honor, Ian Voerster could hear the shrieks of the women on the widows' walks and the moans of terror from the house kaffirs. The ranks of the Wache wavered and stumbled. Even the shimmering blue-white arc-lamps that bathed the airship landing ground in cold, harsh light seemed to flicker as the sonic booms rolled across Voertrekkerhoem.

"Stand fast! Stand fast, damn you!" The Voertrekker-Praesident's voice could scarcely be heard over the rolling thunder from the east.

Ian Voerster was the first to see the descending shuttles, falling like huge, gleaming spearpoints out of the night sky. The spacecraft were shadows on the emerging stars. Ian's blood felt as though it were congealing in his veins. His limbs felt wooden, and his heart labored, as he raised a pair of binoculars.

Lightning raced through the thunderheads moving west. The electric blue light flashed on the carapace of the leading lander. Clearly the thing was made of some heat-resistant material because it glowed white at the leading edges, shading to ruddy red along the ugly, humped dorsal surface. In the field of the binoculars, the vehicle seemed aimed directly at The Voerster and his frightened troops.

It approached, or fell, at a stunning rate. One moment it had passed high above Amity Bay, in the next it was rushing low overhead with a crackling rumble of tortured, parted air. In train behind it came others, all alike, at intervals of perhaps a half kilometer. It was like watching a flight of giant assegai.

As the last sonic boom rolled and crashed across the Sea of Grass, the first shuttle struck the turf of the landing field with incredible violence. It ploughed into the field, turning a long, deep furrow that steamed and hissed with the red heat of the blade that had created it. A ribbon parachute, larger than any similar device ever stored aboard a Voertrekker dirigible, opened and slowed the shuttle to a stop. When movement ceased, the spacecraft lay sunk in the wet soil, surrounded by a fog of superheated water vapor.

The spaceship was far larger than Ian Voerster had thought it would be. Delta-shaped, it was fifty meters from tip to blunt tail, a half dozen meters from keel (now buried in the soil of Voerster) to the thick, darkly blind carapace of the dorsal surface.

The Voerster had only a moment to consider the lead lander before another roared over his head, and another and another, until the landing field of Voertrekkerhoem was littered with red-hot, steaming, hissing spearpoints. There was a smell of burnt metal in the air and Ian Voerster could feel the sweat of fear rolling down his ribs. He took note of the fact that the vehicles were featureless, terrifyingly blind. They lay on the field amid their brightly colored ribbon-chutes, a legion of the most threateningly foreign devices Ian Voerster had ever seen.

The *Nepenthe* had rained no such storm of fearsome devices on Voerster. Ian remembered seeing that Goldenwing transiting the sky, and the descent of a small machine, large enough to carry a single man, that remained on the surface of the planet only long enough to deposit Black Clavius on the ground. Then it had risen, or so the witnesses claimed, silently into the sky to be gone. Clavius' arrival on Voerster had been nothing like this terrifying visitation.

The Voerster glanced back at his house. It seemed smaller, less grand than it had only moments before. The women, servants, and kaffirs had all vanished. Only the Voertrekker-Praesident and his barely controllable Honor Guard remained on the landing field surveying a multitude of still-glowing sky machines with gleaming, mottled carapaces that looked to Ian Voerster as though they were made of porcelain or ceramic. What sort of people owned such machines as these? For the first time, Ian Voerster, his mouth dry with anxiety, thought to ask himself whether or not he had the means—and the courage—actually to do what he intended doing.

No man could live on Voerster without an intimate knowledge of fear. No man could rule Voerster without an equally intimate knowledge of how to control and use fear. Ian shouted an order to Leutnant Benno to advance the Honor Guard until it commanded the forepart of the first vehicle at the far end of the field. Benno barked commands at the Wache troopers and trotted down the long, smoking furrow to where the shuttle rested. The Voerster followed, aware that his boots and trouser-legs were being stained with hot mud as he slogged through the ploughed ground. The dirt reeked of burnt iron.

As he reached the rear of the first shuttle he studied it carefully. He needed to know everything possible about these Starmen and their machines. Protected by a cowl of stained ceramic were six bell-shaped protuberances that appeared to be mounted on swivels. They were still in motion, and obviously superheated. The metal of which they were made radiated heat in waves that made the air shimmer.

Taking care not to get too near the craft, the Voertrekker-Praesident took up a position on the flank of the now somewhat dishevelled Honor Guard. Benno shouted an order. The Wache troopers, to a man white-faced with suspicion of this monstrous visitation from *out there*, assumed the formal guard position. It was a posture out of the Manual of Arms, with their weapons (heavy-gauge shotguns) at high-port. It struck Ian Voerster as faintly absurd to assume a position intended for crowd control of restless kaffirs. The huge, hot spearpoints resting in Voertrekkerhoem's field were unlikely to be impressed.

For a long moment there was no sound but the creak of hot

metal. Then a segment of the spearpoint's ventral surface began to retract. Previously invisible creases appeared, widened. The entire segment sank into the craft, leaving a black hole.

Ian Voerster's breath came hard. His throat was too dry to swallow his frothy saliva. *Have they come to kill us?* he wondered. *Are they truly men, or have they changed into something horrible, something more at home in the void of space than on firm ground?*

After all, what did one really know? Black Clavius was a human being despite the grotesque receptacle in his wool, but that was no assurance that *all* Starmen were human.

Something appeared in the opening of the shuttle. A man. *Thank God,* Ian Voerster thought. Ian Voerster sucked in a deep breath of cold, wet air.

But for his obscenely revealing clothing—a single garment that clung like a second skin and displayed the genitalia in disgusting bas-relief—the man from the stars could have been a Voertrekker. He stood on the tortured soil, looking about with evidence of a huge curiosity.

The Starman spoke. The language was Afrikaans of a sort. Understandable, but absurdly accented and archaic.

"I am Jean Marq, mathematician and syndic of the Goldenwing, *Gloria Coelis,*" he said.

A murmur ran through the ranks of the Honor Guard. The Starman looked at the troops and frowned. "The shuttles contain the cargo ordered by Alfried Voerster. I need men to help with the unloading."

The Voertrekker-Praesident stepped forward and spoke in his most formal manner. "I am Ian Voerster, heir of Alfried Voerster and Head of State, Mynheer Marq. Say what you need and you shall have it."

Another ripple of uncertainty ran through the nervous Wache *lumpen.* Perhaps, thought Ian Voerster, it would have been more practical to greet the Starman with ordinary Trekkerpolizei. But it was too late for that now. The Goldenwing had provided Voerster with a hostage, and when the moment came, the chocolate soldiers of the Wache would have to do.

———

But what weapons did the man in the skintight suit carry? It did not look as though he had any place to conceal anything in that vulgar getup.

The nearby shuttles began to open. The *lumpen* recoiled. From each machine a strange creature emerged, one a meter tall, with six jointed legs, four arms, and no head. The central torso was ringed with what appeared to be eyes.

One of the Wache had had enough. He uttered a cry and leveled his shotgun at the clacking horror. Before Benno could prevent it, the trooper fired. Buckshot clanged off the rounded flank of the thing, ricocheting off without visible effect.

The man called Marq's expression betrayed his contempt. "It is only a machine, Voertrekker," he said soothingly. "A machine intended to make unloading less burdensome."

Ian Voerster flushed. He was not accustomed to being the object of strangers' pitying scorn. *"Leutnant Benno! Take that man's name."*

To Marq, Ian Voerster said, "The man will be punished. Is your device damaged?"

Marq's eyes grew oddly veiled. "A syndicate and its belongings are not so easily damaged." He gave a command. The robot produced a New Earth weapon called a beamer.

A voice issued from within the first shuttle: *"Jean Marq, remember what Duncan said about frightening or offending these people. . . ."*

A bolt of lightning blue light sprang from the beamer's lens and struck the ground at the offending Wache's feet. Blue-violet light whirled and left a smoking hole in the earth.

"Holy Jesus," Leutnant Benno whispered.

The semisentient robots chittered. The Wache flung down their weapons and fled, Leutnant Benno in pursuit.

Ian Voerster stared at the Starman, humiliated and enraged. *Alfried Voerster,* he thought, *what have you done to us?* With all the control he could muster, he walked up to Jean Marq and stood stiffly before him. "That was enlightening, Starman. But come with me so that I can show you the hospitality of Voerster."

Just inside the courtyard wall of Voertrekkerhoem, a more disciplined and less favored detachment of armed men, this one under command of Trekkerpolizeioberst Transkei, fell on Jean Marq and made him prisoner.

The small shuttle, one of three kept aboard *Glory* and variously called the sleds, the jumpers, or the useless toys (mostly by Dietr Krieg), crossed Voerster's terminator at seventy-six thousand meters traveling at Mach 10.

The sleds were not so heavily instrumented as were the larger cargo shuttles. Anya Amaya was flying by wire, unconnected to the computer interface. Her hands rested lightly on the controls. She seemed to be flying casually, almost without attention, yet the craft's descent followed the mission profile created by *Glory*'s mainframe with zero deviation. Beside the girl sat Duncan Kr, and lashed down in the cargo hold lay the corpse of Han Soo.

On a virtual-reality holograph in the sled's instrument panel, Anya and Duncan could see the wireframe images of the landing area changing as the angles changed. Mountains sheltered a valley. In the valley there appeared to be a large, grounded craft of some kind. "I think it is a dirigible," Duncan said. "Have you ever seen one, Anya?"

The girl smiled ironically. "New Earth has its faults, Duncan. Being technologically quaint isn't one of them. But I did see a picture of a dirigible in a book when I was in breeding school. It was called *Hindenburg.*"

"This one is not so grand," Duncan said, studying the image in the display.

Anya Amaya's fingers caressed the controllers she held. *I was a misfit in more ways than one,* she thought. *Even fertile, I would have been a disaster as a New Earth matron. But this is living.*

The sled passed through fifty thousand meters and across a line of squalls far below. The world was blanketed in cloud. The virtual-reality screen ignored the weather and showed a steep line of cliffs extending far to the east. The Shieldwall. The barrier between the grassy heartland of Voerster and a vast, isolated and cold, arid plateau. The Planetia.

Glowing plasmas streamed off the plummeting sled's leading edges. Like all landers the sleds were delta-shaped, with stubby wings and a ceramic outer skin. Inside the shuttle's bobtail, the climb-out engines rested dark and silent. Their only purpose was to lift the sled back into orbit to rendezvous with *Glory*.

The inside of the sled was brilliantly illuminated with red light. Duncan looked gaunt and melancholy in bloody illumination. What a sad, lonely boy he must have been, Anya thought. To be the child of a marriage group must have been very like starting life as a clone. Anya Amaya knew about that. A third of the children born on population-hungry NE were clones. It gave her an unpleasant thrill to know that back on her homeworld there were (*had been,* for they were swiftly growing old and might be dead by now) four others exactly like her. The thought revolted her. It reduced her—a human being—to the nonstatus of a made *thing*.

Skillfully she piloted the sled into the cloud-tops. The wireframe images were all that she needed to keep the shuttle on course. At nineteen thousand meters they were still in the clouds. Radar mapping showed that they had traveled five hundred kilometers along the east-west length of the Shieldwall.

Flashes of lightning speared the blackness through which the sled was descending. A brilliantly starry night suddenly exploded onto the forward-looking monitors. The sled had thrust free of the storm system. Below, the planet's broken surface of granite mountains and sheer basaltic upthrusts gleamed in the starlight. Recalling his eidetic study of topographical maps of Voerster, Duncan named them. The Grimsels. High peaks and sheer valleys cut by the movement of great glaciers ten million years ago. Guarded by those mountains lay the valley with the strange name of "Einsamtal."

Anya Amaya said, "Buckle in, Duncan. We are almost there."

*

The people in the tower room watched while Luyten ruddied the eastern sky. Broni, exhausted by her watch of the Golden-wing, had fallen asleep and had been taken to her room by Star, who carried the young Voertrekker girl easily. Eliana, Osbertus, and Tiegen Roark had remained in the tower through the night, watching each appearance of the *Gloria Coelis* as she swept from horizon to horizon in her low orbit.

The string of golden spearpoints that had separated first had vanished, but a small point of light grew brighter. It left a trail of glowing gasses as it descended the sky.

Sleepless and excited, Buele had lurked in the shadows of the tower room until Osbertus Kloster gave him a turn at the eyepiece of the telescope. The boy grinned at Osbertus and said, "He is coming, Brother. I called him and he is coming here."

Eliana murmured to Tiegen Roark, "Can it be so? Is the Sternkapitan coming to cure Broni?"

Roark was deeply moved by the proud Eliana Ehrengraf's pitiful hope. A hope he himself did not share. He wished he dared say to Eliana that the world was not like that—that one did simply wish something to be true and have it so. The world in which he had lived his life—Eliana's world too—was simply not so kind. If a Starman was coming it was for advantage. And besides, what could another Starman do that Black Clavius had not tried, only to fail? The simple bitter fact was that Broni Ehrengraf Voerster was dying. The only question now was whether she could live long enough to fulfill the Voertrekker-Praesident's design, or, with unimaginable luck, frustrate it and leave her protectors alive.

I was a fool to let my feelings for Eliana embroil me in an affair that will be my death, he thought.

"Listen," Eliana said.

"Thunder," Osbertus said.

A cold wind blew in through the open window. The morning sky was clear, star-filled.

———

"No, Mynheer," Black Clavius said from the doorway. He filled the opening, a massive figure in homespun and black leather, his balichord hanging from his shoulder. "Not thunder," he said.

"Then what?" Tiegen Roark said irritably, his equanimity badly shaken by his thoughts of a moment ago. He was still a young man and a Voertrekker aristocrat, and but for his decision to follow Eliana to Einsamberg he would have had the prospect of a long and comfortable life. This disagreement about thunder only exasperated him. On the one hand was a foolish old man trying to be a scientist on a world highly antagonistic to real science, and on the other a kaffir giant who came to Voerster only to make trouble among the native blacks. "If not thunder then what?"

"A sound I have not heard for ten years, Mynheer," Clavius said. " 'The adversaries of the Lord shall be broken to pieces; out of heaven shall He thunder upon them . . .' "

Tiegen Roark, his nerves worn by a sleepless night and the sullen fear that had been growing in him ever since he had so foolishly set foot aboard the *Volkenreiter*, said irritably, "Make sense, old man. Don't pretend to a holiness you haven't got!"

Eliana said swiftly, "Don't you speak to the Starman in that way, Tiegen."

"No need to protect me, my lady," Clavius said gently. "The Healer is quite right. My holiness is a fraud. I am not an honorable man. Only a homesick one." He walked to the window and stood listening to the echoes of the sonic boom fading among the sheer granite peaks of the Grimsels. " 'Lo, these are parts of His ways: but how little a portion is heard of Him? But the thunder of His power who can understand?' " He stood at the stone sill, looking down the valley of Einsamtal. Something in the air added to his melancholy and made him uneasy. This, he thought sadly, at the very time when the rolling thunder of his own kind approaching should be filling him with joy.

The work by the local kaffirs on the moored dirigible

appeared to have stopped. Where was Luftkapitan Klemmer? The disciplined Klemmer would scarcely have allowed the kraal kaffirs to stop work on his beloved *Volkenreiter*.

Eliana stood beside him. The scent of her hair was like flowers, Clavius thought. What an odd thing to remember on this sere world where flowers were unknown. "Is a Starman coming at our summons, Clavius?" she asked.

"It could mean that, mynheera," he replied, still searching the sudden quiet of the mountain valley.

"It does mean that, Brother," Buele said excitedly. "That is exactly what it means. I know."

"Hush, boy," Osbertus said edgily. "Speak only when you are spoken to."

"Since when, Brother?"

Before Osbertus could reply, a second peal of rolling thunder swept over the valley. Clavius raised his eyes to the zenith, where the sky was thick with stars, and there it was. A sled, its lifting-body contours glowing with the heat of a swift penetration, its swing wings extending into a landing configuration.

Tears rose in Black Clavius' eyes. How could it be that he had ever left his beautiful vastness of stars and darkness? he wondered. What racial madness had driven him ashore to share ignominy with the kaffirs of Voerster? His breast ached with homesickness. *Lord*, he thought, *how well you and The Voerster know me. How well you know my weakness. Selah.*

The sled banked steeply and lined up with the length of the valley. Whoever was flying it was good, very good. *Gloria Coelis* was thrice blessed with such skilled pilots. The sled disappeared momentarily behind a granite dome and Clavius heard Eliana's breath catch. For one who had never seen anything in the air moving at such speed, the Ehrengraf displayed an almost intuitive understanding of what was happening.

The machine reappeared between the mountains and angled steeply toward the ground. At a half dozen meters height, it flared into landing rotation, skids extending from the ventral surface. Next appeared a ribbon chute and the sled struck the ground at a shallow angle a few meters from the moored *Volkenreiter*. Almost instantly it came to rest hissing and steaming.

Clavius looked at Eliana. She stood with a hand at her throat, awed by what she had seen, yet somehow understanding it. Her empathic powers were formidable, the giant Starman thought. *She has leached understanding from me as a mineral is leached from a stone.*

The others in the room, except for Buele, were not nearly so entranced. The astronomer looked frightened. The Healer had paled, but was standing firm as the hatch in the sled opened.

Two occupants, a man and a woman, stepped to the ground. As they did so, the sound of gunfire echoed across the valley.

23

ARE YOU HUMAN?

On the radio Fontein's voice from Winter Kraal was flat and without timbre. The carrier wave crackled and sputtered with the electrical discharges of the thunderstorms out on the Sea of Grass. Ian Voerster had to incline his head to the megaphone to understand what it was Vikter Fontein was saying.

"If you have taken a Starman prisoner, you will have a revolt of the kraals to deal with." The Planetian's manner was contemptuous. "You're a fool, Ian Voerster. You are ripe for the plucking."

Oberst Transkei, flushing at the insolence coming from the radio receiver, moved the microphone closer to the Voertrekker-Praesident. "In here, Mynheer, speak directly into this screened bit."

It frightened Transkei to see the Voertrekker-Praesident in such a state. The Voerster never personally used the radio, and it was a measure of how angry he had become that he was willing to do so now. Some Kraalheeren believed that technology had caused the Rebellion, and that even the lowest level of technology was suspect. Therefore swords were better than energy weapons, shotguns better than automatic rifles, heliographs better than radios. Some of the established churchmen even preached that the Luddite way was the proper way of life. Ian Voerster had never been such a fanatic. But it was true that he, like a long line of Voersters, preferred the old to the new. There was a time for innovation, he thought, but not now, not with Marq a prisoner in the lower cells of Voertrekkerhoem.

Starman Clavius had been a prisoner—and without the mynheera Eliana's interference, he still would have been. But the

Gloria Coelis syndic was a very different matter. Mynheer Marq was a man with a ship and crew behind him, a ship that had been delivering vital cargo to Voerster. There was no telling where all this would lead, Transkei lamented. Now that freak of nature Vikter Fontein was taunting The Voerster.

Ian Voerster said, "Don't start congratulating yourself, Vikter. And above all don't think you can escape the terms of the contract we signed. Now listen to me carefully."

The reply was profanity, but The Fontein was listening as instructed by the Voertrekker-Praesident.

Transkei fumbled in his sabertache for a cloth with which to wipe the sweat from his brow. He had never, in all his life, felt so exposed and at loose ends. When ruling aristocrats break the law, what might not happen? The sky could fall. The policeman thought about the horrifying descent of the cargo shuttles. They could have as easily been loaded with munitions of war. If they had been, the government of Voerster would cease to exist.

Ian Voerster said into the microphone, "My agents in Grimsel tell me that Eigen and Georg, with a gang of *lumpen* cutthroats, passed through there on the way to Einsamberg. What do you know about this?"

"I? Not a thing." The Fontein seemed furious. As well he should be, Ian Voerster thought. Eigen was unhappy with his father's decision to preempt the marriage contract with The Voerster and it appeared he was doing something about it. But was that all there was? There was great guile in the people of the high country. And whatever else Vikter Fontein might be, he was not a fool.

I am about to shake you badly, monster, Ian thought. *Let's see what you really think.* He said, "Broni and Eliana both are at Einsamberg, Vikter." He waited for the explosion. When it finally came, he interrupted the stream of profanity from the Planetian. "Shouting will win you nothing. Be silent and listen to me."

"How could you let the Voertrekkerschatz be so insubordinate?" Fontein bellowed.

What a strange one to speak of insubordination, Ian thought.

———

Vikter Fontein was the self-appointed leader of the Planetian kraalmeisters—the most rebellious and intractable gang of cutthroats on Planet Voerster.

"The machines that descended from the Goldenwing are performing the unloading of the shuttles automatically. I have given orders that no one is to interfere with them and no one has. The Starman is a suitable hostage against any interference by the people from the ship. That only leaves your son Eigen and his pack of delinquents. What do you intend to do about him?"

"Leave Eigen to me, Voerster."

"Will you send a commando?"

Gratingly, angrily, "Yes. Will you do the same against the Ehrengraf?"

"Yes, by airship."

"Talk to your wife, Voerster," the Kraalheer of Winter said in a tight voice. "Control the prideful bitch. If you have the balls."

Ian Voerster's pale cheeks flushed at the insult, but he kept himself tightly reined. "Coordinate your commando's movements with Oberst Transkei." He abandoned the radio. "Deal with this highland freak, Transkei. I want Einsamberg back under control by the day after tomorrow." The Voerster thrust the microphone against Transkei's brass-buttoned chest, rose, turned, and marched through the narrow door of the communications center.

The lead slug struck Duncan's thigh as he reached the ground. A flash of pain and shock jolted him and his leg collapsed. He went down like a stone.

The fisherfolk of Thalassa, engaging as they did in an occupation rife with accidents, had among them teachers of the Zen discipline, a technique used on the Great Sea of Thalassa to cleanse the mind of shock. Though Duncan had not used the Way for many years, it came unbidden as the missile imbedded itself in the muscle of his thigh.

He lay still, controlling first the bleeding and then the trauma. Pain had flared through him and then quickly vanished. But rising to his feet again was more than he could do.

———

Anya knelt at his side in the still-hot earth, stunned and frightened by the wound and unable, for the moment, to understand how Duncan had come by it. A second shot crashed across the valley and buckshot whined off the impervious surface of the landing sled. An answering rattle of gunfire came from the stone manor house at the head of the valley.

Duncan said tightly, "We appear to have come ashore in the middle of a battle, Anya. Take cover."

Anya asked furiously, "What sort of savages live in this damned place? Did you bring a weapon?"

"No," Duncan said.

From the direction of the grounded dirigible came a fusillade of shots directed at the manor. Duncan could see activity in the house grounds. A number of black men were advancing, taking cover where they could find it.

From the foot of the meadow, a single rider mounted on a large rodentlike animal galloped across the open ground in a showy feint toward the advancing kaffirs. To Duncan and Anya, he was a grotesque figure. Short, massive, with a huge chest and a bulging neck topped by a spectacularly ugly face and head. As he approached the blacks, he uttered a savage yell.

There was a shot from the house and the rider fell and lay still. His animal gave a frightened chirping cry and bolted.

Duncan heard: *"Starman! Stay where you are! We are coming!"*

The cry was in the Voertrekker tongue, mostly ancient Afrikaans, and peculiarly accented.

"Damn them," Anya said, angered and frightened by Duncan's wound. "They ask for help and then shoot at us."

Duncan showed his teeth with the effort of controlling the pain. "Help me get behind the skid."

Anya helped Duncan under the sled. She watched him fighting a psychic battle with his own nervous system. "Don't let me pass out," he said, "or the bleeding will start again."

The kaffirs had gone to ground. A trio of bulky men of the same breed as the fallen rider appeared from cover at the foot of the valley. They were waving a white flag.

"Well," Duncan said. "There are some rules, after all."

"Shit," Anya said.

The trio retrieved the body of their comrade and returned to cover. The firing began again. It was answered from the manor house. Anya, who had served in the New Earth militia, recognized the tactic as covering fire. Two black men dressed in homespun and carrying archaic-looking rifles appeared seemingly out of nowhere. They were regular-featured men with skin the color of cocoa, wooly hair, and startling light eyes. Ethnic Voerster kaffirs. The *Nostromo* syndics had reported their appearance and passed it along with the bills of lading for what eventually became *Glory's* cargo.

"Are you badly hurt, Mynheer?" asked one of the kaffirs.

"I can manage with some help," Duncan said.

"Then let us go quickly."

The second kaffir uttered a cry and the facade of the stone house sparkled with gunfire. From down the valley near the grounded airship there were shouts and curses.

Supported between Anya and one of the kaffirs, Duncan limped for the cover of a stone wall separating the house grounds from the mountain pasture of the valley. The marauders' weapons were extremely inaccurate at long range. Heavy lead slugs left silvery streaks of molten metal on the stones; no one was hit.

A stocky blond man appeared. He was wearing a leather sabertache. "Let me look at that wound," he said. "I am sorry to say I know a great deal about gunshot wounds."

He hesitated and then asked: "Are you human?"

"Only too human. This will need binding. I can't control the bleeding alone," Duncan said.

The man opened his kit and began winding white fabric around Duncan's thigh. "It isn't sterile," he said. "I should warn you of that."

"No matter. Infection I can prevent," Duncan said.

The man stared at him. "My name is Tiegen Roark. I am a Healer. A physician. You understand?"

"Of course he understands, you fool," Anya Amaya said furiously. "Let's get him under cover."

Tiegen Roark stared at her. He had never met a woman like this one. And she *was* a woman. Her skintight garment displayed every contour of the body beneath it. She spoke her strange-sounding Afrikaans with an authority that equalled that of a Voertrekker-born.

"And who are you, mynheera?" Tiegen demanded.

"I am Amaya, Sailing Master of the *Glory*. Shall we move my captain now or do you want to stand here babbling while he bleeds to death?"

Duncan, despite his condition, suppressed a smile. Anya had been doing some cramming on the subject of Voerster and its people. Anya bristled at the Voertrekker physician and dared him to take exception.

Roark, for all his Voertrekker peculiarities, was not an insensitive man. The woman from the Goldenwing unsettled him, but he had the sense not to be the Voertrekker aristocrat just now. One could not guess what this Amaya person's reaction might be.

He glanced again at Duncan Kr's tightly controlled face and realized that as a physician he, Mynheer Healer Tiegen Roark, had a very great deal to learn. There were many kinds of medical knowledge. These Goldenwing syndics had their share.

"Bring a blanket," Roark said.

The kaffir he addressed disappeared into the house and swiftly reappeared. With some help from Anya, the Healer and the kaffir rolled Duncan onto the blanket and carried him through the massive, cast-metal door into the Great Hall of Einsamberg Kraal.

Duncan could hear more gunfire from the upper windows. The change of light made him narrow his eyes in the interior shadows of the vast, near-to-empty room.

A rotund man wearing what appeared to be an academic gown over his shoulders and a slender woman entered the hall. The light struck shining black hair, brows like dark wings, skin the color of alabaster. Duncan was struck by the woman's presence and an overwhelming sense of empathy.

"This is the kraalheera of Einsamberg, Starman," the academic declared. "She rules this house."

"Gently, Cousin," the woman admonished. To Duncan, she said, "I am Eliana Voerster. I ask your forgiveness. It is my doing that you were injured. It was I who asked that you come here."

Having taken shelter near the bulk of the captured dirigible, Georg Fontein and his people paused to regroup. Their plan of attack, so typical of the Highlanders, had been rudely interrupted by the sudden appearance of the skycraft. Though Georg's acquaintanceship with space vehicles was limited to one short and badly taught course at University, he had no doubts about the strange machine resting on the churned ground of the meadow of Einsamtal. The thing had descended from the Goldenwing now orbiting Voerster, and the other droplets of light he had seen descending in the west must have also been shuttles from the starship. How many troops could such vehicles carry, Georg Fontein wondered, and what were their weapons likely to be? The machine in the meadow was impressive enough, but hardly the overwhelming threat one might expect from a vastly more technologically advanced society than that of Voerster. What had begun as an enterprise of impatience and greed— Eigen's desire to possess what he felt should have been his—now took on different dimensions. The Fonteins had assumed that any visitors from *out there* would come in strength, prepared to do what they liked with Voerster. But the shuttle had carried only one man and an all-but-naked woman.

If these people were Ian Voerster's allies, then the Fonteins of Winter would do well to reassess all their agreements. Einsamberg was free for the taking—though it disturbed the Highlander that Eliana Ehrengraf had seen fit to arm kaffirs. He had not expected that. It wasn't the Voertrekker way.

Georg coldly considered the body of his brother. Eigen Fontein had been a thorn in Georg's flesh for many years. He had finally committed a capital stupidity with that senseless charge at the space machine. Georg felt nothing at his loss—except elation that he, Georg Fontein, was now the heir to Winter. But Eigen *was* a brother. Fontein blood had been spilled. That made this skirmish important. Georg spoke abruptly. "Bring me the airship captain."

"Sah." A *lumpe* ran to do as he was bid.

Sheltering in the lee of the *Volkenreiter*, the prisoners shared the picket line with the mounts. The riding animals were tethered by halters; the prisoners by cords sewn through their lower lips. Though the Fonteins did not know it, it was a method of handling captives invented by the ancient Assyrians of Earth, a folk with a temperament not unlike that of the Highlanders of the Planetia.

The *lumpen* from Winter regarded the grounded shuttle with suspicion tinged with superstition. They knew, as did all the inhabitants of Voerster, that they were not native to the planet. They had, in fact, a rich mythology about their origins in a land called variously Congo, Lesotho, or Soweto, where black kaffir empires were once available for the taking by adventurous white tribesmen. They knew, as did the mynheeren, that everyone on Voerster descended from First Landers who had come down from the sky aboard landing craft from a great starship like the one now orbiting the planet. Still, the reality of the metal-and-ceramic arrow grounded in the meadow of Einsamtal was daunting. Except for a guard of two men, *Glory*'s sled had been left alone. Eigen Fontein had intended to inspect the craft personally, but not before the matter of the unfortunately alerted occupants of Einsamberg Kraal was dealt with. So the sled stood apart from the men from Winter, an object of immense curiosity and some very real fear.

Luftkapitan Klemmer, bruised and bleeding from a gratuitous beating at the hands of the now deceased Eigen Fontein, was led into Georg Fontein's presence at the end of a bloody tether.

"Can you speak?" Georg asked.

Klemmer glared at his captor. The airship captain was not a

cowardly man, but the throbbing agony of his cruelly mistreated lower lip brought tears to his eyes.

"Cut him free," Fontein said to the *lumpe* who had brought Klemmer into the shelter. The airshipman stood, his uniform bloody and torn, his face swollen and throbbing. His pale eyes blazed with outrage and hatred for the grotesque man sitting on a camp chair, a large single-action revolver in his hand. He had seen Fontein's father before, in Pretoria, where the Voertrekker-Praesident had gone aboard the *Volkenreiter* to a secret meeting. The Kraalheeren of the Planetia were always on the brink of rebellion. Now the Fonteins of Winter had gone over that brink into outlawry. Klemmer was resolved to acquit himself as a Voertrekker and a Mynheer. He could see no end to this but his own death.

"Answer me, *cholo*," Georg Fontein said. "Can you speak?"

The use of the vulgarism for a person of mixed blood was ancient. It was said that *cholo* referred to the Cape Colored of old South Africa.

Klemmer flushed. "Yes." It was pure agony to form words. He glanced out at the wounded bulk of his beloved *Volkenreiter* and wondered if he would ever walk her gondola again, ever see the sun glisten on high clouds. It did not seem likely.

"You will carry a message for me." Georg Fontein's hairy face was crisscrossed by frostbite scars. A terrible man. Cruel, Klemmer thought.

"No," he said thickly. "I carry no messages."

"Consider the alternative," Fontein said, pointing the revolver. "Carry my message and you will go back to your people. Refuse and I kill you."

That was Planetian directness, thought Klemmer. One could not state the case more clearly.

Every movement of Klemmer's savaged mouth sent spears of pain lancing across his face. He wondered, as a vain man would, what permanent damage these highland savages had done to his looks. What would his wife think of his slave lip?

———

Then reality set in and he realized that he was not likely to see his mynheera again unless he cooperated.

"What terms?" he mumbled.

Georg Fontein did not even have the grace to be pleased with himself. To overbear an airship captain of questionable ancestry was, after all, a small triumph for the new heir to Winter Kraal.

"Hear me, Lowlander. These are my terms to Eliana Ehrengraf," Fontein said. "To begin, I will have this kraal and all its kaffirs and chattels." He paused for effect and then said suggestively: "And I will have both women—Voerster's wife and the Voertrekkersdatter."

In spite of his pain, Klemmer snarled, "You're insane."

Georg did not pause. "The girl because she was to have been promised my brother, and the woman because the promise was a fraud. Winter has lost an heir. It is only just that Eliana Voerster spread her legs to supply us with another."

24

SHALL WE FIGHT?

Damon Ng flung himself along the fabric tunnel, his breath coming hard and a cold sweat on his face. The situation seemed to have very suddenly collapsed into chaos. Nothing in his previous experience, either in the forest villages of Grissom or aboard the *Gloria Coelis*, had prepared him for this explosion of gratuitous disasters.

He had spent the last two orbits trying to reestablish contact with Jean Marq and failing. The cybernetically moronic unloaders on the landing ground fatuously reported their progress with the cargo to *Glory*'s computer, but all demands for word from Jean Marq were met with a kind of binary incomprehension. Jean had left the lead shuttle. A weapon had been fired. That was all.

To make matters far, far worse was the static-ridden contact by primitive radio with the place called Einsamberg or Einsamtal— Lonesome Mountain or Lonesome Valley—in the language of Planet Voerster. Damon had only too clear a picture of what had happened there. Duncan and Anya had apparently landed in the middle of some fight between the locals, and Duncan had been wounded. Since that time Anya had used the natives' transmitter to ask Dietr to prescribe treatment for a *gunshot* wound, in the name of all that was holy. For some reason that was not entirely clear, but had to do with the fighting, Anya could not use her drogue, nor could she use the radio aboard the sled.

The very idea that the Master and Commander was injured and, for all that Damon could glean from the conversations between Anya and Dietr Krieg, might be at death's door, shattered all the confidence Damon had recently and laboriously constructed for himself.

He moved through the access tunnels inside *Glory* like a projectile: from the bridge to Dietr's sick bay, then back to the bridge and thence to the hold where the last sled was hangared, and back once again to Dietr. He had left a team of monkeys swarming over the sled, trying to put it back into useable condition. He had forgotten that the sled in question was out of service, and would be until *Glory* reached Aldrin, where the local technology sustained a commerce in components for sublight space vehicles.

He reached sick bay and spun himself into phase with Dietr's vertical. Two of Mira's adolescent kittens took exception to the Rigger's explosive arrival, and jumped for the tube and were gone.

"Shall we fight, Dietr?" Damon demanded. "Can we?"

"Calm yourself, Damon," Dietr said. "Take deep breaths."

"The sled is useless, damn it. I should have remembered, by God, I should have!"

"There is no question of us going downworld, boy. There never was. Duncan wouldn't allow it even if the sled were useable." A sudden burst of noise came from the communications system. "Be still, now. Let me try to get all this."

A woman's voice, overlaid with waves of static (Voerster's magnetic field was almost as powerful as that of one of the gas giants), came from the speaker on Dietr Krieg's console.

"That's not Anya," Damon said anxiously.

"No. Be still and let me listen." Dietr had several recorders running. Damon discerned that the woman was speaking in the native Afrikaans. On the same frequency, a man replied. He sounded angry. Then the woman again. The Rigger could not understand her words, but her tone was unmistakable. It was firm and unafraid. The word that occurred to Damon was *regal*.

The conversation proceeded for several minutes and then stopped. Damon demanded, "Can you understand that?"

"Not at all," the neurocybersurgeon said. "Afrikaans—particularly this Afrikaans—isn't German. I will have to run it through *Glory*'s translation program."

Damon protested, "We must do something about Duncan and Anya."

"Not about Jean Marq?"

"That is not what I meant," Damon said violently.

Dietr said, "Anya will have to get Duncan back to the ship. There is no other option. I think those people below will refuse to cooperate unless I agree to treat one of them. 'The daughter of the house' is the way they put it. Anya says she probably needs a heart valve. I told the Sailing Master all she had to do was get them up here. Then we can worry about what has happened to Jean Marq."

"Can she do it?"

"Why, youngster, she must, mustn't she?"

In the manor house the kaffirs who had arrived on the *Volkenreiter* and the house people set up defenses which dated to the time of the Rebellion. Iron shutters for the larger windows and doors, barricades in the outer grounds, traps in the avenues leading to the house. They might be outnumbered by the Planetians, but no one had ever taken Einsamberg's manor house by storm. For the moment, the situation was a stalemate.

Black Clavius had estimated that the attackers numbered about thirty Highlanders. Eliana had recognized the sons of Vikter Fontein at a distance and had seen one of them fall.

The manor house had radio communication—of a sort—with the world beyond the Grimsel Mountains. Reception was very poor, had always been because of the surrounding terrain. But Ian Voerster had managed to get through, and he had delivered a fulsome tirade of threats and demands. When Eliana had refused to be intimidated, his anger had grown progressively more abusive and violent. Ian Voerster was not a man accustomed to being challenged as Eliana was challenging him now. *Yes, Broni was with her, and no, Broni would not be returned to her father's jurisdiction.* She had answered Ian Voerster calmly, even icily, with a contemptuous civility that infuriated him.

Each exchange had made Eliana more determined, and Ian Voerster more furious. Finally, he had said in a voice trembling with rage: "I am sending a detachment of the Wache by airship to return Broni to Voertrekkerhoem and take possession of Einsamberg Kraal. Do not interfere with them."

To which Eliana replied, "Broni you shall not have. As for Einsamberg, you have no more rights here than that commando of mutants at the foot of the valley. Einsamberg and its lands are covered by a First Lander's writ. You know this as well as I do. You can send force, Ian, but force does not make you right."

The Voertrekker-Praesident's face was livid. "Damn you for an arrogant bitch. I am the law on Voerster, remember it."

"We have killed Eigen Fontein," Eliana said calmly. "He tried to attack the Starman. If you come here, guard yourself."

"You lured the Starman to you," he accused.

"And one of your highland freaks has wounded him. Ian, you are playing with forces you don't understand."

"And you do, shiftless bitch?"

The use of the word "shiftless" had special meaning on Voerster, where by long tradition women of the mynheeren class wore long and concealing quilted gowns with nothing under them. This custom had the force of law, and had ever since the days of the first post-Rebellion Voertrekker-Praesident, who had written in his *Colonial Instructions* that upper-class women should dress in that manner in order "to be both modest and aware of their nakedness." Meaning their vulnerability.

Eliana refused to give him satisfaction. "Shiftless I may be. But I have the right to defy you in this, and you know it."

"Tell the people from the ship that their colleague has delivered their cargo. He is my honored guest at Voertrekkerhoem."

Eliana felt a chill. She had not supposed Ian was so set on having his way that he would risk alienating the Starfolk whom Planet Voerster might need to depend on in future.

"No matter what you do, Ian, you will not get Broni. This I promise you."

"We shall see," Voerster said, and broke the crackling connection.

As the kraalheera of Einsamberg Kraal, the decision to defend or surrender was Eliana's alone. Even Osbertus, who was given to talking matters to death, and Tiegen Roark, who tended to yearn for risk-free solutions, made no offers of advice. For this Eliana Ehrengraf was grateful.

They had put the injured Starman into one of the grand guest chambers, a cavern of stone walls jammed with ancient, ornate, and incalculably valuable carved wooden furniture.

Eliana stood in the doorway, watching the woman called Anya Amaya and Tiegen Roark care for the Starcaptain. By some mysterious black magic of the mind, Duncan Kr had blocked out the damage done his leg by the shotgun. It was a remarkable performance. The Starman, lean and more darkly appealing than any Voertrekker, had impressive powers. Still, it appeared that Duncan Kr was in considerable pain. Tiegen, his skills as a Healer belittled by the strange talents of the people from space, had almost retired to the role of spectator. That was a pity, Eliana thought. Tiegen, the Tiegen she had known all her life, was capable of more than that.

She walked on through the high-ceilinged hallway lined with portraits of Ehrengraf forebears. Many wore the uniform of the planetary militia that had been formed—and had ruled on Voerster—during the Rebellion. The bitter time of Reconstruction came later. It was during this period that her ancestor, who had sided with the rebellious kaffirs, had been disenfranchised, then arrested and finally "rusticated." On this very estate, the property of a more conventional cousin, a member of a less rebellious cadet branch of the Ehrengrafs.

From the upper stories, where her kaffirs manned the windows and arrow-slits, she heard an occasional probing shot. *What we have here is a war*, she thought. *Small, but still a war.* And a stalemate that could not last. If Ian ordered in the Wache by airship, the unsettled weather on the Grassersee was a protection. But if he called for help from Fontein, time would grow short very quickly.

Starman Duncan and the woman had come down from orbit without a single weapon. Such peaceful intent was commendable, Eliana thought, but not helpful in the present circumstances.

She passed a chain-and-counterweight wall clock at the end of the domed hallway. It had been built for Einsamberg centuries ago, as a curiosity. Quartz crystal clocks and the means of making them had been rediscovered, but the antique still worked. It kept track of the hours and the position of the Six Giants. It was cumbersome and anachronistic, and it was a perfect metaphor for Voertrekker society, which had begun to ossify the moment it was planted on this alien soil.

Out of the shadows came one of her house people, a rifle on his back. Eliana wondered: *Have I made a mistake arming my kaffirs?* It was a thought worthy of Ian Voerster and she knew it.

"Mynheera. The Fonteins are sending the Luftkapitan under a white flag."

A truce flag, Eliana thought. What nicety. Just as though Georg Fontein were a conquering general instead of a highland bandit.

The kaffir regarded her with level, pale, unreadable eyes. Peculiarly, the whispers about Otto Klemmer's ancestry had put the kaffirs off.

"Let us see what Field Marshal Fontein wants to tell me," she said.

25

THE KRAALHEERA OF EINSAMBERG

Eliana Ehrengraf met Luftkapitan Klemmer in the outer courtyard of the manor house. She was prepared to see that he had been mistreated. Nothing less was to be expected from Planetians. But she had to steel herself at the sight of Klemmer's battered face and ballooning lower lip. She had heard of the method used by the Highlanders to ensure docility among their prisoners. She had never seen it.

Otto Klemmer, a formal man, refused to be assisted until he had surrendered his white pennant and delivered himself of his message which was sticking like slime in his throat.

"Mynheera," he said, speaking with great difficulty. "I have been commanded to offer you The Fontein's terms for surrender."

"Come inside first, Luftkapitan, and let the Healer tend your wounds."

Klemmer regarded the slender, erect figure of the Ehrengraf through tearing, watering eyes. She was like a swordblade, he thought. Tempered and beautiful and, in certain circumstances, deadly. It would not be out of character for a Voertrekker aristocrat to have a messenger killed if the message was demeaning. A fact that had not escaped Georg Fontein, Klemmer thought. *May his feet and hands be broken, his progeny prove sterile and his sexual organs rot.* An ancient kaffir curse. One worthy of the new heir of Winter Kraal.

"I am dishonored enough, mynheera," the airship captain mumbled. "Let me be rid of the load of bile Fontein sends to Einsamberg."

Healer Tiegen Roark appeared behind Eliana with Black

Clavius at his side. The Kaffir scowled at Klemmer's state and said, in his sonorous voice: "'Know therefore that the Lord thy God, He is God, the faithful God, which keepeth covenant and mercy with them that love Him . . .'"

Tiegen said furiously, "Stop that babble, old man, and help me with him."

But Eliana made a commanding gesture. She knew what it meant to the battered airshipman to stand on his feet and deliver his message. "Be silent, Tiegen," she said.

Clavius, who loathed anyone who deliberately inflicted pain on another, completed his quotation from his beloved Book: "'And repayeth them that hate Him, to destroy them: He will not be slack to him that hateth Him, He will repay him to his face.'"

Klemmer held himself stiffly upright and spoke The Fontein's words. The claim to house and chattels was insolent, but understandable in the circumstances. But when the airshipman reached the demand for both Broni and the Ehrengraf, the words came near to choking him.

He expected the Voertrekkerschatz's reaction of icy contempt. "For the moment that message deserves no answer, Mynheer Klemmer. You have done your honorable duty. Now, Tiegen, attend to him. Then we will all meet in the room of the Starman."

"Tell me, oh, please. What are they like?"

Broni's pale face was alight with anxious curiosity. She sat in her wheeled chair, but only because the Healer had threatened the most dire consequences if she left it.

"They are people," the kaffir serving woman said calmly. "No bigger, no stronger, no different from people here on Voerster."

"But a girl. A *girl*. I didn't know there were space women, too."

"It stands to reason. They have the same two sexes as we, mynheera."

"Don't call me that, please."

The black woman regarded the girl with eyes the color of a

clear winter sky. She did not smile. "Very well, Broni. Just as you say." She busied herself with making up the girl's bed, another of the high, broad four-posters with which the old house abounded.

The cry of a sentry on the highest widow's walk facing the valley of Einsamtal could be heard faintly.

"Has the fighting stopped? Was the Starman badly hurt? Tell me what is happening!"

"The Healer said you were to remain very still, mynheera."

"*Broni!*" The girl stamped her foot in irritation. "Why won't you do as I ask?"

"You ask that I change the way things are on Voerster, mynheera. I would do it if I could, but I cannot."

"I am sorry," the girl said. "I truly am."

"It is not your doing, mynheera."

"At least, tell me if our people are still fighting with the Highlanders. I want to know if the Starman is hurt, and if he is, is he angry with us, and will he harm us?"

The kaffir looked long at the girl. The tone of command was unmistakably Voertrekker. What a pity, she thought, that if she lives she will become one of *them. Ah, Broni,* she thought. *Right now you are only an adolescent girl, pretty in your frail, half-sexed way.* And like her mother, she was amazingly sensitive to the feelings of those around her. What was it Black Clavius called that? *Empathy.* A talent for sharing another's most intimate emotions. It was a gift that was at once touching and frightening. It was odd, but the black Wired One had it, too. So it was not a matter of race.

Of course, on Voerster, *everything* was a matter of race.

"Aren't you going to answer me?"

The kaffir sat on a window seat near Broni's chair. "The shutters are still closed," she said, "because the Fonteins are still camped around the *Volkenreiter.* The Luftkapitan was sent in with a message for the mynheera. No, I do not know what it was, but if it came from a Fontein I am certain it is coarse and badly meant."

———

"The Starman is hurt, isn't he? The Fonteins shot him. Will he die? Mayn't I see him and the space woman?"

"Live or die, that's for the Lord to decide, not for me or you to say. You must rest, now. Healer Roark should be heeded."

Broni's pale face grew somber. "So that I can be given to a Fontein?"

"I think not, mynheera the Voertrekkersdatter. Not while your mother has an Ehrengraf breath left in her body."

A house kaffir stood in the open doorway. "You must bring the mynheera. There is a council in the Starman's room."

In the gathering evening the low light in the great, gloomy house coupled with shadows to make strange forms and patterns on the ancient walls. Anya Amaya regarded her surroundings with distaste. On New Earth nothing was allowed to become old. Buildings gleamed with plastic cleanliness, roads were smooth as butter, trees and shrubs were trimmed and tidy. On NE, disorder of any sort was a sign that the battle against the empty planet was being lost. One grew accustomed to the light of triple suns, to multiple shadows and the brightness of interior scenes. Here on Voerster it seemed to her that the colonists wallowed in what was old, static, and dark.

She had already noted that Duncan was at home here. Despite his injury, the darkness of the house and the somber inner melancholy of the people appealed to the Thalassan dreamer in him.

Against all good sense and Anya's warnings, Duncan was on his feet. His wound was tightly bound, but Anya could see that his control of the bleeding was only intermittent. Bloody spots stained the coarse white bandage Duncan had insisted she wind around his leg so that he could stand.

People appeared out of the gloomy galleries and hallways, silent and attentive. The blacks were unfailingly polite to the people from space, but their reserve was a tangible barrier. *What do they expect from us?* Anya wondered.

———

When a kaffir woman wheeled in a gaunt and pretty blonde girl in an invalid's chair, Anya Amaya understood.

The great high-and-mighty lady who had so impressed Duncan expected her visitors to bring Dietr Krieg down to do whatever he could for the girl they called Broni. What they were not capable of understanding was that Goldenwing neurocyber-surgeons were not heroes who removed malfunctioning organs in daring operations atop computer tables. If these Voertrekkers expected help for the blue-lipped child, the situation outside would have to be improved enormously, and soon.

Anya looked worriedly at Duncan. A flight to orbit—even assuming they could disperse the savages camped near the sled— might be more than the Master and Commander of the *Gloria Coelis* could manage. Unless it happened soon.

Eliana Ehrengraf came into the room, somehow managing to look like an Amazon warrior in a velvet gown. Anya, insatiably curious about these odd people, had made some inquiries and the replies enraged her. On Voerster, a man of the landed class was referred to as "Mynheer," but the proper form for a woman of the same class was "mynheera," without the honorific capitalization.

In a society based on land tenure, the most potent title was "Kraalheer." Even the president-for-life of Voerster was some-times referred to as the "Kraalheer of Voerster." Eliana Ehrengraf Voerster, Anya surmised, had longer bloodlines even than the Voertrekker-Praesident. She was, in fact, one of the very few women landholders on the planet. Yet her title was properly "kraalheera."

Proud as she obviously was, Eliana seemed at home with the slights put upon her—and presumably all women—on this benighted world.

With Eliana came the old astronomer and an armed escort of two large black men. Was the situation really so grave as that? Anya Amaya wondered.

The kraalheera Eliana went straight to Duncan and bowed

her head in a gesture of respect. "Starman, I present my daughter and heiress, Broni Ehrengraf Voerster."

The kaffir attendant woman wheeled the girl forward and she made no effort whatever to prevent her trying to rise so that she could show Duncan the same respect her mother had done. Duncan thought: *These are a formal people. They would be ashamed to die in a disorderly manner.*

To his shocked surprise he caught a strong nuance of comprehension from Eliana Ehrengraf. She had come very near to hearing his thought. The woman was a natural empath.

To Broni he said, "Remain seated, mynheera Broni." He took her slender hand and held it. The girl was regarding him worshipfully. From her radiated the empathic signal, even stronger than her mother's sending.

He smiled and said, "You are rare people."

The large figure of Black Clavius appeared in the stone arch framing the metal door. Duncan knew him for a Wired One instantly. This was the marooned Starman of whom he had been told.

Clavius regarded the newcomers of his own kind with sudden tears in his eyes. *"Lord,"* he murmured, *"it is good of You to let me live to see this day. 'I am not able to bear all this people alone, because it is too heavy for me.' When Your Jews wrote the Book of Numbers You must have known I would need it to express my frailty . . ."* Then he said, "I am Clavius, Duncan. Once a syndic of the Goldenwing *Nepenthe*."

Anya said tersely, "I have never seen a syndic who chose the beach."

Clavius regarded the Sailing Master sadly. "My fellows aboard *Nepenthe* were intolerant of my habit of speaking with God, Sailing Master." He essayed a rueful smile. "We are not all tolerant, Sailing Master, nor all perfect. Perhaps you have noticed."

"He has you there, Anya," Duncan said. To Clavius, he said, "Have you had enough of life ashore?"

"I suspect *it* has had enough of me," Black Clavius said with a shrug of his massive shoulders.

"We will talk of it," Duncan said. He spoke to Eliana: "How many are outside?"

"Thirty. Perhaps as many as forty."

"Are they soldiers?"

Eliana smiled tiredly. "They think they are."

"They have weapons," Anya said. "Therefore, for purposes of this discussion they are soldiers."

"I fear that is true," Osbertus Kloster said in a tremulous voice.

Tiegen Roark arrived, breathless, from two floors above. "They are settling down for the night in tents near the airship, mynheera. They have pickets out."

Eliana said, "The Six Giants are all in the sky. Two will set by midnight. By two o'clock two more will be down and the night will be dark." She looked straight at Duncan. "I am told that you are keeping yourself well by some power you have, but that it will not last. Is that true?"

"It is," Duncan said.

"And that there is a skilled physician aboard the Goldenwing."

"Yes."

"Will that machine carry us all?"

"Seven. It can carry seven," Anya said. "No more." Somehow she did not want Eliana Ehrengraf aboard *Glory*.

"Seven and a child?"

"We can manage that," Anya said grudgingly. She looked at Duncan. "But there is Han Soo."

"A crewman who died during the voyage here," Duncan said. "I owe him a grave. He had a dread of being cast into space. He was an old and honorable man."

"Then we must provide what is needed," Eliana said. She faced Duncan squarely, and suddenly it was as though they were alone in the shadowed room. "If my daughter does not receive the kind of treatment available on your vessel, she will die. Not tomorrow, but soon."

Duncan looked into the wide, dark eyes of a fellow empath and smiled his melancholy smile. "Then we must provide what is needed," he said, and took Eliana by the hand. For the first time in his life, Duncan Kr was in love.

26

TWO MEN OF THE WORLD

The Voertrekker-Praesident, sitting behind his polished slab of a table, regarded the Starman with interest. He dismissed Oberst Transkei with a silent wave of his hand. The Trekkerpolizei, concerned for the Praesident's safety, withdrew frowning.

Ian Voerster said, "The warders tell me you are a Frenchman. I have never seen a Frenchman before. Are you unique?"

Jean Marq sat heavily in the uncomfortable chair. He had never before in his life been restrained from doing almost exactly as he chose to do. Being in custody was almost a pleasant experience for him. For the first time he was not burdened with decisions. He had been looking distractedly at the Zulu weapons on the wall above the Voertrekker-Praesident's table. He knew what they were because he had seen similar ones in the Louvre or the Pompidou many years ago. There was a streak of venality in Jean Marq and he estimated that the relics must be worth a million new francs, possibly more. Yet they were removed from Earth, from France, from the Louvre and the Pompidou by light-years of space and time-dilated centuries. He shivered with a sense of his isolation from his roots.

"France has always been the most civilized nation on Planet Earth," he said, almost defiantly. "In that sense, all Frenchmen are unique. A man of the world would know that." Duncan would be proud of him for challenging this offworld bourgeois authoritarian. The Thalassan, peasant that he was born, brought forth the qualities and bearing of an aristocrat when needed. It was one of the things that made him of such value to the *Gloria Coelis* syndicate.

The Voertrekker-Praesident steepled his fingers and scrutinized the hostage even more closely than before. It seemed remarkable to Ian Voerster that here before him sat a lordly representative of Earth, of the homeworld of all Men. And yet, despite his airs and mysterious skills, he was quite as helpless as any kaffir. *Would that I could dominate the animals of the Planetia so easily*, Voerster thought.

But wait. Perhaps matters were not so simple as they appeared. This "Frenchman" had fallen quite easily into his hands. Perhaps too easily? Ian Voerster was a conspiratorial man. Was there something here that was hidden, and yet sent neural messages to his inner self? Black Clavius had always aroused this sort of suspicion in the Voertrekker-Praesident—a feeling that something was going inexorably awry out there beyond the range of a virtuous man's understanding.

"You understand that you are a prisoner? And a hostage for the good behavior of your fellow syndics?" Ian Voerster kept his voice calm, even friendly.

"I do," Jean Marq said. "I also know that you will have cause to regret what you have done. It may well be a thousand years before another Goldenwing chooses to visit the Luyten Sun. There is nothing here but brutes and truce-breakers."

Ian's reddish eyebrows arched so pronouncedly that they seemed almost to touch his high hairline. "I was not aware there was any truce between your people and mine, Mynheer Syndic," he said.

"Or any war, either," Jean Marq said calmly. "Colonials do not make Starmen into hostages. At least not until colonial science can produce something as necessary as a starship, *Monsieur le Président*."

"Is that a French form of address, Mynheer Marq? I am genuinely interested in the quaint customs of out-of-date civilizations."

"Why have I been detained?" Jean Marq demanded, veering suddenly to near-explosive anger. He was developing a very great dislike for this pale man with his sparse fair hair, his thin lips, and small, alert eyes—like those of a pig rooting for truffles, he thought with a wild impulse to laugh aloud. Where had this rustic creature found the courage to challenge—and capture—a Wired Starman?

"Let me explain matters to you, Mynheer Marq," Ian Voerster said. "You and your shipmates have arrived at a difficult time. There are changes taking place on Planet Voerster, and we are—quite frankly—not a people who take easily to changes. I will not bore you with the whole spectrum of Voersterian customs and political realities. Suffice it to say that I have found it necessary to make certain arrangements and alliances I regard as necessary for the survival of our social order. My wife has chosen to defy me. She has apparently enlisted the aid of a pair of your syndics, who have joined her at Einsamberg Kraal—in the mountains some twenty-two hundred kilometers from here."

"Your provincial politics mean nothing to Wired Ones," Jean Marq said.

"That's as may be, Mynheer Marq. But the fact is that your people have become involved. So it has become necessary for me to involve you."

"There were messages to our ship asking for medical aid," Jean said. "Our Master and Commander is a humanitarian."

The small, bright eyes fixed on Jean Marq. "*You* are not a humanitarian, I take it."

"I am a Starman, not a downworlder."

"That's plain enough. We won't be troubled with sentiment, then," Voerster said. "I approve of the demand for medical aid. I would have asked for it myself, if I had not been preempted. It is of absolute importance to the government of Voerster—"

"Meaning yourself, *Monsieur le Président*," Jean Marq said with heavy irony.

"I do not deny it. I and my family represent the only law this world has ever known. We owe very little to the homeworld, Mynheer Starman. Our people were regarded as enemies and pariahs ever since the more militarily favored nations forced sanctions on us to change our chosen social order. The move from Sol to Luyten was the *second* Great Trek for the White Tribe. We do not change our ways easily."

Jean Marq, Sorbonne intellectual and Gallic snob, regarded the Voertrekker-Praesident with distaste. Dietr Krieg was right in generally choosing not to come ashore on these bumpkin worlds.

"I was about to say that the medical assistance required is needed so that a political alliance can be fulfilled. I won't trouble you further with details, except to say that your well-being depends on the delivery of the aid requested—and the return to my jurisdiction of certain citizens of Voerster who have broken a number of our laws. I shall make that clear to your syndics at Einsamberg."

"I have heard that there is a beached Starman on Voerster," Jean Marq said.

Ian Voerster's smile showed tiny, even, white teeth. They looked like baleen in that large, florid face, Jean Marq thought.

"There is such a Starman. Black Clavius by name. He has been on Planet Voerster for many years. Our years, which are, I believe, somewhat longer than the Earth Standard years used aboard Goldenwings."

Jean Marq was surprised. One didn't expect colonials to be informed about the internals of life aboard lightsailers. He wondered if perhaps he had been guilty of making hasty judgments.

"Until a short time ago, Clavius was my personal guest here at Voertrekkerhoem," Ian Voerster said. "Persons who spoke to the syndics of the Goldenwing *Nepenthe* all those years ago say there are stories on many worlds about Black Clavius."

"There are some, I am sure," Jean Marq said.

Ian Voerster smiled thinly. "He talks to God, you know."

"Qu'est-ce que c'est que cela?"

"Quite literally, I assure you," Ian Voerster said with a thread of scorn in his tone. Ian needed to turn on Marq the same spite the outworlder used on those he obviously thought of as inferior. This was a game Voertrekkers played in their cribs, and they played it well. "Of course, even Clavius is reluctant to claim that God replies to him directly. Or at all, for that matter. You are an odd lot, you Starmen. Do you suffer delusions or great loss of intellectual capacity when you are separated from your—" He made a disdainful gesture about his head. "*Drogue,* you call it?"

Jean Marq looked at the Voertrekker-Praesident with grudging respect. The man was even more cruel and more capable than Marq had first supposed. Duncan was going to have his hands full with this one.

"My mental capacity is adequate to my tasks, I assure you, *Monsieur le Président,*" Marq said.

"Excellent," Voerster said, getting to his feet in dismissal. "You will dine with me tonight, Mynheer Starman. I look forward to it. I am sure that two men of the world can find much on which to agree."

27

A FUNERAL FAR FROM THE YANGTZE

A column of greasy smoke rose from the foot of the valley toward the overcast. Gusts of wind swirled down the palisade of the Shieldwall north of the manor house, scattered the smoke and then, dying, allowed it to re-form its oily path between soil and sky.

Duncan, heavily dressed against the intermittent rain, leaned on the parapet and studied the lower valley of Einsamtal thoughtfully.

"Is there much to the rites?" he asked.

Eliana, dressed much more lightly and quite at ease in the chilly air that was customary so near Voerster's arctic circle, said, "Yes. A great deal. We are a people who value ritual. I am told that on the homeworld there are still ruined monuments on the land whence we came, monuments where my people used to gather to swear loyalty to one another and celebrate the pride of the White Tribe. It is no different here."

"But funerals?"

"Death is our great reality."

Duncan looked steadily at Eliana's fine-featured face, the dark brows and eyes, the ebony hair blowing in the wind. He could feel her within him. He was a trained and experienced empath and yet he had never felt another's gift so deeply. What, he wondered, could this remarkable woman have accomplished had she been found on Search and Wired at an early age?

"Death, your reality, Eliana? I don't sense that, somehow."

She essayed a slow smile, an expression of deep wistfulness. "Perhaps I overstated it, Duncan. We are a melancholy people.

There is a darkness in us. In twenty years or two hundred it will all come to nothing here. We abandoned justice a thousand years ago. That is why nothing changes on Voerster and why we make so grand a business of dying."

She indicated the pyre beyond the rocky ridge at the foot of the valley. "The Planetians are a race of brutes, but they would never deny Eigen Fontein his funeral fire."

"Interesting," murmured Duncan, returning to his view of the rising smoke column. It occurred to him that men had begun to rise above the animals when first they invented ceremonies with which to face death.

"And they honor a white flag," he said.

"More or less," Eliana said. "I would not put too fine a point on that. The Highlanders have their own ways."

"They sent you the Luftkapitan."

"They had two reasons for that. They wanted me to see how they had mistreated him. And they had a message meant for me, personally."

"The Law of Tribe," Duncan murmured.

"You have been studying, Starman."

"You have an impressive library here. And this—" He touched the socket in his skull. "—this helps one with languages."

"So Black Clavius told me," Eliana Voerster said. "How eager he must be to connect again. He once said it was like setting the mind free to roam the stars."

"Colorful. And almost true," Duncan said. *And how you would love it, Eliana—*

Her eyes met his directly, answering him.

"My concern is my daughter," she said. "If you know the Law of Tribe, you know what was promised the Highlanders. Both of the Fontein's solutions are unsatisfactory. But I will submit if that is the only way to spare Broni."

Duncan felt a shudder of revulsion at the thought of Eliana Ehrengraf in the hands of one of the strange men at the foot of the valley.

"Don't judge my people too harshly," she said. "Our laws are what our world has made them. Our ways seem harsh to you, but they were written to help us survive."

"I don't judge, Eliana," Duncan said. "Does your husband know what the man down there intends?"

"If he does not, I will tell him. As soon as Buele and your woman repair the radio. It might divert him from Broni. It may even give him reason to reconsider what he has done."

Amaya would hit flash point if she heard herself referred to as "your woman," Duncan thought. No New Earth feminist ever thought of herself as any man's woman. He wondered what Eliana's reaction might be to the uninhibited way the syndics lived in deep space.

He said, "In the cargo bay of my shuttle lies the body of an old friend to whom I promised a burial. Would the Fonteins permit it—under a flag of truce?"

Eliana considered the outrage Georg Fontein was feeling. The brother lost was hardly beloved. That was not the highland way. Fontein blood had been spilled, and that was a serious matter. "I don't know, Duncan. They might, but I am not sure."

Duncan unconsciously shifted his position to ease the strain on his wounded leg. He felt feverish and the thigh muscle was swollen and throbbing. Whatever was to be done had to be done soon.

Eliana said instantly, "You are in pain."

It would have been useless to deny it to an empath. "Yes."

Her dark eyes were wide and steady. "So is my Broni."

"I know."

"Can you bury your dead and still take Broni with you to your vessel?"

Duncan drew a deep breath and decided. "Broni and all of us, Eliana, if there are more of those—" He indicated the foot of the valley once more—"on the way from the highlands."

Eliana had shared part of Ian's threat with the Starman. That Ian himself would also be on the way as soon as the weather cleared, she did not mention to Duncan Kr. It was the nearest one empath could come to lying to another.

———

Duncan said, "Clavius tells me that he thinks Dietr Krieg can help Broni."

"I told you that when I first saw you," Eliana said.

"That was faith speaking. But Clavius knows what a syndic physician can do." His cool gray eyes fixed on Eliana's dark ones. "We are not miracle workers, mynheera. You must understand this."

"I know what you are, Duncan Kr," Eliana Ehrengraf said.

Duncan made no immediate reply. Of course she knew what he was and who. Her raw talent informed her. She knew, but did not know why she knew. Perhaps this made for more trust than he, Duncan, deserved. He was only a ship's captain, after all. Not a saint. "And if Dietr can help Broni, what then?"

"One trial at a time, Duncan. Save her life first."

Duncan looked again down the sloping valley of Einsamtal. The wind carried the sounds of the Highlanders' funeral chants. And mingled with the mournful piping came the sound of a balichord. Black Clavius stood on one of the corner towers playing for the enemy dead.

"If we leave here, what will become of your kaffirs?"

"They will melt into the mountains. They are all hill people."

"How do you bury your dead, Eliana?"

"We weave a sarcophagus of grass. On Earth we used coffins of wood, but here there is almost none. So we use what we have in abundance. Grass."

"Ask your people to make such a sarcophagus."

"Very well."

"And I will carry a message to the Planetians."

"You? But you are hurt, Duncan—"

"They are less likely to do something treacherous if I ask for a truce to bury my syndic. I come from the sky, remember."

"It may seem that you are dealing with primitives, Duncan. But you are not. Perhaps you need to remember that. The Planetians are sophisticated enough to be treacherous."

Duncan took her hand. The flesh was warm, her grip strong. "Do you know what a Cargo Cult is, Eliana?"

"Is *that* what you think Voerster has become?"

"Hasn't it? Don't you wait for years—tens or hundreds of years—for the Goldenwings to bring what you want from *out there?*"

She closed her eyes and said with deep wistfulness, "My poor Voerster."

She was a Voertrekker aristocrat, and for all her unhappiness with life as she was forced by duty to live it, she loved her homeworld deeply. Duncan still felt echoes of a similar feeling from long ago. He remembered the gray sea and the dark sky of Thalassa. Human beings, he thought, were capable of strange and powerful attachments.

"What does Captain Klemmer intend?" he asked.

"All Klemmer really wants is to fly his airship back to Voertrekkerhoem. I have imposed upon him most grievously."

"Will the Fonteins allow him to go?"

"I think not," Eliana said. "They would try to prevent him. It is their way. By now, Georg Fontein probably believes that *Volkenreiter* belongs to him. Planetians are like that."

"Will they attack us today?"

"Not until Eigen's funeral fire burns down. Georg must take ashes back to Winter Kraal and bury them there."

"'For the ashes of his fathers and the temples of his gods,'" Duncan quoted softly.

"Thalassan?" Eliana said.

"From Earth," Duncan said. "A man named Macauley wrote it long ago about a Roman soldier and what he reckoned worth fighting and dying for. We humans don't change much, do we?" He braced himself for the walk inside. "We had better call a council of war," he said.

They gathered in the room adjacent to Broni's bedchamber. Duncan had asked for a representative from the kaffirs in the manor house, and two were present, standing silently against the wall with Eliana's kaffir handmaiden.

For the last ten minutes there had been an exchange of ideas concerning the possibility of the Fonteins permitting anyone to approach the shuttle grounded in the meadow near the dirigible *Volkenreiter.* Luftkapitan Klemmer, his tattered uniform having been replaced with borrowed clothing from Healer Tiegen Roark, sat stiffly on the edge of his chair. He spoke slowly and with difficulty over his swollen lower lip. "I will not board the starcraft. I wish to return with my ship to Voertrekkerhoem. I can manage *Volkenreiter* alone if I can get aboard her."

"Oh, I don't think so, Brother Klemmer," Buele said without being asked. "There must be someone on the elevator helm. I remember that very well."

The airship captain rounded exasperatedly on the boy and would have reprimanded him had he not been cut off by the unexpected intrusion of Tiegen Roark who, until now, had not spoken.

"I will go with you, Klemmer," he said.

Eliana laid a hand on his sleeve. "Are you certain of this? It could be more dangerous than flying to the Goldenwing, Tiegen."

"I don't think so, mynheera. I would give much to see what wonders a Starman physician can perform. But up there I would serve no purpose. On board the *Volkenreiter* I can be of help." He looked across at the Luftkapitan. "If you agree, Mynheer Klemmer."

Klemmer nodded admiringly. He had never liked Tiegen Roark, but the Healer's decision was an act of courage—the paramount Voertrekker virtue.

Black Clavius said, "I should stay with the kaffirs."

"I want you with us," Duncan said. "To help Anya in case I begin to fall apart. My fever is rising and I may not make it all the way."

Anya Amaya said, "I object to you carrying a truce flag out to those bastards who shot you. I will do it."

"Forgive me, mynheera," the kaffir maid said calmly, "but if you do you will get nothing but a gang rape. It is their way."

"It is true, mynheera Anya," Osbertus Kloster said in a

hollow, trembling voice. "Women—that is women without status on this world—are treated without respect."

"Christ," Anya said explosively, "I can use a weapon as well as any man."

Duncan said. "What we want is the permission to bury Han Soo, Anya. Not to start a pitched battle. I will carry the truce message. If I do not return, I order you and Clavius to get these people aboard *Glory* in any way you can." He forced himself to his feet and stood for a moment, gathering his strength. He looked at the faces surrounding him and tried, as ship captains were supposed to do, to give them confidence. To Eliana he said, "How long before your husband's people reach us?"

"The weather is breaking. It will clear by morning. They will be here by then." She looked at Klemmer. "I apologize to you, Mynheer Luftkapitan, for the trials you have had to face on my behalf. The chances are that you will intercept the Voertrekker-Praesident's force somewhere between here and Voersterstaad. I will give you a letter to my husband. It will absolve you of any blame for our flight from Voertrekkerhoem. By his own standards Ian Voerster is a fair man. I do not think you will lose your command. Is *Volkenreiter* able to fly?"

"Well enough, mynheera."

"And you, Osbertus? What will you do?"

"I am terrified, Cousin. But I would not miss this adventure for all Voerster and the Six Giants thrown in."

Eliana looked long at Duncan Kr and then said, "Then let's begin."

At dusk the funeral cortege left the safety of the manor house and filed past the simple grave of the *lumpe* Airshipman Blier, down the meadow toward the glade near a mountain stream where Ehrengraf kaffirs had dug another grave in the bitter soil. The Fonteins, grim and silent, stood on the ridge at the foot of the valley, armed, immobile, and watchful.

In the windows of the manor house could be seen ambiguous

figures over what appeared to be weapons protruding into the misty evening air. The cortege walked slowly down the valley to the *Glory*'s shuttle, parked near the moored *Volkenreiter*. Tiegen Roark and Osbertus Kloster's boy, Buele, bore the woven grass sarcophagus on their shoulders. It seemed a light load. Duncan carried a staff with a white cloth that snapped and crackled in the wind off the Shieldwall.

Eliana Ehrengraf, as kraalheera of Einsamberg, walked at the head of the column, giving the ceremony and interment legitimacy by her presence. Over her Voertrekker gown she wore the embroidered overcloak of the Kraalheeren, a garment that announced her rank and duties to all in the valley.

Under the truce flag and in his halting Afrikaans, Duncan had explained to Georg Fontein that Han Soo's corpse must be retrieved from the shuttle, laid in the grass sarcophagus that the lady of Einsamberg had so graciously caused to be made, and then, after suitable funerary incantations, put into the ground. "My comrade's soul will rest with that of your companion in this valley. Han Soo was an honorable man who died very far from home. We thank you for allowing us to give him proper burial."

As Eliana had pointed out, the Fonteins were brutes, but not primitives. At dusk, they stood on the ridge, silent and staring at the Ehrengraf kraalheera, her servants, and the pair from the stars.

At the shuttle, the cortege paused while Tiegen and Buele followed Anya Amaya into the craft. As the time lengthened, the Fonteins began to whisper restlessly among themselves, making a show of their weapons.

"What are they doing in there, sah?" one of Georg Fontein's *lumpen* whispered. "Why are they taking so long?"

"Honneger, go down there to the star machine and see what they are doing," Georg ordered another of his men.

But as the *lumpe* began to run across the meadow, the people emerged from the shuttle. This time three carried the sarchophagus. The Starman Han Soo had been put into the grass coffin and brought out into the rainy evening.

Bright light flooded the meadow as the shuttle's landing lights came on. The Fonteins were startled, but held their places. Had the Starpeople brought weapons out of the machine? Georg wondered. The wounded Starman had pledged his honor that there were no weapons aboard the starcraft. Fontein was coming to believe that the Starmen lacked the courage to fight. If they had both weapons and honor they would have fought when the Starman was hit. Since they had not, and did not now, Georg began to think that a sudden attack on the funeral party might be profitable, truce flag or no. He stood, undecided, as the cortege reached the newly prepared grave by the river.

The large kaffir stood and made music on his balichord—sad and mournful music that was much the same as he had sent down the valley while Eigen Fontein burned.

Georg waited, undecided.

At the grave site Duncan planted the truce flag. He could see the Fonteins' restlessness. They fondled their weapons, muttering and whispering among themselves.

Duncan had brought Han Soo's *Book of Common Prayer*. Old Han had been a Christian of many years' standing. Once he had confessed to Duncan that he had joined his first syndicate because of the Muslim pogroms that had still swept China in the Celestial's time. "As a follower of our Lord Jesus," he explained with characteristic irony, "I became fair game for the believers in Allah the Merciful, the Compassionate."

Duncan, who was not a Christian—or a believer in anything but the prodigious nature of Nature—had seen religious wars in the colonies. He could only imagine how much more violent and intolerant they had been in the last days of the jihad and the Exodus. But what filled him with wonder was that Han Soo had stretched his uptime years into centuries. The old Celestial had been an alabaster image, a relic of Earth's long-vanished history. Duncan felt in his deepest being that they might at this moment be burying the oldest human being who had ever lived.

Despite their tense situation, Duncan had selected some of Han Soo's favorite verses. The old man had always preferred the English *Book of Common Prayer* over the Bible because it was, he said, "so much more civilized."

"'Lighten our darkness, we beseech Thee, O Lord; and by Thy great mercy defend us from all perils and dangers of this night.'"

"Amen to that," whispered Anya Amaya.

"'From envy, hatred, and malice, and all uncharitableness, Good Lord, deliver us.'"

Black Clavius raised his face to the deepening night and closed his eyes. "'Behold, I show you a mystery; We shall not all sleep, but shall all be changed, In a moment, in the twinkling of an eye, at the last trump: for the trumpet shall sound and the dead shall be raised incorruptible, and we shall be changed.'"

Otto Klemmer, raised a strict New Lutheran, recognized the verse from First Corinthians, and whispered a heartfelt prayer. He felt nothing for the alien he had helped to lower into the grave, but Black Clavius' sonorous prophecy made him think how near to death they all stood, here under the hostile gaze of these Planetian marauders.

Duncan wished there were more time to speak to Han Soo as they planted him in this alien soil. He wished he could explain to the old man that though it was not the misty valley of the Yangtze River, it was still a part of that same creation. *You may only be dust and energy, old friend,* he thought, *the stuff of stars long dead and awaiting rebirth. If you are sentient, if you exist at all as any part of the man who was Han Soo, then you know and there is little I can add.*

"'O Lord, support us all the day long, until the shadows lengthen and the evening comes, and the busy world is hushed, and the fever of life is over, and our work is done. Then in Thy mercy grant us a safe lodging, and a holy rest, and peace at the last.'" He closed the book and nodded to the others. "Fill the grave now."

Eliana watched the dirt fall on the grass sarcophagus with a certain revulsion. On Voerster not only the Planetians cremated their dead. Some instinctive taboo, brought on the Goldenwing

Milagro, kept Voersterians from rites such as these. She glanced at Duncan and Amaya. She had imagined that as travelers in the vastness of interstellar space, they would set their dead adrift among the stars as men once did in the seas of the homeworld.

Duncan met her eyes. "It was Han Soo's own choice," he said.

Anya Amaya, sensing Eliana's inner shudder, said in a tight voice, "This is *our* way, great lady."

"Enough," Duncan said. "How much time remaining before auto-launch, Anya?"

"Three minutes."

As the grave was smoothed by the kaffirs, Duncan said in a low voice to Klemmer and Tiegen. "Go now. We will follow."

The airshipman and Tiegen Roark made an obeisance to the fresh grave and began to walk unhurriedly toward the moored *Volkenreiter*. They cast long shadows across the meadow as they moved through the lights shining from the shuttle.

Duncan sensed the uncertainty among the Planetians on the ridge. "They will move soon," Anya said. "Can you feel it?"

"Yes."

Unhurriedly, he placed Han Soo's prayerbook on the grave. "Now," he said quietly.

Anya led the way in the direction of the shuttle. She was followed by Buele and the Astronomer-Select, then by Eliana. Farther up the meadow, Tiegen and Otto Klemmer had reached the grounded airship.

That set the Planetians into motion. Someone on the ridge gave a shout and they started down, waving their weapons.

The light vanished, leaving only a star-shot darkness. *"Run!"* Duncan shouted. He began to lope, searing flashes of pain burning through his thigh. He stumbled, felt the grass under his hands. Someone lifted him. It was Buele. They ran on until they reached the shuttle.

Beyond the dark wedge-shape the vast soft bulk of the *Volkenreiter* was floating upward in silence.

The Fonteins began to shoot their blunderbuss shotguns.

———

Duncan heard projectiles whining and ricocheting from the ceramic heat shielding on the shuttle's nose. He could smell the familiar ozone tang of the magnetic resonance engines starting. As he pushed Buele into the hatch and then fell sprawling himself in the cargo bay, he saw the spectroscopic rainbow of the first pulses from the thruster nozzles.

He heard Anya's call: *"Is the hatch clear?"*

He answered her. *"Clear, Anya! Clear!"* and the shuttle lifted.

28

A STAR IS RISING IN THE WEST

The Claw was a long talon of land descending from the northeasternmost coast of the Planetia to the planetary ocean of the Luyten Sea. Standing on a rocky promontory five hundred meters above the crashing surf, Beltram Denebeim searched the star-lined horizon with an ancient brass telescope.

The sky over The Claw was clear for the first time in days, though the wind buffeted Denebeim and lashed the sea into a maelstrom. The sea-spume seemed to glow with a light of its own in the darkness below. The waves striking the continent here had rolled across half a world of empty sea.

Denebeim's family had run hornheads and farmed The Claw for uncounted generations as dependents of the Fonteins, whose holding lay three hundred kilometers west and nineteen hundred meters above the Denebeim Kraal. From his father Beltram had inherited a single high range where hornhead could be pastured, and The Claw from crest to shore, where boats could shelter. Though the living was poor and the land inhospitable, to the barrel-shaped Planetian standing on the cliffs, The Claw had a rare grand beauty.

Starlight illuminated the raging sea. Luyten 726 lay in a thickly populated region of the galactic spiral arm. Bright stars filled the sky. Denebeim had never seen moonlight, but he would have found a clear night with a full moon in the sky of Earth familiar. His heavy-lidded eyes had superb night vision and acuity, and at the moment he was searching the Luyten Sea for the shape of his elder son's fishing sloop, due to return to the safety of The Claw this night.

Denebeim was a superstitious man without education. Only the sons of the wealthiest Planetian Kraalheeren went south to university, across the Gulf of Pretoria. And little enough of value they learned there, Beltram Denebeim thought as he watched the sea. His strong son Orrin was worth a dozen of the highborn swaggerers with their arrogant ways and saber-scarred cheeks.

For a Planetian of Denebeim's caste, life was harsh and simple. There was scarcely air to breathe in the highlands, let alone soil enough to raise proper crops. A man lived with his family, replacing each worn-out wife with the next, sometimes grieving as he lighted the funeral pyres, and always only just scraping a bare living from the barren plateau between the Sea of Grass and the Northern Ice. The hornheads struggled to survive, but like all necrogenes, they refused to multiply. All the native life on Planet Voerster had a maddening way of staying in almost perfect balance with the planetary ecology.

In Denebeim's household there were seven sons, six daughters, and, for now, a young wife—daughter of the shareholder who farmed the Fontein hectares nearest the Ice. Beltram, now in his late fifties, had buried four wives. Childbearing on the Planetia was a life-devouring business. It sometimes seemed to Beltram Denebeim that human beings, having come uninvited to Planet Voerster, were becoming as necrogenic as the native fauna.

Among Planetians, Beltram would have been thought a sentimentalist. He had loved several of his sturdy, vastly lunged and furry wives. He was fond of his children, and he held a special place in his oversized heart for his son, Orrin. One was expected to accept the fact that life was hard and risky on the Planetia, and Beltram did accept it. But as each hour brought the dawn nearer and no sign of Orrin's boat could be seen, Denebeim found himself praying to his austere New Lutheran saints—Matthew, Luke, Armstrong, and Bol-Derek—for some sign of his son's safe return from the sea.

The sign came.

It appeared low in the western sky, a streak of blue-white fire rising from the tumbled clouds hugging the Shieldwall. It soared straight overhead, lighting the barren landscape of The Claw's coastline in a supernatural light the color of the electric bolts that fell from the sky during thunderstorms.

Beltram Denebeim dropped his telescope and stared, open-mouthed, at the sky. The object passed high overhead, soon followed by a rolling crash of deep thunder. It continued to climb steeply out over the sea to the southeast.

The Planetian sank to his knees. He was not a religious man, but he knew that he had experienced an epiphany. He watched, filled with wonder, as the fiery manifestation dwindled and finally faded beyond the southeastern horizon.

And when he fumbled for his telescope, found it, and leveled it once again at the sea, he was in no way surprised to see, bright in the starlight, the sail of his son Orrin's small boat returning home.

The last thing in all the world Ian Voerster wanted at the very moment of armed departure for Einsamberg was an unannounced appearance of an investigative committee of the Deliberative Assembly, led by Ulf Walvis, Kraalheer of Windhoek, and one of the most pompous and stupid legislators ever to sit in the Kongresshalle.

Walvis, a corpulent septuagenarian of impeccable Boer stock, fancied himself a rival of Ian Voerster for the presidency. In fact, Mynheer Ulf was a frequently used cat's-paw, a dodderer who was sent here and there primarily as an expression of the displeasure of the Deliberative Assembly. When used in this way, the Kraalheer of Windhoek was given a portfolio containing a list of questions and demands—none with acknowledged authorship—as a Bill of Particulars, which, if not answered suitably by the party under investigation, could then become a part of a Bill of Attainder in the extremely unlikely chance of such a bill being voted by the full Assembly.

In nearly two hundred years, no such disciplinary action had ever been taken against a Voerster. In the same two hundred years, bills had been presented to a number of Ian's ancestors with blustering demands for answers or explanations of policies disliked by the members of the Assembly. There was no record of any of these demands ever having been met.

This knowledge of Voertrekker history caused the eight members of the investigative committee to defer to their senior member, Ulf Walvis. The committee members arrived at Voertrekkerhoem in the small hours of the morning. The eight members had decided that a more suitable time to interview the Voertrekker-Praesident would be midmorning. But Ulf Walvis, a man who was both conscientious and dull-witted, said (quite accurately) that the Voertrekker-Praesident was obviously about to depart for Einsamberg with a military force of the Wache, and that since it was this very expedition that the Assembly wished explained, he, Ulf of Windhoek, would interview Ian Voerster at once, and if necessary, alone.

It was indeed necessary. The other members of the committee (quite properly in their view) refused to be impolite to the Head of State and remained in their guest rooms at Voertrekkerhoem.

Ulf Walvis, dressed in full legislative regalia, marched out to the airship ground where the troops of the Wache were embarking on an Impala-class police cruiser. Once there, he cornered Ian Voerster and, to the Voertrekker-Praesident's barely contained fury, began his litany of complaint.

"I regret the necessity, Voertrekker-Praesident, but I am empowered by the Committee of Investigation and Inquiry to question you—"

Voerster, interrupted in an exchange with a Wache officer he considered far more important than either Ulf Walvis or, for that matter, the entire Deliberative Assembly, looked up at Walvis with bloodshot, angry eyes.

"Walvis, what the hell do you think you are about? Can't you see that I am busy here?" At the far side of the field a ground crew struggled to maintain control of the loading of the Impala-class airship. The winds were swirling around the stone buildings and across the field where the starcraft stood like rows of huge tombstones. Since the cargo had been unloaded and the odd cybernetic machines that did the work had withdrawn into the shuttles, no one at Voertrekkerhoem had ventured near them. The Voertrekkers feared the shuttles and the kaffirs ignored them. Ian had hoped that the first unpleasant hours of detention would have made Jean Marq amenable to using his advanced machines in what Ian Voerster called his "punitive expedition" to Einsamberg. But it appeared that Jean Marq had never once considered such a course of action. The Starman had, in fact, begun to act very strangely, dropping into sleepless trances at unexplained moments and looking at The Voerster's preparations to regain authority over his wife and daughter with a bemused detachment.

Jean's apparent indifference had enraged Ian Voerster. Who did the Starman imagine he was, not to fear the authority of the Voertrekker-Praesident of Planet Voerster?

This most recent disturbance, in the person of the fat and foolish Ulf Walvis, sent The Voerster into a near-ballistic arc of fury.

"Damn you and damn the Assembly," The Voerster snapped angrily. "Can't you see that I am busy?" Because he was developing a self-nurtured autocrat's rage, he added, "Get off this field now, while you still can, Mynheer Walvis." A more prudent and less self-absorbed man than the Kraalheer of Windhoek would have done as he was bid. After all, the mynheeren of Voerster had had years to become accustomed to Ian Voerster's temper. But Ulf Walvis was not an alert man. He chose to argue with the Voertrekker-Praesident.

"The Kongresshalle has heard disquieting stories about your dealings with the Planetians, Voerster." Walvis stood with his ebray-gloved hands resting on his well-padded hips in an attitude of challenge. From a window on the guest floor of Voertrekker-hoem other members of the delegation from the capital watched and waited for the explosion that was sure to come.

"The Kraalheeren hear rumors," Ulf Walvis declared, "that you have made a marriage contract for Broni Ehrengraf Voerster with Vikter Fontein. That you have promised the Highlanders what is not yours to promise—the First Landers' kraal of Einsamberg, which is your wife's."

To landowners whose holdings were secured by similar or less secure titles, the promise to dishonor a First Landers' Portion was tantamount to a declaration of class war against the gentry. "And the Assembly is also concerned about the reports that you have detained a Wired Starman, one Jean Marq, as hostage for the good behavior of others of his syndicate who landed at Einsamberg—"

Ian Voerster's jowly face grew purple. The ever-restless members of the Deliberative Assembly, afraid to speak for themselves, had sent this fat caricature of a Voertrekker to prod and chastise and even correct the man who had ruled Voerster by decree for nineteen years, as had his ancestors for centuries before him.

Even now Ian Voerster would have been inclined to swallow his anger and send Walvis off with vague promises. This was, after all, the method of dealing with the Assembly Ian had learned at his great-uncle's knee. But the Kraalheer of Windhoek made one mistake too many. In his piping, fat man's voice, he added the final indictment. "Our informants report that your wife has left you, Ian Voerster, and that she has taken the heiress—the Voertrekkersdatter—with her. This requires an appearance in the Kongresshalle and an explanation to the Council of Kraalheeren."

Ian Voerster, eyes ablaze, drew back a gloved hand and struck old Walvis across the face. *"How dare you speak like that to me?"*

Ulf Walvis rocked backward and would have fallen, save for his bulk. Blood smeared his chin from cut lips. His pale Voertrekker's eyes looked shocked and bewildered. He had spent his lifetime telling his betters things they did not wish to hear. Never had he been physically attacked for performing the duties assigned him by a committee of his peers. He tried to protest, but what came from his mouth was a gobbling babble of sounds. He could only think of the other members of his delegation back at the manor house. He wondered if they had seen him shamed and mistreated.

"*Ryndik!*"

The chief of Ian Voerster's bodyguard appeared instantly while the Wache captain to whom The Voerster had been speaking before Ulf Walvis' untimely interruption swiftly and tactfully withdrew.

"Sah," Trekkerpolizeioberst Ryndik reported.

"Take this clown and put him in the cells. Tell the warders that he is to remain there until we are out of here." He glared at the still-stupefied Walvis. "You need to learn manners, old man. And discretion. By all means, *discretion.*"

Walvis could only mop at his bleeding mouth with his expensively embroidered cuffs.

"And tell the Wache I am ready for the Starman now. Send him out. Under guard."

"Sah!"

The Voerster watched the policeman march old Ulf across the airship field. Ian already felt some remorse, but the man had allowed himself too many liberties. His treatment would be a warning to all the members of the Deliberative Assembly, who appeared suddenly to believe that they had a right to interfere in the governance of both the Voerster family and the nation. Let them learn.

He busied himself with details of the embarkation. He knew it was a failing to insist on tending to each task himself. A Head of State should not need to control the scheduling of military games for his troops, supply of his police forces, regulation of supplies into and out of the townships, and now the embarkation of a punitive expedition against his wife.

Yet he had always done such things. He knew that many of the Kraalheeren said—behind his back—that he had the mind of a bookkeeper, and perhaps it was right, but he never felt secure unless he personally guided each and every detail of any project.

The trouble was that it took so much *time*. Departure for Einsamberg was already five-and-a-half hours overdue.

A detachment of the Wache appeared with the Starman Jean Marq.

"It would all have been easier if you had agreed to use your machines against my lawbreakers," Ian Voerster said aggressively.

But Marq seemed oddly subdued and at peace. "I could not do that, *Monsieur le Président*. It would be a violation of my syndic's oath."

"Well, your oath is going to get you an airship ride in irons, my fine Wired Starman. Be assured of that."

Jean Marq made no reply. Instead he was looking at the sky to the west over Amity Bay. A bright star was rising swiftly, leaving behind it a trail of golden ionization.

"I do not know what it is you wanted to do with all this," Jean Marq said, indicating the airship and the embarking troops. "But it is really too late, *Monsieur le Président*. What will be will be."

Ian Voerster looked at the sky. There was a bitter taste of anger in his throat. "I still have you, Mynheer Marq. I still have you."

29

A BROAD AND AMPLE ROAD
WHOSE DUST IS GOLD

Duncan lay on the deck, pinned by the four Gs of Amaya's emergency liftoff. As the acceleration eased, he lifted his head. At the far end of the compartment he could see Amaya, Wired in and contained in her pilot's pod. Beside her, in the open copilot's pod, lay Eliana. He could only just make out above the bulge of G-absorbent gel. Her now-familiar velvet Voertrekker's gown was dishevelled, the long skirt above her knees. It was the first time Duncan had seen the Voertrekkerschatz's legs. The thought brought with it a wry amusement, when one considered the circumstances of the escape from Einsamberg.

In ordinary acceleration couches along the bulkheads of the compartment, the dim light of the radarscope and holocenter showed Broni, wide-eyed, obviously showing the effects of the takeoff. Very pale, silent, breath coming hard. Next to her Buele, also wide-eyed but far less silent. He was uttering strange and inarticulate cries that might have been signals of distress or pleasure. Duncan guessed the latter.

Next to Broni and the boy lay Black Clavius, relaxed in a Starman's takeoff attitude, eyes closed, lips moving in some unknown invocation; and Osbertus Kloster, plainly terrified and disoriented by the pressure of forces on his body—forces that must seem as strange to him as any he had ever experienced in a long life downworld.

Duncan was impressed with Buele. The boy was far less handicapped than he appeared to be. He had assisted Duncan on the run across the meadow in the dark. He had got himself aboard the shuttle with a minimum of guidance from either

---

Duncan or Anya Amaya, and he had made himself at home on one of the padded couches, as though he instinctively knew their purpose.

Duncan rose to his feet carefully. The G-load was diminishing, which meant that the sled was near to achieving orbit. Even as he considered it, the flight holograph shed its resonance and plasma symbols. He felt the twisting moment as the sled assumed orbital attitude, with the planet "overhead."

Anya opened the sliding carapace and there was seen a vast and silvery Voerster, shining in the white light of Luyten. Sundazzle flashed from the tops of great cyclonic weather systems—the same systems that only a short time ago had been wetting the new grave of Han Soo in the valley of Einsamtal.

Acceleration, gravity's surrogate, diminished to nothing, and Duncan floated free of the deck. He crossed the compartment to look closely at Broni. She was trembling, exhausted by the takeoff as well as by the physical and psychological strain of being spirited from the manor house and into the sled in Han Soo's coffin of woven grasses. *We might have killed her*, Duncan thought. But she was looking through the transparent carapace with an expression of utter wonder.

"Broni?"

"Yes, Mynheer." Her voice was thin, thready.

"Breathe slowly and deeply."

"Yes, Mynheer Duncan." Then: "When shall we see her, Mynheer Duncan? When shall we see the *Glory*?"

He caught her hand and squeezed it gently. "Very soon, now, Broni. Two more orbits."

"Will the Goldenwing be *there*?" The boy, Buele, was pointing at almost exactly the place above the curving disk of Voerster where *Glory* would materialize as Anya began her approach to rendezvous.

"Right there, Buele," Duncan said.

The youngster was excited, all-seeing. A talent? Duncan wondered. Well, why not? The gifts one needed to live in space were to be found anywhere and everywhere.

Duncan turned in air and floated toward the controllers. It was an almost sinful pleasure to be weightless again. He crossed above the open pod where Eliana lay in the gel. Her eyes were open and she was looking, fascinated, awestricken, at the shape of her homeland. Duncan caught the edge of the pod and anchored himself near her, looking for any sign of panic. There was none. Only amazement.

"It is so beautiful," Eliana whispered. "How could I ever have known?"

"Welcome to my world, mynheera," Duncan said.

"Is it all like this, Duncan?"

He smiled at her. "Much better," he said.

Eliana freed herself from the nonadhesive gel.

"Any disorientation?" Duncan asked.

"No." She floated clear of the pod.

"Take care. It needs some getting used to," Duncan said.

She closed her eyes and smiled. "It is like a dream of flying."

Duncan unreeled a restraining strap and put the end in her hand. "Go gently," he said.

Broni was sitting up. "Mother," she said delightedly, "I feel so free."

Eliana reached for her daughter's hands. Girl and woman smiled, like children playing a new and fascinating game.

"Oh, God. I think I am going to be sick." Osbertus Kloster, his loose clothing ballooning about him, looked pale.

Duncan located a medical kit and extracted a patch for motion sickness. He stripped the cover from the adhesive and fixed the disk to Osbertus' neck.

"Lie still a moment," he said. "The effect is almost instantaneous."

The astronomer closed his eyes.

"Breathe more slowly," Duncan ordered. "There. Better."

Osbertus opened his eyes again. "Why is the planet above us?"

"We are orbiting in an inverted position for better actual visibility."

———

"Actual?" Motion sickness was suddenly forgotten. Kloster's pale eyes were alert with eagerness to see, to experience.

Duncan indicated the flight holograph. "That is what we usually fly by." He glanced at the silver glitter of Voerster's planetary ocean reflecting the Luyten sunlight. "Sometimes we miss a great deal."

Black Clavius, free of the couch and floating free beneath the open carapace, sang out joyously in his sonorous voice: " '*The heavens declare the glory of God; and the firmament sheweth his handiwork.*' Ah, Master and Commander Kr, I have missed it so."

"Can I come up there, Brother?" Buele was free of his restraints and swimming awkwardly toward the black Starman. Clavius caught him, spun him about so that he floated close to the transparent carapace of the sled. Buele burbled with delight.

Anya, still Wired, but allowing herself to rise from the pod in which she lay during the liftoff to orbit, said, "Damon is calling us, Duncan. The cargo shuttles have returned on automatic, but Jean Marq is not with them. He is still on the planet. And Dietr wants to speak with you."

Duncan looked across the compartment at Eliana and Broni. The two resembled sisters as they watched Voerster spin above the shuttle, the green of the Sea of Grass now as bright as emeralds in the new day dawning across the continent below.

Duncan unreeled a drogue and plugged it into his socket. Immediately, his perceptions widened. *Glory* orbited three thousand kilometers ahead and five hundred kilometers above the sled. The ship was still well below the gleaming eastern horizon, but it called to Duncan with the loom of home after a long and difficult absence.

Dietr Krieg spoke to him as though they were across the compartment from one another. "*That bullet wound, Duncan. How is it?*"

"*Well enough. It will keep until you look at the girl.*"

"*May I register a protest? We are not a ship of do-gooders.*"

Duncan smiled in spite of himself. The remark was paradigmatically Dietr. "*No one would ever accuse you of being a do-gooder,*"

Dietr. A good mechanic, perhaps." Neurocybersurgeons hated being called mechanics. Four thousand years ago, when their cutting craft including shaving and trimming hair, they had hated being called barbers. Many things changed, but human nature did not. *"Be ready to examine her as soon as we come aboard."*

"Is that native quack with you?"

"No," Duncan said shortly. In fact, he thought, Healer Roark and the airship captain might well be dead by now, having bought the rest a few precious minutes of time.

Amaya, in the circuit, said, *"We will rendezvous in a hundred forty-seven minutes. Have Damon depressurize Hold Eleven."*

"Understood. I will be ready for your guest—and you, Duncan. Prepare for thirty hours in a recovery capsule."

"Very well, Ship's Surgeon," Duncan said formally. It was a title seldom used aboard the *Glory*, and one Duncan suspected Dietr, with his Germanic love of protocol, enjoyed hearing applied to himself.

Duncan removed the drogue and turned to see Eliana watching him. Did the sight of a man with a cable connecting his brain to a machine repel her? he wondered. Had she heard him subvocalizing and did she wonder if it were part of some nonhuman ritual?

The zero gravity appeared to have eased the effects of the hard takeoff for Broni. The girl was sucking in great breaths of the oxygen-rich air inside the sled. Eliana whispered to her and the girl responded with a wan smile.

As the sled passed over the eastern Shieldwall, Broni gasped with excitement. "The Blue Glacier, mynheera! Look how the sun shines on it. Oh, how *lovely* it is!"

Eliana looked across the compartment at Duncan with an expression of utter joy. "Thank you," she said silently. "Thank you with all my heart."

Glory's sled passed over the eastern coast of the continent at a height of one hundred eighty kilometers. Black Clavius could see the first wink of the Southern Ice. He shivered in spite of himself.

Against the silvery blue of the Great Southern Ocean, the grays and browns of the Sabercut Peninsula lay like a corpse in the sea. Clavius studied the Isthmus of Sorrow, and remembered the pitiful coffles of detainees on the way through Hellsgate. Clavius had been fortunate. They had transported *him* by police dirigible. The inhabitants-to-be of the more severe clangs in the Friendly Islands were not so favored. Between Hellsgate and the Detention Two complex across Walvis Strait from the Southern Ice lay eight hundred kilometers of narrow mountain road along the southern shore of the Sabercut, a strand known as the "Skeleton Coast" for a similarly inhospitable coast on the homeworld. There were no accurate records on which to rely, but the word was that dozens—possibly even hundreds— of prisoners had died on that journey of despair.

As the sled orbited southeast, the low sun-angle struck shards of cold light from the Sea of Lions and Walvis Sound. Clavius wondered about the detainees he had seen and spoken to in the cells at Voertrekkerhoem, at Hellsgate, and Detention One. What had become of the garrulous *lumpe* Fencik? Was he somewhere down there on the icebound shores of the Skeleton Coast?

Clavius had seen few kaffirs on his short journey through the penal system of Planet Voerster. The word in the clangs was that kaffir miscreants were either dead or immured in the southernmost camps of the Friendlies. It was quite possibly so. It seemed a way of coping that came naturally to the Voertrekkers of Voerster.

Osbertus Kloster clung with a death-grip to the restraints on his couch, but his face was uplifted and he stared open-mouthed at wonders he could never have guessed at in his days—he thought of time past that way—at Sternberg. The view of the heavens through the observatory's small refractor was not a hundredth of what he could now see with his naked eyes.

Out beyond Voerster's southern limb the Astronomer-Select could see four of the Six Giants, enormous and brilliant. Green Erde, the kaffirs' Mandela; yellowish Wallenberg, that the blacks called Tutu. Thor, the war god, whom the kaffirs worshipped as Chaka. And dreaded Drache, the dragon, who was more powerful in his kaffir persona of Angatch, the All-Powerful. And, slowly changing as the sled flew, the curved illusion that was Voerster— the kaffirs' Afrika.

There is so much to know, Osbertus thought breathlessly, *so much to learn. And life is so short. I am so near my end.* He glanced at Buele and wondered why he was not surprised that the boy had been instantly at home aboard the starcraft. Open-eyed and wondering, but amazingly self-possessed and at home. The astronomer looked briefly at Anya Amaya and Duncan; at the moment both were Wired to the vessel and obviously in communication with the great Goldenwing still beyond the curve of the planet. He felt a furious flash of envy. To know what they knew. To be as young as they were. To sail between the stars and live forever. . . .

He reined himself sadly. *Be gracious, Mynheer Voertrekker,* he thought, *and be generous with your thanks for what you have already been given.*

Broni's wan attention was captured by the girl beside Duncan at the control console. The Voertrekkersdatter could sense an aura about the New Earther that was redolent of energy, sexuality, devotion—to what? Was it to her ship that Anya directed all that love? Broni wondered. To her syndicate? Was it to Duncan? It was all of these and more. Anya's personality seemed turned outward, toward the deep between the stars. It was a yearning and a fulfillment. Broni seemed suddenly to know what made Anya Amaya different from the downworlders with whom Broni had spent all her few years. It was a faith, almost a religion, and it held her enthralled by the promise of an endless and ever-renewing unknown.

The Voertrekker girl turned her attention to Duncan. Now that she had turned the key with Anya, had she the instrument with which to begin to know Duncan Kr, and by extension all of the Starmen of *Glory*'s syndicate?

———

For as long as Broni could remember, she and her mother had affected the moods and emotion of those around them. Looking at Anya Amaya and Duncan Kr, Broni understood to what uses such a wild talent could be put. The realization made her pulse race. Anya and Duncan turned as one to look at her, and despite the frailty of her grip on life, Broni Ehrengraf Voerster wanted to shout with joy.

Eliana sensed her daughter's joy. She watched as Duncan and Anya responded to Broni's emotional offering. They sensed it so clearly that it was as though a beam of light were uniting them all.

For a moment she felt bereft, left out. These were deeply personal experiences neither she nor Broni had ever shared with others. Then she felt Duncan's emotions brush against her own. She looked at him. It was a revelation. Other men had fallen in love with Eliana Ehrengraf. But she had never encouraged any of them, not even Ian, for hers had always been destined to be a dynastic marriage. The love between man and woman had seemed forever beyond her grasp. And now, *Duncan.*

What has come over me? she wondered. *Have I become wanton?* She had given herself to The Voerster virginally, as was fit for Boer aristocrats. She had never looked at another man with desire.

A Voertrekker kraalheera kept her bargains.

Until now.

Duncan smiled slowly and moved to her side. "That great sea is like the ocean on my homeworld, mynheera. The sun is brighter here, and it shines more willingly, but an ocean that covers nine-tenths of a world brings memories of Thalassa."

"Did you grieve for your homeworld, Duncan?"

"I think perhaps I did. For a time. But no grief lasts forever."

"A downworlder knows very little about forever," she said.

There was no reply he could make. Seen from her point of view, he and Amaya and the rest were virtually immortal. Did she dislike him for that? No, he sensed nothing of the sort from

Eliana Ehrengraf Voerster. If anything, she regarded him with admiration. With love? His own state of arousal near her made dispassionate judgment difficult.

Amaya, sharing Duncan's feeling through the drogue, seemed to resent Eliana Voerster less. "We will dock on the next orbit," she said. "The western coast of Voerster will be visible again in six minutes."

Eliana said softly, "So precise."

Amaya heard through the drogue, with Duncan's hearing. She said, "It needs to be so. It is *not* a game."

"Forgive me, mynheera," Eliana said openly. "I have much to learn."

"If the need arises," Amaya said drily, "I will try to teach you."

The sled crossed the western coast in bright morning sunlight. Osbertus could see the deep inroads of the sea at Windhoek Gulf and Amity Bay. From this viewpoint, the argument among Voersterian scientists about the origin of many of Planet Voerster's features seemed specious. Both the gulf and the bay were almost certainly formed by the impacts of asteroids or large meteors during the formative stage of the Luyten 726 system. The old astronomer felt a deep, personal gratification at the clarity of the evidence. The Asteroid Collision Theory had been argued as long ago as Osbertus Kloster's time at Pretoria University. As a student he had been a member of the minority, a fervent Asteroidist. This, combined with an absolute refusal to indulge in the sport of slashing the faces of his fellow students with a saber, had earned him a reputation for being eccentric. *Which I was,* he thought, eyes fixed on the continent below, *and for which I am now very grateful.*

He looked at Eliana with a certain pedantic satisfaction. He had lectured the Voertrekkerschatz many times on his vast file of peculiar astronomical and natural theories. He hoped she saw in the crater-shapes of Windhoek Gulf and Amity Bay a vindication of her quaint cousin.

But Eliana was not thinking about geological shapes. What she saw was the brilliant green of the Sea of Grass, the cyclonic swirl of silver-white clouds above the continent, the dark grays and browns of the Shieldwall and the Grimsel Mountains, and the ice blue of the Blue Glacier shading to white as it melded with the dazzle of the Northern Ice.

For a strange moment Eliana felt an almost physical pang of separation and love for the bleak land so far below. She was struck by a lonely thought: *To feel the Nachtebrise once again and see the grasses take wing, yes, I should like to feel and see that at least once more.*

Orbiting between the Tropic of Luyten in the north and the Tropic of Voerster in the south, the sled was above Durban on the Sea of Lions when *Glory* rose above the curve of Planet Voerster's silvery limb.

Broni saw the Goldenwing before any of the others watching through the sled's transparent carapace, and she responded with a tremulous cry of ecstasy.

Glory orbited in sunlit splendor, a long, slender hull surrounded with the lofty spikes of her masts and rigging, all glittering with the laserlike streaks of monofilament rigging. From portside main to starboard mizzen a web of light spread across a gap of twenty kilometers. Zodiacal light framed the ship against the blackness of space and the stars. Directly behind *Glory* lay the constellation of the Ploughman, a stooped figure guiding a diamond-bladed plough through the furrows of infinite darkness. As the sled overtook *Glory*, even Duncan was moved by the sheer size and beauty of his command.

Buele grew wide-eyed and uttered a chortle of pleasure. "She is so *big!* See how very *big* she is!" He tugged at Osbertus Kloster's flowing sleeve, and the Astronomer-Select of Voerster could say only, *"I had no idea, no idea at all—"* The vast ship they were overtaking bore almost no relation whatever to the tiny gemlike miniature he had seen in a telescope field. This was very different. This was—*Glory*.

Eliana caught Duncan's hand and held it. "So beautiful, Duncan. So *beautiful!*"

And Black Clavius, who drank in the sight of the Goldenwing as a man might drink water in the desert, let himself rise almost to the curve of the transparent overhead. *O, Lord,* he thought, *to travel again*—" '*A broad and ample road, whose dust is gold, And pavement stars . . .* ' "

His deep voice broke and he floated without speech, tears of greeting after long separation flowing down his cheeks.

30

A MATTER OF DISCIPLINE

At a distance Jean Marq considered the tired and angry man berating his troops in the meadow below the manor. There was a lack of sophistication common to these offworlders; all of them, he thought, no matter how arrogantly they proclaimed authority. The time he had spent close by the Voertrekker-Praesident of Voerster had not increased his respect for the man. He reminded Jean of a prosperous farmer he had once known, long ago, in Provence. A troubling memory—indistinct, and yet laden with unpleasant emotions for which he had no explanation.

Jean had been studying the situation on Voerster. It was plain to any unbiased observer that Ian Voerster was willful, which was unattractive in anyone and ugly in a ruler, and stubborn, which was dangerous. His Afrikaner ancestors had been forced to surrender South Africa to the Xhosa and the Zulu. Now he saw his task as maintaining Voertrekker domination over Voerster forever, even if it meant allying himself with the no-longer-quite-humans of the Planetia. The man fancied himself a politician and military tactician, and while his skills in both professions might be adequate for ordinary times on Planet Voerster, where men like himself had been writing the rules for generations, there was some question in these extraordinary times.

Somehow the Voertrekker-Praesident had managed to antagonize his entire peer group, the mynheeren class of colonists, by mishandling the freaks from the highlands and alienating his wife and daughter, who were now safe with Duncan—presumably aboard the *Glory*.

Jean Marq paced the upper stories of the manor house at Einsamberg and wondered what Ian Voerster imagined would happen when he informed Duncan that a member of his syndicate was being held hostage. He stood on the high battlements and looked down into the meadow that formed the floor of the valley of Einsamtal. Two airships were moored there—the military craft that had brought him, with Ian and a detachment of troops of the Wache, to this place in the foothills of the Shield-wall, and the other encountered and turned back along the way as it was limping westward. The *Volkenreiter* had been damaged and was being flown by two men when the military force had encountered it and forced it to return. The men aboard the dirigible had been arrested immediately and were now imprisoned somewhere within the manor.

On the valley floor a colony of tents had sprouted—squat ugly things meant to shelter the squat, ugly, sometimes many-fingered men who had descended from the Planetia to meet with Ian Voerster and his troops.

Jean understood that they had rushed to this place intending to capture and detain the Voertrekker-Praesident's women. They had arrived too late. The sled had gone. Voerster's wife had taken asylum aboard *Glory*.

Jean Marq felt a reluctant sympathy for Voerster. His wife had made a fool of him, perhaps even cuckolded him. At the very least she had prevented a dynastic marriage, and who knew what other plans she intended to disrupt.

Ian Voerster imagined he could prevent further catastrophe by informing Duncan Kr that Jean Marq was now officially a hostage. But Starmen did not respond to such threats. Sailing the Coriolis forces would be impossible if every and any gang of colonists could control the movement of the Starmen and their ships by outlawry.

Duncan would do nothing to retrieve Jean Marq and the Frenchman knew it. It was simply a matter of discipline. But did the colonial know it? Jean wondered. It seemed he did not, to judge from the way he was leering up at his captive, showing him off to the thickset Planetian with whom he was speaking. Arguing? Now that did seem likely. It appeared to Jean Marq that every conversation entered into by Ian Voerster turned acrimonious.

The Frenchman left the parapet and sat on a stone bench. He did not feel well, and the nightmares were returning. Apparently the Boche had been doing something right with his treatment of Jean Marq. But he had taken his last dose of medication before leaving the ship. It had been days now and the effects were wearing off. The dreams were returning. The trouble was that Krieg's conditioning had been highly effective in the disruption of mnemonic patterns. He still could not remember the whole content of the nightmares which had been growing so troublesome aboard *Glory*. He remembered piercing hot sun. A rocky terraced hillside. Ancient vines making stark shadows at midday. And a girl. There had been a girl named Amalie, and Jean knew that he should know her name as well as he knew his own.

He lifted his face to the white light of Luyten. Another sun, he thought. Warmer, more golden. . . .

He closed his eyes and reluctantly allowed sleep to draw near.

"I see him well enough," Vikter Fontein said in his rasping voice. "Explain to me what profit you have turned by taking him hostage."

Ian Voerster, tired and in need of a bath after three days in the field, frowned up at the Kraalheer of Winter. "With him I get my women back."

"*My* women," Fontein said bluntly.

"Not yet, Fontein. You have the manor, be content with that for a time."

The Fontein looked about him at the valley of Einsamtal. Compared to his holding of Winter on the high plateau in the shadow of the Blue Glacier, Einsamberg was a paradise. But he knew as well as Voerster that his claim on the estate was tenuous. The Boers who settled Voerster had some peculiar laws, but they

———

lived by them. This generation's Voerster was a dangerous—and opportunistic—deviation from the straightlaced Boer ethic to which all Voertrekkers claimed to subscribe.

"There is still the matter of the First Lander's Writ on this holding," Fontein said.

"Don't talk to me about First Lander's Writs, damn you," Ian Voerster said angrily. "I am buying your loyalty, Fontein, with land and a daughter. Be content with that."

"I might be," the Planetian said flatly, "if the girl were here. Or failing that, the Ehrengraf."

Voerster's florid face went livid. "You'll have Eliana Ehrengraf when Voerster stops turning and not an hour before."

The Fontein looked across the field to where his *lumpen* were engaged in hand-to-hand practice under the command of his new heir, Georg Fontein. "This adventure has already cost Winter a son, Voerster. I want my due."

"You lost your son because both your sons are idiots, not through any failing of me or mine," Ian said. "They had no call to come down to the Grassersee on a fool's errand. I promised the Fonteins should have Einsamberg and so they shall—always provided that the Deliberative Assembly does not take collective action against us for trying to establish some sort of order among our turbulent peers."

"They wouldn't do that," Vikter Fontein said.

"Oh, would they not? I brought your people down to the lowlands. It hasn't been a popular move, Vikter. You can retreat to the Planetia and it isn't likely anyone can follow you. But the combined mynheerenshaft could keep you in the heights until Luyten goes dark. Whatever else you choose to forget, do not forget that." He looked again toward the battlements of Einsamberg for Marq, but the Starman had gone. "As long as we have the offworlder, we have the dominant hand. The Starmen will do anything to get him back—even return my people."

"Do you really believe that?"

"Of course I believe it."

"I do not," Vikter Fontein said heavily, and turned away to

stamp across the meadow grasses toward the ridge where, Georg had told him with funereal face, Eigen Fontein had been properly cremated.

Below the ridge there was a patch of newly turned soil—the cold, wormy grave of the Spaceman. The Kraalheer Vikter Fontein shuddered and superstitiously refused to look at the last resting place of the old Mandarin, Han Soo. In the highlands it was black death and ill fortune to look upon a new grave. The Fontein shuddered, looked at the blank sky, and marched on, thinking that the bargain which had seemed so fine that late night in Voersterstaad seemed a great deal less so here and now in the valley of Einsamtal under the Shieldwall.

31

ABOARD THE *GLORY*

What daunted the downworlders overtaking *Glory* was her vast size. The sled approached the Goldenwing cautiously, as though it were fearful its filial relation to the ship might be forgotten and its tiny existence snapped up and snuffed out by its glorious, diamantine mother. The visitors were made speechless by the dimensions of mast, spar, and rig. Even their sense of distance and proportion was challenged as they approached *Glory*. At five hundred kilometers she was large and seemed nearby. At one hundred, she dominated the sky. At fifty, her furled wings umbrellaed Voerster. She was not only the most beautiful artifact Eliana and the others from below had ever seen, she was the most commanding.

Amaya carefully piloted the sled toward the hatch of hold 11. The sensation was one of entering a cathedral in space. The carapace remained open. Duncan guessed—since it was a choice always left to the sled pilot—that the Sailing Master had left it so to awe the Voertrekker passengers. She succeeded.

Eliana held Broni against her breast. The girl trembled. Buele and the old astronomer turned faces upward and outward, astonished by the patterned intricacies of the iridescent mono-filament rig. It carried light, and it divided the cosmos into uncountable segments, as though some prodigious god were intent on apportioning a mystic judgment. Black Clavius smiled and feasted his eyes on a sight he had not seen for many long downworld years. *Glory* was more beautiful, even, than *Nepenthe*, he thought.

The sled moved into the cavernous interior of hold 11. A

high overhead gradually hid Voerster and the stars. Broni said in a faint whisper, "Mynheera, Voertrekkerhoem and the Kongress-halle could fit inside this place."

The distant fabric walls and overhead were pierced by myriad ports and skylights. Through some could be seen the silvery glare of Planet Voerster, through others only the rig, the sky, the stars, and the Six Giants.

Even Buele was subdued. He murmured to Osbertus that not only would the Kongresshalle and Voertrekkerhoem, as Broni said, fit inside this one empty hold, "But everything between the Kongresshalle and the shores of Amity Bay, as well. Have you ever seen anything so empty, Brother Osbertus? It must be kilometers from end to end. Whatever could they have carried in such spaces?"

Duncan withdrew his attention from the control displays and said to Buele, "She carried people in cold-sleep, Buele. On her first voyage she transported ten thousand colonists from Earth to Aldrin."

Buele was starry-eyed. "She carried a *world*, Brother Duncan?"

"Yes. But only once. On Aldrin, her syndicate took possession of her."

"And she has been in the sky ever since then?"

"Deep space is her home." Duncan glanced at Eliana again. She was watching him with an unreadable expression in her dark, shining eyes.

The sled lurched slightly as Anya Amaya allowed it to settle the last few centimeters to the fabric deck. Turbines and genera-tors unspooled, their flywheels winding down through the tonal scale as they slowed. Behind them, the hold hatch contracted like a sphincter, shutting out the light of space. The walls of hold 11 began to bulge as interior pressure was restored.

Amaya, conscious of Duncan's pain, patched through *Glory*'s interior communications system: *"Dietr, come now. You have two patients here in hold eleven."*

———

Eliana was startled by the chittering babble of odd voices outside the sled. "You have kaffirs here?"

"Monkeys, kraalheera," Amaya said. "Cyborgs. Part machine, part animal. Chimpanzee, actually. I doubt there is any animal quite like them on Voerster."

Several of the small beast-machines scrabbled over the sled, securing it to deck hold-downs. One paused to peer curiously in through the carapace.

"Dear Lord," Osbertus breathed.

"They are harmless, Mynheer," Duncan said. "And we could not sail the ship without them."

"Wonders," the Astronomer-Select of Voerster said. "Is there no end of wonders?"

From somewhere in the vast dark of the hold came flashes of brilliant light. Duncan read the exterior atmosphere values and said, "You can open now, Sailing Master."

"Yes, Captain."

There were sounds behind the computer console. The ventral hatch dropped. Cold air rushed into the sled, together with beams of electric blue light. Damon Ng and Dietr Krieg, skinsuits gleaming, materialized out of the dark. Two medical carryalls waited at the foot of the ramp made by the open hatch.

Krieg rose from the open hatch to float in the microgravity. "Stay quietly, Duncan. You've been in a gravity well for twenty hours. Now where is the girl?" He answered himself by moving skillfully to Broni's side. "This girl is anoxic. Bring a mask."

Outside the lander, monkeys scrambled. Dietr drew a hypodermic airgun and loaded it with a beta-blocker. He smiled distractedly at the wide-eyed Broni. "This is an old remedy, but still a good one. Give me an arm." The gun popped and Broni gasped in surprise. Dietr immediately covered her face with an oxygen mask. "This is just until I can get you into an environmental control unit."

Dietr now looked at Eliana. *"Du lieber Gott,* are you this child's mother?"

_____

Amaya said warningly, "This is the kraalheera Eliana Ehrengraf Voerster."

"Kraalheera Voerster? Forgive me for staring, *Gnadige Frau*, but I was not expecting a beauty." He took Eliana's long, slender hand, and brushed it with his lips in the antique Euroterrestrial style.

It was an unheard-of intimacy for a stranger, but Eliana allowed it. "Aid my daughter, Healer. I ask humbly."

"I will do what I can, *Gnadige Frau*. Be assured of it."

He moved to Duncan. "What have you done to yourself, Master and Commander?"

"A bullet, Dietr. It can wait. Take care of the girl."

"Don't tell me my business, Duncan." The Starmen had switched to Terrestrial Anglic, too colloquial and too changed by time to be easily understood by the Voertrekkers.

Duncan called monkeys into the sled and instructed them to lift Broni onto one of the waiting carryalls.

Osbertus Kloster braced himself unsteadily and declared, "I am Kloster, Astronomer-Select of Voerster. At your service, Healer."

"Clavius. One-time syndic of Goldenwing *Nepenthe*."

Dietr said to Duncan, "You brought the lot, my Captain."

"Not everyone," Duncan said wearily.

"Damn it, Dietr. Get Duncan into sick bay, will you?" Amaya snapped.

Dietr helped Duncan to the ramp. "Get in the carryall, Duncan. The leg is going gangrenous. I can smell it."

"I need to be on my feet in thirty-six hours," Duncan said. "Jean is still down there."

"I see. What you want is not one miracle, but two."

"But Brother Healer, you *can* work miracles, can't you?"

The physician looked down at the unbeautiful boy and was empathically staggered by the strength of his Talent. He clearly did not speak Anglic, yet his empathy was so great that he understood precisely what was said, and what was meant. *This one we must have. To train as Jean's successor. Is that why he was brought here? To serve as payment for repairing the girl's rheumatic heart? Kismet,* Dietr thought.

Duncan would never agree to such an arrangement. A quid pro quo would not even enter the Thalassan's mind. *But it would enter mine,* Dietr Krieg thought. *I am not burdened with Duncan's sense of honor.* He looked at the Voertrekker woman.

She was, of course, an enigma. A beautiful enigma. No surprise, Dietr thought with a wry smile. Offworlders were impossible to fathom. And what beautiful woman was not a sphinx?

Dietr held up forceps with a lead fragment between the tongs. "Your Thalassan black magic did you good service, Duncan. But you didn't get it all and you didn't completely block infection. You have a low-order staph bug rotting your meat. You'll need the full thirty-five hours in a recovery pod."

Duncan, naked and bathed in ultraviolet light on the surgical table, said, "You said twenty-five."

"I said thirty, but I can understand your eagerness to be up and about. The Ehrengraf is incredible. I haven't seen a woman like that since home."

Duncan said, "You have never seen a woman like that, Dietr. Nor have I."

"It is like that, is it, Master and Commander? What an unsuspected romantic you are." He signalled for a monkey to move the immobilized Duncan into a recovery pod.

"Wait," Duncan said. "What about the girl?"

"It is more complicated than I thought. She needs a full heart-lung transplantation. I am not equipped to do that. On New Earth, or Gagarin—but not here. I can give her a prosthesis. That should help . . ." He broke off and said, "What is Voerster like, Duncan? A planet of empaths? The girl and the mother are both sensitives, and that moonfaced boy is a powerful Talent. Can we claim him?"

"We must deal with Osbertus Kloster first, then with the boy."

"He makes me itch to give him a socket. I take it from what Black Clavius says, they think he is retarded?"

"Some do. Not all."

"Duncan, a question. Syndic to syndic."

"Ask, Dietr."

"What's to be done about Jean Marq?"

"I don't know yet, Dietr." He sounded weary and troubled.

"You will decide," said the neurocybersurgeon, and signalled the attending monkey to move Duncan into the waiting pod.

Dietr was about to close the pod and put Duncan into cold-sleep when Black Clavius appeared in the surgery.

"Will his wound heal?" the black Starman asked.

"Of course. What do you take me for?" Dietr snapped.

"*She* is in the passageway. She wants to see him."

Dietr said irritably, "Very well. Bring *her* in."

Eliana appeared, still unsteady in the microgravity. She was an illusion of light and shadow, Dietr thought, with her gown floating about her and her long hair clouded about her pale, narrow face.

She looked at Duncan and hesitated. Dietr realized that she was startled by Duncan's nudity. Of course. Voerster was a planet of prudes. God, what a pity, he thought.

"Shall I cover him?" he asked challengingly. "He is very nearly asleep. Harmless to great ladies." Why, he asked himself, did he always eventually respond with hostility to aristocratic women? He had no such problems with Amaya. But then, Amaya's presence was not so demanding as the Voertrekker woman's. Was she taken with Duncan Longshanks? he wondered. He sighed with envy.

Eliana simply stood looking at Duncan as he sank into the healing gel within the pod, and into sleep as well.

"Thank you, Healer," she said. "He feels safe in your care."

She sensed that, did she? Dietr wondered how strong her empathic sense was. Powerful where Duncan was concerned, that was obvious. The neurocybersurgeon watched her leave the surgery closely escorted by Black Clavius. The *Nepenthe* Starman was teaching her how to move about in the near-weightless environment. She seemed to be learning her lessons well. There had been no hints of motion sickness or panic from either the Voertrekkerschatz or the Voertrekkersdatter. *Lieber Gott,* he thought. Finally. A language uglier than his own native Teutonic.

Dietr Krieg propelled himself into the transport plenum. Mira had appeared from nowhere, as she always did, and now rested comfortably across Eliana Ehrengraf's shoulders.

"Mynheera," he called.

"Healer?"

"I will be ready for Broni within the hour. Please bring her to me then."

Eliana found her daughter with Buele and the young Rigger Damon, in the light-gravity spaces. She was watching them play a strange sort of tennis with nonsymmetrical balls that took weird rebounds from the court walls.

Broni declared, "Damon says that when the Healer finishes with me I shall be able to fly about like they do. Won't that be wonderful, mynheera?"

Mira trilled with pleasure at the sound of Broni's voice and left Eliana's shoulder to leap into the girl's arms.

"A cheet, mother! A cheet like Ylla."

"Not a cheet, love. A cat. Earthborn. We used to have them on Voerster, but they did not prosper."

Broni was fascinated by the hair-thin wire extending from Mira's head. The cat fixed her with an intense look and allowed her to touch the drogue. *A young queen and an old queen,* Mira thought. *Now there was a proper number of females within the great-queen-who-was-not-alive. If they would stay there might be hunting in the deep night.*

Black Clavius said, "It is her own equivalent of a Starman's socket." He touched his wooly hair. "The Healer's idea."

Mira fixed Broni with an intense stare and purred deep in her throat.

_____

Broni ran a hand over Mira's short, silky coat. "You little beauty," she whispered.

"Broni," Eliana said quietly. "We shall take you to the physician within the hour."

"Yes, mynheera," the girl said fervently, "oh, yes. Will you tell the Voertrekker-Praesident?"

"Of course, Broni," Eliana said quietly. "He is your father."

"Does he really care what happens to me, mynheera?"

"Never doubt it, Broni," Eliana said, and held her daughter in her arms.

"But he offered me to the Fonteins of Winter."

"He was mistaken. That will not happen."

Broni, holding Mira, was content with that. For the remainder of the hour she sat with her mother and Black Clavius watching Spacemen's games—games she hoped one day to play.

32

AN EXAMPLE FOR THE PEOPLE

Cursing self-righteous men, Healer Tiegen Roark bent over the mistreated body of his fellow prisoner, Otto Klemmer. In all the world there was no one more certain he was always and forever *korrekt* than the Voertrekker-Praesident, Ian Voerster. It naturally followed that any subordinate—especially one who had benefitted from a close association with Voerster and his family—owed total allegiance to his patron. It made no difference whatever that the Luftkapitan's airmanship had probably saved the lives of the Voertrekker-Praesident's family, or that he had already suffered revolting torture at the hands of the Fonteins. Klemmer had bestowed his loyalty upon the Ehrengraf and not upon her husband. Otto Klemmer—a *cholo*, after all—had assisted her flight into the sky. Now he was paying the price.

But the rumor was out that The Voerster was in trouble with his fellow Kraalheeren. It was said among the new arrivals from Voersterstaad that the members of the Deliberative Assembly, unsupervised in the Kongresshalle, were demanding to know if what was being done to the heiress of Ehrengraf could also be done to any one of them.

The threat to invoke the Law of Tribe did not trouble them, but the thought that First Landers' Writs were now to be considered valid only at the pleasure of the Voertrekker-Praesident troubled them a great deal. If solemn land grants were to be dealt with cavalierly, where would it end?

At Ian Voerster's command, Tiegen was sure, the Fonteins had taken up where they had left off with Klemmer. He had been battered and disfigured by members of Eigen Fontein's com-

---

mando before breaking for freedom in the *Volkenreiter*. He was now undergoing more of the same treatment each time he was taken into the cellars of Einsamberg "for further questioning."

Actually, there was no need whatever to interrogate Klemmer further. He had admitted, as had Tiegen Roark, that acting on Eliana Ehrengraf's specific orders, they had created a diversion that allowed the Voertrekkerschatz and her daughter to escape the Planetians with the Starpeople. Still, Ian Voerster pursued her as best he could, with ranting radio calls—unanswered—to the orbiting Goldenwing. The man was a fanatic.

The Voertrekker-Praesident seemed obsessed with the desire to retrieve his wife and daughter from those who had saved them and deliver them to those who would harm them. All in the name of peace with the Highlanders. Healer Roark was a man of no great intellect, but he was a Boer aristocrat to his fingertips. He was well on the way to developing a treasonous disesteem for the Head of State of Planet Voerster.

He daubed at the airship captain's sweaty, battered face with a cloth moistened in the abominable wine served with his supper of burnt ebray and coarse bread.

"Is it very painful, Klemmer?" he asked. As a favored physician, he had never before had to deal with the effects of fists and clubs. It was sickening. Even the blood shed in his student dueling days had been spilled under almost aseptic conditions. Not like this. What beasts the Highlanders were.

Klemmer had difficult speaking. The puncture wounds made in his lower lip by Eigen's *lumpen* had festered again and the swelling disfigured Klemmer's long, narrow face.

"The Fontein was here," Tiegen said. "He says we must use the radio to speak with the Voertrekkerschatz. He says we must tell her he will kill us if she does not return with Broni."

"To hell with The Fontein," Klemmer mumbled. Hatred burned in his eyes. "And to hell with Highlanders. May their twelve fingers rot and fall off while masturbating." Of all the Planetian attributes, their occasional polydactylism was most offensive to Lowlanders.

"Yes," Tiegen said. "But it would do no harm to speak with the lady."

Klemmer closed his eyes in angry exasperation. *He thinks I am a coward,* Tiegen thought. *But I am not. I flew with him, didn't I? I selflessly helped conduct his pig of an airship over these mountains, at night, in high winds and rain—all so that mynheera and the Spacepeople could take Broni to the Starman Healer. Shouldn't that count for something?*

"They are building a gallows in the courtyard. Can't you hear them?"

"I have made my peace with God," Klemmer said with *lumpen* certainty.

Tiegen bit his lip with mingled pity and exasperation. *Cholo,* he thought. What was there about the slightest infusion of the kaffir in the blood that made a man so stubborn? And so fatalistic?

"The Voerster needs you," Tiegen said. "You can bargain with him."

The airman's voice was all but gone, his battered mouth made clear speech impossible, but he muttered hoarsely, "You can't bargain with a man who will sell his daughter to the Highlanders just to have them at his back instead of his throat."

There was the sound of boot-heels on the stone floors. Tiegen waited with dread, thinking that one of these times the guards would be coming for him—for Healer Roark.

The door burst open. There, like a shrike, stood Ian Voerster, flanked by two brutish Highlanders. "Go back to Fontein. I have no further need of you here," he ordered.

"Sah." The Highlanders, bundled in ebray furs and leather and hung about with hand-weapons, departed. Ian Voerster stepped into the room and slammed shut the door.

He snapped, "Healer, have you patched him up so he can walk?"

"He is badly hurt, Voertrekker-Praesident. He has been tortured."

"He has had just punishment."

Tiegen Roark felt the unfamiliar pressure of blood pounding

behind his eyes. For some unexplainable reason, Ian Voerster's crassness tipped some inner scale in the physician. "That is shit, Voertrekker-Praesident. We were returning to Voersterstaad when we were intercepted. The Luftkapitan was only following orders given him by the Ehrengraf." He could not explain to himself why he spoke of Eliana in quite that way. He knew—had always known—that it irritated the Voertrekker-Praesident to be reminded that his wife was the heiress of a family as ancient and renowned as his own, and was considerably better loved on Voerster.

Ian Voerster's eyes glittered. "I have always suspected that your loyalty was to the Ehrengraf rather than to me. In spite of all our traditions, you have always been ready to betray me." He slapped at his booted leg with the short crop he carried. The impacts were like pistol shots and Tiegen's anger subsided to be replaced with a damp, icy fear.

"You have heard the rumors, have you, Physician?" Voerster asked with an almost demented slyness. "Trouble in Voersterstaad. The legislators getting above themselves. They all favor my wife. They have begun to call her 'the new Elmi.' How would they regard her actions if they were in my place?" He stood over the semiconscious airshipman, prodded his battered cheek with his whip. "Stand, *cholo*. On your feet."

"He cannot, Voerster," Tiegen Roark protested.

"Malingering bastard." Voerster walked to the window and stood looking down at the encampment in the mountain valley. It suddenly came to Tiegen that Ian Voerster was trapped here in the valley of Einsamtal. There was no one to fight, but if he abandoned the kraal to the Fonteins—or even to the mountain winds—his reputation would fall into ruin among the Kraalheeren. And if there was one thing a Head of State on Voerster could not survive, it was a loss of reputation. What the kaffirs called "cheek."

Voerster seemed to feel the physician's scrutiny and he turned. His face was livid, eyes sunken. No, thought Tiegen, his adventure with the Planetians was not succeeding. Eliana had been right, after all.

"What are you staring at, damn you?"

"Nothing, Mynheer Voertrekker-Praesident," Tiegen said.

Voerster pointed with his whip. "Patch him up enough to walk from here to the courtyard."

Tiegen felt the bottom drop out of his belly. "Mynheer—"

Ian Voerster said, "Luftkapitan Klemmer will be hanged as soon as he is well enough to stand on his feet like a Voertrekker. I intend to make him an example for the people."

He slapped his leather boot-top once again, and strode from the room, leaving Healer Tiegen Roark open-mouthed with amazement and dismay.

33

I LONG TO TALKE WITH SOME OLD LOVERS GHOST....

As in a dream, Eliana Ehrengraf floated through the long passageways inside *Glory*. Surrounded by the silence and space of a more peaceful world than she had ever known, her thoughts roamed.

The Starman physician Krieg had insisted that Broni's convalescence would not be long, considering the extent of the surgery he had found it necessary to perform on her. It was true that the girl looked comfortable in her deep coma inside the healing pod. There was color in Broni's cheeks and a deep, easy rhythm to her breathing. Her shallow breasts rose and fell quietly. Her golden hair lay tumbled about her pale face, and her lips were slightly parted, as though she were on the verge of waking.

Eliana had asked, "Does she dream, Healer?"

"Some do, mynheera," Dietr Krieg had said. "Not all, but some."

She regarded him obliquely. "Did Duncan?"

The neurocybersurgeon shrugged. "*Gnaedige Frau*, my Master and Commander is a mystery to me. Who knows if Duncan Kr dreams, or if he does, of whom or what?"

Eliana showed the physician a book. "Anya Amaya lent this to me. She said it was Duncan's. It is very old, I think."

The physician turned the small volume over in his hand. "One of Duncan's antique prizes. *The Poems of John Donne*. Is the poet known on Planet Voerster?"

Eliana smiled ruefully. "Poetry is not much read on Voerster."

Krieg handed the book back. "Duncan would think that

more a pity than would I." He shrugged. "I am not at all like the captain, mynheera. I did not become a wanderer for love of the stars."

"A practical man, Healer."

"I believe in what I know." He turned away from the Voertrekker woman. There was something about her simple elegance that discomfited him. Sooner or later he was going to have to tell her that the transplantation in Broni's chest had not been a true success, and that there were going to be costs. He was thankful that Broni was still deep in her healing coma and that the moment of disclosure was not yet. Dietr Krieg was not accustomed to failure—even to partial failure. It would be some time before he could come to terms with it. Typically, Dietr was more concerned about his own self-esteem than about the potentially devastating effect his confession would have on this unsettlingly beautiful woman.

"Have you seen Duncan since he came out of the pod?" he asked.

"No," Eliana Ehrengraf said. "He has made no effort to see me and I don't want to intrude on his privacy."

"Well, he is a strange one, mynheera. A solitary man."

"Yes."

"If he has been avoiding you, it is because he thinks it best."

She thought of that exchange now, as she drifted, weightless, through *Glory*'s vast, empty spaces. Time was strange aboard the Goldenwing. The Starmen kept a twenty-hour day. It could have been almost any length, she surmised, but twenty hours—earth hours, twelve cesium-clock minutes shorter than the hours which passed on the planet above. She had begun to think in Starman's terms, she realized. "Above" because the *Gloria Coelis* was orbiting in an inverted position relative to Planet Voerster. The silver-and-blue planet could be seen through the many dorsal transparencies scattered throughout the long empty hull. Voerster seemed to blaze with a rush of color and light that was incredibly beautiful.

Eliana found, to her surprise, that she did not mind terribly being alone in *Glory*. Osbertus and Buele spent most of their time with Black Clavius and the young Rigger, Damon Ng, doing the technical and scientific things that commanded their attention. When she encountered the Astronomer-Select and his apprentice, they were euphoric, overwhelmed with new knowledge. The Ehrengraf in her felt a measure of pride. *Colonials we are,* she thought, *and far from a technological people, but the wonders of space are wonders Voertrekkers could grasp and appreciate.*

Eliana longed for the companionship of Duncan Kr. The man had touched her deeply. On the planet she would never have allowed herself the thought. But she was not on Voerster—she was free, in Duncan's world.

The woman syndic, Anya Amaya, was an enigma. On Voerster she had seemed resentful of Eliana. But in her own element she had been generous, even friendly. It was clear that she watched over Duncan intently. But their relationship was oddly like brother and sister—though from what the girl said (and she spoke quite freely of intimate things), they had been occasional lovers. It seemed probable that Anya Amaya had been—was—lover to all the Starmen. With the exception of the one on the planet's surface held by Ian. "Our Earth-born lunatic," she called him.

Amaya had returned to what was her normal Starman's routine of wandering about the vessel nude or nearly so. Eliana flushed the first time she had unexpectedly encountered Anya in what the girl called "her natural state." The Sailing Master was without inhibitions. More than that, she was sharply alert to the feelings Eliana had when Duncan entered her mind. Life in a microcolony of empaths had its rewards, but privacy was not one of them.

When Amaya had delivered Duncan's book of poems to Eliana she took pains to call her attention to the dozen or so verses on certain dog-eared pages, poems lined with yellow marking pen.

"Duncan's favorites," Amaya said.

Eliana Ehrengraf had never in her life read anything about love so earthy, yet so moving.

Come, Madame, come, all rest my powers defie,
Until I labour, I in labour lie.
The foe oft-times having the foe in sight,
Is tir'd with standing though he never fight. . . .

The lines brought a smile and a tingle to her cheeks. She had never heard a lustful man's erection so deftly invoked. Ian would be scandalized.

Your gown going off, such beautious state reveals,
As when from flowery meads th'hills shadow steales.
Off with that wyerie Coronet and shew
The haiery Diademe which on you doth grow. . . .

Anya said, "Poor Duncan. How he must long for someone to love. Look here." She pointed to a pair of melancholy lines Duncan, or someone centuries gone, had underlined in ancient brown ink.

I long to talke with some old lovers ghost.
Who died before the god of love was borne. . . .

"The Elizabethans were outspoken," Amaya said with a sidelong smile. "And who would ever imagine there were such fires burning in our silent Thalassan, mynheera?"

Who, indeed?

Who but Eliana Ehrengraf Voerster?

She arrived silently at the hatch to the compartment where Broni lay in the healing pod. Strange instruments watched over the girl's vital signs. And Mira, *Glory's* cat, lay protectively over the transparent shield that covered her. The small beast lifted her head and regarded Eliana unblinkingly. The tiny wire drogue trembled as she moved. What could she be thinking, Eliana wondered? For the first time Eliana speculated on how it would be to wear a Starman's drogue, to see the vast universe as the ship's computer saw it—and as Mira did. How marvelous that would be, the Voertrekkerschatz thought. To have come from a world of so many walls into a world that was all vast spaces and movement and coruscating light.

Mira appeared to have sensed what she was thinking and she stood, stretched, and then launched herself into a surreal leap that ended on the wall by Eliana's face. The cat's emerald-colored eyes fixed on the woman's. For a moment, Eliana felt disoriented, as though she were plunging into those deep green wells. Mira opened her mouth, bared the Jacobson's organ in the roof of her mouth to "taste" the woman, then trilled with satisfaction. She showed her tiny teeth in what may have been a snarl but was not. She stepped from the vertical wall onto Eliana's shoulder, rubbed against her cheek and was gone in another slow flying leap to her chosen station on Broni's pod.

"It seems the small queen finds you acceptable."

Eliana turned to see Anya Amaya. She was dressed in sweat-damp shirt and workout trousers fresh from the spin-gravity well where she must have been exercising.

Her face was shiny and her hair hung in wet ringlets. She stripped the shirt off over her head and tied the sleeves around her waist. "That's better." Her full breasts were slick with perspiration, the nipples soft and dark rose-colored.

"Come with me, mynheera," she said, and launched herself down the long, empty plenum. Eliana followed. The Voertrekker-schatz had not even the words to describe a sexual attraction between women, but Amaya's nakedness stirred unfamiliar feelings.

Anya turned to address Eliana as she moved down the fabric tube. "You still have not seen Duncan yet, have you?"

"No."

"A self-denying man, my Master and Commander."

"I don't understand you," Eliana said.

"I think you do, mynheera. Aboard the *Glory* you can let yourself understand many things that could never be—up there." Amaya indicated the silvery sea and cloud of Voerster shining through a transparency. "He loves you. Is that so hard to grasp? You're an empath. Surely you feel it?"

Eliana stopped herself with a hand against the curving wall. She said, "This is a different world from any I have ever known, Amaya. I am groping. Feeling my way."

Anya caught her by the hand and pulled her along. She was smiling as she said, "At least you aren't telling me that you are a married woman."

"Did you think I was liable to say that?"

"No. I'm an empath, too, mynheera. And a trained one. I know how things are between you and your husband. There are loveless marriages on New Earth, too."

"I am not yet easy discussing very private matters, Anya."

The girl caught her by the shoulders and spoke with a sudden, almost angry intensity. "My concern is for Duncan. Always for Duncan and *this ship*. Look at me. Do you love him?"

"How can one say—"

"Stop it, forget what is downworld. Speak the truth. The truth. *Do you love him?*"

Eliana heard herself saying, "Yes."

"Then come with me." Anya spun once again and took a different plenum leading toward the dorsal. Eliana followed in silence.

Presently they reached a high, arching chamber whose entire ceiling was transparent. Beyond the skylight rose the masts and the spidery wonder of the monofilament rig. St. Elmo's fire raced along stays and halyards. The pale light of Luyten gleamed on the furled skylar sails. Here and there in the rig, kilometers away from the ship, the tiny lights showed where ship's monkeys were at work. High overhead, almost against the transparency, Eliana could see the spread-eagled shape of a naked man outlined by the sun's glare.

"He comes here to take the sun on his wound, and to look at his beloved stars," Amaya said softly. She cast herself loose from the wall and held Eliana at arm's length. "He comes here to avoid meeting you, mynheera, and compromising your Boer sense of morality." Eliana could see that there was no hint of a smile on the New Earther girl's pretty face now.

"But we know better, you and I," Amaya said. "We know what must be done, don't we?"

"Yes," Eliana said sibilantly.

Amaya's fingers found the ties that held Eliana's Voertrekker's gown in place. She loosed them. In the microgravity, Eliana's disrobing had the quality of a pavane. Anya untied the Boer knots, opened the gown and let it fall away.

As Eliana felt the unfamiliarly cool air on her nakedness, she thought that the ease with which she was made naked was, after all, a part of the Voertrekker ethos. She watched as Anya Amaya bent and removed her Voertrekker sandals. She felt her nudity like a pressure in her loins. Amaya slipped off the polished wooden ring that held her hair. A black mane framed her pale face. Eliana hung in space, back arched, legs spread, eyes half-closed, lips apart.

Amaya put her arms about Eliana and pressed her breasts against her own. She whispered, "Perhaps one day—but not now, mynheera." She pushed gently and Eliana rose through the bright darkness toward Duncan.

He had heard them, turned, seen the last of it. He spread his arms and enfolded Eliana.

Eliana Ehrengraf felt his naked body against hers. She felt him enter her with consummate skill and tenderness. *In all my dreams of love,* she thought, as his mouth found hers and her legs wrapped around his waist, *it was never, never like this.*

34

THE FRIENDS OF ELMI

The Kraalheer of Windhoek looked about the ancient panelled Kongresshalle room so redolent of generations of heavy rhetoric. He studied the faces of his peers with a mixture of surprise and pride. Ulf Walvis, a man in his declining years with an undistinguished history, a balding pate and a sagging belly, had become a hero. His colleagues on the Committee of Investigation and Inquiry of the Deliberative Assembly had just elected him by voice vote to the chairmanship of a new committee—The Friends of Elmi.

No one on Planet Voerster could have been more surprised to find himself leading a movement than the Kraalheer of Windhoek. He had been publicly humiliated by The Voerster on the airship ground of Voertrekkerhoem—with the members of the Committee of Investigation and Inquiry watching from the manor house. That should have ended his career in politics.

It did not.

After Voerster had departed with his punitive expedition to Einsamberg, the jailers of the Wache released Walvis from the cells, and the committee returned in sullen silence to the capital. For most of his seventy-odd years, Ulf Walvis had been thought rather a fool. But now he was the right man at exactly the right moment in the history of Planet Voerster.

Women enjoyed few rights on Voerster, and the Kraalheer of Windhoek was an unlikely feminist champion. But when the woman being wronged was sole heiress to a prime First Lander's holding, a shudder ran through the Kraalheerenschaft. And when the Voertrekker-Praesident struck Walvis before witnesses, he created a necrogene within the body politic.

Wags among the Voersterstaad *lumpen* who loitered near the Kongresshalle murmured that the legislator's courage grew in direct proportion to Ian Voerster's distance from Voersterstaad. There was truth in this. But Ulf Walvis did what came naturally to the old Boer nobility. As the original South Africans on Earth had often done in times of trouble, Ulf turned to Voertrekker legend.

The legend was the symbolic mother figure of Voerster.

Elmi Voerster Ehrengraf was the mythic wife who took her dead husband's place as one of the first Voertrekker-Praesidents, and who lived as a man for what was reputed to have been a hundred-odd years. Opinions about Elmi's tenure varied. But the time was right, the advocate was right, and the symbol was exactly right for a troubled world.

The Kraalheer of Windhoek, savoring his Claudian emergence as a political force, regarded the potential new members of the Friends of Elmi, and welcomed each with relish. He had not realized until now how much he hated Ian Voerster—*had* hated him ever since, as The Voerster, he first stepped up to the Machtstuhl.

The caucus room was crowded, the air heavy with the smell of portly men in heavy clothing. Ulf finished his welcoming remarks, to the newcomers from Durban, Milagro, Capetown, Port Elizabeth, and Pretoria.

The full attendance testified to the fact that Ian Voerster had made a critical error. It was all very well to play tyrant and oppress the *lumpen* and kaffirs, but when one threatened the privileges of one's own aristocracy, one sowed dragon's teeth. The Voertrekker-Praesident, a man of impeccable bloodlines, had become a danger to every landholder in the Grassersee. Rather than scattering to their kraals as they always had when confronted with unpleasantness, the Kraalheeren who had been at Voertrekkerhoem, or who had heard of Ian Voerster's activities, congregated at Voersterstaad.

The populace, both mynheeren and *lumpen*, was becoming

aware that Eliana Ehrengraf Voerster was (by what magic or connivance no one was certain) now aboard the orbiting Goldenwing that could be seen several times each night by every living soul on Planet Voerster. They knew also that Ian Voerster had rashly taken a Wired Starman hostage. Why he had done so dangerous a thing was only conjecture, but the consensus seemed to be that he was trying to force the Starmen aboard the *Gloria Coelis* to return both the Ehrengraf and the Voertrekkersdatter so that he could give one or both to the despised savages of the Planetia. This was a matter of concern to everyone on Planet Voerster.

At the meeting in the Kongresshalle, Ulf Walvis and his coconspirators were delighted to see some fair-weather friends. Among the newcomers in the first rank of furred and brocaded legislators stood Rector Abelard of Pretoria University—the alma mater of all present—and Kraalheer Guderian of Milagro, the sacred land on which the Goldenwing *Milagro* deposited the First Landers, a holy place to every Voertrekker. Both Abelard and Guderian had an unfailing instinct for avoiding schemes with a potential for failure. Their presence in the caucus room was an omen of success.

Outside the Kongresshalle, the kaffirs, aware as always, watched and waited. The legend of Elmi appealed to them because it was the foundation of the Cult of Elmi, which taught equality for kaffirs. To the lowland *lumpen* Ian Voerster's promised infusion of Planetian freaks into an already bigoted society meant a great deal, and none of it good. The townships were restless, having heard that Black Clavius, too, was aboard the orbiting Goldenwing and might soon be gone. The kaffirs had grown accustomed to the Starman's presence on Voerster. His privileges among the Voertrekkers had earned the kaffirs much cheek. His departure was being regarded as a loss for the kaffirs of Planet Voerster.

Ulf felt weighed down by his heavy legislative robes, but he had made himself into an imposing figure because he knew how his peers valued appearances. A month ago not one would have come to hear him speak. Now they stood to listen.

Ian Voerster, he thought, *it is remarkable what a blow on the mouth can do for a politician.*

The Kraalheer of Windhoek drew a deep breath and began to speak treason.

———

35

A NEW LIFE AND AN OLD AFFLICTION

Broni Ehrengraf Voerster, revelling in an unexpected free dom, swam in the cool sunlight entering *Glory*'s dorsal. She could feel Luyten's radiation on her naked skin. It felt best along the thin line of scar tissue between her adolescent breasts. She twisted to look down at Dietr Krieg, the Starman Healer, who seemed to recline on shadows in what he told her was "the spaceman's slouch," a position that the syndics could maintain for hours without effort. She waved to him and he waved back.

Through the transparency overhead she could see Duncan and her mother playing like children outside in the rigging. They wore skinsuits and light bubbles of glass on their heads. Duncan was instructing Eliana on the use of the small reaction device in his hands. Each time Eliana tried it, she was sent spinning through the rig, scattering the monkeys who were at work patching a skylar sail. In the earpiece she wore, Broni could hear her mother's laughter.

There was something else, something that aroused loving pity in the younger woman. Each new experience, each unfamiliar sight, evoked wonder. She heard Eliana say: *"Oh, Duncan— isn't that Port Elizabeth Sound?"*

The narrow limb of the silver Luyten Sea rolled over the horizon, sparkling with wind-patterns and dappled with clouds. As each moment brought a new vista into view, Eliana responded to it with warm and unrestrained delight. The thin film of air and water, of life, which clothed the planet above sparkled in the light of its parent star. From moment to moment, Eliana would pause in what she was doing and exclaim her joy.

"The Sea of Lions sparkles like diamonds."

"You sparkle, Eli."

He calls her Eli, Broni thought with a tolerance beyond her years. *Duncan makes up nicknames for her and she's like a girl, loving it.* The Voertrekkersdatter let herself rise to the transparency and signalled to the pair in the rig. Her mother mimed a kiss. Below her Damon Ng and Buele appeared, g-string naked—probably as a concession to Broni's sensibilities. Silly, perhaps. But how quickly one became accustomed to Starmen's ways. And how absolutely aghast her father would be, she thought with a giggle. So far Black Clavius and Cousin Osbertus had not succumbed to the pervasive nudity, but Clavius had spent ten years among the kaffirs, who did not approve of nakedness before whites. And she could not imagine Osbertus Kloster shedding either his clothes or his academic dignity. Though it amused her to think of the old cousin delivering a learned paper to the dons of Pretoria University wearing only his Master of Sciences bonnet.

She pushed off from the transparency, spinning and twisting in a weightless dance. The scar on her chest pulled slightly, but Dietr had warned that it would, and that it would probably itch until it was completely healed.

It filled Broni with wonder that the Healer had actually opened her chest like a Landers' Day package and done unimaginable things to her heart and lungs. A prosthesis powered by a microdot of nuclear fuel now beat in her breast, aiding the heart whose progressive failure had so nearly killed her.

Dietr signalled for her to come down to him. She took a last look at her mother and Duncan dodging through the wires and halyards like truants, before she jackknifed like a platform diver and pushed off again, moving easily down through the compartment. She passed Damon and Buele on the way. The astronomer's apprentice shouted a greeting, and for him she had a smile. But seeing Damon so nearly naked *did* affect her and she looked away, and then back again, behind her fingers. She could feel what Damon was thinking. His interest in Broni grew stronger each day aboard *Glory*. She would have to speak with her mother and ask about that. Or if not the mynheera (it was increasingly hard to think of Eliana Ehrengraf Voerster as wise and venerable), then Anya Amaya. She would do that, yes, when next she and Anya met for the cosmology intructions she had been taking from the New Earther.

When she reached the Healer he handed her a medical gown. He let a smile touch his thin lips. "To keep you warm, Broni Voerster, not to cover you. I am a Healer and a syndic," he said.

And a man, Broni thought. It was very interesting, the way she now affected the males aboard *Glory*. If Eliana had not been so preoccupied with Duncan, would she be displeased? It was an interesting question. A Voertrekker girl was raised to be silent, to remain in the background, to deny her sex. Until that moment when she was given, body and chattels, to a man whom she probably had never seen before, and who had the right in law to loose the cords of her gown and demand both virginity and sexual fulfillment. *All things considered,* Broni thought, *we do well enough, we Voertrekker women.* But the task was a difficult one.

Dietr Krieg took her by the arm and led her out into the plenum.

"Are you going to be stern, Healer?" Broni spoke ingenuously, aware, and not minding at all, how poorly the hospital garment covered her.

"Don't use your nubile tricks on me, mynheera. I am too old a dog to hunt children," Dietr said sternly.

Broni smiled, far from offended.

The Healer led the way past a branching in the passageway and guided her along a fabric tube she had entered before. In time the way widened into a dark, open-roofed chamber similar to the one above. But this time the transparency in the overhead displayed not the brilliant face of Voerster, but the cold and distant stars. Somehow, during their passage, they had changed orientation, a thing that happened often aboard *Glory*. Motion aboard *Glory* was like venturing onto a Moebius strip. The lack of gravity was both a delight and a perplexity. Did the Starmen themselves ever really become accustomed to it? Broni wondered.

As they entered the large chamber, Broni became aware that Anya Amaya floated in the darkness. She was "shooting stars" with an ancient bubble octant. It was an optical device used long ago by navigators of the homeworld. Amaya said she liked to practice with it, never knowing when the skill might be needed.

Dietr said, "Come down, Sailing Master."

Anya, dressed in half a skinsuit (she had startled Broni by explaining that she dressed that way when her menses were flowing because tampons were in short supply aboard the *Glory*), dropped easily to the fabric deck. She spoke to Dietr. "Now, you think?"

"Yes. It had better be now. We won't get Jean Marq back."

"I should say that's a loss, but I can't," Amaya said.

Dietr turned to Broni. "Look up. What do you see?"

"The stars, Healer." The simple statement left unsaid the wonder of it. The deep, deep black of infinite space, the gem-points of light that lay forever beyond the reach of mankind, and the thousands of worlds which did not—worlds reachable by ships like this one, and by people like these. The girl felt a pang of the most poignant longing. Mira appeared from nowhere, accompanied by one of her kittens. She landed softly on Broni's shoulder and trilled a feline greeting in her ear.

Broni instinctively caught the kitten and allowed it to nestle between her budding breasts.

Dietr said soberly, "There is a thing I must tell you, myn-heera. I considered speaking with your mother first, but decided against it. It will affect you most directly and you have a right to control your own destiny."

The idea of a woman—most particularly a young woman—controlling her own destiny was remarkable to Broni Ehrengraf Voerster.

"You are very solemn, Healer."

At this moment Broni heard the sound of Black Clavius' balichord playing somewhere not too far off. The black Starman had not made music since coming aboard the Goldenwing, seemingly content to feast himself on the sights and sounds he had imagined he would never see again.

"I mean to be solemn," Dietr said.

"You are frightening her, Dietr," Anya said protectively.

"She's a natural empath. She already all but knows."

"What do I know, Healer?" Broni asked.

"That you came to me too late, Broni. That the procedure was not completely successful."

Broni felt a cold chill. She held the kitten's warmth against her skin.

"Am I going to die, Healer?" she whispered.

Anya ran fingers through Broni's golden hair. "Dietr, for heaven's sake . . ."

"You will die in due time, Broni, as we all will," Dietr Krieg said. "But if you return to the planet, your time will be almost at once. You cannot live in a gravity well."

"I don't understand, Healer."

"It is simple. If you return to Voerster, the prosthesis I implanted will not keep you alive. The mass of your body—as little as it is—will kill you. If you remain in microgravity, you will live a normal human life span. I am sorry. I was overconfident, perhaps. But I did give you my best skill. Now you—and your mother—must decide."

Broni said slowly, "Are you saying I can remain aboard *Glory*?"

"The final decision will have to be Duncan's, of course. He is Master and Commander. But even if you were not so valuable an addition to the syndicate, he would never send you back unless you chose to go."

"I could be like you?" She looked from Dietr to Anya and back again. Her hand went to her head.

"Yes," Dietr said. "That, of course."

"Mother does not know?"

"No. We chose to tell you first. Actually, Anya did. It was a feminist decision. Though God knows the mynheera is feminine enough, even for Anya."

———

"She has the right to decide for herself," Amaya said fiercely.

"Of course she has. I don't deny it," Dietr murmured.

Broni looked up at the stars. *To see them close by. To move between them on golden pinions like some glorious bird. How marvelous. How sad for those I must leave . . .*

Dietr looked at Anya Amaya and produced a wry smile. The girl's empathic qualities were remarkable. He could almost read her thoughts. What bloodlines there must be on Planet Voerster, he thought. If the Age of Sail were not ending, syndicates would make Voerster a regular port of call, and human nature being what it was, they would loot the planet of its best and brightest. But none of that would happen. The time of the Goldenwings was almost past, and *Glory* would be the last Goldenwing for Voerster.

"What do you feel, Broni?" Anya asked. "Would you join us aboard *Glory*?"

Us, thought the girl. "Oh, *Anya*."

Dietr said, "Understand that you won't live forever, Broni. We don't, you know. We live a normal span of human years. But we sail on the tachyon winds at almost the speed of light. So the years pass at a different rate for us and for downworlders. There will be no return to Voerster, Broni."

"What will happen to your colleague, Healer?"

"We will never get him back unless your father releases him without conditions. Long ago it was decided that hostages must be expendable among syndics. Anything else would create an impossible situation. You will learn all of these things, Broni."

"And more. Much more," said Amaya.

"Can you choose, Broni?" Dietr Krieg asked.

"I want life," Broni said, with the selfishness of youth, but with her eyes filling. "I want the beautiful stars no matter what, or who, I must leave."

Dietr produced another of his rare smiles. "I'm not surprised."

Broni looked hard at the neurocybersurgeon. "There is something else, isn't there?"

Dietr glanced at Anya. "Yes. But I needed to speak with you first. I didn't want you influenced." He looked up at the distant starlight. "This port call will go into *Glory*'s log as miraculous. I must ask Duncan, but there's no doubt what he will say. We are at war with Voerster. It was your father's choice, not ours. So we will ask the mynheera and Buele to join the syndicate as well. Let's see now what your mother and the astronomer's boy have to say when we offer them a new life."

Since the Great Rebellion it had become fashionable on Planet Voerster to say that a taste for civil war was an old affliction to which both Voertrekkers and kaffirs were susceptible. In the great halls of the kraal manor houses, in the lecture rooms of Pretoria University, and in the caucus chambers of the Kongresshalle, an awareness of history was always a presence. Despite the bloodiness of the past, Voertrekkers had learned to live with their "old affliction." The specter of civil war haunted their dreams.

The chronicles ignored all home-fought battles save the one great confrontation with the kaffirs. But the Oral Histories which were both a Voertrekker and a kaffir tradition urged remembrance of the people's past, both on Voerster and on Earth.

The emergence, during the Voertrekker-Praesident's absence from Voersterstaad, of the Friends of Elmi was only a repetition of similar events, large and small, that had taken place a dozen times since the Goldenwing *Milagro* deposited the First Landers in the Sea of Grass. The Voertrekkers had fought the planet, the kaffirs, and each other for more than thirteen hundred planetary years. Colonists and their descendants who did not succumb to the harshness of the climate and the exigencies of a life of subsistence farming, were savagely culled, generation after generation, by the old affliction. Like his ancestors for a thousand years, Ian Voerster had held these forces at bay since ascending the Machtstuhl.

Now a familiar sense of impending strife had turned the air around Voersterstaad electric. The radio waves crackled with coded messages flying among the Kraalheeren. The Friends of

Elmi movement swiftly outgrew the Cult status. The numbers swelled until they encompassed the fifty most aristocratic families on Planet Voerster. In one day, the word spread from the Kongresshalle that Ian Voerster was vulnerable. In two, the landholders of the western Grassersee were rising in arms. In three, commandos were aboard airships dispatched to the capital.

And on the fifth day the plotters began to quarrel among themselves.

A history of failed coups had taught the great families of Voerster that rebellion could succeed only if it were swift and certain. But this time there were different elements in play: a Goldenwing in the sky and a mood of change among the people.

What came to be called the Elmi Rebellion was swift enough. The country commandos flooded Voersterstaad and confined the Wache garrison. Some advanced thinkers among the lesser mynheeren class actually offered the cholos of the Wache the franchise in return for their neutrality. Few accepted, but the fact that the offer was made in so race-conscious a society was a measure of how swiftly events were now moving.

What the rebellion demanded was *direction*. The aging and corpulent Kraalheer of Windhoek was a highly suitable symbol of ancient privileges in danger; but what was needed now, and quickly, was a leader. Old Daric Koepje, a retired proctor of Pretoria University, and a man given to political epigrams, put it best to the Friends: "We have gathered the power to destroy Ian Voerster and his work of many years. What we must have now is someone who can prevent us."

The self-seeking nature of the coalition, and the genuine need to act before Ian Voerster's infatuation with Einsamberg and the Planetians faded, put hitherto unknown strains on Voertrekker tradition. And with a single, desperate radio call to Eliana Ehrengraf Voerster aboard the orbiting Goldenwing, the brick fortress of Boer-Afrikaans mores began to crumble.

36

I BELIEVE IN THE INCOMPREHENSIBILITY OF GOD

A man so put upon as I, thought Jean Marq, *should understand all about fugue.* Over the years, Jean had grown accustomed to psychiatric terms. He even took pleasure in them. The Boche had enriched his vocabulary. But Dietr Krieg had failed in his true duty as syndicate physician. For Jean Marq, simply understanding the fugue syndrome was not enough. Dietr should have disclosed to Jean what it was that the mind was seeking when it took flight. It would have saved him from humiliation, as in the case of the disgusting paracoita doll. But Dietr had not. Like the worldly priests of Jean's youth, the Boche took refuge in academic cant, so that over time Jean Marq's view of psychiatry became as muddled as the grudging religion that had been a part of his early days.

The Marq family, true to the anticlerical pretensions of French intellectuals, had cautioned young Jean that there was no God, that there never had been a God, that there would never be one. On Earth (centuries after the death of the sainted Karl), Marxism was still a harlot cult among the intelligentsia. Being Marxists, Eduard and Denise Marq were, of course, atheists. Being French, they chose to dither.

If, after all, there *was* a God, He was, as Balzac declared, "incomprehensible." It wasn't the Marqs' responsibility to guard their son's morals if God, who claimed perfection, failed to make Himself clear.

This sort of ethical ambiguity had not served Jean Marq well in his times of need. Neither had Dietr Krieg's dissuasive excursions into psychoanalysis. Time and uncertainty gnawed like animals at Jean Marq's limited reserve of sanity.

Jean's confinement at Einsamberg Kraal had grown onerous. The physical limitations of a shipboard environment natural aboard a Goldenwing were not the same as this claustrophobic detention between stone walls. The presence of the Planetians added to Jean's stress. He had always been a latent bigot, and the physical differences between the Highlanders and the rest of mankind—the great chests, the odd hands, the girth, the sucking way they breathed in the thick air of the lowlands—caused Jean Marq to fear and despise them. Racial diversity held no attractions for Jean Marq.

He watched the activity in the courtyard with rising apprehension. Until now, he fancied he had carried himself well, as a Wired Starman should. But this satisfaction grew less palatable with each gray, wet day in the lee of the Shieldwall. The political authorities on this planet were knaves and fools. How they had managed to survive since First Landers' Day (a holiday, by whatever name, on every colonial world) was a puzzle to Marq. Ian Voerster was a blustering tyrant, exactly like the old-time Afrikaners Jean's instructors at the Sorbonne had described with such contempt.

Marq stood on the inner wall in the misting rain, watching the happenings in the courtyard two dozen meters below. The construction of the gallows had been slow and overly dramatic. It was a stone arch, and it had taken days of hammering, fitting, and mortaring.

Now, in the grim forenoon, both lowland and highland troops were forming into a square of ranks around the ugly thing. It seemed the gallows would soon be used. Jean Marq's troubled thoughts raced.

There is something I did, long ago, for which execution is a suitable punishment.

He did not try to recall the act. The last thing he wanted was to remember. The gibbet was surrounded and ostentatiously tested by repeatedly dropping a heavy sack of sand off the narrow stone step six meters above the cobblestones. It was a sickening business.

Jean Marq tasted bile in his throat.

Death had a stink to it, fetid and bloody.

There was a sweetness in his nostrils that suggested human rot.

Jean looked up into the dark sky as though he had been startled by the beat of wings. But the misty air was empty of life. There were no real birds on this benighted world. The wind, curling down the Shieldwall from the high plains above, was frigid. Elsewhere there might be sunlight and clear air, but not here, huddled against the Grimsels.

He thought: *Death must be cold, yet I remember it hot and bright and terrible.*

He looked again at the preparations in the courtyard. The stone walls, the cobbled *pavé*, the very air of the execution yard suggested another place, in another town.

In France, in Jean's time, leniency for criminals was temporarily out of fashion, and death came to malefactors by hanging. In one rather lurid case of the murder of a farm girl, the hanging was to be done in the town square of Aix-en-Provence. It promised to be an execution worthy of the ghostly Albigensian heretics who had once died there in their hundreds.

Jean Marq recognized the terrible scene. It was exactly as he had imagined it to be for all those horrid nights in prison in Montpellier before his father contrived his release.

The walls and boundaries of reality bulged and trembled surrealistically.

Fear bubbled in Jean Marq's chest, crowding out the air he struggled to breathe. Defeated, he closed his reddened eyes and suddenly fled into the fantastic landscape of his madness. . . .

Healer Tiegen Roark found himself between fetid-smelling Planetian escorts, herded, like a frightened ebray, out into the wet courtyard of Einsamberg. The enclosure was crowded with

Ian Voerster's and Vikter Fontein's commandos. Despite the cold, the air was thick with the smell of unwashed men. The Planetians glowered at the lowland *lumpen* and Tiegen was dismayed to see that they had newer and cleaner weapons than the police commando Ian had brought from Voersterstaad.

The physician still could not believe that Ian would be so rash as actually to execute Luftkapitan Klemmer. Other considerations aside—and they were legion—Otto Klemmer was a hero to the recently formed *lumpen* and *cholo* segments of the Voertrekker population, a man who proved by his example that good things came to those who were hardworking and loyal.

To kill such a man in a fit of rivalry brought on by the victim seeming more loyal to one's wife than to one's person would be the act of a tyrant. But it appeared as though an execution was exactly what Ian Voerster intended.

Until this dreadful, rainy moment Tiegen Roark had never really permitted himself to think of Ian Voerster as a killer. To be sure, The Voerster had, like all Voertrekker-Praesidents before him, dealt ruthlessly with kaffirs and criminals. But this was different. Otto Klemmer was a white man and a Voertrekker who had broken no law.

The gossip was that only the admonitions of the commando's chaplain prevented Ian from revenging himself on the offworlders by digging up and dishonoring the corpse of the Starman buried by the river. True or not, Tiegen was aware that that idea had, in fact, occurred to Ian. To his credit, he had not acted upon it.

But problems multiplied. The air between Einsamberg and Voersterstaad was suddenly alive with radio messages, many mangled by the weather, but most clear enough. Ian's supporters in Voersterstaad were frantically warning that rebellion and treason were in the wind. They begged him to return at once to the capital to face down a restless gang of seditious Kraalheeren. Tiegen had no way to know what was true and what false, but he had heard rumor (passed on by a grinning Highlander) that elements of the Wache, those not under arrest, were fighting in the streets of Voersterstaad with rebellious commandos from the Grassersee kraals.

Tiegen had neither political cleverness nor military proficiency, but common sense told him that if half of what was being said was true, the administration and presidency of Ian Voerster was in deep trouble. He absolutely must abandon Einsamberg to his erstwhile allies—no matter what the cost—and return to Voersterstaad to rally his loyalists.

The physician had been separated from Klemmer soon after his last interview with Ian Voerster, and the sight that now presented itself filled Tiegen with despair. He had no particular fondness for the airshipman (who was, after all, a person of mixed race if the stories were true), but since the ill-fated departure from Voertrekkerhoem's airship grounds—it now seemed an eternity ago—Tiegen Roark had developed a grudging respect for Klemmer. For that reason he wanted to avert his eyes as Klemmer was brought into the courtyard supported by two of Ian Voerster's Wache adjutants.

It was obvious that Klemmer had been denied even the most rudimentary medical assistance. His face was distorted by the swelling of his lower lip, where an infection had obviously set in. Both legs had been so badly beaten (repeated strokes of a rod across the hamstring was a favorite highland torture) that he could not walk. His eyes were invisible under swollen lids and there were bruises and unhealed cuts on both cheeks.

Did I bring that on, Tiegen wondered, *by accusing the Planetians to Ian Voerster?* It was unlikely. The Highlanders needed no challenge to make them despicable. The stony, airless land they had been given, long ago, by the First Landers had produced a race of brutes. *By all that is sacred,* Tiegen thought, *these are the people to whom a man would give his daughter—or even his wife—for peace in our time?*

Tiegen stood in the path of the prisoner's escort. "Stop, damn you," he shouted at the Wache commandos. "This man needs attention."

———

"Stand aside, Healer," the officer said. "He's about to get all the attention he will ever need."

They shoved Roark aside and mounted the scaffold, dragging the almost comatose Klemmer.

At that moment a sound that was more animal than human reverberated within the stone courtyard enclosure. Everyone about the gibbet looked up at the source.

Two dozen meters above them, there stood the Starman Marq, poised like a bird about to take flight.

On this strange day there was no sun. The light hid behind a high overcast that drained land, sky, and even sea of color. Jean stood— walked?—on bluffs that overlooked the tideless waters of the Côte d'Azur. All around him were the vines planted generations ago by Amalie's grandfather and great-grandfather. He noted that the grapes had been harvested and the vines pruned to low bushes of blunt, ugly branches.

He looked about for Amalie but somehow, and with a sick certainty, he knew that he would not find her. In his right hand he held a smooth stone, slippery with blood. Red had stained his fingers. He uttered a chirp of mingled horror and disgust and dropped the stone at his feet. It rolled over the cliff's edge and fell bounding toward the distant sea.

He looked back toward the terraces of the vineyard to see if he had been observed. But there was no living thing in sight. No man or woman, no farm animal, no birds or insects. He glanced fearfully upward. Black carrion birds often soared along these cliffs. But the sky was blank and the landscape immobile, like a painted backdrop on a stage. Yet he was not alone. Jean could hear the soft, susurrating sound of a silent crowd, expectant, waiting.

He would not believe the evidence of the stone. Amalie would soon appear, running down the terraces, hair flying, her naked legs and thighs flashing in the newborn sunlight.

I am cold, ma chérie, he thought. Bring the warm sun and blue sky. *But she did not appear. Instead he began to discern a crowd in the marketplace of Aix. The terraces had vanished. Jean did not consider that strange. Nor was it strange that there was a gallows in the square below. A noose blew in a wind that Jean could not feel.*

His heart began to thud heavily in a panic reaction. His breath came swiftly and shallowly, making him feel light-headed. There was activity below. A police van drove slowly though the crowd, which parted like a human Red Sea before it. Jean watched in horrified fascination as the van stopped and gendarmes *dismounted.*

The condemned man was taken from the van and half-carried to the gallows steps. Jean felt the blood rising behind his eyes. Surely they would fill and burst, bathing him with blood and serum. The pressure within his head was more that any man could bear. He moaned. "Wait! In God's name, wait!"

The funereal procession below stopped. The condemned man looked up. Jean stared. The face raised below was his own.

"Not me," the condemned screamed. "Take him. He is the one!"

Jean Marq turned, ran three steps and dove out from the steep cliff over the sea. As he fell, slowly twisting, the sun emerged and bathed his sweat-streaked face with light. Somewhere in the turquoise sea below, Jean Marq knew, Amalie swam, naked and golden, waiting for him at last.

The Voertrekker-Praesident emerged from a small postern door just in time to have the Starman's socketed skull burst like a melon as it struck the muddy cobblestones at his feet.

The courtyard erupted into riotous confusion. Tiegen's eyes were drawn to Ian Voerster's livid face. *The eyes,* the Healer thought, *are enormous and as cold as the ice-strewn Southern Ocean.* The courtyard was vibrating with shock, but something different was taking place inside Ian Voerster. Tiegen Roark could see it, feel it.

The Voerster stepped over the corpse at his feet, bloodying his boots in the spilled contents of the Starman's Wired head. Tiegen held in an urge to spew. At this moment it was the Voertrekker-Praesident who dominated the scene and imposed order on the confusion. He stared at Otto Klemmer with a look of such hatred as Tiegen had never seen.

Ian Voerster stepped to the base of the gallows and began to issue orders in a frigid, almost inhuman voice. "Clean up this offal, and take the *cholo* back to the cells," he commanded, "and tell my people to begin boarding the airships. We return to Voersterstaad today."

37

AN ISSUE OF WAR AND PEACE

Hold 120, a vast, dark emptiness aboard *Glory*, had on Duncan's command been hastily converted into a holographic theater. The imaging cameras, which had not been used for more than three years, were all activated now. Monkeys swarmed busily through the rigging. Amaya had rotated the ship so that the camera ports in the hull had a clear view of the planet below.

Inside the hold now, Anya, Damon, and Dietr floated, Wired, in the reflected light of the scene of fumbling warfare that filled the volume of hold 120. Duncan had chosen to remain unconnected to *Glory*. Under severe Thalassan self-discipline, he forced himself to see the display as Eliana must see it.

An image of the scene far below played out the beginnings of a spreading tragedy. Osbertus Kloster watched, horrified. There had been no organized war on Voerster since the Great Rebellion, and there were no holo images of that terrible time. Buele and Broni floated in the microgravity near Duncan. He could see, in the play of light across their faces, that they understood what was taking place in the Grassersee, but as children. There was a curious detachment in their expressions. A decision had been made about the two adolescents. The choice for Buele had been touching. He had been wildly eager to stay aboard *Glory*, but he did not want to leave Osbertus. To the old man's credit, he had insisted that Buele remain "—and see the stars, boy, and see the stars for me."

For Broni the decision had come more easily. The medical record was unmistakable. Stay and live, return and die. Duncan looked at Eliana with an ache in his chest. Her choice had been

---

to stay aboard *Glory*. But as she watched with horror the killing that had just begun on Voerster, Duncan felt the return of an old loneliness he had foolishly thought a thing past.

He forced himself to look away from Eliana. She had come to watch in Voertrekker dress. Duncan tried not to recall her nakedness, the soft feel of her inner thighs, the taste of her lips and tongue, the warm pressure of her breasts. *It was all a dream,* Duncan thought. *It never happened at all.*

He made himself look away and at Black Clavius. The large man was moving his lips in prayer—or in conversation with God. The acts were synonymous with Clavius. But his eyes were sad. The battle they were watching in the holograph was being fought over the fields of a township. Airshipmen on a dirigible bearing the marks of Windhoek were trying to rise above a craft from Joburg, on the southeastern coast of Windhoek Gulf. The commandos of Windhoek dropped burning thermite on their enemy, and fire rained down onto the kaffir fields below. *Glory*'s computer saw the scene from above, but at an oblique angle that made the fiery deluge stand out sharp and deadly against the dusty green of the Sea of Grass.

Eliana reached for Duncan's hand in the semidarkness. She gripped it with astonishing strength. It was the first physical contact they had shared since the messages had begun to pour in—first from Voersterstaad, then from kraals across the Grassersee all the way to Pretoria, begging her to return.

"Action elsewhere," Dietr reported for *Glory*'s computer.

"Voersterstaad," Eliana said, tightening her grip on Duncan's hand.

The city was under cloud cover, but the infrared images showed red crowds clotting the streets between the colder, blue buildings. A momentary break allowed *Glory*'s computer to show the scene in true color. There were barricades going up in Voersterstaad. *They were closer to this suicidal behavior than we offworlders realized,* Duncan thought. He looked at Eliana's pale face. *But she knew. She always knew.*

As they watched the display, the terminator moved across

the Planetia, the Sea of Lions, the Sea of Grass. For a moment the land below was bathed in the pure, whitish light of Luyten. Suddenly, out of the grasslands, rose wave after wave of emerald green. The phenomenon took place across thousands of kilometers of empty savannah. Green gems glistened in the low-angled light of the westering sun. It was a startling and beautiful sight.

Eliana whispered, "The night breeze is blowing, love, and the grasses have begun to fly."

When Duncan Kr looked at his Voertrekker beloved, her eyes had closed and her cheeks were wet with tears.

38

GLORY

In the unfamiliar garb of a Voertrekker commando, Ulf Walvis stood his post on the level ground between Voersterstaad and Voertrekkerhoem, backed by a thousand men from Windhoek and half that many others drawn from insurgent kraals all across the Grassersee. A hundred meters from his station, a ditch had been dug by the engineering force from Pretoria. Sharpened stakes had been emplaced, and mines had been planted. The university commandos were well into their fantasy of playing soldiers.

Beyond the rather primitive works lay another set of almost identical fortifications protecting a smaller force of commandos and Wache from Voertrekkerhoem. The summer winds were thick with flying grasses and it had begun to rain still again. Old Ulf shivered in his commander's furs and wondered how he came to find himself here. It was true enough that he had been at the heart of the coalition of Kraalheeren who formed the Friends of Elmi. But he had been a disinclined messenger to Ian Voerster on the day before the Voertrekker-Praesident departed for Einsamberg; he had been an awkward (if excited) conspirator at the meetings where the Friends of Elmi took shape; and he was now an extremely reluctant amateur warrior.

He had done these things, the old Kraalheer thought, because the world was in great need of a radical change of direction.

With each decade that passed after Landers' Day, Voerster had sunk deeper into iniquity. Ulf was only a mildly religious man, and he was by no means a progressive (the thought made him shudder), but the fact was that Ian Voerster's rule was iniquitous.

The Kraalheeren who officered the *lumpen* ranked between Ulf and the outskirts of Voersterstaad chose to defy Ian Voerster only because he challenged their old privileges. But no matter why they fought, the Kraalheer of Windhoek considered, the important thing was that they *would* rise against the government. Such a thing had never before happened among the whites of Planet Voerster.

But oh, lord, Ulf thought. *I wish I were younger and a better soldier.*

Across the wet field which was turning into a soupy sea of mud, Ulf could see Ian Voerster. His staff seemed badly under-manned. Were the rumors true, then? Were his loyalists holding back and waiting to see if a force gathered behind the figurehead of the Voertrekkerschatz Eliana Ehrengraf?

Ulf looked up at a sky filled with flying, mating grasses. Blades had broken free of the wet soil and were rising all over the Grassersee. From Sternberg to Milagro, the grass was flying in a millennial dance that was ancient before the first necrogenes had developed on Voerster. In spite of himself, Ulf Walvis was moved, and he knew that every person on the field shared his response to the most indigenous of Planet Voerster's botanical mysteries.

Ulf raised his field glasses. If he was a general he would act the part, though he knew nothing about organized fighting. The Voerster knows very little more, he thought, and instead of being a comforting thought, it chilled him to the bone.

He tried to pierce the curtain of rain and grasses. The air glittered and coruscated with green fire as the shiny leaves spun swiftly in the wind. He lowered the binoculars and wiped the lenses. Was she coming? Had her ambiguous answer been a yes or a no? Would the Starmen aid her? He thought not. He had read the credo of the Wired Ones. It was said they honored a Universal Directive not to interfere in the politics of less techno-logically advanced societies. Ulf's studies suggested that the Starmen had few weapons. But "few" could be catastrophic. Ulf Walvis had not seen the thing they called a *beamer* used on the day the Starman Marq delivered the animal embryos. But he had heard stories. Apparently it had terrified the Wache. With such energy weapons, the men from space could decimate Voerster. But the Starmen did not sail the deep of space in warships. Perhaps that was a blessing. There were weapons too horrible to be used. The homeworld had been ravaged by them. Not once but three times.

High in the air over Voersterstaad there was a sound like that of ripping cloth, followed by a rolling sonic boom. *Eliana,* old Ulf thought, hitching up his weapons. The Starmen were returning Eliana Ehrengraf to the planet of her birth.

With its ceramic skin still glowing with the heat of atmospheric friction, *Glory*'s small landing sled furrowed the wet black soil between the forces drawn up outside Voersterstaad. Steam roiled into the air, emerald leaves, flushed with mating hormones, swirled and flew from the atmospheric bow wave ahead of the sled.

The machine came to rest facing Ian Voerster's hastily assembled commandos. The ranks wavered, but did not break and run. Ulf Walvis' troops ran forward exultantly. The *lumpen* accepted immediately what the Kraalheeren only hoped was true. The New Elmi was aboard the spacecraft. The lady of Ehrengraf was once again on the soil of her homeworld, delivered in Voerster's time of travail by the almost mythical Wired Ones. A thousand armed men formed a half circle around the hissing, steaming ceramic spearpoint from space and began to chant.

"*El-mi . . . El-mi . . . El-mi!*"

Ulf Walvis felt himself being pushed forward. Suddenly his colleagues in rebellion had appeared on the field, ready to greet the New Elmi.

The ramp dropped on the sled and Eliana Ehrengraf stepped onto the wet ground. She was dressed as no Voertrekker had ever seen a Voertrekkerschatz dressed, in skinsuit and environmental unit. Behind her towered the large form of the black Starman, Clavius. At her right stood her cousin, the Astronomer-

Select of Voerster, and at the head of the ramp leading from the spacecraft stood the Starman female Anya Amaya.

The insurgents waited, but there was no Broni, no boy Buele.

A stillness fell across the field. The only sound was the hissing of the rain and the soft whispering song of the grasses.

When she spoke, Eliana's voice was amplified by the helmet that covered her dark fall of hair. "I did not wish to return. But you asked me and I am here."

Ulf Walvis stumbled forward, suddenly feeling foolish in his warrior's garb. "Voertrekkerschatz, kraalheera, the Committee desires—"

"Mynheer Ulf," Eliana said firmly. "I have accepted the Committee's invitation to govern, not to pretend. I have not come home to create a new myth. I intend to be the New Elmi in fact, not legend." She indicated the Starman who stood looming over her, silent and somber, with an ancient balichord slung over a massive shoulder. "This man will speak for me to the kaffirs. If that is not satisfactory, clear away your men for I intend to return to the *Glory*."

"*Kraalheera*—!" The old Boer had never heard a wellborn woman speak so. He was shocked to the core.

Eliana said, "Call my husband. I want to speak with him."

Ulf Walvis felt a weight being lifted from his shoulders. He called an adjutant and issued his orders. The people waited in silence as a delegation departed for the loyalist lines.

Eliana stood, as still as a statue. She could see the group across the field, Ian at its center. *I spent my life with him, bore him a child. But I feel nothing.*

A messenger arrived from the rear and whispered in Walvis' ear.

The old man said, "Kraalheera, across the Grassersee the kraals are declaring for you and against Ian."

Eliana regarded him without expression.

The discussion among the loyalists ended. Eliana could see Ian Voerster looking across the lines at her. *What does he feel,* she wondered. *I am taking from him the only thing he values. Will he live and die hating me?* Ian began to march in her direction, flanked by Trekkerpolizeioberst Transkei and a young Wache officer. He looked weary. There were deep shadows under his eyes and etched lines in his face. *Things have not gone well for Ian,* Eliana thought. *Nor for me.*

She could feel, among all who watched her, the particular attention of Anya Amaya, standing in the open hatch of her space machine. *What would it have been like to wear the drogue?* To share an intimacy she could even now only imagine? *To see and feel and know all that Buele and beloved Broni would soon see and feel and know. Ah, Duncan,* she thought, *Duncan my love . . .*

Ian Voerster, wet to the skin and bitterly angry, stomped through the mud and stood before her, arms akimbo.

"So you've come back, have you?"

When Eliana Ehrengraf spoke it was in a voice that rang with authority. "No, cousin, I have *not* come back. This is all new. Now hear my terms."

And behind her she heard the familiar deep and resonant whisper of Black Clavius speaking the words of the Preacher:

" 'So I returned, and considered all the oppressions that are done under the sun: and behold the tears of such as were oppressed, and they had no comforter—' "

And what had Duncan once said of Voerster? "Your world is an attempt to turn back a universal clock. It can't survive." *Would he have been so frank if he had known I would stand here now? But I am who and what I am.*

Welcome home, Elmi, Eliana thought sadly, *welcome home.*

As the Luyten sun rises swiftly above the curve of Voerster, the Goldenwing Glory prepares to depart from orbit around the silver planet. For the last twenty hours the Starmen aboard have watched the grasses of Voerster change the color of the single continent. Now the emerald green is fading as the grasses finish their aerial mating dance and die, falling from the sky in a desiccated rain of spores which can wait a season or a century to germinate. In their way, the grasses of Voerster are like the necrogenes, conforming to a millennial imperative that is deeper than instinct, more inbred in the genes than the urge to survive. The grasses of the Grassersee will perform their seasonal pavane ten thousand years after men have vanished from the planet.

Aboard the Glory, *the monkeys race through the rig, loosing vast mirrors of skylar to the tachyon winds blowing from the galaxy's distant center. Damon Ng lies in his rigger's pod, Wired, but aware of the two newcomers he is bound to instruct in first principles.*

Buele will be Wired first, as soon as Glory *clears the orbit of the gas giant Wallenberg which the kaffir call Tutu. The girl, Broni Ehrengraf Voerster, will be made a full syndic when her convalescence is complete. She lies comfortably in the microgravity, aware that she will live many years.* Glory *has given her the gift of life.*

Broni is aware, too, that she will never again see the mynheera who bore her and loved her. Intellectually, she is fascinated by the activity that has invigorated Glory. *Emotionally, she is bereaved as she looks for the last time at the planetary seas and the single great continent of the world on which she was born.*

Neurocybersurgeon Krieg is in his surgery, Wired, like the others, and watching closely the signals from the biomedical sensors he implanted in Broni's open chest only short days before. Krieg is well satisfied. The profit from Goldenwing voyages is often difficult to measure. This port call at Voerster Dietr considers a success. We buried Han Soo, *he thinks,* and lost mad Jean. But we found two young Starmen. A more than fair exchange.

Anya Amaya is at the helm. She is, of all the people aboard, most closely connected to Glory. *At the moment she is* Glory, *and will be until the great starship clears Luyten 726's inner space and is outward bound. She is just now the least human of* Glory's *syndics, but a part of Anya shares Duncan's grief and loss.*

The Master and Commander lies in his bed of gel, Wired to Glory *as are the others, but far away in spirit. He idly caresses the sleek, furry shape of Mira, who senses his grief and will not leave him.* Be content, old tom, *she thinks.* I am here, and the great-queen-who-is-not-alive will guard us. *Duncan half understands the cat's offer of comfort and his long fingers knead her fur at the base of her small, feral head.*

———

Duncan is remembering. What he remembers happened days and hours ago, but the events seem as distant now as history.

She read from the book of Donne that he gave her:

> Sweetest love, I do not goe,
> For weariness of thee,
> Nor in hope the world can show
> A fitter Love for mee. . . .

He looks through the overhead transparency at the hectares of extending skylar. Glory is spreading her golden wings. Anya, naked in her pod, twists unconsciously, her fingers twitching as she feels the sails cup to the timeless winds.

Duncan searches the planet, whose aspect is beginning to change as Glory acquires delta-V. But there is no sign of the Voertrekker commandos, the highland invasion that Ian set in motion. No sign of cities or conflict. None of those things can be seen from space. Climbing above the horizon now the green point of light, Erde, which the kaffirs call Mandela. The planet shines brilliantly through the monofilament halo of the rig. And Duncan is reminded of Black Clavius, who wanted more than almost anything to stay aboard and return to space.

But Clavius has chosen instead to remain on the world of exile, which his people call Afrika, not Voerster.

The name sends a thrill of human jealousy through Duncan. Will she make her peace with Ian Voerster? Or will she live and die now as the New Elmi?

He hears Dietr whisper in his mind: "That no longer concerns you, Duncan. Let it go. She chose. Let it go."

Glory begins to tack across the solar wind pouring outward from the corona of Luyten 726. The aurora borealis paints the sky with rose and pink. More skylar spreads and Glory's wings gleam with the light of heaven as she prepares to leave orbit.

At Sternhoem on the Sea of Grass the night is still. The Nachtebrise has dropped to a whisper. It only stirs the dead wings fallen from the spores dusting the dark ground around the observatory.

———

On the wall just under the dome of the building, Eliana Ehrengraf Voerster stands, face uplifted. She sees the change in the brightness of the golden star racing across the night from northwest to southeast.

"They are going, Cousin," she says to Osbertus Kloster.

"Be not sad, Elmi," the old man says.

For the first time she does not say, "Don't call me that."

Osbertus lays a hand on her wrist. He feels her pulse, strong and firm under the soft leather of her glove. "When will his child be born, Elmi?"

Eliana regards Osbertus Kloster with affection. "How did you know, old cousin?"

"You would not have left the Glory without that."

"In the spring, when the spores bloom," she says, and resumes her vigil, watching until the Goldenwing Glory disappears at last beyond the southeastern horizon of the Sea of Grass.